To: Britt(
My new 'U'

PHOBIA

A NOVEL

BY
DANIEL LANCE WRIGHT

Danny Wright

booktrope

Booktrope Editions
Seattle WA, 2012

Cover Design by Greg Simanson

Edited by Rachel Brookhart

This is a work of fiction. Names, characters, places, brands, media, and incidents are either the product of the author's imagination or are used fictitiously. Any resemblance to similarly named places or to persons living or deceased is unintentional.

ISBN 978-1-935961-45-1

For further information regarding permissions, please contact info@booktrope.com.

Library of Congress Control Number: 2012937905

DEDICATION

This latest work of fiction is dedicated to the memory of my father, Kenneth William Wright (1923-2012). He arrived at the end of his personal journey on earth this spring, just as the first bluebonnets appeared. He is missed.

ALSO BY DANIEL LANCE WRIGHT

Annie's World: Jake's Legacy (ATTM Press)
Six Years' Worth (Father's Press)
Paradise Flawed (Dream Books LLC)
Where Are You, Anne Bonny (Rogue Phoenix Press)
"Trouble", in CrossTIME Science Fiction
    Anthology, Vol. IX
Dancing Away (short story - Untreed Reads)

CHAPTER 1

Nick Brandon sat cross-legged on the polished tiles of the department store floor, hands forced to relax and draped over the points of his knees. Body language had to be just so, non-threatening in every detail.

He could not dispel fear of a problem growing exponentially just out of sight around corners and beyond walls – a gathering crowd murmuring, wondering, pressing forward, wanting to see; held away by the thinnest of threads, two inexperienced mall security officers. The pair had already offered cause to grind his teeth in frustration and he had only known them for a few minutes. If all those curious people knew the danger of what was unfolding where he sat, they wouldn't be so eager for a better look, only wondering whether he'd succeed or people would die.

Red and green tinsel, hanging overhead, fluttered and then flashed light reflected from a dangling sign that touted last-minute savings. It captured Nick's attention. He glanced up, but not to see the holiday decoration; he sought divine help beyond it, an indication, an idea – anything that might point the way to his next step. His focus remained far from symbolism of the season. The urge to jump and run tugged at him, as if he'd never noticed and gotten involved. For a fleeting second, it seemed possible.

At eye level, from where he sat on the floor, a colorful array of sleeve ends, pant legs, and dress bottoms were scattered through this section of the store like a chrome forest in full brilliantly colored leaf. He slowly ducked his head low and looked beneath and across it all as if an answer might barrel at him and he wanted to be ready when it did.

Racks of women's clothes were strewn randomly – or so it seemed – arranged to encourage shoppers to stay longer, a labyrinth born of marketing genius to slow shoppers down. The arrangement of racks must be figured out in order to escape. The answer he looked for didn't come.

Christmas music piping throughout the store offered no joy, virtually meaningless at the moment; the light-hearted melody drowned in the amalgamation of many conversations by that throng of people he couldn't even see. There was no one from his vantage point except the girl. Her situation had to be his sole focus. Distractions threatened to lure his attention away. *Damn it! That music and all that noise needs to just go away.* He didn't have the luxury of showing that desire and frustration in his demeanor. He struggled to focus; thinking quickly and clearly might save her life, and his. Regardless of his wish, the music turned his ear, reeling him back to his original purpose in the store.

In a coarse whisper from some distance away, "Doctor Brandon?"

Turning his head smoothly, Nick met the voice with a slow, cautionary hand. One of the two mall security guards glided on the tips of his toes toward him, as if that made him less noticeable – idiot.

Suddenly, Nick was irritated again by inexperience as the young man approached during this extremely delicate time. "Not now," he hissed. As he was waving the young man away, he added, "Go on, control the crowd and leave us alone."

That boy and the other green-as-a-gourd security guard had been grossly ineffective, but maybe they could keep onlookers – mostly curious teens – from pushing for a closer look until Houston police arrived.

The young man nodded, backed away, and left as ridiculously as he'd arrived. *What a moron! The janitorial staff probably has more sense.* Head still turned away from the girl, he clenched his eyes shut and pulled a slow breath. His anger eased as he struggled to again relax facial muscles for a pleasant, non-threatening façade.

Being at the wrong place at the right time had put Nick's psychology training to the test. He didn't know how long it'd take for police to arrive. It didn't matter. Remaining as chief negotiator was his only choice, possibly the only way to resolve the situation – whatever that resolution might be. But, arrival of officers might serve as a psychological crutch that he wasn't alone in this ordeal.

He needed their presence so that he might address the problem more calmly. Just an appearance of calm was taxing his ability to the limit. Several critical minutes remained before police could make it to the scene. The weighty responsibility of preserving a life sat squarely on his shoulders.

Again, that illogical but incessant thought intruded on an already cluttered mind. It was only a flash of a thought that disappeared as quickly as it materialized, but for that fractional second, it seemed doable: Get up and walk away. That may have been Nicky Brandon's way at age fifteen, but certainly not Doctor Nicolas Brandon's way at age thirty-four. Still, this situation scared him to that degree. Even training that prepared him for life-and-death encounters while serving in the army hadn't prepared him for this fragile state of affairs.

He finally opened his eyes, as the receding young security guard disappeared around a corner. Perspiration dampened his forehead despite the cool floor he sat on and the air conditioning that breezed across his body – one indicator of fear he just couldn't conceal. Slowly, calculatingly, he began turning back to the problem at hand. As he did, he glimpsed his image in a mirrored support column. His usually well-combed, long, dark hair had fallen across his forehead. He still wore a sport coat, but the tie had been shoved into the coat's side pocket. He surreptitiously smiled at his reflection. It was not a vain thing; he rehearsed a passing look of sincerity that had to be conveyed.

As his face squared with the girl, the smile broadened, but only slightly. He tilted his head affably. The necessary look came together.

Nick locked eyes with the young girl huddled tightly beneath the jeans under the rack. Denim legs of designer pants hung down hiding the left side of her face. He saw enough to discern beautiful, youthful features: seventeen years old, perhaps, with silky blonde hair, parted at the center, hanging off her shoulders, and the unobstructed portion of her face clear and smooth, stress distorting natural beauty. Strands of that honey-colored hair had abandoned the center part and been forced at an angle across her face. Ruddy cheeks glowed below wrinkles pulled tight across her forehead and a wide, blood-engorged eye. The other eye was hidden by a dangling pant leg.

Holding the muzzle of a snub-nosed pistol to the soft area beneath her chin, her fingers shook, even the one against the trigger.

A trembling hand holding a deadly weapon kept Nick's gut knotted. Each unwarranted move by the gun hand caused him to flinch. Even so, her loveliness shined through. He envisioned his daughter Alli looking much like this troubled child in ten years. He hoped the other security guard did as promised, keeping a watchful eye on his daughter while he took care of business on the floor of this sprawling Houston department store inside Bayside Mall. He assumed Alli and the guard stood safely in the court area outside the store's exit in the main mall, a safe distance away.

Just a quick trip to buy a last minute gift – that's all it was supposed to have been; run into Bayside Mall, buy a gift and be gone. It had been a promise to Alli so she might find something special for her mother that'd be a genuine surprise Christmas morning, two days away. The shopping trip soured fast when someone yelled, "Gun!" The crowded store came alive like startled ants deserting a mound. That's when the two young security officers came running to the scene, only a few feet from where he and Alli stood when alarmed cries rang out; they were near ground zero, pure happenstance. A sudden sense of obligation caused him to take charge and push six-year-old Alli to go with one of them. At first refusing, she held her ground and looked up at him, tugging on his index finger, lower lip quivering. "Aren't you comin'?"

He wrenched his finger from her grasp. "I'll be along in a minute or two," he'd told her. "Stay with this man. Okay?"

"Okay." Her voice trembled.

He stroked her hair. "Go on now," he whispered into her ear. "I have to help this girl if I can. I'll be along in a minute or two… okay?"

She pouted but nodded, reluctantly allowing the mall officer to guide her away by the hand. She watched as long as she could but was eventually swallowed by store fixtures on her way to the main entrance.

The other Bayside security man then forced customers from the interior into the mall outside. Holiday shoppers from the other side of the store began congregating, forced to stand away around the center island of the store, out of sight. Nick suddenly found himself alone in a cavernous department store with an armed and very frightened young girl cowering beneath a rack of designer jeans.

As his mind raced, one thing needed no interpretation: The girl was wound tight – too tight, tears exploding from her eyes and veins standing proud on her neck and temples. Although her posture indicated suicide, he remained aware that he could become a target if some scale of mental stability tipped. Forcing distractions aside, he focused on a pleasant, relaxed appearance – eyes not wide, lids blinking slow, and methodically. Relaxed facial muscles only hinted a smile.

Although less than a minute since it began, it might as well have been ten. Enough time to notice the fear he felt to be reminiscent of impending armed conflict. The rush of adrenaline and fear for his safety were identical.

Preparing for battle sitting in a tank on the Kuwaiti/Iraqi border, he waited for the order to escort ground troops into Iraq. Then, as now, he didn't know what to expect other than that he might not make the return trip alive. His wife, Julia, was home pregnant with Alli, and the muster of courage didn't come from a gung-ho desire to defeat an enemy, but instead from a longing to keep family intact – and that meant surviving.

The same logic motivated him now. This time it wasn't his family but that of the terrified young girl cowering mere feet in front of him. If she pulled the trigger of that pistol pressed under her chin, a family would be devastated and left with a psychological scar for a lifetime. *I can't let that happen.*

The girl forced a deep guttural whimper through clenched teeth.

From somewhere near but out of sight around the central island of dressing and storage rooms, another young girl's brazen high-pitched voice shook him from his thoughts. "Where did Debbie get a gun? Did you know she had it?" she asked some unseen companion.

Nick couldn't see the girl or hear the response, but he learned two things: This troubled child's name was Debbie, and she hadn't come alone to the mall. He then heard the same voice, sounding closer but still out of sight. "Stop acting crazy, Debbie! Put that gun away. You're being stupid!" Then her voice dropped a few decibels. "She's such a dweeb."

Disgusted by the comment, Nick ground his teeth and watched the girl's reaction to the insensitive remark. She pushed deeper under the rack, pulling her knees tighter yet against her breasts with the free arm, and pushed the pistol muzzle deeper into the soft tissue under her chin.

The girl he now knew as Debbie wailed, "You don't understand! Nobody does!" The gun hand shook.

He bit the inside of his cheek to keep from showing a reaction that might be construed as an attempt to stop her.

Outwardly, his pleasant face remained, and he turned his head away from Debbie. But the only person he saw was the young security officer standing at the corner of the central cluster of rooms the store surrounded. His sole task was to keep the crowd at a safe distance, out of sight and line of fire. Judging by the increasing volume of voices, he was doing a poor job of it.

The young security guard's inexperience kept him angling for a better view. His youthful curiosity was as strong as any of those teens he was charged with controlling. For every step forward, the crowd surely followed, judging by the increasing noise. Any nearer and faces of the crowd would appear, putting people in danger of catching a stray bullet.

And, as feared, the security guard appeared, shuffling half a step at a time into full view with a clutch of faces right behind him.

Nick's smile wavered and his brow pulled down in frustration. He lost control. "Get them out of here!" he shouted to the security officer armed with a flashlight and walkie-talkie.

Nick forced a smile to return, wasting no more time with the mall brat just out of sight around the corner or the uniformed man.

"I'm not stupid and I'm not crazy!" Debbie yelled as a final response to that crass remark.

It angered him to think a companion, close friend or not, could respond to a person's agony in such a way. He spoke his first words. "You're Debbie, right?"

With fast chin bobs, she nodded then raked tears from her cheeks with two nervous swipes.

"Don't pay any attention to talk like that. It's just you an' me, sweetie."

It appeared that becoming smaller was her goal – but smaller by how much? It could've been defensive; less of a target against the tart tongue of a peer or maybe she wanted to disappear altogether. It troubled him. She seemed intent on using the gun on herself, no one else. But the mystery was still unfolding. Staging it in a crowded mall may have been a way of begging for someone to step forward with a solution, and fate made him the one to offer it. It took no special training, psychology or otherwise, to see that a young girl's life was in his hands.

Then that mouthy girl bent on exacting some perverse gratification had to toss in her two-cents-worth again, "Can't you see that it's just a showy grab for attention, Mister."

Nick snapped his head around.

The girl now stood in full sight and not that far away.

The security officer had her by the hand but seemed impotent to check her advance. She now had become a clear target if Debbie should explode in anger. At the moment, that seemed likely.

"Someone to pay attention to her," the girl said. "That's all she wants... I don't know why you can't see that."

Nick watched Debbie move her free hand to surround the gun-hand, adding resolve to follow through on a threat to end her life right here, right now. He estimated the bullet would enter through her throat and exit the top of her head. She cowered and sobbed.

Imparting a sense of calm was all he could think to do. But, he couldn't achieve that as long as that idiot girl kept up the shrill taunting. The girl, standing dangerously close and unprotected, clearly had no clue. "I want to get to know you, Debbie. But first, I need to have a chat with your... *friend* over there. Okay?"

Debbie didn't answer or show any indication.

"Please relax and breathe deep. Don't pay any attention to what she said. Her talk... those words... they don't mean a thing. I'll be right back." He scooted backward on his butt and came to his feet slowly. He made no sudden moves as he walked away, but glanced back often.

Teary eyes followed him.

Staying on the tiled walkway between carpeted shopping areas, Nick picked up the pace and crisply advanced on the loudmouthed girl. As he approached, he held out a stiff disciplinary finger on a fully extended arm and pointed it inches from her nose. "Not one more word! Just keep your mouth shut!" He pushed his face to within inches of hers. "Got it?"

He had her full attention. Her arms fell limp to her sides and her mouth fell open. She stepped back putting distance between his fingertip, his face and her. Otherwise, she didn't respond, seemingly in shock. The girl obviously was unaccustomed to discipline and stunned by a strange man telling her what to do.

He held a hand to his side in a balled fist. Although he had no intention of hitting the girl he wanted her to know in a fast way that he had no time to debate and certainly wasn't moving until he had an answer and a promise. *Freakin' spoiled mall brat!*

"Okay, okay." Like a small child she crossed her arms, huffed, pulled her chin into her chest and pouted.

He took a one-step lateral move toward the mall security guard. "You've got to keep these kids out of sight. That girl over there is blinded by whatever's troubling her and may do something with that gun, unintentionally or otherwise. Either way it's a dangerous situation. Is that so difficult to understand? That kid… " He flicked his chin toward the bratty girl, "… would be a likely target if that one beneath the jeans begins spraying bullets. Yell, scream obscenities… I don't give a damn how you do it; just keep them at a safe distance. For God's sake just get it done!"

The spoiled teen pressed her lips into a stiff angry line. The mall security guard appeared just as perturbed about becoming the brunt of discipline alongside a teenager. Still, he nodded, grabbed the girl's hand and yanked her in tow behind him.

"Hey! Get your hand off me," she protested.

He didn't let go, and they disappeared around the corner.

Considering circumstances, hurt feelings were of little concern. Nick sighed, relieved over that resolution, but relief was short-lived as he turned to face the reason for the problem.

Debbie, the shrinking girl, peered with frightened eyes from between the jean legs unchanged from a moment ago. He had no choice but to start the process over and not assume familiarity with the troubled teen.

Cautiously, he approached and stopped at a respectful distance, bending at the waist and placing his hands on his knees. "I'm sorry about that." He spoke in low even tones. "My name is Nick Brandon." He squatted to eye level and settled gently back on his heels. "I'm a doctor. I know your name is Debbie, but what's your last name?"

She sniffed. "M – Miller."

"It's nice to meet you, Debbie Miller. I'd really like to know what's troubling you."

"I'm scared."

"Of what?"

"I – I don't know." Her stomach did a double-pump spasm between sobs. "But I'm so tired of it; I don't want to live this way anymore."

On that comment, his gut tingled. *I have to downplay it, change the subject.* "What were you and your friends doing when you became scared?"

"Shopping for jeans… that's all, just shopping. Then Missy made fun of the clothes I'm wearing. It took my breath. I don't know why."

"Is she the one with the loud mouth over there?"

"Yeah," she said, glancing at the spot Missy had stood seconds before. "That's her."

As her eyes came back to meet his, he noticed the expression was distant, appearing detached from the present. It was as if she looked right through him to another place and time.

What are you seeing, Debbie?

"Don't worry about her," he said quickly. "She's not at all worth thinking about. She pisses me off, too." As a gesture of support, he glanced in the direction where the girl had been standing with a clear look of disgust on his face, blowing a frustrated snort through his nose. "Go ahead, tell me your story."

The added hand fell away from the pistol; the other relaxed, although the girl refused to remove it from her neck. "Missy kept on making fun of the way I looked. Then I couldn't breathe!" A sob squeezed off anything she might have added to the comment.

Unspeaking, she spent long seconds trying to establish even breathing. "Like... like someone poked me in the stomach with a red-hot branding iron. It burned and I couldn't breathe. The more she joked, the louder she laughed; and the louder she laughed, the worse I became. I couldn't stand it. My knees gave way. I fell. And now I can't get up. My legs won't work," she wailed.

"Listen –"

"Don't you understand? My legs won't move!"

"Debbie, listen to me. What you're experiencing is a phobia. It's a very real problem that needs to be addressed but, Hon, you're not crazy. There are ways to control it."

She said nothing, just cried.

He inched nearer.

"Don't come any closer!"

"Easy."

"I swear I'll pull this trigger!"

He made another calculated move.

"I'm not joking! I'll kill myself!"

Nick held up an open palm. "I'm not moving any closer. Okay?"

"Just don't." With a fast shaky hand, she swiped at tears obstructing her vision.

"Would you mind telling me what you're doing with a pistol?"

"It's my dad's. I took it from a drawer in the table next to his bed." She pushed back deeper under the rack.

"Why would you do that?"

"He said mean things about a failing grade I'd made on an English test. He told me that I must be the dumbest thing on planet Earth." She cried harder. "I did the best I could, really." Her face screwed down as that memory added a dangerous layer to her distorted perceptions.

"I know you did." To keep her talking became a droning mantra in the back of Nick's mind. It wouldn't stop the fear but might bring it down to a manageable level. He feared that an involuntary muscle spasm during one of those gut-wrenching sobs might send an unintentional bullet through her brain. "Go ahead. Tell me about it. I want to know and understand what it is you're dealing with. I want to be your friend and I want you to see me as one; I want it very much, please believe that."

Following another convulsive jerk, she drew a full breath. "I couldn't... handle it. The thought of him saying it again scared me. I wanted to be prepared if he did. So, I took the gun."

"Prepared?" He nodded at the weapon in her hand. "You mean using that on him?"

"Only at first; after I thought about it, I felt silly for thinking such a thing, but I had already slipped the gun into my purse. I meant to put it back in the drawer when I got home this afternoon."

Fear of ridicule. This is the first time I've seen this one. He struggled to remember his book of phobias to recall the name of this rare condition. "Can I sit beside you?"

"No!

"Easy. I'll stay right here." He continued sitting on his heels about six feet away.

The general din of the out-of-sight crowd changed. It captured his attention. He looked to see the security guards escorting two approaching police officers. They exchanged whispers. The officers responded by staying at a distance, helping to order people away. Nick relaxed a bit and turned his attention back to the girl.

"Debbie, tell me about your friends."

"I really want them to like me but..." she whimpered and renewed the grasp on her knees, pulling them into her flattened breasts. Sweat and tears streaked her face. "I'm just amusement to them."

How could this girl not be popular? He wondered. He thought of Debbie's so-called friends and took a renewed look at her face. It couldn't have been about looks; this girl was gorgeous.

Nick sought a sign – anything positive he might build upon and work to his advantage in the negotiation for her life. Uncertainty dried his mouth. His lips stuck together. If she chose to follow through, it could happen within the blink of an eye. *Stay calm, Nick.*

Suddenly it came to him: *Catagelophobia.* "Catagelophobia, Debbie," he blurted. "That's what you're suffering from. I can help you. Would you let me?"

"*Cata*...what?"

"Catagelophobia; it's a treatable disorder. And you seem to have a rather severe case of it, but you don't have to live like this. I can help. Would let me do that? Would you let me work with you to put it out of your life forever?"

She kept her eyes closed, but the deep lines of stress leveled out.

"Whaddaya say?"

"Ya mean it?"

Nick smiled. Tension began draining away. "Yes, I do. You have my personal guarantee. I want to get to know you, Debbie... the real you. In time, I can make it so you'll never have to be afraid again. All I ask is that you believe it as much as I do. Trust me. And, please, hon, believe in yourself?"

She began lowering the pistol from her neck.

"You and I can work this out together."

"Serious?"

"Serious." He flashed a relieved grin.

Behind the sweat, reddened cheeks, and streaming tears, Nick detected a smile trying to get through on one of the most beautiful young faces he'd ever seen. As she relaxed, so did he.

Releasing her knees, she allowed her legs to drop and splay in front of her, easing the pistol to the floor between them.

Suddenly a distant voice rang out that made Nick's blood run cold. It was Missy, Debbie's friend. "Quit being such an idiot, Deb! Get out from under there and let's go home! You're gonna get me in trouble if I'm not home by six."

In a flash, Debbie's eyes hardened. Her brow pulled down. The rose on her cheeks turned deep crimson and veins again popped out on her neck. She stopped breathing and then closed her eyes. Her lip quivered over a set jaw and new tears escaped in torrents from between clenched eyelids.

As if a tranquilizer suddenly took effect, she went expressionless, letting out a measured exhale. She whispered, as softly as a bedside prayer, "Forgive me. I just can't take it anymore."

She snapped the pistol back to her neck.

Time slowed.

"No!" He lunged as the gun fired.

He blinked and felt spatters of warm fluid across his face as his hands reached her feet. He felt her toes twitch inside her shoes. When he looked again, he saw Debbie's eyes wide, pupils rolling back.

She wilted over.

The gun clanked against the metal leg of the jeans rack.

She convulsed once, and then life left her.

As the hard ring subsided in his ears, the sound of Jingle Bells took its place. There was no sound anywhere in the store. Nick stared in disbelief, thinking momentarily that it was not too late. He started to move but stopped. He began to speak, but did not. His mind raced, unwilling to concede that he was out of options. Several seconds passed before the finality of what had just happened finally stuck. He fell back on his heels and buried his bloodied head in his hands.

The comparison of Alli in a few years to this girl brought on a sudden, clear image of how beautifully and simply this outing had begun.

***

"Please, Daddy, tell me what I got for Christmas. You and Mommy won't tell me anything." Six-year-old Alli refused to allow her father to pass lightly over her curiosity. A wide grin revealed the freshly pulled tooth in front that caused a lisp. Cottony blonde hair danced upon her shoulders as she maneuvered around to walk backward in front of him. He walked around her without breaking stride.

Nick breezed past a mechanical dancing Santa; tinny sounds of "Here Comes Santa Claus" repeated in an endless loop from the cherry-faced elf with the eternal smile. Velvet-covered mechanical hips rotated in time with the music.

Nick glanced around and grinned as Alli tugged on his pant leg.

Skipping ahead again, she turned and stopped to block him.

He sidestepped her. Nick couldn't be annoyed, eyes fixed on the twinkling lights of a decorated department store entrance just ahead on the right. He snagged her hand and briskly walked by. "Honey, how much fun would Christmas morning be if I told you what was in that *huge* box under the tree?" His eyes widened as if it were the best gift ever.

In favor of allowing this time to be Alli's, Nick suppressed nagging thoughts about the future direction of his career, about whether to remain in general practice or to specialize. He had visions of becoming an expert in a narrower field of psychology; he just didn't know what that might be. At thirty-four, he felt pressure to make a decision. But today was not the time. These precious days belonged to Alli and her mother – a joyful occasion that should not be infringed upon.

She sighed and conceded, "I guess it wouldn't be as much fun." She then turned and bounced on her toes. "But I think I'll bust if I don't know right now. I gotta know whatchya got me. I just gotta." Her eyes sparkled above a Christmas grin. Alli was Daddy's girl, giddy at the opportunity to spend this special day at his side.

Nick laughed and turned sideways, through an oncoming rush of people scurrying to get last-minute shopping done. Christmas day was only two days away. Nick grabbed and held tight to Alli's hand, pulling her close then breathing in the sights, sounds and smells of the season, still child enough to join a six-year-old in her excitement.

Everything glistened, decorated in reds and greens; sparkling tinsel matched the twinkle in his eyes. The air was laced with mixed aromas of fresh-cut pine, cinnamon and candies of all sorts. He looked down at her. "You can find patience somewhere inside you, sweetie. I know you can. This trip is for your mother. Let's think about her this time. Okay? It might be our last chance to get her something wonderful. Christmas is almost here ya know."

Alli stuck out her bottom lip. "Oh, all right."

"You wouldn't want us to miss our chance, would you?"

"I guess not."

"That's my girl."

This time he didn't simply glance down at her; he stopped and looked at Alli, realizing the blessing she was.

***

The vision faded, but Alli's face remained, now superimposed over Debbie's lifeless one. Billowing anger rumbled within him. He turned in time to see the security guards and two police officers race in his direction, but the danger had passed, and he felt no obligation to wait. He sprung to his feet then, walking straight for Missy, who had come around the corner to see what the gunshot was all about. She no longer looked belligerent or defiant – just horrified.

He quickened the pace to confront the spoiled brat. "What did you expect?" He approached with an open palm raised, fully intent on slapping common sense into her.

She covered her face and cried, "I'm sorry! I didn't know Deb was serious." She hunkered low, bracing for a stinging hand across her head.

Nick stood over her. His lip curled and quivered in anger. He held his arm high, muscles twitching, ready to strike, but he fought the urge to hurt the girl. He wanted to. He wanted her to feel pain, for Debbie's sake.

Finally, he took a swipe at the air over her head. "Aw, hell! Go on, get outta here, kid. Go home and think long and hard about how you treat your so-called friends."

He spun away and went looking for Alli. Once he caught sight of her, he pushed through the throng and broke into a trot. He couldn't get to where she stood fast enough. He dropped to his knees in front of his frightened daughter. He held her head between his palms and then lowered his hands to her shoulders and pulled her to him.

"Don't be afraid of anything, ever. Okay?" He held her tight.

CHAPTER 2

Ten Years Later

Azziz Baruk gazed from the third floor window of his apartment. "It would seem Lebanon, the land of our fathers and forefathers, has fallen into quiet subservience. The world ignores us... our problems, our needs. Would you agree with that, Sahid?"

Maintaining the thoughtful examination of his homeland, he didn't face his compatriot; he just continued looking through the window. Mood contemplative, body relaxed, he studied the contoured skyline of Beirut, a city torn by centuries of off-and-on violence. Azziz casually wiggled a finger that intertwined with the others at his back. His head tilted. "You seem slow to answer. Did the assessment offend you somehow, my brother?" He still did not turn to address Sahid directly.

Azziz, an imposing man with a beard full but trimmed to strict definition and razor outlined, stood over six feet tall. His features were angular, with a hawkish nose and swarthy skin. He wore a sleeveless tunic of broad earth-tone stripes over a white linen shirt with loose-fitting, long sleeves.

Sahid stepped forward, joining him at the window.

Azziz offered an affectionate smile.

Sahid acknowledged Azziz's quiet, brotherly greeting with a warm smile of his own. "It was not offensive at all, though it does give me pause. The profound nature of your wisdom astounds me to silence on occasion. Yes, it seems 'subservience' does describe Lebanon at this point in our history. It indeed makes abundant sense."

Of a slighter build, Sahid Arrani mimicked Azziz, espousing the same politics. Sahid fed off Azziz's confidence; he always had, even in childhood. Over the years, adulation became too easy for Sahid.

Agreement on every issue and continual exaltation swelled Azziz's ego, bolstering him to believe he could accomplish anything. Azziz filled with pride at the thought that he'd done such a grand job of molding his friend into the perfect person to be at his side.

Abdullah el'Aknar entered the room stirring a small cup of tea. The older man's shoulders slumped with the weight of age. He lived in the same building and shared similar ideologies, spending considerable time in the company of Azziz and Sahid. The much older man assumed the mentor role – a position Azziz quietly protested, believing he deserved that distinction. As the elder's opinions grew bolder, even laced with sarcasm, Azziz's annoyance had recently crossed the line into anger several times. Little of his patience remained for the old man.

Twice their age, Abdullah, once upon a time, was instrumental in political uprisings, but his advancing years had begun to squelch the fires of dissent. He no longer cared to participate in dangerous pursuits; he now preferred quiet debate with a good cup of warm tea in his hand. Azziz did not abide by empty chatter.

Holding the dainty teacup near his lips, Abdullah asked, "Does silence trouble you, Azziz? I suppose peace in our time could, possibly, have a negative impact on war-weary ears that still ring from bombs and artillery." As he brought the cup to his lips, a wry grin sprouted. He sipped his tea. Abdullah's beard was salt-and-pepper gray, ragged and sparse, in sharp contrast to those of Azziz and Sahid.

Azziz interpreted Abdullah's questions as rude and argumentative. "Peace?" He looked to Sahid. In a measured move, he turned to face the older man. Although he remained calm in appearance, a small flame of anger had just sprung to life. Azziz squinted at Abdullah. "Do you call a moment's quiet in a troubled land 'peace'? Do you call America's colonial attempts in the region 'peace'? Is it possible you are that naïve? Or is it that the passage of time has taken your edge, even your sense of direction? Abdullah, you should know better than most; once their flag flies over military bases throughout our lands, the death of our Muslim ways will not be far behind. Teachings of the Holy Quran are openly mocked; believers of the true faith are denigrated. Narrow-minded Christian missionaries will come. They'll not respect our ways. Eventually we will be outlawed in our own land, forced to bow to their false god… the crusades all over again. Open your eyes…" He fanned his arms wide. "…look around, and reawaken to reality, my salty old friend. Christian zealots place passion at the tips of missiles and enjoy aiming them at the hearts of Muslims. Passing centuries have changed nothing. Christendom conquers, then converts, all the while espousing peace and democracy – two words that mask the desire to build and extend empires. Can't you see that? It's a matter of winning or losing, using the name of God as an excuse. It's their shield *and* their sword."

As Azziz spoke, he'd begun to stalk Abdullah, balling his hands into fists, his anger spiking. He no longer felt obligated to show the old man any respect whatsoever, and he took steps to show it. "If it is in my power, I will serve Allah as a willing weapon of the jihad. As He is my witness, so shall I fight to prevent His people from enslavement by pagan theology!" Huffing through flared nostrils, he glanced about and realized that his escalating temper served no purpose.

Apparently intimidated, Abdullah stepped back to maintain a buffer. He sipped his tea, but the act seemed to hold a pretense of calm. Abdullah's words had plucked an angry nerve. "Yes, it – it seems many religions use the name of God to justify illicit goals," he said with a hint of smile that came up and disappeared too quickly, like a nervous tic. It was clear he sought to re-establish common ground. "Please Azziz, don't misunderstand; I am in full agreement. My intent was only to provoke conversation, not anger. I meant not to diminish problems that I, too, know exist. The west has reduced our ideologies to inconsequential by-products of a never-ending quest for a smelly, slimy black substance flowing from the earth. Yes, I know they take us for fools. The American spin machine tosses out phrases like "human rights" and "democracy" and then expects the world to believe they care about us as a people. Their sincerity is a sham… just as are the intentions that drive the deeds. When, in fact, they have designs only on forcing their will. In the final analysis, oil is key, the motivator of all statements of good will and all action that follows. There is nothing else in the deserts of the Middle East worth that much attention. That's plain enough to us all."

Abdullah set his teacup on a small table and then clasped his pleading hands together. He took a gentle step toward Azziz. "My friend, I know the problem and its source as well as you, but bloodletting is not always the answer. Centuries of wars and death have changed nothing. After each conflict, the loser vows revenge, and it begins anew."

Sahid Arrani stepped in to join his friend and mentor, compelled to speak. "Even if there is sense to be made of what you say, old man, talk and diplomacy has lost effectiveness over the centuries, manipulated by lies and deceit. We must stand strong and united so that our sons and daughters, our grandchildren and great-grandchildren will be singing the praises of Allah in centuries yet to come, not hiding in caves marked for destruction by Christian zealots intent on slaughtering believers of the true faith. And let me be clear on this point: Slaughter does not have to mean the shedding of Muslim blood; it could as well be the attempted murder of Allah in the hearts of men..."

Azziz nodded in decisive agreement.

"...and that, Abdullah, would be no less devastating than a bloody war. While we sit at summit tables, at their request, it is they who quietly sharpen weapons in preparation for our destruction–"

"Swords of ignorance wielded by a powerful nation will flay our very souls!" Azziz blurted, interrupting Sahid, while grinding a fist into his open palm. Although he spoke to Abdullah's assertion, he looked everywhere except directly at him, as if his eyes swept a crowd of eager supporters hanging on his every word. "That is why the fight must be taken to them, before we fall to conquerors while we sleep." His voice hit a higher note. "It seems clear enough Abdullah that you are slumbering now. Know this well: They will swarm over us like blowing desert sand before we know to defend ourselves."

Azziz panted as if the proclamation robbed his energy. He closed his eyes and tipped his head back, drawing a deep breath. In a calculated way, he straightened, brought his head down and opened his eyes to glare at the old man. He then turned his head toward

Sahid, but his eyes were slow to follow. He finally abandoned the contentious stare at Abdullah and placed a firm hand on Sahid's shoulder. "My brother is right. It is by *their* hand Jihad has been forced. We may not match their brute power, but we can strike small, brutally, and often. Operations must be fast and winnable. Lining up on an open battlefield against them would be suicidal foolishness."

Azziz dropped his hands, lacing his fingers once again behind him. "Israel, too, takes land that does not belong to them. They are American puppets, nothing more. This 'peace', as you call it, Abdullah, is merely the calm before the holy storm."

"Holy storm?" Abdullah mumbled. He grew visibly uncomfortable. His voice lost the resonance of a political debate and took on a fatherly tone. "It has always been my belief that we are united in a common cause, a brotherly bond of ideologies. But I'm hearing a divide in our once-shared beliefs. Do I detect a shift in your intentions? We're still of like mind in purpose, are we not?"

Azziz saw the old man's questions as combative, and his eyes narrowed. "Some of us are, yes." He turned to look again through the window to the street below, and across to a bombed-out building left over from the Israeli invasion of 1982. Rubble had been dozed back into the shell of the structure and left untouched since. Many such stories were scattered throughout Lebanon; there was nothing unusual about this shell of a building. But the mere sight of it reminded Azziz that it was time to take the conflict to the enemy, to their backyard.

"We must join the ranks of Hezbollah, Hamas, al 'Qaeda and the disenfranchised Taliban on the world stage. With the help and financial support of our Syrian and Iranian brothers, it is now possible." Holding a fist high, he continued, "Solidarity with our neighbors is the only way, but we cannot acknowledge that support unless it is they who wish it known. This is our strength: deniability. If we appear as rogues, then the Americans will never know whose finger is on the trigger or where their guns should be pointing. In their confusion we enjoy sympathy of liberally biased American news media that lingers too long on casualties of war. There can never be open multi-lateral resistance. The cause you and I share is indeed the same, Abdullah. In that we agree. It's the method we are discussing."

Abdullah retrieved his teacup from the small table and sat on a well-worn divan, sipping. He seemed to relax when Azziz agreed on a point. "And what political maneuverings do you suggest we employ to accomplish such visions of grandeur? Shall we request a moment at the podium of the United Nations Security Council and roundly condemn the Americans for egotism and unwanted intervention?" He formed a slow, patronizing smile, taking another dainty drink from the tiny cup. His boldness to debate was returning.

Through steely eyes, Azziz determined that the conversation was headed for a dead end. The old man had moderated too much over the years, desiring words over bullets to get the world's attention. He preferred diplomacy, and Azziz didn't appreciate the old man's sense of humor. His weariness of the old man's calm impertinence was peaking. "Politics are slow and ineffective. Our beliefs slip into the muck as positions are debated. The years have softened you too much, Abdullah."

"Soft? Is that what you think I've become?" Abdullah showed his first signs of perturbation. He stroked his long, sparse gray beard and thought. "Maybe. What you say may hold a thimble of truth."

He took a sip, placed the cup on the low table beside him, and stood, pacing two steps one way and two the other. He partially shrugged and gestured toward Azziz. "How old are you? Thirty, thirty-one perhaps? You have the fire of youth still in you." As Abdullah took time to choose his words, he continued stroking his beard. "Yes, I have age working against me… an irreversible tragedy of humankind, I'm afraid." He sighed. "As you can see in the lines upon my face, my years are many upon this earth. But with age comes wisdom, knowing how to benefit the most people to do the most good, while preserving precious human life…"

Azziz's lip twitched angrily at Abdullah's comment that implied he might be less wise than someone of more advanced years. As Abdullah continued to speak, Azziz glanced to Sahid. It concerned him that such talk may plant seeds in his friend's mind.

"...It is clear that success to you means taking it by force and not negotiating for an equitable solution. If you should 'take the fight to them', as you say, then you and your followers," Abdullah punctuated with a sweeping gesture, "will flame across the sky like a comet and be gone for all of eternity." He blew into his fist as a magician might, then opened it to show an empty hand.

"I believe Azziz can bring that comet down on those who wish us harm!" Sahid said.

Abdullah remained dispassionate. "I'm sure of it," he replied offhandedly, "and he will kill many who wish the Muslim world nothing but peace and goodwill in the process. You can't put them all in the same porridge pot. That's a recipe for a bitter stew indeed."

The old man turned his back to Sahid in order to face Azziz. He clasped his hands together. "Please, do not allow anger to blind you. There are answers to this problem of colonialism by the Americans, and they should not always be spattered with blood."

"You talk as a man of experience," Azziz said. "I respect that. I also think you are a man that accepts logic." His voice remained tranquil but his demeanor was calculating, his eyes narrowing.

Abdullah nodded. "I would like to think so, my friend." He looked away for a second and then glanced back. "That is, of course, if our definition of logic is the same."

"Good enough," Azziz said. He began turning away from the old man slowly; his stare remained fixed until his body forced his eyes away, as if he distrusted the old man not to pull a weapon. He walked to a world map pinned to the wall. It was yellowed, tattered and curled at the edges, pinned against wallpaper no less aged and puckered, that separated along its seams with rust-colored streaks from a leaky roof. "Look at what has happened in Iraq. Feuding factions using crude bombs have captured the attention of the world. America's mighty war machine cannot cope with such street fighting. In Afghanistan, the Taliban has taken the cue; they fight the Americans in the same style. And it's interesting to note that the people of America don't just mourn there dead; they go to extremes to honor each fallen soldier. The greater goal becomes obscured, and questions arise. The media relishes planting seeds of fear. Bleeding hearts mean more viewers, and that means more dollars flowing into media coffers." After a quiet second, "Can we agree that this is so?" He looked over his shoulder, refusing to continue until he had a reply.

Abdullah nodded and rolled his hand from the wrist. "Continue... please."

"All those improvised bombs are of little relevance in the overall scheme of things. Yet America and its heathen spawn – the news media – are compelled to focus on each one. Have you considered the powerful advantage this provides us?"

"I'll give you that."

"Now, my wise, old friend, consider this..." He threw his chin out and looked to the ceiling. "...Before September 11, 2001, the name Osama bin Laden was known only to a handful of intelligence organizations." His voice rose. "Today, there isn't a schoolchild in the entire world who does not know who he is." He smashed a fist into the map on the wall. "He is a living martyr, deified and exalted the world over... a phantom of immeasurable power. Even though bin Laden is dead, it does not matter. He still is the most powerful force against colonialism in the world today. It's the pinnacle of what the American news media can do *for* us... not *to* us." He pulled his eyes down from the ceiling to connect with Abdullah's.

Abdullah showed no concern, since he clearly assumed he was not the target. He maintained an appearance of neutrality, an angry distraction to Azziz who then took aggressive steps away from the map toward the old man. "If crude car bombs in Iraq, and children wrapped in bombs walking into crowded markets in Tel Aviv, or in any of those war zones, can capture the attention of the world, the magnitude of what I have in mind will resonate for centuries: a series of events planned at intervals. But it would all begin with a single spectacular operation designed to focus on the cause." Azziz struck a pose. "Just imagine... centuries!"

Sahid drew a faint, smug smile. "Listen to him, old man. You may yet have the opportunity to witness history made."

Taking offense at Sahid's inflection on "old man", Abdullah glared for a second before returning his attention to Azziz. "You force my hand," Abdullah said. "Now I must ask the difficult question: Is what you're proposing for the glory of Allah or the glory of Azziz Baruk? I'm not hearing glory being given to God in your words."

Rage pushed blood into Azziz's face, his nostrils flaring. An eye twitched, bouncing his right cheek. He breathed deeply. As he exhaled, his fury subsided to within manageability.

Abdullah sighed. "I'm sorry, my friend. I see that I have angered you, but we must be clear on this point. I only seek clarity, not your ire. How would you answer?" He casually stepped past Azziz to study the map as he waited for a response.

Azziz cut a glance to Sahid, who stood between him and Abdullah.

Sahid nodded almost imperceptibly, and then tapped fingertips on his tunic, where a knife was concealed.

Azziz returned a measured nod then again faced Abdullah's back.

The old man's eyes remained on the map.

"Your question is valid," Azziz said, "and deserves a definitive response. I promise, my dear Abdullah, the answer you seek will be compelling and undebatable."

Abdullah smiled as if a wayward son had seen the light. He spun around and stepped away from the map on the wall past Sahid, ignoring him altogether, to hear what Azziz had to say.

Without warning, Sahid wrapped his arm around Abdullah's throat from behind and jerked his chin upward, exposing the tender part of his neck. He pressed the knife blade firmly into the area below the Adam's apple. The razor-sharp blade drew a trickle of blood.

"The answer you seek, *old friend*, is that once the names Azziz Baruk and Sahid Arrani are on the lips of the world, we will indeed praise Allah for such a grand victory." Azziz relished the fear in Abdullah's eyes; the sudden absence of disrespect was immensely satisfying. Smiling, he stroked the old man's face with loving hands, "Now you will live forever as a martyr, giving glory to God. I suggest you offer up a quick prayer of acceptance and forgiveness for interfering with His will."

Abdullah gurgled, trying to speak – clearly to beg for his life – but the pressure of the blade against his throat prevented even a single comprehensible word. The only evidence of his desire was in his eyes, wide enough to see into eternity.

Azziz nodded to Sahid.

Sahid pulled the knife solidly into Abdullah's throat, sliding the blade's full length across his neck. Blood gushed down Sahid's arm and dripped off his elbow.

Abdullah's arms shuddered outward from his body, searching for relief.

Sahid held him until the old man weakened and became limp, and then let him fall. Going down, Abdullah made a final grab for his throat to stop the bleeding, but his arms had gone useless. In a pulsing geyser, blood spurted from between his loose fingers. His eyes flickered; life faded as his head hit the floor.

Azziz knelt beside Abdullah. Blood pooled beneath the old man's head. He stroked Abdullah's face with a loving touch as death throes ended in a final, full-body shudder. The air filled with the metallic stench of fresh blood. It smelled of promise, of great things to come – of victory. "Praise be to Allah, my friend," he whispered in his ear. "Go be with God."

Sahid cleaned the blood from his knife on the old man's tunic. "Azziz, my brother, now that we have no more interruptions, I am eager to hear your plan."

Azziz sprang to his feet. "Yes," he said with joyful crispness, feeling no more concern for the old man than he would for an incised boil. He stepped briskly to the map. His extended finger led him as he headed for a specific place in the southern United States. Without slowing, he stabbed at the spot confidently. "Here's where the plan begins – the first of eight strategically positioned around the globe. But this one, the first, is designed for maximum exposure to world media. The ten of us will travel to the Port City of Galveston in the state of Texas."

"What consequence is that place to us?"

"It grows in popularity as a place where cruises depart, and few eyes are on it, although the wealthy from every country in the world gather there for decadent pleasures. Major news organizations and Homeland Security stay focused on major metropolitan areas, not on Galveston."

Azziz became excited, turning to Sahid and placing his hands on his friend's shoulders. "By this time next week, my brother, we will have the cruise ship Ocean Dancer under our command and all its guests and crew at our disposal." Azziz's eyes vibrated with orgasmic excitement.

He walked to the window and looked across Beirut. But it wasn't the Lebanese city that interested him; he looked farther and saw so much more than what lay before him. "Most importantly, Sahid, we will bring America to its knees." He lifted a tight fist of defiance. "They will soon plead for us to allow them to do whatever we ask. The eyes of the world will be on us. The scale of wills will tip in our favor and be locked there, while the power-mongers in Washington grovel at our feet." He glanced over his shoulder and down at the lifeless Abdullah. "Our brother was right; the names Azziz Baruk and Sahid Arrani will be glorified."

He walked back to the world map pinned to the wall. He extended his arms and placed an open palm on each end, holding the world between his hands. "What we will accomplish next week, Sahid, is only the beginning."

CHAPTER 3

Houston, Texas

"Marrying you was a mistake. A big one." Evie blurted out the cruel comment. She clearly took no time to think before she spoke.

Nick made a move to cover his wife's mouth. "That's enough," he hissed. "Keep your voice down."

Evie twisted her head away before his hand could reach her mouth. "Don't touch me!"

He frowned and huffed through flared nostrils, and whispered from the corner of his mouth, "This is a television studio, not our home. None of these people need to hear about our problems." He smiled nervously at the approaching floor director and dropped his voice to an even quieter range. "That's a conversation for another time, and most assuredly a different place, but one that's sorely needed."

Evie turned her back to him but otherwise stood defiant.

The pretty young floor director ignored Nick's wife as she wrapped her hand around the microphone attached to her headset, pushing it up away from her mouth. She signaled Nick to lean over. The girl's proficiency astounded him; she appeared to be in her teens.

He suddenly felt old. Still, he offered as warm a smile as possible. His anger at Evie hadn't subsided, but the longer he looked at the young girl, the less he cared about Evie's tantrum. His fascination with this gorgeous young creature came with a twinge of guilt; admiration was tainted by a lusty tingle. *For heaven's sake, Nick, get a grip; she's not much older than Alli.* The gawkish stare had less to do with respect for professionalism and much more to do with the girl's physical attributes – no doubt a response to his marital problems. He shook off the lecherous leaning and focused.

The girl whispered into his ear, "You'll be on next, Doctor Brandon, in the featured position surrounding the mid-break."

"Thank you," he mouthed. He shot a final, furtive glance at those tight blue jeans as she glided away across the studio floor, clipboard in hand, to speak to a member of the crew. He heaved a sigh and averted his eyes, taking in a visual sweep of the cavernous studio.

The scan stopped at Evie. She still fumed. He wished Douglas Mathews, his longtime friend and the host of *Good Morning Houston* had not invited her to the television station to watch – but he had. Now all Nick could do was make the best of it and try not to let her insecurities sour his mood. Seconds before a live television interview was not the time to analyze his wife's mysterious discontent.

Movement beyond Evie caught his eye. He looked to the porthole-like window in one side of the double doors separating the darkened studio from the noisier but less hectic side of television – the business offices. A familiar face peered through it like a fish pressed against aquarium glass. It amused him. His worry lines melted into a smile.

Opening the door, his sixteen-year-old daughter Alexandra – Alli, as he called her – confidently strode in, Dr. Pepper in hand, unable to function before noon without one. Nick didn't know whether it was the sugar, the caffeine, or the taste that appealed to her – maybe all three. She drank too many – that he did know.

Suddenly, Nick heard Doug say, "Please stay tuned. Coming up next on *Good Morning Houston* is Doctor Nicholas Brandon, noted psychologist specializing in groundbreaking phobia therapies. You're watching KPRC Television, Houston."

Doug's microphone clipped, and then audio from speakers positioned near the ceiling blared out bumper music segueing into a car commercial.

The floor director shouted "Clear!" and trotted up onto the stage.

The studio transformed into a buzz of conversations that a mere second ago had been inaudible. People darted about. The young floor director stepped off the stage toward Nick, but Alli hurried to get to his side first. "Make me proud, Dad."

He pulled her into a buddy hug and pressed his cheek into the top of her head. "I always try."

"I know." She patted his belly. "That's for luck."

"Excuse me, Doctor Brandon," the floor director said, "but we have less than ninety seconds. Please follow me."

Hooking fingers around his arm at the elbow, she courteously – but insistently – guided him up onto the foot-high platform, a mock-up of a living room intended to appear cozy. To television viewers, it probably did. Every angle was bathed in light from the grid of suspended scoops and spotlights fitted with brilliant quartz halogen bulbs, with not a shadow anywhere.

Nick trailed the floor director closely. She escorted him down to the empty chair and took time to pose him at a three-quarter forward angle toward the camera, facing Doug. As he allowed himself to be positioned, he again noticed Evie standing at the edge of the light, offstage next to one of the cameras.

The girl fastened a microphone to his lapel. He flashed a weak, insincere smile at her as she took a step back to get the full picture of his appearance. She moved back in and smoothed his lapel, whispering into his ear. "Relax. The camera will love a man as handsome as you." She squeezed and then patted his shoulder.

"Thank you," he said, meaning it. She couldn't know that his split attention had had nothing to do with nervousness about the interview – but now it did. He fidgeted, needing to focus. He didn't appreciate Evie's distraction.

"Ten seconds… stand by," came a shout from the silhouetted figure behind a floor camera. The cameraman stepped into full view at the same speed that Evie backed out of sight into the darkened studio. The cameraman lifted a finger high over his head, ready to bring down the cue.

Again the studio became a beehive of activity. In short order the confusing blend of chatter became whispers. Footfalls in the studio went the way of voices. Activity ceased. It was utterly quiet.

Nick couldn't see any of the crew, who had shrunk into dark recesses away from the lighted set. All distractions ceased, save for one. Evie had stepped back into view at the edge of the light. Nick wished she'd stay out of sight.

A flash of anxiety flushed a rose into his cheeks when he realized that all eyes were on him – not just those in the studio, but every viewer in Houston with a set tuned to this station. It was not a new experience, but he had yet to become comfortable with it and figured he never would. Doug Mathews, on the other hand, just sat there like the stately, seasoned professional he was. Nick admired his friend – a man who had spent years under glaring lights, scrutinized by a fish-eye lens with a touch of envy. For Doug, this was just another day at the office.

Nick struggled to bring his racing heart under control. Audio clicked on mid-stream and blared from the speakers overhead. Startled, he flinched, hearing the final few seconds of a weatherman's spiel from an audio booth or another studio: "...and even though it's the middle of May, you might confuse it for August as temperatures are expected to rise well into the nineties today in the Gulf Coast region of Texas. Now, back to Douglas Mathews, and a special guest."

Theme music played for a second and then clipped. The studio again fell quiet. Nick assumed that his microphone was live and focused on the interview. The fifty-two-inch high-definition monitor near the stage caught his eye as a two-shot of them sitting together appeared – his cue to look warm and friendly.

"Welcome back," Doug said. "With me this morning is Doctor Nicholas Brandon, a clinical psychologist with an office in downtown Houston. Doctor Brandon has pioneered innovative therapeutic techniques for the treatment of phobias that are now common in practices across the country... methods documented and certified to have successfully brought back patients from the brink of insanity."

Nick smiled, first for the camera and then at Doug, dipping his brow courteously at both. "Thanks for having me."

"Dr. Brandon, the word 'phobia' is a cliché in today's conversational lingo, but a very real psychological disorder."

"Oh yes. It's misunderstood by those who have never been afflicted and not taken seriously as regards to damage it can cause. This underestimation makes it a source of jokes and a label for any uncomfortable situation. To the uninformed, the disease at its worst may appear irrational. It might even look like a demonic possession to the extremely uneducated. If you ask a sufferer, they might agree; even to the phobic, it's no less absurd. Those afflicted usually don't know what's wrong, terrified of odd things, and unable to understand the source of the problem. Fears that seem so unjustified that many victims go decades before seeking help. Sadly, some even take relief to extremes..." He glanced to the floor and recalled the beautiful young girl holding a gun beneath her head in Bayside Mall ten years ago.

"You mean... like suicide?" Doug asked.

He looked to the camera then back to Doug. "Exactly... like suicide." He held a finger up for emphasis. "I want to make it abundantly clear that a phobia is an overpowering fear. Sufferers who refuse to accept the disorder as a genuine disease possess the worst form of it. They ignore it and try stamping it from their mind. The fact is: Ignorance makes it worse."

"What are the mechanics of it, Doctor Brandon? What makes a phobia? Why do they exist? Why do they afflict some and not others?"

"The simplest explanation is that it's a short-circuit in the brain, between the animal-like response generated by the amygdala and hippocampus and the analytical cortex. When the three work together as they should, responses to stimuli are automatic. In the case of a phobia, uncomfortable situations remain trapped and never make it to the more rational cortex to be analyzed and acted upon logically or dismissed entirely as non-threatening. To those afflicted, all situations that are less than cozy are interpreted as potentially life-threatening. As a result, a phobia is born from common, everyday things that simply make normal people feel a little less at ease."

"Everyday things? Give an example of one of the more bizarre cases you've dealt with?"

Nick's eyes drifted to the floor. "That's a difficult question. The irrationality of a phobia makes them *all* bizarre to the unafflicted. Take asymmetrophobia, the fear of anything asymmetrical. I had a patient refuse to sit in a room in which one of two chairs facing one another was askew or maybe a few inches too far apart. Remember, a phobia is not an annoyance. It's a debilitating fear. Physical changes within this person included cold sweats, a tightening in the chest, difficulty breathing, and a strong desire to run, to get as far away from the problem as possible – but even the patient realized how illogical escape was. This inclination toward *flight* is common to most sufferers, but when there is nowhere to run, the person is crushed under the weight of inescapable fear. By the time help was sought, the lady I'm referring to wasn't able to leave the carefully sculpted world of home for fear of seeing something out in the world that was imbalanced. Too many things aren't symmetrical," he said, adding flippantly, "Take a look at how people park in a Wal-Mart parking lot."

Doug laughed. "The study of phobias sounds fascinating."

"The less common ones are, but the majority of phobias people are familiar with – claustrophobia, fear of confined spaces; acrophobia, fear of heights; and agoraphobia, fear of open spaces or crowded places – are still the ones I deal with most. It's worth pointing out that within each one of these broad labels are a myriad of related conditions. For example, aeroacrophobia: It's not so much a fear of heights as it is a fear of *jumping* from great heights."

"I understand you have a graduation of sorts for patients who've responded favorably to therapy."

Nick hesitated. He didn't expect the question, having only spoken casually about it prior to the show. "Well…" He paused and looked to his feet, not certain he wanted to address it on the air. He searched for words that wouldn't bind him definitively. "…I'm still formulating a plan, but I believe it could be a legitimate therapeutic tool. If I can take these people and put them in a situation that would be fun under normal circumstances… something totally out of the question at the beginning of therapy… then, maybe, it'll aid in completing a rewire of their brains."

"Interesting use of the word 'rewire', tell us more about that."

"It's well-documented how a stress-free environment filled with goodwill and laughter can physically alter health for the better. I want to put willing patients in a fun situation. Given a reason to focus on something other than fear, they should feel like a set of helping hands is pulling them out of that dark place. Take a short cruise maybe. But it's still just an idea I'm floating – excuse the pun."

Doug laughed.

Nick grinned. "But I have to add that this so-called *good time* is serious business, planned as affirmation of the patient's desire to lick the problem and put it behind them once and for all. Each one of the patients must make the decision for themselves whether they're ready to take that leap of faith to a new life. To you and me, it doesn't seem like such a big step, but to them it's huge. I won't insist that any of them go; I might as well order them to magically be cured. I will be presenting the idea at my weekly group therapy session later today and...well, I'll just have to let you know what happens."

Nick noticed movement offstage, at the edge of the light. Evie dropped her hands onto her hips for a second and then folded them over her breasts, her nostrils flaring over clenched lips. The only thing missing was cartoon-like steam billowing from her ears.

Suddenly, Nick's personal problems came rushing back to the forefront. "Like I said, it's just an idea. I'll need a consensus among group members and... others. Stay tuned." Nick grinned at his host over his use of the common television idiom.

Doug laughed and reached over, patting Nick's knee. "That's a great reason to have you back. Would you do that? Would you come back for another visit soon?"

"Sure. Thanks for having me."

Doug wrapped up the segment by introducing the sports guy who, apparently, was ready and waiting in another studio to fill out the hour. As microphones were turned off, audio blared from studio speakers. Fluorescent lights above the harsher grid lights came on, and the noisy clunk of an electrical breaker signaled the death of the brighter halogen lights. It now seemed almost dark in comparison.

Alli skipped toward the stage. "A cruise? That idea rocks, Dad." She met him as he stepped from the foot-high riser.

He gave her a quick hug. "Thanks sweetie. I think so, too."

The hard heels of Evie's sandals slapped the studio floor as she came at him, not stopping until she was directly in his face. She swung both arms as a flashy gesture of discontent. "You could've let me in on it before you announced it to all of Houston, for Christ's sake!" She turned to march away, took a step, stopped and whirled around, unwilling to let it go. "Damn it, Nick, don't I matter? What I may think about it or have to say doesn't mean anything to you, does it?"

At the moment, not so much, Nick thought. He had many comebacks for that question. None flattered his wife, so he kept his mouth shut. Her anger baffled him. He then became aware of a lack of talk or movement in the studio and noticed people listening to this soap opera in the making. He stepped nearer Evie and wrapped an arm around her shoulder, pulling her close.

She shrugged off the embrace, ducked from under his arm, and then backed away.

"I just thought you wouldn't object to going on a cruise," he said softly. "It'd be fun. Just think about it, okay?"

She didn't afford it even one full second of thought. "I'm not about to get on a ship under the ludicrous guise of a good time and then watch you pay more attention to your patients than me for four days. I can stay home and get that treatment."

"Evie, please—"

"No!"

He sighed and stopped trying to reason with her.

Alli locked eyes with her stepmother and stepped between them, forcing Evie and Nick farther apart, making sure Evie was the one made to step back. The teenager stared her down as she commented to her father, "Dad, you've always been on the cutting edge. Before she died, Mom thought so, too. I have the same faith in you. Don't let anything stop you." Her stare at Evie didn't waver. "Excuse me," she said venomously, "I didn't mean any*thing*. I meant any*one*."

Evie threw up her hands and marched away.

Nick allowed his daughter's show of disrespect to go undisciplined, since it came in his defense. He kissed her on the forehead and embraced her, stretching tall to prop his chin on top of her head. "She didn't seem to like what you had to say."

"Sorta looks that way," Alli said.

"Maybe you shouldn't have said it."

"Humph!"

Watching Evie storm across the studio, Nick wondered what he could've said differently to change the course of her reeling anger.

The woman could have drawn no more attention than if a flashing red neon arrow followed her. It was as if she wanted the world to know her displeasure; but why? What was its source? When she disappeared from view, he pushed Alli back to look into her face and saw Julia in his daughter's smile. He missed his first wife. Alli had grown into a beautiful young woman with board-straight blonde hair, parted at the middle and extending halfway down her back, with a few wisps draping her shoulders. The resemblance to her mother was striking, except for height – that, she inherited from her father, standing five-feet-nine. *Jules, why did you have to leave me? Alli needs you so much right now. Hell! I need you.* Had he entered a relationship too soon after her death? On days like this, the question haunted him. He'd been dazed by Julia's rapid demise due to breast cancer and, at that time, did many things without thinking them through. But now he couldn't afford to get mired in it; it was done. He had to do the right thing and make the marriage to Evie work, but she made it difficult. She had a life outside their marriage; he just didn't know what it was. *I'm going to follow through on my plan, regardless of what Evie thinks.* He nodded decisively.

"What?" Alli asked.

"Nothing; just thinkin' how much I love you."

CHAPTER 4

Benjamin Robenstein, silver-wire-rim reading glasses low on his nose, carried a book with a finger between pages. He wore a bathrobe, untied and open, exposing a favorite t-shirt and long pajama bottoms that swept the floor as he shuffled across the glossy hardwood beneath his feet. The faded words "Diamonds are a Jew's Best Friend" were barely legible across his chest. It had been a gag birthday gift received over twenty years ago and showed its age in ragged seams across the shoulders. Sagging socks, flopped at the toes, completed the ensemble. A scruffy face was the final touch of the visual tale he told: He hadn't been out of his condominium and away from the perceived safety of home in days. It was as clear as the whiskers on his face that hygienic pursuits had slipped down a few places on his priority list.

In her usual tizzy to get things done, his rotund housekeeper Carol Rourke had, moments before, hurried past him to the bathroom, clutching the handle of a plastic tray loaded with cleansers and brushes. Now, with equal verve, she scurried back through, but stopped abruptly in his path. Mrs. Rourke's strawberry-blonde hair, streaked with gray, had been pulled back and fashioned into a bun, but errant strands hung loose down the sides of her heavily freckled face. She wiped her palms and the backs of her hands on the short apron she wore.

Squaring her stance to Benjamin, she placed her hands upon ample hips. "Mr. Robenstein, do you realize you haven't left your home in... well, quite some time? I can't remember the last time... no, wait," she said with a finger snap, "it was your group therapy session last week. Good gracious, have you been cooped up without so much as stepping outside for that long?" The Irish accent was strong. She placed a finger to her lips and tapped them as her eyes drifted upward. After a moment, she continued: "My heavenly word, I do believe that's right: an honest week since you've been out." She squinted and wagged a disciplinary finger at him. "That's not good… blessed be the saints, not good at all."

Benjamin's hands, one empty, one with a book, came up slowly. He pushed out his lower lip and shrugged. "Eh, it's not such a big deal." He reached out and patted the back of her hand, which was holding the container of cleansers. "And, it's certainly nothing for you to be worrying about."

"Now you hear me," she said, again wagging that finger, "it's not healthy. You need to be gettin' out. Good heavens, don't you ever get cabin fever? Aren't these walls closing in on you? It can get cramped in here, ya know."

"Cramped? Maybe. Safe? Absolutely!" His expression softened to a smile. "Besides, cramped spaces are not my problem; cozy surroundings comfort me. I really haven't given my confinement any thought…" He then made a point of gazing into her eyes as his own widened. "Mrs. Rourke."

She scowled. "After all these years and you're still callin' me Mrs. Rourke? By the saints, Mr. R., my name is Carol. Stop bein' so formal."

"Yes it is, and I will…*Carol*." An easy smile came up and a knowing glint followed, as he took steps to shuffle around her. "And my name is Benjamin, not Mr. R., Mr. Robenstein or… Mr. *anything*."

"You're a sly old dog; always makin' your points in clever little ways."

"Sly?" He pretended to think about the preponderance of the word for a second and then pushed a limp-wristed dismissive wave toward her. "I should be so lucky." The slight-built man continued sliding his socked feet across the hardwood floor in a choppy glide away from Mrs. Roarke. He was short at five-foot-eight but had maintained his original hairline, though it was thinning.

"Please, Benjamin, all kiddin' aside: You need to get out. All I ever see ya do is walk from one end of this house to the other, occasionally sittin' to read a page or two." Then, with a sideways grin, she added, "I must admit though, your excellent housekeeper has created quite the tidy and inviting living space for ya."

Benjamin tossed a fist in her direction, as if casting a line, and then made a buzzing sound, pretending to turn the crank on a reel.

"And just what's that supposed to mean?"

"You are attempting to reel in a compliment, aren't you?"

"Did it work?"

"Of course, it always does." He turned and walked back to her. He touched her lightly on the shoulder. "I could've searched the world over and not found anyone to equal your domestic abilities. You're a fine housekeeper, but that's not what you're really good at."

"And, just what do mean by that?" she asked with indignant flair.

"You make a much better friend."

She deflated. "Oh."

"And I mean that."

She shadowed him into the living room. "Somehow, we've gotten away from the point of this conversation: I worry about you."

He glanced back on his way to his favorite chair. "What have I done to deserve such concern?"

"Sometimes your head can be as thick as my arm." She held out the appendage and shook it, loose skin on the underside flopping. "As ya can see, that ain't nothin' to be sneezin' at."

He suddenly stopped before sitting. "I have been feeling more courageous. Doctor Brandon seems to be helping me corral the worst of my fears."

Turning to sit, he saw a question in the portly redhead's eyes and remained standing. "What's on your mind now?"

"Curiosity is all. It's the curse o' the Irish. Aren't you sufferin' from more than one phobia?"

Benjamin breathed deep then let out an extended sigh.

She recoiled and began waving him away. "I'm sorry. I didn't mean to pry. It's none of my business."

"Oh hush! You're like family." He picked up a scrap of paper with something scribbled on it from a small, decorative round table next to his reading chair and used it as a bookmark, and then set it on the table. "According to Doctor Brandon, I showed symptoms of six separate conditions – starting with acrophobia, the fear of heights; then that grew to include aeroacrophobia, the fear of jumping from great heights. Being the lucky guy that I am, it didn't stop there.

Once those two were out of control, I picked up bathmophobia, the fear of stairs or steep slopes, and even a rarer one called batophobia, the fear of standing next to tall buildings."

Carol shook her head and then, through circled lips, "Whew."

"I know, I know. I'm a weird old duck."

"I'm sorry for not rememberin'. But, ya know what? It's no wonder I couldn't remember them all."

Benjamin's head wobbled, becoming vaguely embarrassed.

"You said six. I only heard four."

"Let's not forget I showed signs of cremnophobia, the fear of precipices, and illyngophobia, the fear of vertigo."

"I'm surprised you can remember all those long words."

"It's not difficult. I've been living with them for ten years. Ever since..." He abruptly stopped talking. His chin slipped down to meet his chest. "...since my sweet Rachael passed." The lines in his face went hard, the memory far too clear to ignore.

"Damn my stupidity. I'm sorry for puttin' that horrendous day back on your mind."

"It's not your fault. You may not have intended for it to happen, but sometimes it's inevitable. On the upside, Doctor Brandon says it's part of the healing process. I just have to remember it in a certain way, sort of like putting the memory in a box, always available for my perusal, but so that it could then be put away."

He turned away as a sour face betrayed his thoughts. The memory unraveled like a hideous movie in his mind's eye. He didn't try to stop it, just attempted to stay in control as the scene played out.

Clouds hung low on that cool autumn day in Houston and kissed the ground not far up the street from where Benjamin walked. He left Rachael, his wife, in their twelfth-floor hotel room near downtown, a convenient accommodation for two nights since the couple only lived another half-hour away in suburban Spring Branch. He wanted to be close to the site of the annual jewelry wholesalers' exposition he came to participate in. Working as a jewelry and diamond broker for twenty-seven years gave him an edge in finding new markets. The goal of the trade show was to entice a particular up-and-coming chain jewelry store he sought to do business with. Even as he neared retirement, Benjamin remained analytical, thinking through every angle – no gemstone unturned. He competed against masters of negotiation, yet often walked away with favorable deals. It had become more joy than need, like a game of chess; he planned and rehearsed every move.

Before leaving the hotel, he had stopped and asked the desk clerk in the lobby to put his sample case in the hotel safe. Once on the sidewalk outside, he pulled the collar of his black trenchcoat high to block the damp, cool breeze on his neck. He walked down the street to the convention center to prepare for the show scheduled to begin the following morning. Once inside, he headed directly for his booth.

He fussed over every detail, holding his own diamond ring at tabletop height and moving it about until a beam of light found the brightest sparkle in the stone. He then marked that specific location with a piece of tape on the table. That signified the featured spot for a three-carat, marquise-cut yellow diamond wedding ring with which he planned on dazzling wholesale shoppers.

An hour zipped by, and he left the convention center to stroll back to the hotel.

It was the week before Thanksgiving. A cool mist persisted. Clouds obscured the tops of buildings, taller structures disappearing altogether. An occasional drop of rain hastened his step as he neared the hotel.

Suddenly, a female scream came from somewhere overhead. It jolted him.

His face tingled. His heart stuttered. His head popped up from the collar of his long coat like a prairie dog from its hole.

Thin gray hair reacted to the breeze as he caught sight of three people with terror-streaked faces, standing on the sidewalk and looking up. One man pointed to a specific place somewhere on the side of his hotel. Benjamin's eyes followed their gaze and the man's extended finger.

At first, the mist obscured his vision, but then it cleared somewhat. His jaw dropped and he clutched his chest as if he were having a heart attack when his eyes connected to the grisly scene above. In the haze, twelve floors up, Rachael struggled with a man on the small balcony outside their room.

Before Benjamin could yell out a plea for mercy with outstretched arms, the man shoved her backwards. The force tipped her over the top of a wrought iron rail too short to prevent a fall. Rachael reached, first with one hand then the other, missing with both, and fell, plummeting and screaming.

The heart-wrenching shriek stopped abruptly as her body slammed onto the concrete sidewalk with a sickening combination of slapping flesh and breaking bones. Had he not seen it up close, he wouldn't have believed a human body could bounce. She was dead by the time she hit the concrete the second time.

The grotesque image seared indelibly deep.

Her body rested mere feet from where he stood, its gruesomeness destined to taint most every thought in the years to come and, ultimately, be responsible for the birth of a phobia that grew like a tree, branching into other areas of affliction.

Benjamin later discovered from the district attorney's office that the man had been caught and interrogated. He'd become angry when Rachael couldn't say where the sample case of jewels was located. The thug didn't believe her and tried scaring the information out of her by threatening to throw her over the balcony. The plan to force information from her became a struggle that evolved into a clumsy murder. But it was all lawyer-speak, after-the-fact armchair quarterbacking. Details simply didn't matter.

How the would-be thief even knew about the gems never came out, and Benjamin didn't care – just another unimportant detail, possibly the work of a jealous competitor. His success had always attracted resentment among peers.

Ten years later, the man remained on death row, awaiting execution. The murderer's imminent demise was no comfort. Rachael was gone. No amount of eye-for-an-eye would bring her back.

Countless times he watched her plummet, and it was always the same – hands flailing and grabbing for something that might break the fall. But the only thing her reaching hands touched that day was the grace of God.

Carol's voice pierced the memory he was trapped in. "Sit down," she said. "Please."

His breath had quickened, his brow glistening from popping perspiration. He became dizzy and faint. His knees weakened. He listed sideways and stumbled.

"You're teetering, Benjamin." She grabbed his arm and helped him into his chair.

Reaching for the armrest, he knocked the book from atop a small round table beside it.

"I should have thought of something cheerier to talk about. I'm sorry for my thoughtless lapse."

Between breaths, Benjamin responded, "It's okay. It's nothing new, and certainly not your fault."

She guided him partway down, and he dropped into the chair. "I'm taking you to the grocery store with me."

Still breathing hard, he replied, "As long as you're with me, I guess I can do that."

"It's only a block away. We can walk. The time outside will do us both good. You can help carry grocery bags. You'll not be gettin' out easy… you'll have to work for that fresh air."

Still bringing his breathing under control, Benjamin looked up into her bright green eyes set in a matronly freckled face with rosy cheeks, thanking God for her presence. He calmed and nodded. Carol was his anchor and his guide back to reality. "I'm afraid to think what might have become of me if you hadn't waltzed into my life when you did."

"You best not be forgettin' that," she said in her best Irish brogue. "Go shave that scraggly face, change clothes, and grab your hat. We have errands to run. Afterwards, I'll drive you to group therapy at Doctor Brandon's office."

***

"Thirty five years of marriage doesn't have to end like this, Lydia."

"You still don't get it, do you Bruce?"

Bruce Hansard crossed his arms over his chest and turned his back to his wife. "Maybe not, but what I *do* get is that you and I are sitting in an attorney's office about to finalize a divorce, an obvious overreaction to a few stupid comments I may have made." He took a couple of steps toward the open conference-room door in the suite of law offices. "I, frankly, see what we're doing as an unacceptable way to handle a minor marital problem."

Premature gray hair topped a face that showed little appreciation of his predicament, maybe even full denial. He'd even dressed casually, in tan khaki pants with a well-worn, faded golf shirt, as if this was just another honey-do chore he had to endure before they went home together to resume life as usual.

Lydia's anger billowed. She slapped the tabletop. "A *few* stupid comments? *May* have made? And, what the hell do you mean by 'minor marital problem'?"

Clearly realizing he'd danced over the situation too lightly, he quickly looked back at her then spun to face her. "Calm down," he said, glancing toward the door. "Okay, comments I *did* make." He pulled a chair back and sat across the table from her. "It was just frustration. Can't you see that? It wasn't hate or anger and certainly not because I don't love you." He snaked his hand across the table and covered the back of hers.

Although the smile that came up appeared contrived, Lydia was still stunned by the sincerity in her husband's tone. How long had it been since he told her that he loved her? She couldn't remember. And that simple word caused her to settle into silence. It turned into a needed moment of reflection; she had to bear part of the responsibility for the string of events that brought them to this moment, the brink of terminating a marriage that'd endured for over a quarter century. But it didn't change her conviction that her part in all this was unworthy of Bruce's total lack of support, or that he still seemed to deny her a reasonable level of concern for a condition she had no control over. It was clear: He believed her to be a drama queen – nothing more, nothing less.

After a moment, she pulled her hand from beneath his and rose, needing to step clear of affection that could crush her resolve to follow through with ending the marriage.

She rubbed her shoulders as if chilled. "Look, Bruce, I know you made sacrifices because of my crazy fears, maybe more than I realize. I'm not sure. But not once did you take my claustrophobia seriously." She pinched the bridge of her nose and then swiped the air with that hand. "You joked about it, for Christ's sake! And what

about all those crass remarks and heartless jabs about how much
therapy costs?"

Without warning, she sank into an emotional meltdown. Her
voice cracked. "God, Bruce, you laughed at me. Laughed!" Her lip
quivered. "When I needed you most, you just… laughed."

She was losing control and, realizing it, pulled her frame
straight. She squeezed her eyes shut, refusing to shed more tears; she
didn't want to lose the rage. She needed it to get through these
proceedings. Turning her back to him, afraid of where to draw the
line on that anger, she asked, "Did it ever occur to you how much
the *lack* of therapy would cost *me*?"

Lydia considered letting it go, like she'd done so many times
before, but was overpowered by a need to take her thought through
to conclusion. She snapped her head around long enough to fire off a
stern gaze. "I'm not sure if we can ever get back to where we were. I
refuse to ignore your heartlessness any longer."

Flashing a mischievous grin, he responded: "I have to admit,
therapy is less expensive than this divorce folly we find ourselves in
the middle of." He looked proud of the comment, as if delivering a
world-class punch line.

She whirled around. "Folly!" She dropped both arms to her
sides. Her fingers rolled into hard fists. "You think all this is folly?
Bruce!"

She shoved her chair back. It slammed the wall and rattled the
framed picture on the wall above it. "Damn that crack and damn
you, too!"

She closed her eyes and breathed deeply and hard, trying
desperately to bring her reeling anger into check. After a moment,
she opened her eyes. "That's exactly why we're here, crap like… like
that thoughtless, no-class joke! This is the only way to make it stop!
Are you really that blind? When is it going to get through that thick
head of yours?" She paused and dropped her voice an octave.
"There are things I need to put behind me, and this marriage is the
biggest."

One of the two attorneys appeared in the open doorway of the
conference room looking concerned, his eyes darting between them.
"Is everything okay in here?"

Lydia turned her back on the lawyer and her husband.

"Yeah, we're fine," Bruce mumbled.

She heard the door shut. Panic was instantaneous when she noticed no windows, and now the only exit had been closed. Glancing to the four walls one at a time in rapid succession, she felt them begin to move inward. Her breathing became shallow and fast. Her knees wobbled. Her heart pounded, drumming in her ears. Her hand shook as she groped for the chair still against the wall. She clumsily centered her body and fell into it.

In a frustrated huff, Bruce asked, "What's the matter now?"

She pointed with frightened fingertip flicks. "D–Door… "

No response.

Louder yet, but barely able to get the words out, "The door… "

Bruce did not attempt to hide disgust and moved in slow motion to comply.

"Open the goddamn door, Bruce!"

Bruce continued on with no sign of urgency. "I just don't understand." He reopened the door to the small conference room adjacent to the attorney's office.

Lydia settled, nodding, swallowing repeatedly, refusing eye contact, staring beyond the open door, giving time for her world to once again open up. Finally, she looked to the legal papers in front of her. The explosive, pent-up pressure subsided. She began coming down and glanced again to the open door, as if she had to be certain it would stay open. After a time she whispered, "Yeah, I know you don't understand. I'm thinking you never will."

An uneasy silence settled over the room. She noticed tears glistening in his eyes. Lydia's resolve ruptured, seeing in her husband's face a glimmer of the Bruce Hansard she'd fallen in love with while still in high school. *Can I ever make him understand? Maybe with a little more time…*

In an effort to absolve Bruce of guilt, Lydia began placing it in another time and place. She ground her teeth, remembering where it all started – the seed that grew into a phobia. *My stepfather has been dead for forty years and I'm fifty-six; God help me, I still blame him.*

Left in the daily care of an unemployed stepfather while her mother worked to support the three of them, five-year-old Lydia

Flint protested, cried, even threw tantrums. No matter; she couldn't convince her mother that she'd been locked in a darkened closet, sometimes for hours, every day that her mother worked, left alone with a stepfather she hated. In retrospect, she came to believe he had another woman in the house during those frightening times sitting in the dark. The scarring was deep. Even the passing years had not softened the pain.

Lydia believed she improved with every visit to Doctor Brandon's office, and that he indeed made a positive difference. Only a few months ago, she couldn't remain confined in a car for over a few minutes without succumbing to claustrophobia. She looked forward to every session to clear her mind – truer today than at any other time. She had a decision to make – maybe a simple attitude adjustment by her, Bruce, or both. She wasn't sure. Doctor Brandon's sessions had opened her world, and she put faith in them beyond the obvious.

One of the attorneys reentered the room. "If you two are ready, we can discuss the terms of your divorce now."

Lydia came to her feet in a calculated ascent. "I'm sorry for wasting your time, but I've decided I'm not ready to take this final step just yet."

Bruce looked up at her; this time, the smile was clearly real and warm. He mouthed, "Thank you."

Clumsily, she shoved her chair aside, "I have to get away and think." She stumbled from the office and down the hall to the elevators. When the doors opened, she hesitated. She saw an elevator as another nemesis in her war against claustrophobia. She looked back to the office she had just exited. *I've got to get out of here.* After a stuttered step, she tentatively stepped in and selected the ground floor button.

The usual symptoms of confinement began to manifest – shortness of breath, pounding heart, and cold sweats. She rounded the elevator compartment like a caged animal, trying not to think about it in terms of captivity, concentrating instead on her reflected image in the mirrored wall. She stopped pacing and came to realize that walking in a circle only heightened the fear. Then it occurred to her that the elevator didn't seem as closed-in as the conference room she'd just walked out of.

Remembering Doctor Brandon's advice, she closed her eyes and began deep, even breathing. After a time, she'd become convinced that she was in a wide-open meadow filled with lush green grass and butterflies darting about. She kept her eyes closed and wondered why the elevator, as cramped as it was, felt more spacious than where she'd just come from. What trick was her mind playing on her now? A curiosity that deserved analysis, but this was neither the time nor place for it. She had to get past the next few moments teetering on a phobic meltdown.

She pushed her thoughts beyond the elevator. *What if I did get a divorce?* She took a chance and opened her eyes to see her reflection in the elevator's mirrored wall. A tall, well-preserved, slender woman looked back. She'd always taken care of her appearance; she was very attractive, with few lines on her face and shoulder-length blonde hair with no curl to it. *Even if I could attract another man, would it end the same way? Is Bruce's attitude unique, or would I relive the scenario? Am I better off remaining within a comfort zone that is more predictable than comfortable?*

The quick ride to the ground floor seemed too long. The elevator stopped, thudding decisively. She stepped sideways through the parting doors into the less menacing expansiveness of the lobby. Even the air seemed fresher and freer as she raced past the concierge desk across the welcome area of the thirty-two-story office complex, her eyes fixed on the revolving door.

Never slowing, she pushed into the door until it regurgitated her from the building onto the sidewalk. She immediately began hailing a cab as she ran to the curb. Waiting impatiently, the sights and sounds of a busy city surrounded her. Diesel fumes rode the warm spring air and cars honked, jockeying for position in traffic.

Although she'd planned on skipping group therapy, it was now abundantly clear that she needed it, to be near people who understood. There was still time, but she must hurry. Before the taxi came to a full stop, she opened the back door of the first one to pull over and slid in. "Take me to the Methodist Medical Tower. Hurry please. I'm late."

As they drove away, Lydia looked up at the high-rise building she'd just come from, to the floor where the attorney's office was located. She muttered, "If our marriage has a chance at all, therapy had better work."

***

How did I get to this point? Trish Campbell thought as she pondered the circumstances guiding her life. She picked up the pace on the exercise bike. Facing her bedroom window in her sister's apartment, she looked out across Memorial Park and listened to a mix CD of hard driving tunes. Perspiration gathered on her eyelashes and dripped to the floor. *It makes no sense, yet I'm afraid of crowds. Thank God I found Doctor Brandon when I did.*

She let a clear vision of the doctor roll over in her mind and clenched her teeth as her pulse quickened. She flexed jaw muscles and pushed the whirring machine faster – the hum of it moved into a higher pitch. The breeze from the spinning wheel whipped the long, sloping bang of hair up and away from her eyes.

She peddled hard, but once the song on her favorite CD changed and Bryan Adams' "Eighteen 'Til I Die" began blaring directly into her ears, that was her cue to take it up yet another notch. She was nearing exhaustion but sought a second wind, aided by a mental glimpse of the good doctor.

Sweat saturated the towel around her neck. Perspiration tracked in jagged streaks on her arms, coming together at bent elbows and dripping into puddles on the floor. The bike hummed and whirred, even whistling at times. The weighted front wheel spun faster and faster. Energy ebbed along with worries. This chosen regimen worked well to allay her many worries, but only for a short time following each exercise routine. It was nice that she now had Doctor Brandon's group therapy sessions to augment the effort.

Punishing physical exercise had become ingrained, part of who she was, a vital element in the control of her agoraphobia. Exhaustion made the disorder less frightening, but it always lurked. Even at low ebb, anytime she happened to become caught in a crowd, a twinge remained – always. It was like outwardly realizing the monster in the closet didn't exist, yet being unable to ignore the closet door.

Before she'd given in to therapy, exhausting physical exertion only delayed the problem, which would inevitably resurface at inopportune times. Still, it helped.

A side benefit was the athletically charged physique she sculpted, accentuating a lithe five-eight frame. Very short, dark auburn hair lay matted with perspiration, except at the crown, where it had been cut too short to lay over, even wet. Her bangs, purposely left long, swept at a gentle angle across one eyebrow all the way down near her ear. They clung to her forehead, giving the appearance that she'd just climbed out of a swimming pool. The hairstyle compromised athletic necessity and fashion.

Hearing a noise, she pulled out one of the ear buds. The apartment door shut with a resounding thud and click. She stopped pedaling and turned in time to see her sister, Sandy, appear at the bedroom door. "What're you doing home in the middle of the afternoon?" Trish asked. "Are you sick?"

Gliding into the room and then over to where the exercise bike had been positioned to overlook the park, Sandy came to stand beside her sister, as if making a stage entrance. Only then did she consider the question, shrugging. "Sick? In a manner of speaking, I suppose." She grinned. "I got horny. I think I might even call it an attack... yes, definitely an attack. I guess that could be a health issue in need of immediate attention. I can't seem to get enough of the cure." She snickered.

Trish came off the bike so fast she almost tripped over the spinning pedals. "Horny? Is that what you said?" She wiped sweat from her face with the towel around her neck.

"Horny is such an adolescent term; let's call it a chronic disease. Fortunately, I didn't need a prescription. I knew exactly the medicine I needed." With a satisfied sigh and dreamy lilt, she added, "I'm fine now. But thanks for asking and thank you for your concern."

"Are you telling me you took the afternoon off just to find a man-slut to bang?"

"Actually, it was the other way around. My boss took me to lunch and then the afternoon-off thing just sort of... happened." She laced her fingers together down in front, like a shy little girl would. "It worked out great, don't you think?"

Trish rolled her eyes, disgusted with her only sibling's devil-may-care attitude. She snatched the towel from her shoulders and mopped sweat from her arms and then bent over and wiped the collected puddles from the floor. "I can't believe you."

"Funniest thing, I can't remember what I ate for lunch." She unclasped her necklace as she sauntered to a mirrored dresser across the bedroom. "Afterwards, I told him I had a little headache and wouldn't be back at the office this afternoon." She unbuttoned her wrinkled blouse. "When I told him, he just smiled and nodded." She again feigned shyness, bouncing her shoulders. "Humph. Go figure. I guess that meant it was okay." She removed her blouse and tossed it playfully at Trish.

Trish snatched it in mid-air and threw it back. "For God's sake, Sandy, you're thirty-one years old. Don't you think it's about time you took life, and your career, seriously?"

Sandy's dreamy amusement vanished. "Don't start with me." She threw the blouse onto the bed with decisive attitude. "You're my older sister, not my mother. Why do you have to be so anal?"

"Anal?" Trish exploded. "I can't take a job for granted! I can't even find a job! Even if I could, I'm not sure I could hold it, because of this... this idiotic phobia."

A moment many years ago popped into Trish's mind: she was a young child standing beside her mother in a crowded airline terminal, needing to go to the restroom, begging. That moment, along with similar times branded her. She tugged at her mother's jacket, pleading to go potty. The line was long, and check-in for the flight moved slowly. She cried. Unable to control it, she urinated. It pooled at her feet. She crowded her mother, hugging her leg and wanting to be very small and unnoticed, but her mother pushed her away. Two older children saw what had happened and laughed, pointing at her, drawing attention to her embarrassment.

Even her mother showed no compassion; the chastisement had been no less embarrassing. A mother's words should've been supportive and nurturing. Instead, she scolded Trish. Many others standing in line and nearby heard and then noticed, becoming involved in the spectacle that was Trish. It was a single episode in her life – important only because it was the first. That alpha moment was followed by a series of confidence-robbing events, all taking place in large gatherings of people, eroding self-esteem until nothing was left but a cranial short-circuit called a phobia.

"Oh yeah, the phobia," Sandy said as she removed her earrings. "That does provide you with a neatly packaged excuse." She flashed a catty grin. "Doesn't it?"

Trish wrung the towel around her neck and clamped her teeth together, fighting the urge to lash out. Jaw muscles worked overtime to keep her mouth shut so she wouldn't say something she might regret, but she couldn't prevent a squinty stare at her younger sister.

Sandy was shorter at five-six, but buxom, soft and curvy with a thick head of flowing blonde hair – blonde by choice, the quintessence of every man's sexual fantasy. She seemed to have it all, and could get more any time she desired.

"Look Trish, you're welcome to stay here as long as it takes to get your life on track and back to work. I don't even care if you help with the rent or not. I'll give you money any time you need it, just stop trying to dictate how I live my life." She didn't cower from Trish's gaze. "Okay?"

Trish finally relaxed her face. Her hands fell away from the towel around her neck. She rubbed sweaty palms on the hips of her black spandex shorts anxious and fast. "I'm sorry. You're right." She resigned to the wisdom of her sister's words. "It's not my place to criticize. I'm mad at the world, myself, and, by extension, you. I have no right to interfere."

Trish turned and looked out the window, across the natural beauty of Memorial Park. A glimpse at what was right with the world on this mid-spring day might take the edge from her frustration. It didn't work. She spun back to face Sandy, wanting to argue, but didn't. She turned and walked away, snatching the towel off her shoulders as she went. "I'm gonna take a shower and get out of here for a while. I can't be around you right now. I might say something I'll regret." She marched to the bathroom.

"Be careful when you go out," Sandy said in singsong fashion. "You might have to stand in line somewhere. Ooh, scary."

Trish had just stepped through the bathroom door when she heard the insensitive remark. She whirled around and pointed an angry finger , but all she could think to say was, "Shut up!"

She slammed the door, shutting out her sister and the world, shaking mad. She planted both hands on the lavatory and leaned on it. *I'm so looking forward to therapy. It's the only place I don't feel like a sideshow freak.* She looked back at the closed bathroom door as if it were Sandy. *Why can't you understand?* She threw the towel at the door.

CHAPTER 5

Chin in hand, Nick Brandon entertained a three-ring circus of thoughts, but no single musing leapt to the forefront to demand immediate attention. He looked across the vacant chairs circled beyond the desk in his office as he waited for his therapy group to arrive. His gaze shifted to a window offering a view across the concrete-and-brick canyon framing the skyline of downtown Houston. Warm, humid spring air combined with smog to create a layer of haze that hung a hundred or so feet off the street.

His eyes wandered. Where they settled didn't matter; the looks were empty, just different things to occupy his eyes, as his fingers drummed the desktop and that overlapping parade of thoughts marched on.

One reflection stuck momentarily. The rhythmic beat of fingertips stopped, suspended inches above the surface of the desk. He wondered how well he'd done on the television interview earlier. No one but his daughter Alli had offered feedback – positive or otherwise.

He frowned, his thumping fingers again setting the rhythm for thinking, as he was reminded that Evie didn't seem to care about his career. She never offered positive reinforcement about it, but he shied away from doling criticism for that misgiving. The career had already been established when they met. He wished, though, she'd take the initiative as his partner, his teammate, his wife. To his way of thinking, it should be Evie's duty and desire to offer opinions and advice whenever and wherever possible for continued success because, where his career goes, so go both of them.

Although only a minor annoyance, it was another reason that he missed Julia so much. She had been with him in the beginning and had always been there with kind words and encouragement, even the occasional hard truth if she viewed what he was doing or saying as idiotic. Remembering a few of those times brought a smile to his face.

But the smile wilted away. Evie was self-indulgent; he knew it and had learned to live with it, but lately it had become something more than childishness. Always fiery during arguments, she'd recently become even more combative. It appeared as though she didn't know what she wanted out of the marriage – something different, maybe? Could it be that an idealized opinion of him had worn off and the reality of who he was wasn't good enough? Her comment at the television station was uncalled for, but she may have been right; the marriage may have been a mistake. That needed to be explored.

As desperately as he wanted not to pit Evie against the memory of his first wife, the second anniversary of Julia's lingering death from breast cancer was six weeks away, making neutrality impossible. Regardless of whatever else was going on in his life, he had quietly observed the date last year and would again this year. The plan was to do so every year the rest of his life. On that day, two years ago, the color of his world drained to shades of gray.

Julia kept the news of her disease a secret, refusing chemotherapy or radiation when the doctor told her that chance of survival was less than fifty-fifty even with treatment. She wanted her remaining time unencumbered by weakness and didn't want him doting on her. Those few months were amazing; the three of them were inseparable – laughing, playing and loving. Nick remembered thinking that it was too good to be true. Life was rich and full; Julia had made certain of that. Only later did he find out that it all had been carefully orchestrated. At first angered, he later came to realize she'd given him the greatest gift of all – a light heart – even as she was dying.

Nick checked his watch; a couple of minutes remained before the scheduled start of the session. The rhythm of his tapping fingertips took him right back into his thoughts.

After Julia's death, he drifted, having no tether that might restore life's delicate equilibrium. It was as if he walked on the heaving deck of a ship in a hurricane, never achieving surefootedness.

Then, late one night at a hotel bar, Evelyn Sparks came in and took the stool next to him. Conversation came quick and easy.

Everything happened fast. It seemed as if he woke up one morning and was married. There'd been no courtship and precious little time to learn her relationship-scuttling flaws. In that bar, that night, all he wanted was intimacy, closeness, and the warmth of a woman – someone to fill a void. It now seemed as though he got exactly what he bargained for: a void-filler.

Now he had a wife with a bad attitude that he didn't know very well. But how could he be any less willing to give up on a shaky marriage than on a difficult patient? There had to be an underlying problem. All he had to do was find it and fix it. But, a question circled him like a pesky gnat buzzing in his ear: Would it be worth the effort?

That troubling question was encouragement enough to focus on the situation at hand. Just prior to group therapy was an inappropriate time and place for spiraling sentimental gloom.

Nick resurfaced from his thoughts, chin coming off his palm. It was time, and no one had shown up yet for the session. He wondered where his therapy group could be. Although eager to reveal the cruise plan, he questioned the wisdom of chaperoning thirteen phobics. Keeping a watchful eye on that many at once could fast become overwhelming if things didn't go as planned. *What if I tip Pandora's Box of lawsuits with this idea? It'd ruin me. I'd be labeled a dangerous quack.*

Although sweating details, Nick remained convinced that buried within reservations lay a brilliant concept. Bringing any new idea to fruition required risk. Innovation often came at a price, always did, and always would. The only absolute certainty was that he wanted to try, to press the envelope.

On that fateful day in Bayside Mall ten years ago, he'd vowed to do whatever necessary to cure phobias and raise awareness of the dangers whenever and wherever he could. He thought that the cruise idea might be a gem waiting to be polished. If it worked, new light might be cast on the subject of phobias; it might become reason for many more interviews like the one with Douglas Mathews on *Good Morning Houston*. It could even be the genesis of government funding for broader studies, but first, it had to happen successfully.

He checked his watch again; now two minutes after the hour, and no one had arrived. He heaved a sigh but was in no hurry to call a halt to his ponderings.

There are some in this group definitely right for it. He slumped back in the chair. Worry wrinkled his brow. *But... what if some of those struggling most decide to go?* A few who were not ready for such an experiment might believe it to be some miracle cure. Nick was fair to a fault: If the offer was good for one, it should be good for all. This is where his idea might jump track. He'd need a small army of support staff, and that just wasn't economically feasible.

He pushed his chair away from the desk just as a woman walked through the door, followed by a pre-teen girl that walked so close to her mother they could have been conjoined twins. "Please come in." He sprang to his feet and gestured toward the circle of chairs beyond his desk.

The woman whispered into the girl's ear and peeled the youngster's hands away from her arm. Continually murmuring words of encouragement, she backed out of the room, throwing kisses until disappearing out the door. The girl whimpered and sat on her hands. Although she was on the verge of tears, the youngster didn't attempt to make her mother stay, only watched her leave from the chair. She seemed to be holding it together. That alone showed progress. For the first three sessions, the mother had to stay at her side for the entire time or she'd scream nonstop.

Benjamin Robenstein and his housekeeper Missus Rourke walked through the door together. Nick heard her say in that wonderful Irish accent, "You'll be fine, Benjamin." She reached for his hand and squeezed it, patted the back of it as well.

Benjamin kissed her hand. "Thank you. You make an old man feel important," he said with a wink.

"Enjoy the session. I'll run some errands and be back in an hour." She gave his hand a final firm pat.

A morbidly obese member waddled sideways through the door, daubing sweat with a wadded handkerchief. Nick wondered if the afternoon heat outside was that intolerable or if the grossly overweight man simply struggled against his girth. It could be that he had had an episode and hadn't completely resolved it. *Over-indulgence in comfort foods doesn't appear all that comfortable.*

From behind the large man, Trish Campbell appeared, the man's polar opposite. She smiled and nodded to Nick. He returned the unspoken greeting, admiring her taut frame. He couldn't resist repeated glances long after the courteous time limit for looking had passed. She could easily be mistaken for a woman much younger than thirty-six, wearing snug hip-hugging jeans with a short white tank top scarcely covering her midriff. Her thin-soled white sandals clicked and clacked on the floor tiles as she walked over and filled the twelfth of thirteen chairs. He saw in her shifting eyes that the growing circle of people affected her calm.

Nick eyed her physique, but there was nothing clinical about the analysis. He suddenly realized that he was staring, actually leering. But just as he was about to look elsewhere, he noticed her eye movement accelerate, darting side to side. At first he believed she responded to his gawk, embarrassed perhaps. But then he noticed heaving breasts pressed that tight shirt faster and faster as her breathing became increasingly shallow. "Are you okay, Miss Campbell?"

As she closed her eyes, she nodded rapidly. "Just give me a moment to practice the imagery you taught us." After a short time her breathing evened out.

It was notable that some of the others had taken her cue and were doing the same. She was loaded with charm and natural charisma. People migrated to her in thought and deed. It was a shame that agoraphobia got in the way of letting too many people into to her life at one time. *She'd make a great leader.*

He looked around the ring of people as they toiled to be okay with their surroundings, each with an idiosyncratic fear. His eyes stopped at the empty chair. "Who's not here?"

"Missus Hansard hasn't made it yet," one said.

"Of course. Missus Hansard. Well, we'll begin and hope that she–"

"Sorry I'm late, Doctor Brandon," Lydia said, rushing through the door.

"You're not. You're just in time."

Sitting next to Trish, Lydia offered a fast friendly greeting.

"First," Nick said, "I want to tell all of you that I'm tremendously pleased with the progress we've made during our time together. As you know this is the last planned group session for a while." He paused as a collective sigh went up. "I know… there's still work to be done. But we'll address issues one-on-one for a time and then, down the road, we'll have another series of sessions, complete with exercises designed for each of you."

Nick walked within the circle, hands clasped at his back, making eye contact with each patient, and said, "As you know, I've never been one to stand on tradition. I'm always searching for new therapies and ways to deal with problems such as yours." He abruptly stopped walking and went silent; reservations about the plan momentarily robbed him of speech, but after a quiet few seconds he finally blurted, "I'm going to throw an idea into the center of this circle and hope it doesn't land like a sizzling stick of dynamite. How about we, as a group, go on a four-day cruise out of Galveston? Think of it as an end-of-school party, something fun. I want each of you to realize that beyond your fears, out there," he said, pointing out the window, "is a fascinating world that you're missing out on, every day that your condition keeps you isolated from it. If you want life to be complete, *you* have to take charge. It's the only way to break out of that safe little cocoon each of you fashioned and chose to reside in. I believe most of you have just now begun to peek out. Now I'm asking you to step out."

A negative buzz went up. Whispers exchanged.

Nick let the mutterings continue uninterrupted, allowing time for the idea to sink in.

One finally said, "There's no way I'd do that."

"There's no way I *could* do that," another said.

"That idea is crazier than I am," a third voice said, topping the second.

Nick smiled. "Maybe the dynamite analogy wasn't far off the mark after all."

Trish sprang to her feet. "Wait a minute! How can you condemn the idea so fast? I, for one, am painfully aware how much I've missed by allowing fear the upper hand. And I'm not gettin' any younger."

A few snickers went up.

"I'm *so* ready to start living again. And now may be the time." Her voice dropped an octave as she re-established eye contact with

Nick. "Maybe I *can* do that...with Doctor Brandon's help of course."
With a toss of her head, she slung that long, dark, angling bang of
hair away from her eye.

The look intrigued Nick. His head sagged sideways into a
dreamy tilt.

"Come on guys," she continued, "isn't there someone else here
that can see what a magnificent light of opportunity this is? There
may not be another chance to do something like this with a group
that understands the problems we deal with." She held her hand
high. "I'm in. Who else?"

Benjamin slowly raised his hand. "Light of opportunity, huh? I
noticed the light. But I was afraid it was *that* Light. You know, the
one I shouldn't be going into just yet."

More snickers – one laughed aloud.

"I'm sixty-six years old and I've never been on a cruise. I think I
could handle wearing a Scopolamine patch for a few days. Who
knows, maybe new love will blossom at sea."

Nick applauded. "That's the spirit."

"I don't know how ready I am for having a good time," Lydia
said, "but I do have a desire – correction, a *need* – to be out of town
and out of touch for a while. If a good time happens... well, I
suppose that'd be a plus." She stood as a show of her vote for
inclusion, fingering away strands of fine blonde hair from the corner
of her mouth and blowing away the ones she missed.

Nick looked around the circle. "Anyone else?"

Others shifted nervously in their seats, looking about, but no one
else spoke.

Nick held out his finger and turned a three-sixty within the
circle. "I don't want anyone feeling forced to go or feeling bad about
not going. As I've said all along, only *you* can tell when the time is
right. So, whenever the rest of you are ready, I'll be your biggest
cheerleader."

He waited for comments before proceeding but received none.
"Okay then, it'll be a cozy little crew of four. When would you three
adventure-seekers like to go?"

"The sooner the better," Lydia said.

"That goes for me, too," Trish said. "There's certainly nothing holding me back."

Nick thought he saw a twinkle in her eye directed at him. Or was that infatuation causing him to read something into her expression that did not exist?

Trish added a smile. "I have to admit, I'm a little excited now."

"I have no one I need to ask permission," Benjamin said then sheepishly added, "But, I'd better ask my housekeeper anyhow." He pushed out his lower lip and began nodding. "I have a feeling she'll be okay with it. Whatever is agreed, I'll go along with."

With an enthusiastic handclap, he blurted, "Great! From this point forward, I'm no longer Doctor Brandon, but Nick. And if I can get reservations on the Ocean Dancer out of Galveston for next week, that's what I'll do."

Nick looked to his shipmates-to-be, admiring their tenacity and willingness to press on, to try something new and untested – to be pioneers. The three he believed had progressed most in the least amount of time were the three who'd accompany him. All the misgivings that had given him pause melted away when he realized that he'd only have three and not thirteen to deal with.

As he folded his hands over his chest, he scanned the faces of his cruise mates. A satisfied smile came up. *This might be fun.*

CHAPTER 6

"How many, Dad?"

"How many what?"

Alli trotted to greet her father as he walked through the front door of their home. "Come on, you know what I'm talkin' about! The cruise, how many took you up on it?"

"Only three, I'm afraid." He tossed his sport coat over a chair next to the umbrella stand.

She wiggled a proud thumb up. "Hey, that's not bad... not bad at all."

"Maybe not." He began to smile, since he believed it was actually great that three, and only three, had opted to go. He pulled the knot loose on his tie as he looked at her for a moment, grinning. "Then again, three might be too many. We'll just have to wait and see." He left the tie draped around his neck, letting his hands sink slowly to his sides as he now considered the predicament of Evie. The smile disappeared quite suddenly when that problem occurred to him. An argument he didn't want to have with her loomed over the cruise issue.

"Okay," Alli said, eyebrow lifting, "what the heck is that sad look for? Gotta problem?"

"Oh, sorry, no... just working through potential problems, that's all... didn't mean to let it show." He leaned in and pressed his lips onto her forehead, smacking loudly. "This actually was a very good day for me."

"Ooh ick! That was wet!"

He laughed. "That proves how much love there was in it."

"Oh, you..."

Evie appeared, peeking around an open door down the hall, and then stepped out into plain view. Nick's face went expressionless.

"Honey, I want you to think again about going with us," he called out. "Would you do that?"

She stepped back and seemed as though she were about to ignore him and his question.

It confused him. He wasn't sure how to respond.

She turned and took another step back toward the door to the room from where she appeared, but then stopped and looked at him. In descending inflection, she spoke: "I have things I need to take care of here." The last words of the sentence were barely understandable.

Nick had just witnessed yet another side to his wife's increasingly odd behavior – bland disinterest. Fiery and argumentative was the better alternative, because that indicated interest in their marriage, their relationship. But in that one otherwise innocuous comment, Nick read volumes about her true disinterest in whatever he did. An uneasy twinge tickled his stomach when he considered that another man could be the source of her recently abnormal ways. Whether it happened to be that or another problem, he was moving toward the inevitable confrontation – but he refused to rush into it. He had the trip to consider and wasn't emotionally galvanized enough to handle the possible revelation of an affair. "Okay," he said as she again began walking toward the door down the hall, "but you and I need to have a serious discussion about things, and soon, too."

Evie hesitated briefly before disappearing through the door to nod reluctantly, and then went on into the small study down the corridor opposite the stairs.

Nick leaned in to Alli and whispered, "Any idea what's going on with her?"

Alli glared at the door Evie walked through with obvious contempt. "No, but she's been acting weird the last couple of days."

"I think so, too. It's starting to bother me."

"I *can* tell you she leaves the house a lot and never tells me where she's going or when she'll be back. I think she's–"

"Stop right there. It's not that I don't trust your opinion. I just don't want my head muddled by something that may or may not be true. Whatever the truth is, it has to come out between Evie and me at the proper time and place."

"Okay," she said in singsong fashion and then threaded her arm through her father's. "I hope you know what you're doin' with that woman."

"I'm not going to respond to that right now," he said with an edge. "And don't call her 'that woman'. Please respect her." He smoothed her long sandy blonde hair down over the top of her head. "Besides, I'm not so sure I'd be discussing it with you if I did have the answer." He scrunched his face into an apologetic twist.

Alli suddenly withdrew her arm from around her father's waist like he'd taken sides against her.

He stroked her hair again then patted her on the back. "Don't look that way. You know that I love you and nothing will ever change that. I've never insinuated that Evie should replace your mother. She can't. But she deserves respect as my choice for a mate." He pulled her chin up to look into her eyes. "Would you do that for me?"

Alli remained quietly defiant for a time and then finally mumbled, "Oh... all right." Then came the quick caveat, "But I'm doing it for you, not her."

He held a stare, and tried not to smile but failed. "Good enough for now."

Alli squeezed him tight and grabbed a handful of his shirt, pulling him lower to whisper in his ear. "If she doesn't stop actin' so suspicious and start acting more wife-like, I'm not gonna keep that promise." She kissed his cheek.

Nick snapped his head back, ready to mete out discipline. But he held in the retort on his lips and said nothing. He realized that how he felt about Evie hinged on understanding what she did with her free time. In the end, he might not respect her as a mate, either.

A car honked from the driveway outside.

Alli pulled away from her father's embrace. "That's Pam. We're going over to Jacque's for a while. Okay?"

"Sure. Just be home by nine. Deal?"

"Deal." She bounced high on the tips of her toes and kissed his cheek a last time. The car honked again. Alli threw open the front door and trotted across the yard. "See ya later," she said over her shoulder as she ran to her friend's car.

He followed her as far as the open door and waved to Pam, then watched them drive away.

Sudden loneliness set in. It was an unusual sensation, considering Evie was home and just down the hall from where he stood. It was definitely worth a clinical psychologist's analytical processes kicking in, because if his marriage was solid, or he at least believed so, loneliness should not be an issue. *Avoiding that was the reason I married her in the first place, for Christ's sake.*

He thought about what Alli had said of her stepmother and whether or not she belonged in this family. Hesitantly, he was drawn down the hall and stood by the closed door of the study for a moment, wondering if he should be attempting, yet again, to reconcile a problem he didn't start. His desire to put off the confrontation dwindled. It irked him that he couldn't think of a good reason not to forge ahead and mix it up with her to get everything out in the open. *Why am I suddenly compelled to do this?* He tentatively held the doorknob and began to turn it. *One thing's for damned sure; I don't need to be hesitant.* He opened the door and walked in. And, with that simple gesture, he broke a vow only minutes old to put off a talk with her until after the trip.

The opening door revealed Evie standing with her hands behind her back peering through a bay window at a rose garden and seemed to be watching a bee dart from one blossom to the next. Without turning, "How many did you say?"

"Three."

Keeping her back to him, she said, "So… you're going through with it, shutting down your practice for at least four days for just three patients." She finally faced him. "It's absurd, you know." The words were provocative, but the tone didn't support interest. She shook her head slowly, disagreeing with his plan but obviously not caring either.

He took a fast swipe through his hair with his fingers. "No… no, it's not. You still don't understand if you think that." He wanted to ratchet up intensity into a true exchange of hidden thoughts.

Evie waved him off. "Regardless of what I think or say, you'll do what you want." She again presented her back to him, showing more interest in the insects, buzzing around the roses through the window in the garden outside, than in him. Quiet tension between them persisted, and the longer no words were exchanged, the more awkward the situation became.

Maybe she feared exploding into a tantrum or simply wasn't prepared to offer up the truth yet. He couldn't tell, but whatever was on her mind motivated her to put distance between them. Still facing away from him, she was finally motivated to glide laterally toward the French doors out to a deck bordering the garden.

"Look at it this way," he said watching her step through the door, "Three people won't take that much of my time. You and I could still find plenty of time to enjoy one another."

"I don't think so." She closed the ornate door behind her.

Nick wanted to shout in anger for her seemingly profound lack of interest in their marriage. He let his head fall back and looked to the ceiling. *What now? What the hell do I say?*

He looked around the room, searching for answers but noticing, instead, rows of pricey volumes lining richly stained cherry wood shelves, wingback chairs covered in tapestry upholstery, and French provincial tables polished to a high gloss adorning the comfortable space. He wondered how an expensive house and lavish furnishings could mean anything without a supportive spouse. It was just stuff, things that didn't matter without a caring partner to share it all with. If, in the end, he should find himself single and alone, then living in a one-room efficiency or even a rundown shack of a house would be all he'd want. Life without love is no life at all. *Thank you, God, for giving me Alli.*

Nick stepped toward the window and observed Evie staring down at a cluster of yellow chrysanthemums. He studied her actions. *My give-a-shit factor is on a collision course with rock bottom. Maybe a few days apart will do us both good.*

Suddenly timid and uncertain of what to do, his feet did the thinking for him, and he rode them out onto the deck without a plan. She sat on a bench that had been built around a sprawling live oak tree. He sat beside her and said, "You know, I bet this old tree had to endure a few bad years."

She rolled the petals of a rose between her thumb and index finger, mauling it until silky red bits of the flower began raining at her feet. He stared at the back of her head for a moment and then again looked to the big tree behind them. He ran his hand over the rough bark. "This tree didn't get this big and strong without weathering difficulties."

"What's your point?"

He placed his fingertips on her chin and tried to pull her face around to meet his. She jerked her head from his loose grasp, choosing instead to watch the mindless work of her hands on that rose.

"My point, Evie, is that our marriage could be compared to that tree, years from now, if only we can weather our problems... whatever they are. It can be that strong, but it won't come easy. That's my point."

She kept her head down.

His voice clicked up to a higher octave. "Look, marriages are tested all over the world all the time. There's nothing unique about ours. All relationships are cyclical, many ups and many downs. We shouldn't be trying to throw in the towel at every low point, that's all." He patted her on the leg patronizingly and stood, "But you have to come to terms with what's bothering you, or this marriage goes nowhere fast."

He walked away, leaving her with thoughts that clearly tormented her. He glanced back to see her finally looking at him. Her eyes were red and tear-filled.

***

Lydia Hansard unlocked the door of the modest ranch-style house that'd been the only home she'd known for twenty-two years. She walked in on weary legs and with a heavy heart. She tossed keys and then her purse onto a small credenza beneath an ornate mirror near the front door. The clunk and thud of the items echoed. Hard heels echoing off Mexican Saltillo floor tiles fueled despair – a reminder of how ear-ringing quiet the house had become now that she occupied it alone. An antique clock chimed the hour in throaty bongs. Impending life changes that may not be reversible remained at the top of her mind, and that alone seemed to add crushing weight to her entire body.

Sunny skies outside contrasted with a dimness inside the house that the flick of a light switch couldn't override. Her mood was stuck in a hole she could not climb from as she looked around at all the familiar things with memories attached – chapters of her life. One specific item happened to be an enshrined baseball encased within a clear dome. She picked up her son Eric's twentieth homerun ball that he'd hit during his senior year in high school, still a school record. He and his young family lived too far away to visit more than twice a year. *Oh Eric, if only you were younger and still lived at home, the decision to stay with your father would be so much easier to justify.*

Everywhere she looked, items assaulted her judgment and threatened a decision to leave the ailing marriage behind. Starting over scared her, and the life she had had remained a powerful inducement to maintain status quo. Good memories came close to balancing the scale. But, even on the brink of divorce, her husband Bruce refused to take her claustrophobia seriously. She looked forward to a few days in the company of people that understood what she was going through. Given the chance, maybe her mind would clear, and the choice would become easier.

The phone rang.

Shaken by the abrupt noise in the hollowness of her home, she snatched up the receiver. "Hello."

"Well?"

"Well what?"

"Are you thinking about it?" the familiar voice asked.

"As a matter of fact I am. I've decided the only way to make the right decision is to be away for awhile."

"What do you mean?"

"I mean an opportunity to go on a four-day cruise out of Galveston has presented itself, and I'm withdrawing some of my savings and taking advantage of it."

After a lengthy pause, "Have you... found another man already?"

She shook her head then forced a cutting laugh. "In a manner of speaking I suppose I have."

Bruce said nothing.

"Don't get silly on me. It's Doctor Brandon and two other patients. It's kind of a field trip. I thought it'd be a good way to clear my head, since the doctor will be with us to help me through any problems with my phobia."

"Oh yeah... the phobia... right."

She should've been angered but wasn't. "There you go again. That tone of voice is the very reason I'm getting out of town. Right now, I'm not sure what I want to do, but I can't figure it out around you."

"Come on, Lydia, you know I was only joking."

"Like always." She hung up without malice. As she did, she realized she'd lost her anger, just laying it out for him as if she were explaining what the problem was to a child for the umpteenth time. There had to be a story in her sudden lack of passion for yet another argument. It gave her pause.

***

Sandy, pretending heart failure, stumbled sideways with one hand on her heart and the other swinging wildly for balance.

"Put a lid on the melodrama. I'd appreciate some seriousness," Trish said.

Sandy stopped teetering in a circle, dropped her hands, and then with a smirk said, "Okay, seriously, why do you need a thousand dollars, for God's sake?"

"You told me just this morning that you'd give me money if I'd stop dictating how you lived your life. Isn't that what you said? Or did I hear it wrong?"

"Well... yeah. That's what I said, but I was thinking more like a hundred bucks, or less, for shopping, dining out, or... well, you know what I mean."

Trish dropped on to the sofa, glass of wine in hand. Light from the setting sun streamed in around cracks in the drawn blinds. She took a quick sip. "I realize it's a lot of money, but I have a chance to go on a four-day cruise with Doctor Brandon and two other patients. It seems like the perfect way to restart living. Plus, the other patients going, Lydia Hansard and Benjamin Robenstein, seem really nice. In fact, Mr. Robenstein has a terrific sense of humor." She swirled the wine in her glass and took another sip. "Besides, it takes nearly all of my unemployment check to cover the deductible on my therapy expense. I don't think the insurance company would spring for a cruise."

"Doctor Brandon, huh? Got a thing goin' there?" Sandy bounced her eyebrows and licked her lips seductively.

"No, nothing like that." She sipped wine. "Not that a thing with Nick Brandon wouldn't be something worth going after." She sighed. "But, he's married with a teenage daughter still at home."

"Too bad."

"Yep. Too bad, so sad." She put the wine glass to her lips and this time gulped it. "I want to go so I can come to grips with these irrational fears. Would you help me do that?"

Sandy smiled and playfully demonstrated an arm twisting behind her back. "Under the circumstances, I guess I'd better."

Trish rolled her eyes. "Shut up."

Sandy scratched her head, paced to and fro, and pretended to think about it.

"Come on, I need to know. Yes or no?"

"Oh all right. I think it's probably a good thing for you and maybe a good investment for me." Sandy flashed a conniving look. "I might need you someday." She raked her chin with the backs of her fingers and offered up a Don Corleone impersonation. "I may come to you someday for a favor." She spun whimsically. "Now if you'll excuse me, I have a date to get ready for."

"Of course you do. I'm surprised you don't have two dates lined up for tonight."

"Is there something in what I said that makes you think I don't?" She disappeared through the bathroom door.

***

"I can't do that, Benjamin," Carol said. She steered the car up onto the entrance ramp of the loop enroute back to his condominium.

"Please, I owe you this for all that you've done for me." Glimpsing the busy street below as they drove across the overpass, he gulped then looked back at his housekeeper, trying to remain focused on the conversation and not the height of the bridge.

"Are you forgettin' a minor detail? I have a husband and two junior high boys full o' meanness at home. How'd it look if I waved goodbye to them and climbed aboard a cruise ship for four days with you?"

"Inappropriate?"

"By the saints, Benjamin! Of course!"

He rubbed his cheek with one hand while pecking his leg with a finger of the other as he considered the predicament. Then he snapped his fingers. "How about I buy a gift certificate for you, your husband and the boys to all go on a cruise anytime you can afford taking the time to do it?"

Carol's eyes widened with shock. "Oh, Mr. Robenstein, that's far too generous. How about just dinner out somewhere? That's all it'd take to keep these old Irish eyes smilin'."

"Just because I'm Jewish doesn't automatically make me stingy. Dinner just isn't enough. And stop with the Mr. Robenstein already. It's Benjamin." He smiled then made a joke of her overly formal manner. "*Mrs. Rourke*, you may have been hired as a housekeeper, but you've certainly become much more to me than that. Anyone can clean a house. But you, dear heart, are a real gem. You're my friend and no better friend could I ever hope for. That means, my dear, there's no way I can be too generous when it comes to you and those you love."

She continued staring at the traffic ahead, tightening her grip on the steering wheel as tears began filling her eyes.

"Well… say, 'Yes, the gift certificate would be a lovely gesture,' and then follow that with 'Thank you'. Until I hear it, I won't be changing the subject."

She cut a glance and quickly swiped away a tumbling tear. "If that's what you want, it certainly would be a lovely gesture."

He clapped once. "Good. Now that that's settled, I can turn my thoughts to finding a rich widow."

"Widow?" She bobbed her head side to side. "Maybe. But rich? I don't think ya need to be concerned about that."

"Think not, huh? I just thought that rich and widow went hand-in-hand when an old guy is on the hunt on a cruise ship. I've always heard that. Am I wrong?"

Carol looked at him and gave him a disbelieving headshake.
He snickered.

"Well as long as you're dreamin'," she said, "why don'tcha make it a *young*, rich widow?"

Within a sigh, he said, "Ah, yes... a young one." He shook his head and cut a sly glance at her. "I'd better just keep that desire in my dreams. The spirit is certainly willing but the flesh is weak."

"Meaning?"

"Meaning I don't think I want to chance heart failure."

They shared a laugh. The conversation turned to dinner.

CHAPTER 7

The monotone voice of the pilot interrupted the constant hum of jet engines, "Egyptair flight 985 will be landing at JFK International in New York shortly. Please fasten your seatbelts." After a slight pause, a feminine voice repeated the announcement in Arabic. Sahid Arrani and Azziz Baruk sat with their heads close. The passenger load was light; no one filled seats in front, behind or next to them. The arrangement was ideal for whispered conversation without fear of eavesdropping.

Sahid leaned across the armrest and, in a barely audible voice, said to Azziz Baruk, "It was genius to have the ten of us enter the United States at five different airports." He leaned back then spoke up, "Since we were kids playing football on that dusty rubble-filled lot near the shore of the Mediterranean, I've known you were destined for great things. I saw your genius even then."

Azziz pressed his head into the high-back seat and drew a proud breath, filling with Sahid's adoration. "Genius?" he breathed, and then leaned sideways to keep spoken thoughts between only them. "Possibly, but we'll have to wait for history books yet to be written to record the true tale of what we do. That's when the whole world will know beyond all doubt that what we do is justifiable and necessary and...yes, for its genius." He placed a finger to his lips and then pulled it away to release a thought; "How does one quantify genius...by executing a plan years in the making? Or, perhaps, saying and doing things that ensure a successful conclusion to a long-held dream?" He paused. "Maybe it was merely a flash of enlightenment ripping away a veil concealing secrets of heaven, hell and all things in between?" Facing Sahid, his smile broadened as he placed a hand on Sahid's wrist that lay upon the armrest. "What we do is good and right."

Azziz lowered his voice. "And, to handle the operation any other way than the plan would have risked too much; flying as a group we would have been detained. There is no doubt about that. American customs officials would find no reason to hold us for long, but our mission would be delayed while they checked databases because we fit a closely observed profile. We should not underestimate the Americans."

Sahid shrugged high and held his shoulders there for a second. "Necessary? Probably so. But your command of logistics is genius; for example, ordering each pair of operatives to use connecting flights to yet another five airports then staggering driving times to Galveston. The brilliance is in the plan's intricacy. Red flags will never have cause to go up."

Azziz again placed a finger to his lips, held it for a second then wagged it. "Think each contingency through; ten Middle Eastern men entering Galveston at the same time; that would be a classic fit into their profiling routine. True or not, we must believe that we will be observed, even arriving only in pairs. If we think the Americans are too stupid to notice then it will be our arrogance that brings us down. The idle dog may seem to doze but he possesses wary eyes that follow our every move. But even the twin towers incident has not taken away their lofty attitude of impregnability. Know this well, my brother, the American government is large and lumbering, fattened by greed and easily corrupted. In that weakness lies *our* strength." He paused then held out a cautionary finger. "But never confuse prideful complacency with dim-wittedness. Let's not kick that dog until the goal is within easy reach."

"Forgive me, Azziz, but I can't help but question the difficulty in controlling two thousand or more tourists and crew with only the ten of us."

"It's simply a matter of perception, my brother. Yes, there is strength in numbers. But, there is just as much strength in perceived numbers. We will never all be in the same place at the same time onboard and we'll be well armed to add fear to that perception. Even if some believe we are few, they will still respect our weapons. They'll have no way of knowing how many of us there are. It will be our job to create an illusion that hundreds more are scattered throughout the ship." Azziz's voice took on an edge. "If we instill fear quickly, uncertainty will take care of the rest for the time we need to accomplish our task."

His head suddenly filled with a sense and scenes of superiority. Power lust set up a primal rumble in his gut, yearning for the global spotlight. It excited him. Anticipation felt sexual as it fluttered through him. He would have been no more aroused than if a young maiden had suddenly disrobed and lay spread for him. He could already taste victory and smell it in the air.

He studied the face of his friend then glanced at the stylish sport coat and silk tie Sahid wore. The many faces of Azziz Baruk took yet another turn, jabbing a playful elbow into Sahid's arm. "You look like the school boy I remember from years ago. Without your beard you look younger."

"As do you, Azziz." Sahid showed dimples in a rare smile of such proportions. He patted his sport coat, producing a ticket for the connecting flight to Atlanta then read the printed information within the form blocks. "We must head for the Delta gate at JFK. There we must look for flight number 4437. We have less than an hour to make that connection."

Azziz nodded. "You are a good friend. We may be of different blood but you are truly my brother."

"Next stop Hartsfield-Jackson International Airport in Atlanta," Sahid said. "It's this confidence that compels me to ask again that you refresh my memory of the plan. I do not want to be responsible for a mistake. You wouldn't have to raise a hand against me. I'd end my own life if I should falter."

Azziz placed a firm hand on Sahid's knee, squeezed then shook it slightly, smiling all the while. But then his smile dropped as his gaze lifted to the overhead compartments while he organized his thoughts. "We take a commuter train called Marta to downtown Atlanta and stay in the Radisson Hotel for two nights, no more, no less. Then we rent a car and drive straight through. We'll be the last to arrive in Galveston." Turning to Sahid, "Then we do what?" Azziz asked, testing his friend's memory.

"We contact an Egyptian-American by the name of Hassan Eldar, who owns and operates Gulf Coast Wholesale Foods in

Houston. As we speak he should be preparing a shipping crate large enough to hide ten men and the weapons he'll have ready for us. He'll never see the other half of that fifty thousand dollars he has been promised. Hassan Eldar will be sent to be with God and his body kept with us in the crate, leaving no chance of betrayal, dead or alive. That same day we'll be delivered to the docks in Galveston and fork-lifted into a refrigerated cargo hold aboard the Ocean Dancer with direct access to the food preparation area."

"Like the Trojan Horse," Azziz said, "loaded with their worst nightmare." He glanced across at Sahid. "There may be things to concern me but your grasp of the plan is certainly not one of them."

Azziz felt a presence and jerked his head around to see a small child at eye-level standing beside him in the aisle holding the armrest next to his elbow with both tiny hands. The youngster playfully swayed side to side. He eyed the youngster with the stern expression of a disciplinarian. "You should be sitting with your seatbelt fastened," he said, no longer whispering. He then smiled at the child who was three, maybe four. The little boy said nothing, only grinned. The kid's smile was so wide that it disappeared into shiny pudgy cheeks. Azziz became captivated. "Do you like horses, little one?"

The youngster nodded enthusiastically.

As Azziz looked fondly at the boy it reminded him of another young boy many years ago, a boy that trusted implicitly, that had no enemies or even knew what the word meant – a foreign concept to a youthful mind. A stranger had asked the youngster if he wanted to see something magical. That little one, too, enthusiastically nodded. But his nod gave a ruthless killer permission to slit the throat of the youngster's own mother and gloat, "See, I have released a spirit into the air, poof!" Then he laughed. That man thought no more on what he'd done than if he'd sliced a tomato. And to what end, a few coins and a loaf of bread? The young boy felt as though his heart had been ripped from his chest. Sinking to his knees, he cried and held his dying mother.

The scenario scarred Azziz. It was only a moment in his life but shaped who he'd become. He grew into just another remorseless aggressor in a country where have-nots preyed upon one another invoking the name of God. Azziz differed in that his aspirations were grander. Petty theft never interested him or felt it necessary, but the mindset was the same.

Azziz ran fingers through the boy's hair. "So do I, my little friend. I like horses, too, very much...especially horses that carry surprises. Do you like surprises?"

The boy nodded. His dimples deepened, eyes sparkling with anticipation. The youngster seemed convinced he was about to be offered something good – candy maybe.

A young woman appeared above the boy. She glared at Azziz then snatched up the child. "Don't touch him," she demanded rudely, then walked away not caring what, or if, Azziz had anything to say.

Azziz's eyes narrowed, neck muscles tightening. He wanted to spring from his seat and slap her to the floor. He drove anger down to remain in control. "I hope I'll be seeing you on a cruise," he hissed barely above a mumble. "It would be my great pleasure to introduce you to manners for women the way Allah intended."

He studied the young mother as she strapped the boy in then snapped the seat belt buckle. She rushed to get seated, too.

Azziz continued glaring at her. *You must be taught manners. And I should be the teacher.*

Tires squawked, the jet pitched slightly right then left, eventually stabilizing for the taxi to the terminal. Egyptair, flight 985 from Cairo was now securely on the tarmac of JFK. Thrusters reversed. The plane whined then shuddered.

Still angered, Azziz stared at the back of the head of the rude young mother who sat across the aisle and ahead three rows as he spoke to Sahid. "It is almost time to set our feet on soil of the country that will soon be paying us homage."

The jet taxied to a specified gate, preparing to dock with the loading tunnel. A steward stepped into the passenger area of the plane from near the exit door and removed a microphone from its hook on the wall. "Thank you for flying Egyptair. We hope your flight was pleasant and that you fly with us again soon."

Azziz unfastened his seatbelt and stood. He stretched tall and flared his nostrils as if he'd picked up the scent of something new.

"Come, my brother. Let's begin this journey toward immortality. History books will indeed record this grand undertaking." He stepped into the aisle cutting off an obese woman, making her wait while he allowed Sahid in line ahead of him. As Sahid stepped past him, "Glory awaits. Praise Allah."

CHAPTER 8

As Houston's skyline slowly began to sink into the horizon behind them, Nick relaxed more with each passing mile. His mind skipped from one random thought to another – snippets of events that held no relevance, little things riding a carousel of thoughts. Easing of anxieties carried him to a rare state as the chartered shuttle van approached Galveston.

The hum of the engine at cruising speed and tires thumping over seams of the concrete freeway added to the waning stress and wooed him. He became drowsy. The sky was clear above a summertime haze that softened the blue into hues of gray, dotted with cotton-ball clouds partially obscured as if seen through a loosely woven linen veil. Unobtrusive music wafted from the radio, scarcely loud enough to discern melody. A cool breeze from the air conditioner brushed his cheek.

With his head back against the seat, he turned to watch the passing scenery; every uneven place in the highway translated into the gentle, rocking motion of his head against the cushion. His lazy eyes blinking slowly, he gazed out the window to the shallow water of the bay. Families enjoyed a day of fishing, most standing in waist-deep water watching the line from their rods as if a fish would be hooked at any second. Farther out, boats skimmed the water like aquatic insects, while barges in the deeper water of the channel went about the daily business of carrying cargo here to there, with tugboats helping get it done. Nick's eyes were drawn to movement, forming no opinions on what he saw, he all the while absently picking at the cracked blue vinyl on the door panel. *All those people have stories; I wonder what their dreams and problems are?*

Finally breaking with rambling thoughts, he pulled himself forward for a better look at where they were headed. Napping may have been the preferred thing to do, but he realized it was also rude to his companions. The van crossed onto Galveston Island and headed straight for the seawall on the opposite side of town.

Lydia's breathing caught his ear, a raspy spasmodic draw that quickened.

"Everything okay back there, Lydia?" He turned to see her eyes shut tight. Benjamin stroked her shoulder. She smiled at the sound of his voice.

"Just a claustrophobic flash; I'll be all right." She opened one eye and looked at Nick. "God help us all, though, if I'd been driving when it came over me."

"Remember the images you chose to replace fear with. Pick one of them and concentrate on it."

She closed her eyes again. "There he is."

"Who?"

"Brad Pitt, of course."

"That's an image that works for you?" He laughed. "I would've figured that guy would induce the heavy breathing, not calm it." He paused. "But, I can't debate that he is an excellent distraction."

Nick glimpsed Trish sitting next to him, smirking. He then turned to see Lydia wearing a faint smile, though she was still grappling with leftovers of the phobia.

His cheeks reddened. "I meant a distraction for Lydia, not me. I'm straight. I'm not... I wouldn't... I think I'll shut up now."

Nick faced the street ahead. In passing, he saw Trish's smirk transform into a wry grin. He took note but didn't linger, although he was intrigued by her expression, wondering what, exactly, was on her mind. He looked again for a stolen second. *I wonder if a girl like her could be interested in a guy like me.* He faced forward and squeezed his eyes shut. *Why am I even thinking that? I'm married, for God's sake.*

The van came to the intersecting street that ran along the top of the seawall and turned onto it. Nick saw open gulf waters and drank in the sight of rolling surf. There were times he'd spent hours just sitting on the beach watching and listening to waves crashing. He slid to the edge of his seat.

"I'm glad we left early enough to drive the wall before heading to the docks."

Looking back in the direction of the mainland, he saw the pyramids of Moody Gardens some distance away and noticed Trish looking, too.

She glanced across to him. "This is my first trip to Galveston."

"Ever?" Lydia asked.

"Afraid so."

"Only fifty miles from home and you've never been here?" Nick asked.

"Nope, never had the urge...or opportunity. Remember, I came to Houston from Chicago three years ago for my job, not the beach." She sighed. "But I can't say that about my younger sister, Sandy. After my second year in Houston she came to join me. With her it was *all* about the beach and other adventures that..." She paused but finally waved off hesitation. "...Well, let me just say her idea of adventure is wearing pants." Her eyes did an embarrassed dance before averting to again look out the window at endless beach umbrellas and tourists off the seawall. After a time she faced forward, her expression sullen.

Nick noticed. "Bad thought?"

"I miss that job. But I can't blame anyone but myself for losing it. It's my own phobic fault. Oh well, maybe things are about to change for the better."

If it was excitement he saw in her, he shared it. When he assumed her unaware, Nick took surreptitious glances, studying her profile, amused by the twinkle in her eye at each landmark they passed. Her eyes hung on every restaurant, curio shop, and young stud in a Speedo walking the seawall sidewalk next to the street. It occurred to him that he wasn't as much interested in her fascination with the sights as he was in her – Trish, the woman. This time, he didn't try to look away. *Oh, what the hell.*

Super short auburn hair over flawless smooth, tanned features made for a fetching sight. Long locks of hair swept from her forehead to partially cover one eye. Heightening his hormonal buzz were her skin-tight clothes; she was dressed as though she'd just stepped into a gym. She wore a low-cut top held loosely by spaghetti straps, and shorts that accentuated muscular striations along her outer thigh.

With lower lip hanging, his thoughts turned lecherous. He must have looked like Homer Simpson drooling over a donut. Finally, he realized that he'd better get his head somewhere else. "If you've never visited here before," he blurted, "then I assume you've never delved into Galveston's history."

Still looking out the window, Trish shrugged. "No."

"Have you ever heard of the pirate Jean Lafitte?" Benjamin asked from behind. He pulled forward to the edge of his seat, poking his head between them.

"Sure," she said, still gazing out across town.

"There you go."

The vague comment succeeded in drawing her in. "Huh?"

"That's a famous name Galveston is known for," Nick said.

Benjamin nodded agreement. "Some might say infamous."

"He and his brother, Pierre, swore allegiance to just about any sovereignty that benefited them personally. Oddly, I know businesspeople in Houston right now like that. The only thing that's changed is the style of dress and the object of greed. Lafitte set up the first government in Galveston and turned it into a bastion of piracy and privateering around 1817."

"If Galveston is such an interesting and historic place, why don't we spend four days here? Why do we need to get on a cruise ship? We can get rooms at the Sheraton, paddle in the pool, and drink Piña Coladas all day."

Lydia, sitting next to Benjamin, finally became engaged in the conversation. "Oh, no; I've set my mind and heart on cruisin' the Gulf of Mexico. I don't want to spend time learning Galveston's history. I just want to feel a warm, salty breeze for a few days, hold sweet alcoholic drinks... something with a paper umbrella in it, and give my aching head a rest." Although the words could have been argumentative, Lydia offered them with a smile. Letting down her window, she sucked in an exaggerated amount of the salt-laden air blowing off the surf.

Nick couldn't determine if she simply wanted to sniff the air and get a feel for the open water, or if it might be a control measure countering claustrophobia. Maybe confinement in the van negatively worked on her more than he realized. "I agree, Lydia." He kept his eye on her for a moment longer, just to make sure she was okay.

She responded to his silent gaze with a smile.

"But if the cruise turns out well," he added, "there's no reason we can't come back and spend the day another time."

On that comment and for the first time, Trish looked at him differently. She bore an easy smile. Nick inadvertently bobbled his head and flashed a boyish grin, hoping that new look on Trish was interest in him.

"Galveston is close enough that we might get together for a day trip and dinner down by the docks and enjoy the Strand," Benjamin said.

Trish looked straight at Nick, "Sounds good... sounds *really* good. Let's hang on to that thought."

Nick didn't look away. He stared as she turned away to again view the sights, and then let his eyes trail down.

The libido-driven gaze was interrupted from behind. Lydia smiled knowingly. Her eyebrow rose. "Let's see how the cruise goes first," she said.

Nick blushed and suddenly felt the need to start talking. "Uh, anyway, Galveston is known for more than just a place to dock cruise ships. The hurricane of 1900 was the deadliest in history, killing over six thousand. And the merchant ship Elissa is open for tours. It was the quintessential merchant ship of the nineteenth century." He looked in the general direction of the docks. "There," he said pointing. "You can see The Elissa's bare-mast standards."

"Okay, but I'm still looking forward to the cruise," Lydia said.

The driver, disinterested by the conversation, remained quiet as he steered the van into a queue of vehicles where ship's personnel scurried about, collecting luggage from cars and trucks lined up awaiting their turn. The Ocean Dancer stood tall, five or six stories above the waterline by Nick's reckoning.

"Oh my," Benjamin said as his eyes moved upward, hitching at each row of windows on the ship's side and stopping at the deck rail high above.

Nick saw a glow developing on the old guy's forehead. "There'll be no sugar-coating this. Each of you will face things on this trip that'll test your resolve. It's part of why we're here. Benjamin is looking at his first big obstacle – the height of that ship. Our task is a final, all-out, no-holds-barred confrontation of fear, a chance to see it clearly and how unimportant it really is when dragged out to face the light of day. That ship represents a delivering beacon of that. All I ask is that you let it shine. Don't lose sight that there is a world of fun about to be served up on a silver platter aboard that ship. All you're required to do is partake. Just be aware as we embark that we'll encounter plenty of height obstacles," he said, looking at Benjamin. Then his eyes swept from Trish to Lydia, "and you two will have a dose of closed-in places and crowds to contend with. This is why I consider a cruise ship an ideal place for this. Let's set some ground rules. We'll be buddies, because when you have fear kicking in, most likely the other two will be in a position to lend support. Of course, I'll almost always be nearby, too."

"Did you really think we wouldn't help one another?" Lydia asked.

"I feel better knowing you already assumed it."

"For four days we'll be as close as family," Trish said.

"A better family I wouldn't find anywhere," Benjamin said, eyes still closed, his head back against the seat. He then opened one eye and lolled his head to the side, glancing again at the ship. "You huge lovely beast; you're not that scary... I guess."

Nick got out and helped the driver unload luggage. They walked to the check-in area in tight single file, taking short, choppy steps like awed schoolchildren walking into summer camp for the first time without parents. They waited in a line that inched its way into the air-conditioned building to check passports before boarding.

Once checked in, they entered a clear-Plexiglas-domed gangway, and the thought struck Nick that it was probably designed and approved by OSHA. His whimsical grin fell quickly when he realized he had a problem developing behind him. His buddy system might be in jeopardy from the get-go.

Benjamin stood in the center of the walkway looking pained, hunkered forward as though someone held a branding iron to his chest. The clear safety of the Plexiglas shroud provided a good view of the dock and water about twenty-five feet below where they stood – a view Benjamin could not appreciate. He began stumbling forward.

Nick dropped his carry-on bag and raced back to him. "Just a little farther, Benny. You can do it. No big deal."

People began bunching up behind them as Nick encouraged the old guy along. Speaking to the crowd at large, "I apologize for the hold up," he said, waving at them. He snatched up his bag in one hand while holding Benjamin around the waist with the other.

Trish began reacting to people crowding closer. Her knees wobbled and her step slowed, providing yet another obstacle to a smooth-flowing line of tourists. A jumble of increasingly irritated vacationers began to push closer. Tempers flared fast after such a long time outside in the sweltering heat waiting to check in. The gangway was not intended for dawdling – no air conditioning. The sun beamed harshly through the Plexiglas, even though it was tinted.

"What's the matter?" came a taunting voice from farther back in line, "Are there retards up there or what? Let's get this line moving! It's hot in here!" Emboldened, others tossed out unflattering comments, too. Trish's uneasiness added awkwardness to her step as she hurried to Nick's side, coming into bodily contact with him. She clutched his arm and whimpered.

While still holding onto Benjamin on one side, he reached for Trish to lend what support he could. He found himself pinched between agoraphobia and acrophobia.

Trish appeared as though she might burst into tears. Her lower lip quivered. She looked up at him. "I'm sorry, Nick. I'm trying."

Lydia seemed no better off. The closeness of the covered gangway stifled her. Her face reddened. Perspiration popped, and she groped for and grabbed Trish's hand.

Nick became concerned. All three succumbed at the same time to different phobic afflictions, and they hadn't even boarded yet. *Oh, Lord, have I screwed up?* he wondered, but he didn't expect clouds to part and drop a divinely inspired answer on him.

As he considered the problem, he noticed on the dock below that three forklifts carried immense wooden containers into the ship's cargo hold. They appeared as a well-choreographed dance of machines. The spectacle intrigued him; it was reminiscent of ants bringing in supplies for winter. Suddenly, one of the large shipping containers shifted atop the tines of a forklift tractor. It rose on one end as if about to fall from its perch. It seemed to contain fluid, or maybe loose cargo. It began wobbling. Curiously, it seemed to right itself before tumbling from the forklift, even before the operator made a fast corrective move to prevent it from toppling.

Nick didn't have time to consider it further. "Come on, guys. Just a few more feet and your problems will vanish."

Finally emerging from the gangway into the interior of the ship, Nick saw a foyer area with elevators; it was not spacious, but a damn sight better than the gangway. Personnel in starched white uniforms answered questions and pointed the way for confused guests. A rush of cool air and the dispersing crowd settled Nick's charges. He breathed a sigh of relief. "See? Just a little test... that's all it was. But don't go searching for the next one, please. Just concentrate on having a good time."

Nick was enamored with the brightly colored carpeting, polished brass detail on walls and support columns, and spiffy accommodating ship's staff. As people waited for elevators or directions from personnel, the room buzzed with many conversations. People became talkative as anticipation built; a smattering of laughter added a festive feel.

He saw pleasant, relaxed looks on the faces of Lydia and Benjamin. Trish seemed to be having a small problem but was, for the present, holding it together. Lydia pulled her close and put an arm over her shoulder.

"Thank you," Trish told her, squeezing her hand.

Nick looked up the stairs to his left and couldn't see beyond the first landing where the steps turned ninety degrees, but what he wanted to see, he did: opportunity. He glanced at Trish.

CHAPTER 9

Cursing in Arabic under his breath, Azziz jammed a foot into the wooden floor, pressing both palms into the top of the shipping crate and wedging his body in place as the container began to rise on one end. The forklift had turned too sharply. Five fully armed men sat on each side, pressed together on narrow benches nailed in place. A corpse that had been rolled and bound in a small rug lay at their feet. Inertial force of the turn had moved the entire crate off-center.

"The body is sliding," Azziz said quickly, "Pull it back to the center."

No one snapped to action fast enough to suit him.

"Do it now, hurry!"

He looked directly at a very young co-conspirator on whose boots the body lay. "Now, you idiot! The crate is off-balance."

Afraid of Azziz's anger, the young man still did not make a move to comply, just sat with fear frozen on his face as the crate sank precipitously on the right end. The corpse slid faster, right over the boy's feet. The forklift operator seemed not to have noticed and was turning even sharper, apparently lining up the loaded tines to the steel plank that bridged dock to ship.

Azziz bore down on the young man. In the dim green light of the glow sticks, his face turned malevolent. He ground his teeth and growled, "Now, you fool!"

The boy flinched, frightened by such intense anger.

Sahid, sitting next to the young man, saw that he'd become terrified beyond good sense and remained unresponsive to Azziz's angry order. He reached past the boy with his foot and stopped the dead weight from sliding any farther. The crate continued rising on the left side, and Sahid leapt past the boy, adding his weight to counter the shift. The crate reluctantly settled.

"You idiot," Azziz said. "There is no room for hesitation... in this matter or any other. The plan almost ended before it began. If this crate had hit the concrete, it would've splintered, spilling us out like bumbling clowns."

Sahid watched the face of his friend and mentor in the dim green glow and saw a familiar expression – hard and determined. He knew that look well and emulated the expression as his own resolve deepened to follow through on the order he knew was coming.

"I'm sorry. I'll pay closer attention. I'll not let it happen again. I promise," the boy babbled. "You are my master and teacher. Please, Azziz, do not lose faith in me. I've still much to learn, but under your tutelage, I will. I swear it."

Sahid watched Azziz's face go calm as a parent might look before counseling a child. "On the contrary, my young friend, I have not lost faith. I now have tremendous faith you will not make any more mistakes."

The boy relaxed. "Thank you, Sir. Thank you for your confidence."

Sahid received a nod from Azziz.

The boy glanced between them. His eyes grew large when it became obvious what those shared looks meant. He whimpered. "Oh, Sir. No. Please no." The boy began to cry.

"Go be with God, my son. Be brave and do not be concerned. We'll all be together again someday soon."

The man beside him held the boy's mouth as he squirmed and resisted. Sahid, sitting next to him on the other side, drew his knife. With surgical calculation, and ignoring the young man's whimpers, Sahid placed the tip over the boy's heart and found the soft cartilage between the ribs. With the heel of his hand, he shoved it to the hilt into the boy's chest. The lad continued resisting as his strength drained away. After only seconds, his head slumped forward and twitched a final time before going limp.

Sahid saw the reaction of another boy near the same age who was sitting at the end, the fifth on his side of the crate. That one clutched the fabric of his vest as if the knife had plunged into his own chest. Sahid felt compelled to answer the boy's expression. "When Allah speaks through Azziz, we must listen. Your future and ours depends on it." As Sahid spoke, he held the knife handle, still deep in the boy's chest, giving time to be sure there would be no noise.

The other man kept his hand over the boy's mouth.

Sahid flicked his eyes toward Azziz.

Azziz nodded and looked to the unnerved boy on the end. "It's the way it must be. The time for training and gentle discipline has passed. Learn by what you've seen. Pay strict attention to the plan, but remain flexible if a deviation is called for." Azziz looked at the dead boy. "Our friend failed to see the need for rapid modification. He failed the test of flexibility. His failure almost doomed the entire operation. Remember this well: It only takes one small mistake to bring down what we seek to accomplish. Remain calm and alert, my son. And, at all times, be prepared to react according to the situation. If you do as I say, you'll be fine."

"Now we are nine," Sahid said, pulling the bloodied knife from the boy's chest.

The muted rumble of the forklift changed as hydraulics engaged and the Trojan horse lowered. As soon as it bottomed out, shaking them side to side, a metal clang signaled closing doors behind them. They were again rising, this time tractor and all. "We are on an elevator," Sahid muttered.

Azziz looked up, as if seeing the direction they moved. "Yes, to the refrigeration unit in the main food distribution area. From there, all foods are sent to the various kitchens onboard."

Shortly, doors on the opposite side opened. The forklift throttled up. The crate jerked as the tines lifted it up, and the tractor moved forward a short distance. It again lowered, and the forklift backed from under it. A monotonous beep sounded the reverse warning on the small machine. Engine noise faded, and the metal clang of the closing elevator doors was followed by silence. They heard men talking in the distance, and then the heavy thud of a shutting door. It became very quiet.

"I feel cold penetrating," Azziz said. "We are in the refrigeration unit. The virtue of patience will now be tested while we wait for the Ocean Dancer to become a floating island in the Gulf of Mexico." Azziz sighed; seemingly satisfied that things were back on track and going well.

Sahid grew proud while watching his friend pose, as if waiting for a portrait painter to immortalize him in oil.

CHAPTER 10

Nick leaned against the starboard rail near the stern of the cruise ship's upper deck, his outstretched hands resting upon it. He watched a shrinking view of Galveston as roiling blue water foamed from beneath the hull and then fanned into a widening white wake. Hundreds of people crowded the rail around the ship. The Ocean Dancer sliced through swells powering south, farther into the Gulf of Mexico.

Trish, a few feet back toward the stern, happened to be standing in the direction he looked. She repeatedly drew glances from two men standing nearby, and from others walking past her. He couldn't claim his own behavior to be out of the ordinary after witnessing so many men obviously admiring Trish's tight, athletic frame. The sinking Galveston skyline wasn't interesting enough to keep him from joining them in the more enticing view of a beautiful woman. She leaned into the rail, eyes closed, head thrown back, letting the stiff, salty breeze have its way – his perfect opportunity for a long, admiring, analytical look. He took his time, drinking her in without fear of being discovered. But it wasn't an unobstructed view.

Between them stood a woman, obviously a young mother; next to her knelt a man pointing things out to a small boy. For a moment, Nick became enamored with the Norman Rockwell-type picture of a family on vacation.

But his searching eyes were on a mission that had nothing to do with skylines and families. He leaned back, still clutching the rail, and craned his neck to maintain a view of the true object of his fascination. Unwilling to look away while the opportunity existed, he indulged in what had only been stolen glimpses before now, examining Trish from top to bottom and back up. Adoration came complete with fantasy, as he studied the contours of a near-perfect feminine form.

Only then did he notice Lydia standing back a couple of paces. It abruptly occurred to him in a most embarrassing way that, as he lustfully watched Trish, Lydia watched him, and she was clearly amused.

Mortified to a deep crimson, he averted his eyes from both of them, turning back toward the open water beyond the ship. He squeezed his eyes tightly shut. *Oh crap! What is Lydia going to think of me now? If she has an inkling of what was on my mind, she'll probably spend the rest of the trip avoiding me.*

Although he couldn't deny that he was checking out Trish, he hoped Lydia had not recognized the lusty aspect of it. But, once again, honesty became his nemesis. A neon sign might as well have been glued to his forehead that flashed *LUST* in bold red letters.

Lydia snickered.

He heard it and glanced to see Lydia grin so big that it left no doubt he'd been found out – caught red-handed, hand in the cookie jar. He was left with no choice but to grin with her. His head bobbled upon his shrugging shoulders like a humiliated child, adding to what must have been a really stupid smile.

"Sorry, weak moment."

She stepped to his side and put her lips to his ear, "It's okay, Doctor Brandon. She's beautiful. I've taken long looks at her, too. But it's envy for her youth and beauty that I suffer from."

"I'm afraid it's not okay," he said, polishing the deck with the tip of his shoe. "I'm married. My wife and I are going through a rough patch, and I need to be working on that. Just the thoughts I was having run counter to that intention." He looked again to Trish. "Oh, Lord… that is such an understatement." He took a long, deep breath.

"I'm certainly in a position to sympathize. I know your dilemma well, believe me. But if I'm to become your friend and traveling companion, this is where I, the patient, advise you, the doctor, to relax and enjoy this trip. If you need a prescription, I'd be happy to jot something down." She patted his hand upon the rail. "Go ahead, Doctor Brandon, let your mind and this ship take you where they will. I plan to. Maybe both our problems will become clearer than that blue sky up there."

"Call me Nick."

"Okay... Nick. Remember, Las Vegas hasn't cornered the market on dissolving inhibitions; cruises have a way of doing it, too, I bet." She paused and winked, then quickly added. "I'm not saying that's bad or good, mind you... just that it's so. But, no matter which way it goes, I'll certainly not be the judge of you; I'll just be your friend."

His sudden embarrassment drained away, and tension from it eased. He offered an admiring glint and pulled her into a side-to-side buddy hug. "You're a good person, Lydia Hansard, ya know that?" He lifted her hand and kissed the back of it then squeezed it between his palms. Nick felt the onset of a comfort zone with the woman ten years his senior, almost as if he had acquired a partner in his desires. At the least, he felt better knowing that she was already aware and wouldn't condemn his actions one way or the other.

Beyond Lydia, Benjamin stood firmly against the cold metal wall of the control room at the farthest point from the rail, as near to the center of the ship as he could get. He clutched the welded mount of a fire extinguisher on the wall. His legs wobbled.

"How ya doin', Benny?" Nick called out.

"Frankly, I'm not sure. My legs don't seem interested in carrying me away from here. Too close to an open, high place, I guess." A distinct vibrato rose in his voice that attempted humor couldn't mask.

"I'll help him," Lydia said. "In the meantime, go get to know Trish." She pushed him gently on the shoulder and smiled. "I have a feeling she'll appreciate the attention." She then wrinkled her nose. "I'm intuitive that way."

As Lydia walked to where Benjamin stood, Nick thought about his attraction to Trish and how easygoing Lydia was toward the notion of it. It all seemed too easy. His sense of professionalism told him to resist, but the concern was fleeting. Lydia's gentle shove was too much like permission.

Nick watched Lydia move to Benjamin's side and speak soft words of encouragement. He felt comfortable turning his care of Benjamin over to her.

The man, woman, and young boy that'd been standing between him and Trish finally sauntered away – the perfect opening to make a move. He stepped laterally, sliding his hands down the rail, coming to a stop next to her. She stood at the back corner of the starboard side.

"Tranquil, isn't it?" he said. "Almost mesmerizing I'd say." He sighed and continued looking beyond the rear of the ship.

She maintained a gaze down at the water over the rail, standing on the tips of her toes. "Indigo swells splashing high into lighter shades of blue, brushing the side of the ship and then rolling away with that rhythmic whoosh... oh, yes, definitely hypnotic." She glanced up. "It's music and a dance hard to ignore. That's a good description, don't you think?"

He nodded.

"I'd add that it's a strong inducement to throw caution to this gentle wind." She glanced again – this time with a smile. "How about you, Nick; what's your story? You already know mine."

"There's not much to know."

"Believe me, I'll appreciate whatever you care to share."

He looked out across the open water, fully conscious that she held him in an exploratory gaze. He couldn't resist subtly puffing out his chest and pulling in his stomach, offering his best profile. He saw the tallest buildings in Galveston finally disappear below the horizon. "I married right out of college, we had a daughter, Alexandra, and then my wife died of breast cancer a little over two years ago. I remarried a year later, and now I specialize in phobias. Today, I'm trying to hold a marriage and a career together."

She made no immediate response, waiting for more.

He glanced sideways. "That's about it."

"You don't waste words, do you?"

"I might... if there was anything more interesting to tell you."

"Somehow, Nicholas Brandon, I think you have a lot of interesting things to say, but are not ready to say them."

"I'm glad you think so."

She took a step closer to him. "Tell me... why phobias? What is the appeal of them for you?"

The memory elicited a skyward gaze. "I watched a young girl become so overwhelmed and scared by a phobia that she took her own life right in front of me." He brought his eyes down to meet hers. "There's no greater motivation than to witness total helplessness and feel impotent to do anything about it. That's where it started. People not afflicted can be so cold about it, even to the point of thinking it's funny, watching some poor soul react like that to everyday things. I bet you know the feeling well."

"You're right. The way my sister treats me confirms that. She laughs and jokes about it all the time. She has no clue how bad it becomes and the suicidal thoughts it puts in a person's head. She can make me so angry."

"Pisses you off, does she?"

She jerked her head back, surprised by the course language.

"Believe it or not," he said, "your anger is a good thing... in small doses, of course. If you're mad, it overrides fear."

"Hmmm. I've never thought of it that way."

"I came to know in that moment ten years ago in Bayside Mall that more needed to be done to make the world aware of, and sympathetic to, the disease. And I knew I needed to go about devising better ways to treat it... case in point, this cruise." He became aware that, as he spoke, his eyes were doing their own thing again, outlining the contours of her body. He struggled against it, eyes darting about, searching for something else to focus on. Finally, he had no choice but to simply look away. "You, Benny, and Lydia, in this place at this time is one more baby step in that direction."

The speaker suspended from the overhang of the deck above them crackled. A voice with a heavy Italian accent announced, "This is your captain, Antonio Mariostansi. I have a rather unusual demand I must make. All passengers please report to the auditorium located mid-ship. The main entrance is located on level three... the mezzanine entrance is on four. Check with your cabin steward or any nearby ship's personnel for the quickest route from your present location. A fast, orderly response is mandatory and will be appreciated by your captain and crew." The announcement was repeated in several languages by different voices.

"What's that all about?" Trish asked.

"Beats me; I've been on a couple of cruises, but besides the lifeboat drill while still in port, I've never experienced an order for a full muster anywhere else. Let's get Benny and Lydia. We'll all go together."

A uniformed man stood some distance away at an open door, motioning everyone over.

Nick gathered his team and urged them to blend into a moving stream of people, passing the young ship's mate dressed in uniform whites. "What's going on?"

"Sorry, Sir, I have no idea. I'm just following orders to get all the passengers there as soon as possible. The crew has been ordered to respond, too."

As people bunched up in the narrow corridor, Trish began showing initial indications of hyperventilating. "Breathe deep and even," Nick told her. "Once we get into the auditorium, people will spread out, and it won't be so crowded."

Digging her nails into his forearm, she breathed, "Don't you dare… walk away… from me," she said between breaths.

"Not a chance."

Her grimace turned into a smile as he pulled her nails from his flesh and patted her hand.

Ahead of Trish, he saw that the tables had turned for the other two. Now, it was Benjamin helping Lydia cope with closeness in the hallway, whispering into her ear as they were swept along with the moving mass of people.

The crowd bottlenecked at the double doors to the auditorium. As they emerged on the other side, it indeed opened up. "Let's find a seat that feels good to us all, not too high, not too crowded, and not too closed in."

Guiding them, he found a place halfway up that seemed perfect: pedestal swivel chairs bolted to a riser with a narrow table in front, facing the stage and covered with a crisp white linen tablecloth. Air conditioning vented out below the riser, pushing the bottom of the tablecloth in gentle undulations. *That should keep us cool and calm*, he thought. From experience, he realized this was a reservation-only VIP table for the scheduled shows, perfectly situated to see the stage in uncrowded comfort. A brass tubular rail ran in front of it to keep passersby in the lateral aisle clear of the table. The aisle was a wide walkway separating the theatre-type seats below them from the reserved section that began where they sat.

As passengers and crew jammed into the theatre, it became clear that the space was never intended to hold the entire ship's population at one time. Seats filled, and people squeezed shoulder to shoulder in the aisles. He thought it'd be some announcement of general interest, and then everyone would be dismissed, the discomfort brief.

People packed tighter into the cross-aisle. Below the bunching crowd in front of them, the rows of theatre seats, already filled, extended in a gentle descent, ending at the stage. They sat high enough to see over the heads of those standing in front of them, but barely. Discontent permeated the grumbling crowd for the inconvenience in the rapidly warming air.

As more people came in, Nick became concerned, glancing at Trish. He watched her breath quicken, eyes dart, and cheeks twitch. "Whatever this is all about, it probably won't last long. Hang in there."

A swarthy-skinned man came in from stage left and walked brusquely to center stage. He held a machine gun.

The sight of the firearm brought forth a collective gasp.

"Is that thing real?" Trish asked.

"I – I don't know," Nick said. "If it's a joke, it sure as hell isn't funny." An uneasy tingle knifed through his gut like an electrical charge.

Suddenly, two men in white uniforms were pushed stumbling onto the stage by two other gun-wielding men. Behind those two, another dark-skinned man appeared holding a pistol, with a machine gun on a strap thrown over his back.

The sound of many subdued conversations blended into a low rumble.

One of the uniformed men approached a microphone, and in that now familiar Italian accent, "Ladies and Gentleman, I am Antonio Mariostansi, captain of the Ocean Dancer cruise ship. With regret, I must inform you that this vessel has been commandeered. I am no longer in command." Glistening perspiration dampened the captain's face.

One of the gunmen shoved the captain aside, taking control of the microphone.

"My name is Azziz Baruk," he said in thickly accented English. "This vessel is now under my control, in the name of the Middle Eastern Liberation Front."

"Who?" Lydia whispered.

"I'm not familiar with them," Benjamin said. "But their presence makes an old Jewish man very, very uncomfortable." He looked to Nick.

Nick frowned and offered a quick shake of the head. He'd never heard of the organization either.

"I have armed men on every level, strategically positioned throughout the ship, and if any of you have thoughts of taking our presence lightly, I have no problem detonating a bomb that will send this ship and all of you to the bottom. To further my point, if even one of you has designs on becoming heroic, I have something I must show you."

The armed man behind Baruk shoved the captain to a position beside the other crewman in dress whites. Baruk walked behind and between the two while he held the microphone. "This man, Captain Mariostansi, is a person of value to me," he said tapping the side of the captain's head with the muzzle of the pistol.

The captain closed his eyes and stiffened, turning his head away from the firearm.

Then the gunman tapped the side of the other man's head. "On the other hand, this man is of absolutely *no* value. Now that we've established that, I have chosen him to prove my point."

With no hesitation, Baruk squeezed the trigger, blowing the side of the man's skull away. Perfect acoustics made the blast as loud throughout the auditorium as it must have been on stage.

A gasp went up. Some shrieked. Others dove for the floor.

Trish and Lydia screamed and covered their ears.

Benjamin pulled his head down into his shoulders.

Before the noise died away, Nick sprang to his feet and shouted, "What the shit's goin' on?"

The killer stood silent for a second or two, letting the crowd wallow in shock, and then yelled into the microphone, "Quiet! Everyone sit!"

Nick slowly sank back into his seat as noise grudgingly died away.

"It is with great regret I had to do that," Baruk said. "But there was really no other way to make the seriousness of my quest known as fast as it needed to be made. I have demands I'll be making of the U.S. government. Once they are made, for each hour my demands go unanswered, one of you at random will be chosen to join this man." He pointed the pistol toward the body of the man lying in a pool of his own blood. "It's a simple, efficient solution to get answers without delay. No one will be allowed to leave this auditorium. Get comfortable. You'll be here for a while... maybe days."

Nick went numb. But he couldn't have been any more shocked than his companions or the three thousand or so people who joined them.

A lady fainted nearby. Her husband dropped down, tending to her.

As Nick looked around, moisture leached from his throat, and he wondered if being killed one by one would be their fate.

Everyone in this substantial auditorium was armed with little more than flip-flops and cameras, a poor defense against automatic and semi-automatic firearms. They were at the mercy of people whose objectives he couldn't guess, but who had made it clear they were willing to do anything to reach them. The only certainty was that he'd had enough combat experience along the Kuwaiti border in Desert Storm to know that sitting back and hoping for the best was the fastest way to get killed.

CHAPTER 11

Sahid roughly shoved Captain Mariostansi into the hands of a co-conspirator offstage and out of sight of the crowd jamming the auditorium. He returned to center stage.

Looking across a sea of frightened faces – three-thousand, Sahid guessed – the enormity of what they were doing hit home. His courage wavered. *Can we control such a crowd with only nine men?* His eyes swept the lower level then reversed it, scanning the mezzanine above. Even open floor space was difficult to spot. People stood or sat on every square foot.

Now that Azziz's demonstration of control had finished, dispatching the first mate with a single bullet to the head, Sahid's arrogant confidence deflated. An involuntary twitch of anxiety fluttered in his cheek, and numerous ways to fail whirled about in his head. But respect for his mentor's ability prevented him from caving to anxiety. His admiration for Azziz ran deep – respect that, itself, had elements of fear attached. He picked at the cuticle of his right thumb with the index finger, continually shifting the machine gun suspended around his neck by a leather sling. It suddenly felt cumbersome – a strong symbol of complicity. It was ludicrous to think otherwise; still, questions spun out about how he might get away should things not go as planned, or if Azziz should get killed. It was a waste of brainpower to even consider, but at the moment, he had no control over where his mind took him.

Azziz stepped to his side and whispered in their native language, "As long as the passengers and crew are unaware of our number and believe we have many men, our plan will work fine. Do not worry." He held a gaze on Sahid's stiffened posture for a moment. "Relax, my friend. A bold show of confidence will carry us through." Azziz glanced at Mariostansi. "That is why it's important we keep them together and ignorant of our number. Should anyone be caught roaming the ship, that's when problems begin."

Azziz watched Mariostansi forced away by his men. He stepped even closer to Sahid. "Pass the word to the men; take no chances, listen to no excuses. If anyone is found outside the auditorium, give the order to slit throats. They have been fairly warned. That is the extent of our obligation to them. Fire weapons only if absolutely necessary."

Azziz turned to another of his men and barked in Arabic, "You. Come here."

"Yes Azziz."

"Remain on stage. Do not leave this area for any reason. Keep your eyes open for unusual movement within the crowd. Allow no conversation. We needn't worry too much about anyone engaging you in conversation since Arabic is all you speak. Still, allow no talk. Even if someone should speak our language, do not allow that person to question your motives. Let no one move about. Do not allow clustering of people. Most important: No one leaves. Kill if you must. Do you understand?"

"Yes... perfectly." He bowed slightly, then respectfully backed away a step before straightening.

"To better emphasize my point," Azziz said, draping his arms over the young co-conspirator's shoulders, "If a restroom is needed, have them do it where they stand. No one leaves. No exceptions."

"It will be done. Praise Allah," the young man replied crisply. He bowed again and turned to carry out the order.

"Yes, praise Allah," Azziz said with a dismissive wrist flip. "Sahid, come with me to accompany the captain to his quarters. We have an important phone call to make to Washington."

Sahid walked slightly behind Azziz as they followed the route the captain and his guards took. He glanced back at the young man that Azziz had ordered to stand guard over a theatre full of people. For the first time in his life, Sahid questioned the wisdom of Azziz to leave a single guard with a machine gun to keep so many people under control. But it was a misgiving he'd take to his grave.

Azziz plainly had no such reservations. He walked with a confident gait.

CHAPTER 12

Nick never thought he'd find himself in another life-threatening wartime situation. Strictly speaking, he still wasn't; this was in no way similar to his tour of duty in the Middle East. He had neither preparation nor training of any kind for a terrorist hostage situation. But the feel and flavor of this dilemma was definitely war-like. The dangers he and his companions now faced were potentially just as lethal as anything he'd confronted in the Iraqi desert. Making things worse, he had no weapons or anything to defend himself with. All he had were the clothes he wore and a keychain with a flashlight on it. He felt naked. His only advantage was an ingrained ability to control anxiety, keeping the mind working on solutions and not dwelling on problems to the point of inducing a seizure of good sense. His training for Desert Storm had left him with at least that much.

He scrutinized everything within sight to determine the value of each thing according to how far it might go in helping save lives or escaping. Not drawing unwanted attention had to be at the top of his mind at all times. Still, he had problems no one else in the auditorium had to deal with: three people suffering from very different phobias. There was no choice. Whispered conversations would have to be part of keeping his charges alive. He prayed that whatever talk they shared would be heard only by his band of four. Those maniacs would end him, and maybe his friends, too, if they even suspected that he was attempting an escape. He kept his eyes on that lunatic-with-a-cause, holding a machine gun and pacing the stage – a vital necessity if he didn't want to end up as coffin bait. In fluid fashion, he surveyed the auditorium, wishing he'd chosen the highest seats of the upper deck near the ceiling in case the guy went wild and began spraying automatic gunfire. He saw three exits: one each at the left and right sides near the rear of the stage; the main double-door entrance up the stairs behind them, between a wide arc of theatre-style seats; and the mezzanine entrance one level up. He had to assume all exits were covered with at least one armed guard apiece, maybe more. But that didn't matter. The exits were too far away to be of value – all within easy view of the man on stage.

Watching the machine-gun-wielding man pacing as a lone sentinel, he wondered just how trigger-happy he might be. *If he starts shooting, how many others will burst through those doors? Twenty? Thirty, perhaps?* The crowd in front obscured Nick's view of the man. It occurred to him that the occasionally obstructed view of the thug worked both ways. Any conversation could be timed so that it was only when the guy disappeared from view.

Like rats crowded by rising flood waters, it seemed everyone stepped back as far from the stage as possible, as if those few extra inches would make a difference in his ability to hit them with a hail of bullets. The crowd pressed together in front of the shiny brass rail that separated them from the table that he and his traveling companions sat behind. He understood the tendency, but it was a nuisance, making it difficult to get a measured look at all he needed to see in this giant makeshift holding cell. He glanced to the rear, but his view was entirely blocked by a large support column for the mezzanine seating overhead.

"If people begin spilling over that brass rail, invading our space…" Trish whispered with a shaky voice, "… I'll beg the bastard to kill me."

Trish's comment was like ice water injected into his veins. It flooded his head with a ten-year-old memory of a time when a similar comment ended in suicide. Her battle was on two fronts: the guy with a gun, and the internal struggle against pressurizing anxiety. If preventive measures weren't taken soon, it would certainly end explosively. Putting on his clinical game face – calm and relaxed – for her benefit, he studied her in a diagnostic way. He had to establish a much-needed time line where her problems were concerned. Exactly how much time did she have, did he have, before panic redlined?

Her skin glistened. She appeared closer to that line than he'd hoped. Her eyes darted from head to head of the people scrunched together in front of them and appeared terrified that one of them might turn and attack her. Muscles twitched in her tensed body; veins in her neck and temples had begun to engorge.

Watching the guard pace on stage, Nick waited until he disappeared behind a bouquet of heads and then leaned into Trish. "Close your eyes. No matter how curious you are about what's going on, keep them closed. Repeat to yourself: *The only people near me are Nick and Benny to my left and Lydia to my right.* Chant it under your breath."

Like some resistance held her head, she stiffly turned to look at him. Fear had frozen her eyes wide. He put his cheek against hers so she might feel the warmth of another human, and then put his lips to her ear. He whispered soothingly, "Fear is only a state of mind, a condition you have the power to deny."

When he pulled away from her ear, he saw her eyelids droop then close.

"That's it. Keep them closed. Deny the fear. Don't allow it to control you."

Nick then heard a gentle whoosh of air conditioning. The tablecloth reacted to the push of cool air from the register vent in the carpeted face of the riser beneath his feet. The stools they sat on were bolted to the top of it. The riser stood a couple of feet higher than the level of the aisle that crossed in front of them, and four to five feet back from the heels of people crowding nearest them, held away by that tubular brass rail.

In a flash, it came to him. The frustration of obscured vision caused by the crowd might be more of an ally than a nuisance. A human shield might provide cover. The column behind him would serve the same purpose. "Benny... Lydia... push this tablecloth forward until it conceals the underside of the table."

Lydia jerked her head around and glared at him. "What do you think you're going to do?" she whispered, almost frantic. "You heard what that ruthless bastard said about heroics."

He put a finger to his lips, frowned and gave her one quick headshake to hold the voice down. He reached across Trish and squeezed Lydia's forearm. "Look, if I don't get Trish out of here, I'm afraid she'll break and run." Only inches from Trish's nose, he paused and took another calculating look at her, searching for additional signs of deterioration. "If she does, that guy'd kill her. Her coping skills are eroding fast."

Tears were now escaping from between Trish's closed eyelids. "I'm so sorry," she muttered. Her face reddened more – breathing remained shallow and fast. She squirmed in her seat and held a white-knuckle grip on the edge of the table in front of her.

Nick touched her cheek with a butterfly stroke. "Don't worry. I'll get you out of here. I promise."

Her lips moved in rapid fashion, likely chanting away the crowd and trying desperately to visualize what he suggested behind those closed eyelids.

Benjamin lifted his arms from the tabletop and began pushing the cloth forward. "Hold it together Trish," he said, and then to Nick he added, "We'll do what we can."

Once the cloth had been lowered to the floor in front of the table to provide a suitable cover against curious eyes, Lydia and Benjamin rested elbows on its backside edge, holding it in place.

Nick began to examine the gunman's pace as he walked from one end of the stage to the other and then back repeatedly. As he turned and walked away, there was about fifteen seconds before he turned and walked back. That should be enough time to sink beneath the table. He also noticed how people stood so close together in front of him that they all moved laterally each time someone shifted from one foot to the other. Nick waited for something to prompt another shift in the line of people.

A young boy forced his way between two people to stand next to a woman, probably his mother. All the bodies shifted left. The machine gun wielding man on stage had just turned to walk the other direction. For a precious few seconds the view of the entire stage disappeared. This was the chance he'd been waiting for.

Nick was now hidden from view; but for how long he didn't know. He wilted over and slid beneath the table, slithering down to the top of the two-foot-high riser at the base of his stool, and then finally off it to the floor below. Lying on the garish purple, yellow, and red carpet on a black background, careful not to move the cloth concealing him, he studied the air conditioning vent cover and saw that it was held in place by two brass Phillips-head screws. Pulling a penny from his pocket, he attempted working one of them out, but the bite of the coin was insufficient. It was too large and the metal too soft. He tried the key to his BMW. It seemed a more appropriate size and slipped readily into the screw's slot. Methodically he turned it until it fell to the carpet at his elbow. Then he worked the other screw. It was more difficult. He fought it and overdid it, twisting the tip off the key. His nostrils flared as he clenched his teeth. *Damn!*

He switched to his house key. He held it with an almost angry intensity as he slowly turned the screw. A blood-bloated blister came up on the pad of his thumb. Finally, the screw fell out.

With raw and overly sensitive fingertips on his right hand, he tugged the louvered cover.

It didn't move. He repeated it – this time with more force.

It gave with a metallic clank.

He froze.

Fear raced in a tingling rush from his stomach right to his head as unfettered cool air came out with sufficient force to push loose hair across his forehead. Holding the lightweight metal cover motionless, he waited and listened, trying to hear telltale noise or voices.

The next three or four seconds passed like tree sap on a frigid January morning. He didn't move. It was vital that he be sure; he listened for incriminating chatter from beyond the concealing tablecloth inches from his back. Finally, he released the held breath as a thankful sigh that he'd avoided discovery.

Sweat popped as he rolled his head and shoulder to look up past Trish's thigh to her face. She remained as she was – terror stricken, eyes shut tight. He reached up and stroked the calf of her leg then patted it. She responded by reaching beneath the table and squeezing his hand. He channeled her anxiety in that shaky grasp. Time had become a commodity he didn't have the luxury of wasting.

And then he heard a child's voice. "Momma, what happened to that man sitting there?"

Someone had noticed him gone. He held still, beading sweat trickling into his fluttering eyes.

"Oh, baby," came the mother's terrified whisper, "please be quiet."

A bit less concerned, Nick breathed relief and then carefully laid the vent cover aside.

Without warning, the tablecloth lifted beside his head. He looked around into the grinning face of a boy not more than four years old, the tablecloth draping around his little head. The youngster appeared totally unperturbed. Nick held his finger to his lips and released a soft, "Shhh." He motioned for the child to come closer. "Want to play a game?"

The youngster nodded enthusiastically and opened his mouth to speak.

Nick put his hand to the boy's lips. "An important part of the game is not saying anything… nothing at all. All right?" His words were more breathed than whispered.

The youngster looked confused at first, then nodded.

"If the man down there on that stage finds out what I'm doing, I've lost the game. You don't want me to lose, do you?"

The boy pushed his lip into a pout and shook his head.

"Good. Want to help me win?"

The boy's frown transformed into an enthusiastic nod and smile.

"Then your job is to stand in front of this table and not let anyone see me. If you do a good job, we'll win the game, and I'll give you a prize. How about that?"

The boy's grin widened more. He then dropped the edge of the cloth. Nick saw his tiny silhouette. The youngster's legs were spread wide, standing guard.

Nick sucked in a big breath, and as he let it out slowly, his head slumped to the carpet. When he opened his eyes, he looked into the throat of the air conditioning duct, measuring roughly two feet wide and eighteen inches high. He shone the tiny beam of his penlight into the duct and saw that it ended about fifteen feet in. There, it appeared that a larger duct intersected it, running at right angles in both directions.

He flicked the light off and briefly wondered how best to get Trish under the table without being noticed, even by the people standing in front of them. If they noticed, it might cause a stampede of people wanting to follow.

Then the most dangerous of all enemies reared its head – hesitation. He wondered if he was doing the right thing. He looked up at Trish, assessing not only her condition, but also the chances of success with the perilous adventure he was about to include her in. *I have no choice. Or do I?*

Nearer the stage, he heard a male voice ask something he didn't understand, but the response from the armed man was unmistakable. The guard shouted an order in Arabic. Nick didn't need to understand what the words meant; inflection indicated that it certainly wasn't a statement of respect.

Nick wormed back up onto the riser then pushed his head above the tabletop, like emerging from a pool without making ripples, making certain he wasn't being watched, gradually coming all the way up to sit. He turned to Benjamin and whispered, "Who had the balls to speak?"

The old guy shrugged. "It would seem there's a man of privilege sitting down there that feels he should be treated better than the rest of us."

The man spoke up again. "You need to know that I am the personal attaché of the American Ambassador to Lebanon," he said to the man on stage. "Whatever it is you and your compatriots seek, I can expedite for you."

The guard waved the machine gun in an upward fashion, indicating he wanted the man to stand.

The man looked around, as if suddenly unsure to whom the gunman spoke, and rose haltingly.

The guard allowed the machine gun to hang loose from the strap around his neck and smiled at the man who now stood next to his wife. They were in the third row near the stage.

Obviously seeing the guard's smile as headway, the man returned the smile and crossed his arms over his chest. There was distinct smugness in the man's mannerisms.

In a flash, the guard pulled a pistol from a holster at his side and fired two quick rounds through the man's folded arms right into his chest.

Screams reverberated throughout the theatre. Every head went down as the man collapsed back into his seat.

The man clutched his chest and grimaced. His mouth opened wide as if wanting to speak, or scream maybe. It was clear the instant life left him. He then slumped forward and moved no more.

The woman that had been sitting next to him wailed as she fell to her knees beside him, "You've killed him! You've murdered my husband!" She snarled, "You ignorant piece of shit! Charles just wanted to help you. He meant you no harm."

The gunman, never having dropped the pistol, swung it, leveled it and squeezed the trigger once more. Nick saw a neat hole in the woman's forehead when her head snapped back.

The force of the projectile went all the way through and into the shoulder of a teenage girl behind her, who instantly squealed in pain. The girl and those on both sides were sprayed with bloody gray matter.

The woman's eyes rolled to white. She fell at her husband's feet, both dead.

Nick looked to the exits and saw a single face appear in one of the porthole windows of the double doors, further evidence that the exits were indeed covered by at least one man apiece.

The man shouted something in Arabic. Even with the language barrier, the crowd knew instinctively to be quiet. Silence came fast.

Nick saw Trish flinch. Her eyes were still closed. He reached for her arm. "Trish?"

Her eyes snapped open. She stared forward but clearly saw nothing. She panted like a dog.

He jerked her arm hard enough that her head lolled sideways and, with all the intensity he could muster in a whisper, ordered: "Listen to me. You've got to hold it together."

In halting jerks, her eyes came around. "I-I don't think I can."

"Bullshit," he hissed through clenched teeth. He put his arm around her shoulders. She quivered. Her skin was clammy.

Turning to Lydia, he said, "That air-conditioning vent below our feet is big enough to crawl through. I think I need to get Trish through it first, away from these people crowding the table. You and Benny follow me into it." Terror suddenly splashed across Lydia's face. "I can't, Nick. Inside that duct, I'd be no better off than Trish is right now... maybe worse. I'd become paralyzed and start screaming."

"How about you, Benny?"

"Someone has to help Lydia hold the tablecloth. I'll stay."

"It's not what I'd prefer," he said, glancing at Trish, "but I don't have time to debate. She's about to lose it."

"Just go," Lydia said. "Take care of her. We'll be fine."

He tugged Trish's arm once, then again. He tried a third time. She remained unyielding.

"Relax," he whispered. He felt the muscle flex in her arm soften. "Now, lean over until you're under the table. Be careful not to disturb the tablecloth. Quietly crawl into the duct. I'll be right behind you."

Trish nodded – it looked more like a twitch – as she finally yielded to his tugs on her arm. He watched as she flowed under the table and off the seat riser to the floor below. She then disappeared into the duct. It seemed effortless for her. Nick leaned sideways to begin the descent to the floor, but he paused and sat upright.

He looked to Lydia. "Are you sure that staying here is the safer choice?"

Gently, Lydia pushed him and mouthed *Go*. She then whispered, "Take care of Trish. She needs you."

Sinking once again below the surface of the table, he had become thoroughly convinced it was a one-shot attempt at saving Trish's life. Crawling into position, he twisted until he was inside the duct, arms fully extended like Superman in flight. He pushed along with his toes while pulling with his fingertips. The metal was smooth and even slightly downhill, but it became dark once his body blocked the light from behind. He couldn't see and was unable to determine Trish's exact location, although he heard muffled clicks, clanks and dull thuds some distance ahead. He then became aware of another problem that likely hampered Trish the most right now: the temperature. It was very cold.

CHAPTER 13

Guarding against sudden moves, Lydia pushed her upper torso against the backrest of the tall stool she sat on, trying to get a better view of the goings-on beneath the table. Her right hand remained firmly in control of the tablecloth – draping the front and extending to the floor, concealing the escape route. She spread her knees wide and looked down between her legs to watch Nick and Trish slither into the ship's air-conditioning system.

Her eyes hitched on the darkened patch on her gray Capri pants where perspiration soaked her inner thighs – a stark reminder that nervousness worked on her and was taking a physical toll.

It crossed her mind that once Nick and Trish were gone, the open duct was evidence of collusion and would put her and Benjamin in danger. But, for now, concern was focused on her two friends. To her way of thinking, they were the ones taking the greater life-threatening risk by crawling through that air-conditioning duct. If caught, they'd be executed on the spot. They would have no say and probably no time to even speak. She knew it. Nick knew it. For her and Benjamin, choices remained a question mark, even their ability to survive. And that, amazingly, seemed the safer choice.

She shifted her head slightly to see one of the beams from a halogen spotlight far overhead illuminate the area beneath the table. The small spotlights in the domed ceiling were scattered at random to simulate stars in an open sky. It would've been nice to appreciate that under different circumstances. She sighed, realizing that a cruise could never be associated with a good time after this – that is, if they should live to remember it.

She moved her right knee a bit more and there, below the riser to which her stool was bolted, Nick was just then disappearing into the duct below her feet. The sight should have been humorous: His toes did the walking as he began a rhythmic rocking motion from the ankle, pushing his body forward an inch at a time. Her misplaced tendency to smile forced the opposite reaction – tightly pursed lips and a frown.

Benjamin leaned into her. "What's with the worried look? They'll be fine. And so will we." He patted her free hand, which was clutching the inside edge of the table.

Lydia's right hand and Benjamin's left still supported the cloth at each end. It occurred to her that they couldn't hold on to it for an extended period but, for now, she and Benjamin had no choice but to hang on to it, so as to keep the area beneath the table concealed and not let it slide off onto the floor.

She tried mimicking Benjamin's confidence, mirroring his smile, but her sense of foreboding deepened. She saw husbands and wives hugging and children gripping their fathers' legs. Many cried. A smattering of muffled sobs and the occasional diaphragm spasm sounded off at random throughout the otherwise quiet theatre. It was death to anyone choosing to speak or even making an obtrusive noise. A man and his wife gave their lives to prove that point. She offered Benjamin a nod. "Yeah, I think we'll be okay, too. We have to believe that."

Benjamin faced her.

For the first time, she noticed his pale blue eyes set in a colorless but smooth face. She sought hope in it but saw something almost as good – blessed calm. It was plain upon his face that he cared for her and seemed to study her.

"I've been curious about you, Lydia. Very soon, I want to know all about you, your hopes and dreams," he said, breathing the words. This sweet little man had dimples in his slightly drawn slender cheeks.

She saw immediately what he was doing, projecting contagious calm. It worked. She returned an unforced smile.

The two most ruthless of the terrorists, Baruk and his number one henchman who seemed to follow him in lock-step everywhere he went, appeared on stage. Baruk whispered to the assigned guard and abruptly turned, leaving his friend behind with the guard and disappearing through a door offstage. Whatever Baruk told the guard was clearly all business, something pre-planned, because Baruk spent only enough time to whisper a few words before turning to leave. The guard's features hardened; still, he smiled. He stayed behind onstage with a machine gun held at the ready while Baruk's friend turned his attention to the crowd at large.

The man took the two steps down off stage then started up the steps in the center aisle between the arched rows of theatre seats. His advance up the broad, carpeted stairs was casual –a saunter, really – as a shopper might walk in a market. At almost every step and every row, he hesitated and perused faces left then right, before moving up one more. The casualness was a disgusting display of arrogance. He bore the look of a man seeking a melon at just the right stage of ripeness. He continued, finally stopping just down from where she and Benjamin sat holding the tablecloth.

Lydia checked her watch. Over an hour had elapsed. Her gut tightened. "God help us. It's time," she breathed. She looked to Benjamin. "He's looking for someone to kill."

Benjamin grabbed and squeezed her forearm when her whisper became too loud.

The terrorist, Baruk's closest confederate, stopped at an obese man wedged into an aisle seat – the quintessential tourist. The man wore sandals and Bermuda shorts over pale feet and legs. His hair was strawberry blonde and curly, as was the hair on his large freckled legs. A tropical shirt with bright yellow orchids splashed over its surface appeared ready to slide off a rotund belly onto equally gaudy plaid shorts. The two garments clashed in a dizzying display of over-the-top kaleidoscopic colors that in no way coordinated. She couldn't see his expression, but lack of movement by the big man indicated that he was staring straight ahead, hoping not to be noticed. If so, sheer size and those clothes made that wish impossible. It was as plain as the flowers in electric colors on his big stomach why the would-be murderer noticed him and, apparently, made the fat man his mark for execution.

"Identification," the terrorist barked.

"What?"

Sahid jammed the butt of the machine gun into the side the man's head. "Identification!"

The man moaned in agony and grabbed the point of impact near his eye but quickly fished through his hip pocket, producing a wallet. He handed it to the gunman, who went directly for the driver's license, throwing the wallet back at the man. He drew his pistol and raised the muzzle inches from the man's temple. The fat man whimpered, pulling his head as far down into his chubby jowls as possible. His face turned a crimson that clashed with his curly orange hair.

Lydia gasped, groping for Benjamin's arm.

Then Benjamin did the unthinkable. "Sir?"

The gunman retracted the pistol and pointed it up. He scanned the rows of seats for the source of the voice, looking over the wrong shoulder.

"Shut up," Lydia hissed.

Benjamin patted her hand and forged ahead. "Excuse me, Sir?" He meekly waved to the gunman.

"No, Benny, no."

The terrorist finally locked eyes onto Benjamin. The old man made it easy by again raising his hand and waving like a school child knowing the answer to a teacher's question.

Benjamin then pressed fingertips to his lips preparing a thoughtful comment of some sort. But there was nothing he could say to change what was about to happen; one way or the other, someone was going to die. All he accomplished was inviting hell to rain down on him instead of, or in addition to, someone else.

He calmly pleaded, "Isn't there a way of handling this as gentlemen. Is it really necessary to kill people to make your point?" His face remained calm, inviting conversation. "I bet if we talk this over, a better way of handling the situation would come to us. What do you say?"

The quiet that befell the crowded auditorium made it clear that no one breathed. In this overly crowded place, even when no one spoke, it was still noisy simply due to shuffling bodies –until now.

The guard that remained on stage must have sensed that this gunman might need help. He came off the raised platform and trotted up the steps to join him. Baruk's partner swung the pistol, now pointing it at Benjamin. He drew an evil grin. Then, without looking again at the fat man, he dropped the driver's license into the recoiling man's lap. He began walking up the stairs. "Identification." Tears welled fast in Lydia's eyes. "Oh Benny. What have you done?"

Calmly as possible, Benjamin pulled a money clip from his pocket with credit cards held together along with cash. "Will these do? I have no driver's license."

The man stepped over the tubular brass rail, reached and yanked Benjamin out of his chair. The old man landed on his side on top of the rail, knocking the wind from him, and then rolled on over it, thudding to the carpeted aisle.

People shoved one another, clearing a space.

Benjamin was now alone to face the consequences of his big heart and bold intention. He gasped, laboring for a single breath.

Lydia held fast to the tablecloth, now occupying both her hands at each end of the table. She couldn't let it fall, making her helpless to go to Benjamin's aid.

The man picked up one of the cards shaken loose that lay on the floor. "Robenstein? You are Jewish?"

"I… am an American… citizen," he said between gasps.

"An American Jew makes it better," he said, and then snarled, "Pig!"

Although the guard, standing back a few steps, spoke no English, he reacted angrily to the word "Jew". That one stepped around his compatriot and kicked Benjamin hard in the head.

Lydia screeched. "Benny!"

The man swung the pistol and pointed it at Lydia. "Control yourself, woman! I have no order preventing me from taking two lives… or three, or whatever number pleases me. Do you understand?"

Through his pain, Benjamin held up a feeble arm for her to say no more.

Lydia's mouth remained open, poised to hurl obscenities. After tense seconds, she forced her mouth shut and lowered her chin to her chest, finally understanding that if she looked at the two terrorists any longer she would indeed say something regrettable.

"Very wise, old man," the pistol-toting terrorist said. "You just saved your friend's life." He then turned his back on them both, whispering something in Arabic to the guard. As a final insult to Benjamin's heritage, the guard stomped Benjamin's ribcage.

The old gentleman let out a mournful wail then groaned. He rolled into a tight fetal ball, the pain clearly intense.

Lydia flinched, ready to come out of her chair before realizing it'd place her directly in harm's way and give up Nick and Trish's escape route at the same time. Cry was all she could do. "Please, God, help him," she whispered.

Benjamin seemed to be losing consciousness. His arm fell outstretched and limp on the floor.

Showing no more consideration than he would for a cockroach, the gunman stomped the exposed arm, breaking it.

On that sickening sound, a collective groan went up from the nearby crowd as Benjamin's loud, agonized moan drove them farther away, stumbling over one another, to put distance between them and the violence.

All the while, the man still clutching the pistol had his back turned, sauntering down the steps. He obviously thought so little of the situation that he didn't look back.

Lydia's first thought was why no one offered to help or say anything, but it was preposterous to even consider such a notion. Everywhere she glanced, people stood or sat with arms and legs pulled in close to their bodies. No one wanted to be heard or noticed at all. In this place, at this time, garnering attention was a death sentence. She held no doubt that Benjamin had sealed his fate by speaking without invitation.

The man finally stopped and looked back, speaking directly to Benjamin. "My name is Sahid Arrani. I, along with Azziz Baruk, will make the West pay for their interference with and indiscretions against our people. And since Israel is a big part of that, you would be my choice for death, but I think I'll save you for Azziz." He turned and began walking briskly down the stairs toward the stage and, without even breaking stride, raised the pistol to the side of the fat man's head and fired, blowing bloody tissue on the woman next to him. After passing through the man's head, the bullet embedded in her leg.

The guard snatched the driver's license from the man's shuddering fingers, caught up to Sahid and handed it to him as they both marched to the stage. The guard stopped to remain on the stage, but Sahid kept marching to the curtain in the rear, throwing it aside. He looked back at the crowd a last time. He smiled and bowed his head as if he were a performer just finishing an award-winning performance. That driver's license in his hand must serve as a vile proof of performance. He left, disappearing behind the curtain.

Once again, as if nothing had happened, the gunman paced the stage.

CHAPTER 14

Lying prone, stretching long into the darkness of the rectangular air conditioning duct, Nick touched the sole of Trish's sandal with the walking fingertips of an extended arm. "How ya doin' up there?" He heard chattering teeth and gave her chilled ankle above the sandal strap a squeeze of encouragement.

In whispered vibrato, she replied, "It's damn cold and dark. I don't need to see them to know my freakin' lips are blue. The chill bumps on my legs are so big I can feel them pressed against the metal. Still, I'd rather be here than in that theatre. Drowning in people is worse... much, much worse, I'm afraid."

"That sounds poetic... in a morose way." Nick felt her feet rocking methodically, as were his. They inched ahead. "You know this, but I need to say it anyway: This is not at all what I expected from this cruise. I, somehow, thought it wouldn't be quite so adventurous."

She stopped crawling. "Humor? Now's the time you to decide to show a sense of humor? Are you nuts? Aren't you scared out of your mind?"

"Scared? Yes. Out of my mind? Not yet. Of course I'm afraid. Only a fool wouldn't be."

She began moving forward again. "Well, at least you've confirmed it."

"Confirmed what?

"That you have a sense of humor. Of course, it seems to be laced with an unhealthy dose of bad timing. I'm sorry I can't appreciate it. All I can think about are psychopaths with machine guns and finding a warm, well-lighted room somewhere. My head is terribly pre-occupied at the moment. So, work on that timing thing, would ya?"

"If I whimpered and cried, would that seem more appropriate?"

Still inching forward, "Careful, buddy. I'd be justified in calling you a wiseass right now."

"Yeah, well… let's not lose sight of the goal. You should be coming to a larger horizontal shaft soon. And lower your voice; you're getting too loud. This duct is like a megaphone. Our conversation can be heard as easily fifteen feet away as we hear each other, so keep it down to breathy whispers only."

In lowered voice, she responded. "Okay, but I – hey, I think I've made it. It drops down a few inches here… more headroom, too." She tapped the metal enclosure above her to get a size reference on the larger duct that opened into the one they were exiting. It sounded like a bass drum.

"Don't do that," he hissed. "That sound carries right back into the auditorium, and the last thing we should be doing right now is sending out tom-tom alerts."

"Sorry."

"Just… don't."

"Okay, okay."

"Once I make it into that space with you," he said, "I can get this key ring flashlight out of my pocket. That should help. At the moment, my arms are over my head, and that's where they'll stay until I have more room to maneuver."

His overworked calf and forearm muscles had begun to cramp in the cool air. Even without light, Nick knew the instant Trish cleared the smaller duct into the larger one. A rush of chilled air hit him in the face. It then occurred to him how much colder it had to be leading than following in the tiny galvanized metal duct.

He finally worked his way to the intersecting main air duct and pulled his body free from the smaller one that was a straight shot back into the auditorium. He quickly began experiencing a greater sense of calm due to progress made. He lifted up onto hands and knees. The cold air moved his hair and tickled his forehead even as he faced away from the flow, blowing across his bare belly above a drooping shirttail. Now he could crawl faster.

Pulling the tiny light from his pocket, he flashed the beam behind him and saw spots of light from feeder vents similar to the one they'd just crawled out of, every ten feet or so, evenly spaced.

The other direction was a similar view, except duct openings also lined the opposite side. "Keep crawling the way you've started," he said. "Maybe we can find cabins or rooms a safe distance from the auditorium."

He couldn't help but notice Trish in the beam of light as she rolled onto hands and knees to again crawl. The skin on the rear of her thighs, that portion he saw below her shorts, was roughened by gooseflesh. She shivered, occasionally escalating to a full body shudder. "We'd better keep moving before the cold renders your fingers useless," he told her. "I know it's difficult, but try to be quiet. We don't know who's above or below us. In this manmade tunnel, every noise will carry to every vent register for hundreds of feet."

"Remaining quiet isn't easy while my hands and feet are numb."

Nick studied the feeder ducts they passed. Each time he hit the light to do so, the sight of Trish's well-toned rear end greeted him. With that view, the cold had no lasting power over him. Finally, to his left, he saw that one of the ducts happened to be larger than the others, ending in a register vent with light coming through it about five feet out. "Hold up," he whispered. "I want to check this one out." He struggled to bend his body into it.

She reached back and hooked a finger in one of his belt loops. She carefully turned and crawled back and put her lips to his ear. "Let me do it. I think I might be faster and quieter. You've made it clear several times already how important that is."

He nodded and backed out, allowing her access.

She snaked her way in.

He waited impatiently for a report. Sitting alone in the dark, he now felt the effects of the constant cold rush of air – ears brittle and nose dripping. Shivering for the first time, he grew eager and did not want to sit and wait. As fidgeting became action, he poked his head in over that portion of her legs that still lay in the main duct where he was. Before he could crawl any farther, she reversed and began backing out, forcing his head to the side. "What? What did you see?"

"It's some type of meeting place… a conference room, maybe. There's a long table surrounded by chairs with a large coffee urn and pastries on a single sideboard at one end," she said. "It appears the room had been in use when the occupants were called to the auditorium. The light on the coffee urn is lit. Oh, God, Nick... hot coffee." She rubbed her shoulders, still shivering. "I couldn't see or hear anything else." She looked around as if trying to see through the metal walls. "Where's the auditorium from here?"

Nick glanced around, too. "We should be above the starboard corridor of the deck *below* the main entrance to the auditorium."

"Starboard? Do I look like a sailor to you?"

"Sorry. I just meant the right side of the ship as you face the bow." He began making his move. "Let me in there. I'll see if I can get that vent cover off so we can get out of this refrigerated air."

He quickly discovered just how inflexible his back was, but he managed to get his body fully into the right angle duct. Still, one blessing had to be counted – they had more headroom than where the journey had begun. Trish was at his heels, clearly wanting immediate access to a warmer place once he'd cleared the way.

Nick scooted on his belly to within arm's reach of the louvered vent face and saw exactly what Trish spoke of: a long table and chairs. The tabletop appeared to be four or five feet below them and closer to their side than the opposite wall. He made no move, just observed and listened. Finally, not hearing anything coming from the room or anywhere within earshot, he took a deep breath. *It's now or never.* Clicking his teeth together and waiting another couple of seconds, giving it one final measure of caution, he concluded that additional waiting would offer no advantage. "Okay," he breathed. "No time like the present."

Placing the heels of his hands on the vent cover, he pushed. His face tightened, engorging with blood. The soft threads of the brass screws seemed to have loosened somewhat. He pulled the cover and felt the slack, realizing that completing the job without noise wouldn't be possible. Holding his breath, he again positioned his hands and tossed up a quick prayer. *God, I hope I'm right and there's no one close enough to hear this.*

He slammed it with a sharp rap, using the heels of both hands. It popped out with a clunk then clanged against the wall, swinging free in a pendulous sweep and grated beneath him. It hung by a single shard of brass.

He didn't move, not even a twitch – just listened. In that moment of gut-tightening apprehension, a number of things shot through his mind should this go badly and someone bursts in on them: He thought of Alli, wondering what she was doing at this very moment, hoping Evie had the good sense to be looking after his daughter. Then the thought of getting killed without ever having the opportunity to know Trish better crossed his mind. It obliterated all other randomly spinning thoughts. But, it was then that he realized that if he were killed, she would certainly be also, and that sent an electrically charged blend of sadness and fear through him. His body involuntarily quaked. Suddenly, he clearly understood why Trish couldn't appreciate his oddly placed humor. He felt a little foolish.

After several breathless seconds, he came to believe that he may have pulled it off undetected. "Whew." *Thank you, Lord.* Poking his head into the room, he took his first good look at the space. A windowless interior room roughly ten by twenty was below a low ceiling – no more than seven feet. Papers lay strewn across the tabletop as if a meeting had been interrupted in progress. The door was not the standard cabin-type. It was unadorned metal covered in glossy white paint. The utilitarian appearance of everything meant that none of it was intended for the guests to ever see.

Now confident that the heavier door masked the noise, he chose not to wait any longer and began snaking out. Once his upper torso cleared, he reached for the tabletop and walked his hands across it to control the fall of his legs. He landed with a soft thud and rolled off the table to his feet. A blizzard of drifting papers settled on the floor. "Your turn."

Reaching for Trish's shoulders, he held fast. She squeezed his arms. The sight reminded him of childhood trips to his grandparents' farm near Navasota and watching his Grandpa help an old mother cow deliver a calf. He gently pulled her free. One leg and then the other fell in an awkward drop. She automatically wrapped her arms around his neck to stabilize cold-weakened knees. Her icy nose touched his cheek. He didn't pull away, just pressed his flesh into hers a little tighter. "You did get cold, didn't you?"

"I probably would've broken my arm if you hadn't been here to catch me. It'll take a few minutes before my limbs warm up enough to be useful." She squeezed his neck. "God, you're warm. If it's okay, I'll just hang on a few seconds." She snuggled her cold nose into the softness below his clavicle. After a moment, she pulled her face away. "Well, Doctor Brandon, once again I find myself propped up by you… so to speak. You've done that a lot in the past few months."

Momentarily losing himself to her, he wrapped his arms around her waist and hugged. He watched her eyes as her breasts flattened against his chest. She reciprocated by pressing her legs into his. That long sweeping dark auburn bang, partially covering one eye, made for a charming sight. While mapping her face, she clearly studied him, too, as if searching for clues. The unspoken question *What next?* floated in that space between them.

The danger of their shared predicament suddenly seemed abstract, distant. His examining gaze settled on her chestnut brown eyes. A rush of sexual arousal bubbled then simmered in his gut – at a time and in a place it didn't belong. The desire was strong but the inclination to follow through was not. Such feelings in this time and place were absurd.

Sense of their dilemma returned, and he gently peeled her arms off his neck. "We have to help each other. It's the only way we'll get through this. Whenever you need help, you've got it. I promise."

"That's comforting to know," she said, inflection trailing down.

Is that disappointment I just heard?

She rubbed her arms and shivered as she backed away from him.

"Go get a cup of that coffee. And, I can tell by looking that you're not into them, but eat a donut, too. The sugar will do you good since there doesn't seem to be any blankets around."

"Now there's a twist… a doctor prescribing a donut. I bet that can't be found in any medical journal."

"Aren't you the one that, just minutes ago, chided me for a misplaced sense of humor?"

"Sorry."

"Besides, I don't prescribe. Let's just call it a helpful suggestion."

Nick looked around, but there was little else to see. His eyes stopped at the door and wondered what, or who, might be on the other side. "You know, Lydia made the right choice by not following us. That duct and this windowless room might have been more than she could cope with." But then he remembered where he'd left them trapped. "God, I hope they're okay."

CHAPTER 15

"Sahid, if you please, fetch the good Captain a cup of hot tea. He seems tense."

Sahid walked across the captain's quarters to a small table near the desk beneath an oversized rectangular window with thick double-paned glass. Compared to other windows on the ship, the size of this one alone might indicate a space of significance if seen from the outside. It offered a sunny panoramic view of the swells of the Gulf of Mexico smoothly rising and falling, far gentler than the churning emotions that plainly emanated from the captain, along with beading perspiration. Azziz's plan – to maximize the captain's usefulness by instilling horrific fear – seemed to be working, but it had to be managed closely. The request for tea was more of a warning to the captain to keep his wits, and a way for Azziz to remain in charge of the man's terror, to manipulate as needed.

From an ornate cut-crystal decanter with a sparkling bell-shaped lid, Sahid removed a teabag and dropped it into a cup. He drew hot water from the electric urn next to it.

Azziz watched him swim the teabag in the cup for a few seconds and then turned back to the center of attention in this life-and-death game that was now underway. "Captain, I fear the call you made for us was not done with an acceptable level of compassion for your passengers... a real shame. I'd hoped for more and, blast my optimism, I expected more. Really, Captain, was it too much to hope for?" He paced away two steps then glanced back.

The captain didn't respond, nor did he move at all; he just stared down at the desktop he sat behind.

"No matter; your performance was inadequate. I simply did not detect an appropriate level of concern for your guests' safety. And, they are your guests, are they not... their safety your responsibility as captain of this vessel?" He whirled around to square his body to the cowering Captain Mariostansi.

The captain didn't lift his head, just his eyes. He nodded once, but hesitantly so. His face glistened with accumulated perspiration. "Surely, you must be worried for the lives of those that trusted you with theirs?" A malicious smile came up on Azziz's face. "Now, I must deal with an American negotiator that doesn't share our sense of urgency. What to do..." He clucked his tongue then tapped his lips with a thoughtful finger, "...what to do, indeed?"

"But, Sir," the captain said without looking up again, "If I may be so bold without angering you, it's American policy not to negotiate with terrorists. To assume they'll bow to demands simply dooms everyone... us by your hand and you by theirs."

Azziz's mild amusement with the situation disappeared in flash. An angry lower lip pushed forward and quivered as it pressed against his upper lip. He slammed the desk in front of the captain with the side of his fist. "We are not terrorists! That implies generalized violence and lack of purpose with no other goal than to terrorize people. Our cause is specific, driven by a clearly defined goal of liberating the entire Middle Eastern region from American colonialism, and we are using the only means we have available to us. That should not and will not be defined as terrorism! I will not allow it!" Azziz snorted through flared nostrils like a raging bull.

When Azziz lost his temper, Sahid became a bit nervous as well. It was nothing new; even back into childhood he worried when his friend began losing control. Sahid always thought he could see something in his eyes that indicated Azziz might not be able to reel it back in. Somehow, though, he always did. Still, Sahid questioned the continued ability of his friend to do so.

A few moments passed, Azziz's reddened face dimmed then relaxed. "If you do not wish to anger me, then you are indeed doing a poor job of preventing it, Sir."

The captain's chin sunk lower yet, appearing as if he'd just provoked a rabid dog.

"I'm so sorry. It was not my purpose to demean your cause," he muttered. "Forgive me, please." He pushed his chair back and rose.

Azziz stepped around and positioned himself between the

captain and the desk. At close range, he lifted the captain's chin with a lover's touch.

"Though we treat *you* with respect for your position, that same respect I simply do not feel coming *from* you. In your speech and mannerism, I sense disgust with us and our cause." Azziz left the captain standing and sauntered away to look out the window.

Steaming cup in hand, Sahid bobbed the teabag in the hot water a few more times and then leaned across the desk and placed it in front of the standing captain.

Azziz turned and held an intimidating gaze on the captain. "Sahid, the card please."

Sahid retrieved it from inside his tunic and placed an American driver's license in Azziz's hand.

Azziz came up behind the captain and pushed the chair into the backs of his knees, and then with a firm hand forced Mariostansi down. "Have a seat. You wouldn't want your tea to get cold." He flipped the card on the desk beside the cup. "As you savor your drink, I want you to reflect on what your lack of commitment has cost... so far. The price is high and we'll have no choice but to continue exacting recompense until conditions are met. It matters not whether it is by your hand or by those from the American government with whom we negotiate."

The captain's face screwed down tight. His eyes filled with tears as he looked at the smiling pudgy pale face of a man with curly strawberry blonde hair.

Azziz saw that his tactic had worked, and he smiled, satisfied.

As the burden of the captain's perceived lack of action hit home, he covered his grief with both hands. His shoulders rose and fell as he quietly sobbed over the loss of a life for no good reason.

"Captain, I need you wholeheartedly in this negotiating process, otherwise much blood will be spilled on your ship in your name and will, Sir, be on *your* hands. You don't want that. Do you?" Azziz's voice took the timbre of a whine. He then smiled. "It is an unusual thing to contemplate – that our fingers are on the triggers, yet it is you killing your passengers. Your lack of compassion frankly astounds me."

As if his head had tripled in weight upon a weakened neck, Mariostansi pulled his face out of his hands and looked up at Azziz, but for only a second. He dropped his chin to his chest and sobbed, defeated.

Azziz nodded. "Yes, I can see it. You are just now beginning to see and understand how important you are in what we must do. Please, Captain, enjoy your tea."

CHAPTER 16

Lydia searched for anything to hold the tablecloth in place to maintain the secrecy of Nick and Trish's escape route. Although important that it remain concealed, it had suddenly lost some of its significance. She frantically sought a way to help Benjamin. He lay helpless on floor, possibly unconscious. She couldn't see well enough to know for sure. His injuries had to be life threatening and she had to, somehow, get down there on the floor to check him out, to help him.

Hardly anything she did would go unnoticed in this crowded auditorium. Plus, by merely screaming on Benjamin's behalf, she had marked herself as a person to watch. The bright white linen cloth's position must be held in place somehow. It'd mean a quick execution for her and Benjamin should the opened air conditioning duct be revealed, and death to Nick and Trish should they be found.

"Give me a minute, Benny," she whispered, voice cracking as she realized he probably couldn't hear the comment. She choked back a sob. Although he lay mostly out of sight below the table's edge, she saw his unmoving upturned feet – not a twitch, not a tremble. Had he succumbed to his injuries and died? She had to find out and quickly.

After nerve-racking seconds, she couldn't think of a way to hold the cloth in place. Then she noticed the inside corner that Benjamin held had ripped when he was yanked from the stool to the floor. She began working it over the sharp inside corner of the table and the hole grew larger fast. She then pulled it against that corner and it began to rip. Continuing what she had begun, a two-inch tear eventually slipped over the rectangular table's sharply squared back edge. She did the same to the other inside corner. After a minute of working it over the pointed edge, she had worn it enough that it had begun to fray. She then ripped it open and forced that corner of the table through the ragged hole, providing a satisfactory and stable drape to cover the front of the table all the way to floor. She didn't have to hold it in place any longer; her hands were free.

Her attention turned to the guard on stage. She began getting the rhythm of his pace, almost like playing skip-rope in slow motion, determining when to jump in. She saw the instant his eyes turned, followed by his body, to methodically stroll back across the stage. Beginning the instant his eyes broke contact with her side of the auditorium, she slid from behind the table, off the riser, and down to the carpeted floor of the walkway separating the theatre seats below from the reserve tables higher up. The backs of those seats concealed her movement as long as she remained on hands and knees.

The crowd pushed even farther away, as if remaining too close to her and Benjamin would involve them when killing-time came. All faces turned away, none willing to watch what she did. Their actions made it clear that they did not want, in any way, to be associated with someone blatantly taking such a life-threatening chance as this. Most sat or sprawled in any available space, since moving about was forbidden. Lydia crawled toward Benjamin, never raising her head above the backs of the seats in front of her.

His hand was twisted at a grossly misshapen angle to his forearm. Blood trickled from his nose and mouth. Some of it had begun to darken and crust over. His breathing was dangerously thin, more of a pant. Broken ribs could be pressing his lungs and may have pierced one of them. He was definitely unconscious, but she realized the advantage it provided.

With trembling fingers, she slowly turned the hand of Benjamin's broken arm, aligning it then gently lifting it. Feeling the separated bones raised acid into the back of her throat. She carefully moved it close to his body to rest at his side. As she withdrew her hand, it inadvertently touched the protruding skin that the splintered bone pushed against. Placing a hand under his head, she cradled it and stroked his cheek with the other. "You sweet, courageous man." Her lip quivered. She pushed her cheek into his. "You're also an idiot." She cried.

After a time, his breathing changed. Eyelids parted. His eyes searched to find focus. He then became aware of the pain. He threw his chin out and groaned.

"Shh. Quiet Benny," she whispered, as a mother soothing a hurting child. "I'm here." She breathed each word slowly and directly into his ear, smoothing sparse strands of gray hair back over his head.

The nod was faint but clear. He swallowed hard. His eyes again closed.

"We have to be quiet… very quiet. Can you understand what I'm saying?" She searched his face for recognition of the warning.

Again, he nodded – more suggestion than movement.

"Good." She stroked his cheek and daubed blood from below his nose with the lapel of her white cotton blouse. "We'll get through this together."

Lydia suddenly felt a tug on her collar. She gasped and turned to face a young boy.

"Are we still playing the game?" he asked.

She pressed a finger to her lips. "Shh." Unsure what he meant, she nodded anyway.

The youngster squatted to be closer to eye level with Lydia. "I did my part," he said with pride. "That bad man didn't look under the table." He thumbed his chest. "I guarded it."

Again she warned him. "Shh." In a flash, Lydia realized it must have been something Nick had told him. "Oh yes… the game." She pulled his head closer and put her lips to his ear. "Just keep guarding the table but be very quiet."

"Will I still get a prize if I do good? That man under the table said I would. Will I?"

"Sure you will. I'll give it to you myself. How's that?"

The boy grinned big and rose. Chest out, he marched a couple of paces away then stood, hands behind his back, legs spread as sentinel in front of the tablecloth. Like a pint-size soldier, he guarded the table, looking the part, right down to the serious expression and wary eyes.

Beyond the youngster, Lydia noticed the woman who must have been his mother. She sat on the festively colored carpet with multicolored swirls on a black background, leaning against the riser with her knees pulled up and head hung low. It was obvious she hadn't noticed that the boy had wandered away. She wallowed in gloom, just like three thousand others jamming this theatre.

Lydia eased up, looking over the last row of seats between two heads in front of her, and saw the guard still pacing the stage. She breathed a sigh of relief and, again, sank down beside Benjamin. She brushed his cheek with light soothing swipes.

His eyes fluttered open. He grimaced.

"Oh, Benny."

CHAPTER 17

Bite crammed in her mouth, cheek bulging, the uneaten portion of a donut dangled from Trish's sugar coated fingertips. "Do you think the Coast Guard, or the government, or somebody out there is planning a rescue?" She smacked and licked the powdered sugar from her lips.

Nick didn't look up. "Bet on it." He leaned over the conference table supporting his upper body with one hand, while shuffling through papers scattered about, reading some of one and then sliding it out of the way to look at the next one. "What do you think they discuss when they meet in here?"

With no pretense of manners, she gulped down the big hunk of donut then shoved another gluttonous bite into her mouth. She stepped in close behind Nick and looked over his shoulder, resting the donut-wielding hand on the other shoulder next to his head. Powdered sugar rained down on the paper he perused. "Oops." She flashed a shy smile when he glanced back and quickly brushed it from the document. "Sorry."

"Not a problem."

She turned and leaned back against the table to face him.

"I suppose they discuss everything from how many rolls of toilet paper per cabin to how many gallons of diesel fuel they'll need." She swallowed and retrieved the Styrofoam cup of coffee, blew the steam from its surface and took a sip. "You know… the kind of stuff passengers would never think about… or want to."

"You're probably right. Here's a copy of an invoice for a large plywood crate of meats delivered from Gulf Coast Wholesale Foods. Different cuts are itemized. It's certainly something I'd never think about if it weren't in front of me." He flipped over the invoice and abruptly stood. Scribbled on the back of it was a note that read: Not on food requisition order. "Well, I'll be damned."

"What?"

"I think I just figured out how they got on the ship. They came hidden inside crates forklifted into the cargo hold. I saw one of them shift as if it were about to fall off the tines of a forklift when we were on the gangway boarding this morning."

"Sorry, I didn't notice."

He grinned. "I'm not surprised."

"Hey, I was a bit preoccupied at the time."

"I was just kidding. I know you couldn't help it."

"Thanks. But how is that information going to help us at this point?"

He drew a big breath, held it a few seconds then exhaled in a huff. "I can't think of a way it would, I'm afraid. Mainly because I have no idea how many crates of them there were or how many men were in each crate." He paced away. "I wonder if the cruise line brass ever discussed terrorists and what to do in situations like the one we find ourselves in now?"

"If they had a plan, it didn't work," she said.

"Yeah, I think that's clear enough."

A thought struck him. He stopped walking and spun around but was forced to move back when he saw that Trish had paced him step for step and found her nose to his chest. "Uh... excuse me," he said.

She didn't attempt to step back.

He hinted a smile as he walked around her and leaned over the table, supporting his weight on widespread hands. "I'm hoping to find a memo... or something among this crap that has an outline of action. But if I found it, I'm not sure how that could help us either." He straightened and dropped his hands on his hips, blowing a frustrated snort through his nose. "One thing's for damn sure: This is a problem passengers shouldn't need to be worrying about. But here we are, waist-deep in a terrifying dung heap."

"Dung heap? What's the matter, afraid of offending me? Call it what it is... some really scary shit!"

He glanced sideways. "Okay, scary shit."

He went back to shuffling papers, reading bits and pieces and shoving them one at a time down the table. Some took flight and fluttered to the floor. "I guess it'd just make me feel better to know that some plan is underway and that we just don't happen to know what that is yet." He finally gave up, abandoning the stacks of inventory lists, memos and weigh bills and stepping toward the door. He put an ear to it, listening. "What I really want to know is how many of those guys are out there, and if there's anyone besides them and us *not* in and around that auditorium?"

Trish shrugged as she topped off her cup from the black plastic spigot at the bottom of the tall stainless steel urn. "Can't even give you an educated guess..." she paused, "Are saying that if you knew it was only a few, you'd race out there like Rambo?"

"Not at all... just one more fact in my plan-formulation arsenal, that's all. The more I know, the safer I'll feel and, possibly, the safer we'll be."

She examined an outstretched arm. "I'd feel much better if these chill bumps would disappear."

Nick abruptly pulled his ear away from the door. "Come to think of it, have you heard noise of any kind since we dropped in here?"

She slowly pulled the cup from her lips. "Interesting question. Can't say that I have. What do you think that means?"

"I think it means that I might be able to open that door and see where we are without a bullet whizzing by my head or, worse yet, through it."

"Okay... should you luck out, then what?"

"I'm not sure. Try to contact someone off the ship, maybe?"

Trish rolled her eyes and set the coffee cup on the table. "Oh, really? Now, I want to say something." There was a distinctive seriousness about her.

"Go for it."

"Let's say we find the key to the magic kingdom, like a satellite phone, the radio room or... you know, something like that. Now, since we're deep into make-believe, let's assume we happen to see a phone number on the wall in large red digits for the Coast Guard, the Navy, or some other helpful government-sanctioned organization. Doesn't this sound like a really wonderful fantasy sprinkled with pixie dust yet?" She shook her head.

"But–"

She held an open palm to him. "Hold on. I'm not through yet. We've come this far, let's take it all the way to its fanciful conclusion." She lightly slapped a cheek and dropped her jaw in mock surprise. "We actually contact and talk to someone who can make things happen. What do we tell them? Duh, we're trapped on a cruise ship, held hostage by terrorists in the middle of the Gulf of Mexico."

Nick saw he'd punched her button. Fear began spilling out as sarcasm, but he figured he might as well let it play out.

"When we tell them that, Nick, do you know what they're going to say? I do. They're going to say, 'We know.' That's all, just, 'We know.'"

Nick looked around as if someone might magically appear in the room with them. "You're getting a little loud."

"Yeah, well, we'll be getting a little dead if we don't have a better plan than going out there to make a phone call just to hear some jackass say, 'We know.'"

Nick had no response, because her rant was right on the mark. "Well, it seemed like a good idea while it was still in my head."

He saw in her changing face that she realized how far she'd gone. The expression transformed into astonishment. Her head went limp. "I'm sorry. I didn't mean to snap at you." She tried to smile. "Although, if it were possible, I'd be racing you to the phone to call a water taxi so we could go home."

"It's okay."

"I've always had an overactive imagination," she said. "I think it's partially responsible for my phobia."

"In this case," he said, "it's a good thing. We shouldn't be reacting without first considering consequences – *all* of them."

Arms hanging limp, she tapped her fingertips together. "Have any other ideas I can blow up for you?"

"No, but hang on to that budding humor; you'll need it." He rejoined her at the table. "I believe we need to think about what you said. Maybe we should determine how many terrorists are on board, and where they're all located. Then we'd have solid information to pass on to those working to rescue us or help us devise our own escape plan. I propose we go on a fact-finding expedition… a recon mission."

She flew a hand from her nose to full extension. "Frying pan right into the fire. I should've kept my mouth shut and just gone along with hunting for a phone."

"Seriously, let's think about this for a moment. If they do number twenty, thirty or more, did they *all* come inside those crates? If so, how could the dock supervisor not notice an unusual number of crates that size? One maybe, two possibly, but three or more?" He stabbed the air with a finger. "Unless... it was indeed just that one crate." He stepped quickly to her and grabbed her upper arms. "Do you know what that'd mean?"

"No, but judging by the bruises you're raising on my arms, you're pretty excited about it."

"It means that that one crate is likely all there was. One could be considered a mistake or overlooked altogether and loaded anyway. And, according to that invoice there was only one. Did you happen to see another invoice?"

"No."

"I believe there was, indeed, only one. Two or more would mean a problem that the ship's personnel might investigate right away, and leave them setting on the dock." Nick released her and began pounding a fist into his palm. "How many men could that crate hold?"

"Can't help ya there either. I never saw it. I was a little busy at the time having the breath scared out of me."

Nick put his palms together and pressed the edge of his fingers to his lips. He thought for a moment. "That crate couldn't have been more than eight feet long, and if men lined each side of it, I can't see a way more than about twelve could have been in it. If I'm right, that makes the odds a little more favorable."

"Pretty good sleuth work. Only problem is, they're carrying serious firepower. By my way of thinking, that doesn't make the odds look much better. Each one of those goons could take on fifteen or twenty angry tourists throwing ashtrays and lamps."

"True. But another advantage for the good guys is that none of the bad guys look like tourists... more like guerillas. As a group, they'd make a dandy political cartoon of the stereotypical terrorist. They're easy to spot."

"I'll give you that much." She pushed her finger into his chest. "But it doesn't help much if I recognize the one shooting me two seconds sooner than I would have otherwise. Are you trying to make a point that I'm just not catching?"

"Not sure." He massaged the nape of his neck and nodded. "But it makes sense. What if the total turns out to be only those guarding the auditorium and the two or three that escorted the Captain away? How many would that be? Ten... twenty tops?"

"Don't forget the guns."

"The alternative is waiting. And knowing the U.S. government doesn't negotiate with terrorists, the chances of something awful happening to Lydia or Benny... or both, goes up fast." He quickly added, "And, what about all those other people with them?"

Trish shrugged. "I don't know, Nick. I just don't know. The best I can offer is playing Devil's advocate because I'm such a coward."

He couldn't determine if it was self-pity or the thought of the worst happening to Benjamin and Lydia that he read into her expression. "I think I know... lambs to the slaughter. In the end, whether those thugs get what they're after or not, they'd scuttle this ship and all the witnesses with it just to make some demented political statement. My observations of Middle Eastern ideologies have shown me that those people have no problem blowing themselves up, along with as many non-believers as they can."

"Okay," she said. "Point made. But I'm no heroine. What if I panic and, God forbid, cut and run? All it'd take is someone getting in my face, invading my personal space, and I might lose it. Nick, I could get you killed. Don't you understand that?" She turned away, hugging herself, rubbing arms rippling anew with goose bumps.

"Don't think of this as a way to go out in a blaze of heroic glory. If we stay focused, then being heroes has nothing to do with it. It's just a job to be done. We have to be extra cautious, that's all. If we find out the exact number we're dealing with, options may spring from that information."

She looked back over her shoulder at him. "Speaking of blowing things up, you have no idea how badly I want to blow that idea up. That's more of that scary shit I was talkin' about. Why do you have to make so much sense?"

"Jumping into the middle of problems, usually someone else's, is what I do. But I don't know if I should call it a gift or a curse; how about a compulsion?"

"Gift, curse, compulsion... doesn't matter. If I'm going to hang around you, I'd better embrace them all."

"Let's sit, put our feet up on that table, and let these considerations marinate for a while. Maybe better ideas will come. Then again, maybe they won't. It could be that we'll act on what we've already discussed. Either way, let's rest for now. A chance to sit and think things through is a blessing that may not come again until all this... scary... stuff... is resolved, one way or another."

CHAPTER 18

Hearing muffled conversations from where she lay near Benjamin, Lydia lifted her head from behind the theatre seats and looked beyond the descending rows toward the stage. At first, it seemed that it was just tension that caused her to perspire, but she came to realize that the number of people jamming the auditorium was taking the temperature up. The smell of faltering deodorants permeated warming air. She watched the lone guard onstage talk to the leader. That's what the crowd had begun responding to. He and his right-hand man then came down off the stage and walked up the broad, gently sloped stairs between the arcs of seats on both sides. She heard a rustling sound and saw that Benjamin heard the same thing.

He wheezed, laboring for breath. "What's the matter? What do you see?"

She dropped down onto the carpet, frantically pressing a finger to his lips. "Shh." Once certain he'd remain quiet, she pushed herself upright and sat. As she did, a shadow moved across Benjamin, blocking the light above her. Her heart skipped, and a tingling flush reddened her cheeks. As her eyes pulled away from Benjamin to look up, she sent out a quick prayer. *God, please let that be Nick.*

The shadow stopped moving.

All it took was a glance – her prayer had not been answered. Two armed men stood hovering. The murmuring crowd receded farther away. She closed her eyes, summoning courage that had not yet arrived. She was in dire need of it – immediately. Finally conceding it as unavoidable, she lifted her head and looked up directly into Azziz Baruk's eyes. For the moment, composure held. "May I stand?" she asked in faltering voice.

"Please do," Azziz said. "I want to apologize to you and your husband. We are not here to torture. That was never part of our plan.

If a life must be taken, then it's to be done quickly and humanely. Those were the orders that I issued to my people."

Refusing the hand he offered, she rolled to hands and knees then came up unsteadily to her feet. Feeling older than her fifty-six years, she swayed momentarily with a light head, holding a hand to her forehead until equilibrium returned. "He's not my husband but has become a dear friend. I can't bear to see him in pain. Is there something you might allow me to do to ease it?"

"Be careful what you wish for," Azziz said. "Alive and in pain may be better than the alternative." He looked to his compatriot. "Sahid here has reprimanded the guard for insolence. We are doing what we must, no more. The attack on your... friend... was regrettable, although I'm sure you understand my man's reasoning."

She'd prayed for courage, but what possessed her instead was quick anger over this sociopath's nonchalance in the face of savagery.

"Reason?" she blurted. "There is nothing reasonable about any of this! There's no acceptable rationale for how demands are forced upon us. It's brutal, for God's sake. I can't understand any act that cheapens human life to the point of spilling blood in order to force political favor."

He threw his chin out and glanced to the ceiling, then coldly brought his eyes back down.

She had angered him, but no greater was his anger than was her contempt for his actions. She glared at him.

His lips pressed tight. But, after a moment, he seemed to relax and turned away, clasping his hands behind him, slapping one into the other. He then threw his head back and whirled around to again face her.

"Then you are ignorant!" His anger reeled, but he constrained volume, going the other way – intense and slow. "Whether you are a willing participant or not, and whether you attempt to understand or not, does not change the legitimacy. But I'll tell you anyhow. You need to hear it, because there is no one in a position of authority in the West that will tell you the truth. Everything you hear is glossed for effect to cloak the profit motive that lies at the core of what they say. Your government has enjoined a war that we will not walk away from. The jihad is waged in the name of Allah. He is a vengeful God when imperialistic forces with colonial intent threaten his people's lives, lands, and heritage. America is empire-building at our expense. We will not tolerate it!"

Lydia felt something. She looked down and saw Benjamin had reached across with his good hand and clutched her ankle. He shook his head. The unspoken message was clear; say no more, or risk being the next casualty of this crazy man's jihad.

She understood but couldn't hold it in. "If that's so, Mr. Azziz, then vengeance should be left to Allah to exact, not you. You're just a man. If –"

With lightning speed, the back of Azziz's hand connected with the side of her face. She whirled around, stumbling and falling face-down on the floor. A woman nearby screamed before she could check it. Otherwise, there were no sounds. It was as if all the people had disappeared – so quiet that the sound of her own breathing coming back to her from the carpet next to her mouth was all she heard. She rolled onto her back.

Benjamin lifted his head and strained to look around, despite his pain. "Lydia!" He pulled his broken arm into his side and tried crawling toward her, pitifully inching along in her direction.

"Go to her, old man. You deserve each other," Azziz said, turning then to the crowd at large. "In fifteen minutes, we are expecting an answer. If there isn't one, then you know what we must do. Allah as my witness, we will not be ignored!" His voice carried throughout the acoustically enhanced theatre.

He whirled around and marched down the stairs toward the stage, suddenly stopping to address his shadow, Sahid. "Throw that woman in the equipment closet by the stage. Let her sit alone in the dark and think on how she has misbehaved. A woman ranting like a child should be treated as one."

"Please! You can't!" Benjamin said. "She's claustrophobic. That's the ultimate inhumanity to a person with that affliction."

Although limp-wristed, she held up a cautionary hand. "No Benny, stay where you are. Say no more." She lifted her aching torso to sit upright. A warm ooze of blood trickled from her nose. With a fingertip, she probed a deep raw scratch on her cheek from Azziz's ring when he backhanded her.

"In that case," Azziz said, "it makes a wonderfully fitting punishment for such disrespectful behavior. If confinement is agonizing, then we may grant her the gift of eternal peace of mind in fifteen minutes. I'll think on that. It would, after all, prove my... humanity. Don't you think?"

Lydia began crying, her fate seemingly sealed.

Sahid came back to escort her to the closet. He stopped and straddled her splayed legs. "Claustrophobia? That's just one sign of a decadent society, a disease of the mind brought on by weak wills. If you people took time to open your eyes, you'd see signs of degradation everywhere – a people becoming fat, lazy, and uneducated, wanting everything handed to them, working for nothing, demanding more for less. Your so-called phobia is but one example. We are on the front lines of stopping virulent behavior before it infects the entire globe."

Lying on his side, Benjamin looked up at the man and, with much effort, said, "You're right. We have become a nation showing ill side effects of generalized wealth, but you're forgetting one very important factor." Benjamin placed the good hand over his chest. "Heart. There is no stronger weapon than understanding. Please understand our fear; you and your friends cast a blind eye to the humanitarian nature of our actions and see only geopolitical aspirations. Sometimes, my friend, a helping hand is just a helping hand."

Angered, Sahid snarled, raising his machine gun, fully prepared to slam Benjamin's head with its butt.

Benjamin seemed freakishly calm but covered his face with his good arm.

"Please, sir. Don't," Lydia said. "I'm ready to go. I'll do as you say."

Sahid, clearly bested in the debate, likely realized he shouldn't have engaged them in conversation. He yanked Lydia to her feet.

"You have a date with an evil I have no part of; the darkness waits to devour you in the confines of that closet." Jerking her in close, he shoved her. She stumbled down the steps. Walking past the stage, he said something in Arabic to the guard still pacing back and forth across it.

Glancing a final time to Benjamin, Lydia wanted to present him with the face of courage, but she couldn't conceal the terror of what awaited her in that small dark closet.

CHAPTER 19

Gently rocking in a swivel chair she had pushed back away from the conference table, Trish emerged from quiet contemplation as her sandals clicked the floor with each thrust.

"Ya think they're okay?" Her eyes darted over the litter of papers atop the table and settled on a stare at some obscure point within it all. She fretfully nibbled a cuticle. Nick didn't answer; he just waited for her to focus on him, which she finally did. "Benny and Lydia I mean. Do you think they'll be all right?"

He leaned back against the edge of the table, partially sitting, partially standing, and crossed his legs at the ankles. He faced her, but his head was down, arms crossed over his chest. His neck tightened as he considered her question, because any answer would have to be a no-win scenario, or a flat-out lie complete with an encouraging smile. His true feeling about Lydia and Benjamin's ability to survive would be clicking downward the longer this situation dragged on. "Don't know. But I'm worried, too. Those gun-happy thugs are void of conscience. To them, human life is a negotiable commodity, and that's about it."

She continued rocking, acknowledging with the faintest of nods, and her eyes seemed to examine something over his shoulder. He knew the wall behind him to be bare. She pushed that long, sweeping bang, as if trying to wrap it around her ear, but it was obviously a mindless gesture because it didn't reach that far. She was looking, but not at the wall. It was clear that she pondered something, maybe attempting to see things impossible to know in a windowless meeting room on the lower deck of a cruise ship. Finally, she slapped the armrests of the chair.

"I feel so damn helpless!"

Coming away from the table, he knelt beside her.

"Look Trish, coming up with the perfect plan may not be in the cards, but if we sit here any longer, we'll dream up all kinds of unimaginable gore, not to mention a ship-load of *maybes* and *what ifs*."

"I think you're right."

"I've already conjured a couple of images that I don't want crossing my mind again – both worst-case and bloody. It's probably best we do what it takes to contact crew or someone onshore."

"Oh, so we're back to the idea of leaving the cozy confines of this room, are we?"

"Reality is hardly ever as bad as what the imagination cooks up."

"Well that was a wonderfully clinical way to sum up the situation, and quite sterile, too. In fact, it'd make a great bumper sticker." She ratcheted the sarcasm up. "I'm sure you're loaded with wonderful personal experiences that back up that assertion. Right?"

Nick sprang to his feet. "Well… yeah, as a matter of fact I *can* back it up."

She suddenly stopped rocking. "I'm sorry. I'm just scared." Then her expression turned quizzical. "Are you serious? You've been involved with experiences like this?"

"Not exactly, but there was a time in the summer of '91 about five miles north of the Kuwaiti border in Iraq that I really thought I was going to die."

"You were in Desert Storm?"

"Yeah; I guess I've never shared that with you, have I?"

"No, you haven't."

"It was night. I had been assigned to escort troop carriers in the tank I commanded. It was supposed to have been a routine sweep to secure an area that American bombers had just pounded… a quick-in-quick-out operation, simple and by the book. It was to have been an outpost, a remote ops base. The tank was equipped with night-vision cameras. I saw hundreds, maybe thousands, of human forms coming up over a hill about three hundred yards out. I shut the tank down and radioed troop carriers to hold their positions. My imagination went wild. I envisioned my unit slaughtered, body parts strewn everywhere. Every bloody thing I could have possibly imagined, I did. That was as close to a phobic episode as I've ever had. About the time I thought I'd wet my pants or choke from a perception of dwindling oxygen, American jets returned for a final flyover, dropped bombs, and came in low to attack survivors. The threat was neutralized."

"Just like that?"

"Just like that." He stood and again leaned back against the table and crossed his extended legs. "A perfect example of a man's imagination creating horrific scenarios when reality turned out to be not much at all... for *our* troops anyway.

Nick saw that Trish's eyes had stopped roaming the room and had locked onto his. Her interest didn't seem quite so casual anymore as she focused on his face. Startled by the expressive intensity he asked, "Are you okay?"

Her stare, though unmoving, began to change with the sound of his voice. It softened. He sensed that she looked directly into his thoughts. Nick felt magnetically drawn and fell stumbling into her eyes. In the span of a second, all problems, all danger seemed moot. Everything faded away. His vision narrowed, tunneling until her face was all he saw. Unable and unwilling to control it, he stood and took the one quick step to her chair, leaned over and kissed her.

Trish met the advance.

Nick's lips explored hers.

Her breathing quickened.

Abruptly he pulled away and straightened. "What the hell am I doing?"

He stepped quickly away and then stopped and faced her. "I'm sorry. I don't know what got into me." Running fingers through his dark, mussed hair over and over, he paced, two steps away two steps back, like a caged animal.

She rose and tentatively stepped toward him. "It's okay. I wanted it to happen."

"No, it's not okay. It's the wrong time, the wrong place, and you're the wrong woman."

Nick saw that he had touched a nerve and abruptly stopped pacing. "Oh no, I didn't mean that the way it sounded. It came out all wrong."

A tear tumbled down her cheek. "It's true. I am the wrong woman. I – I just don't want to be. Forgive me for my thoughts." She took a fast swipe at that tracking tear, as if she could catch it before he noticed.

"I'm so sorry," he said, putting his arms around her. "You could be the perfect woman, I don't know." He walked up to her and hugged her, pressing tightly against her body, afraid he may have lost a once-only chance. He wrestled with whether he even wanted any such opportunity.

"I let myself have thoughts I shouldn't have," she said. "I'm the one who should be apologizing."

Nick savored the scent of her hair and began slipping right back into romantically dangerous territory. He pushed his nose closer, drawing long and slow, losing himself to the erotic scent. Holding her body against his, he finally realized how futile it was and dropped his arms. In a forced and calculating fashion he backed away. "Maybe I need to put raging hormones to good use in other ways."

"Maybe so," she said, taking another nervous swipe at tears that now streamed. She laughed nervously.

Still backing away, as if he might be sucked back in, he spoke. "I'm going to listen at the door and, you know, see if I can hear anything."

"Yeah, I think you should."

He backed all the way around the table, feeling a near-overwhelming compulsion to race back into her arms. The line between right and wrong, where it concerned Trish, had rolled totally out of focus. Marital fidelity didn't seem to matter so much anymore. Trish seemed so right – so damn perfect. *Do I really want to walk away from her?* A swirl of thoughts, including his wife Evie, his daughter Alli, and Trish, made for a confusing and most unwelcome entanglement heaped upon an already dire situation.

He clenched his teeth and flexed jaw muscles, beginning the difficult task of setting aside feelings. Stopping at the door, he placed a hand on the cool metal and finally tore his eyes away from her.

He put an ear to the door but heard nothing. As he listened, he glimpsed something beneath a coat that had been carelessly flung across it. It was similar to an umbrella stand near the door that held wide rolls of paper upright. "I wonder...?" he said, reaching for one.

"Wonder what? What'd you find?"

"Not sure." He unrolled one of them on the table. It was a blueprint. Across the top it read: AIR CONDITIONING AND VENTILATION SYSTEN, OCEAN DANCER. "Hey, look at this."

As Nick held the roll open atop the table with a hand on each end, Trish leaned in behind him, her chin nearly on his shoulder and almost cheek to cheek. "What is it?"

"It's a schematic for the air conditioning system." He flipped a page, stabbing a spot with his finger. "See that? It's the duct we used to get out of the auditorium." He took a moment to look it over. "Ya know what? I have a feeling we need to find a way to go up. If we crawl back into that duct, all the easy routes appear to be lateral or down."

"How about this one?" She dropped another roll bound with a rubber band on the table.

"Let me see." He unrolled it. "It seems to be a blueprint of just the deck we're on. See this?" His finger traveled a line on the air conditioning schematic then referenced it to the blueprint of the deck they were trapped on. "I think this is the room we're in. It's labeled *PLANNING*."

"Sorry, but that's the only other blueprint I see," she said, looking around the room but keeping a hand on the one Nick studied.

He nodded and continued a visual sweep of the one before him. "It appears that at the end of the corridor outside this room, there's a narrow stairwell behind a bulkhead." He crossed his arms over his chest and leaned against the wall to consider the information. "But there's no indication what's at the top of those stairs. I suppose it's for crew only. It certainly doesn't appear wide enough to comfortably accommodate guests, probably more like a ladder than stairs. Maybe it's for utility purposes."

"So it would appear," she said, as she released her hold on the blueprint and it snapped back into a roll.

"And maybe it's only for emergencies, because it's so narrow and can be sealed off by a bulkhead door."

"You mean… like a sinking emergency?"

He nodded. "Yeah."

"I don't think I want to know anymore about that," she said. "We know the main entrance to the auditorium is above us and down a ways. Did you happen to notice what was down the hall in the opposite direction just before we passed through those double doors we were herded through?"

"Afraid not. At the time, I was worried about you and didn't notice."

She blushed. "Oh… right."

"Besides, at the time, who knew then that I'd need to know?"

"I guess that's right, too."

"But you know what? It makes sense. Stairs at both ends of *this* deck might also be at the ends of each corridor of *every* deck – emergency access and exit with bulkhead doors to seal off each layer in case this tub does go down."

"You've been on several cruises, haven't you?" she asked.

"Yeah."

"Any idea where all the maintenance areas and crew quarters are located?"

"Not a clue. I've always been more interested in pegging the location of all the bars. I was intent on having a good time, not seeing what the crew was up to."

"Okay," she said, "then let's get back to those stairs."

"At the moment, I think there are only two considerations: one, which stairwell will put us farthest from the guarded doors of the auditorium, and two, do we even have to stop there, or can we climb all the way up? And, if we make it topside, then what?"

"That sounds like three considerations."

Pulling his gaze down from the ceiling, he cast a crooked grin. "Don't count problems; tally solutions."

"Sorry, couldn't resist."

"Are you ready to find out if any exist?"

"Problems?"

"Solutions."

"Oh." She took a deep breath and exhaled . "I suppose so." She reached for and squeezed his hand.

Nick tingled from the touch. He shuddered. *That's just what I don't need.* For the first time in his life, he considered the prospect that near-perfect chemistry with a woman was a bad thing, possibly a fatal distraction.

CHAPTER 20

Applying a bruising grip on her arm, the guard yanked Lydia to a standstill and reached across her body to the door of the storage closet next to the stage. He flung it open, slamming it against the wall. The tiny space was not a closet at all, but a cabinet-sized storage unit. She questioned whether her body would fold tight enough to fit in it. Lydia remembered rent lockers at the airport with as much interior room. The guard, mumbling something in Arabic, brusquely yanked costumes, a trumpet case, and a whiskbroom from the interior and tossed them aside. The space appeared to be a perfect cube, measuring no more than three feet in all directions.

Seeking courage, Lydia looked back at the crowd. Seats of the theatre were filled. People crowded every aisle, some lying down, some sitting, some standing, but no one made a move or a sound to support her in this moment of impending horrific misery, most averting their eyes altogether. The only thing to do was plead with her captor. But to speak would surely draw a fist or gun butt to the face. He didn't understand or speak English anyway. She looked at him, eyes imploring – an expression that to any humane individual would've been interpreted as a plea for leniency. But it was clear in his perfunctory nature that his orders from Azziz were as good as blinders, overriding any and everything she might do to prevent this cruel confinement. It was clear that avoiding the torturous confines of that storage cubicle was impossible. Her eyes darted to all five visible surfaces of its interior, sweeping top to bottom and left to right, and panic began to tighten her gut.

She began whimpering as he grabbed her arm. A sob escaped her throat, along with a worthless whispered appeal. "Please, no," she said, voice trembling. She leaned against him, hoping a simple touch might unlock a glimmer of concern in her captor for a fellow human. But he went about his business mechanically, even annoyed at the closeness, shoving her to arm's length, squeezing her upper arm with painful pressure.

One courageous voice went up from the audience. "Be strong, hon."

Her captor responded to the voice with an arm snapped to full extension and a rigid pointing finger, as if to say, "Watch out, or you might be next." It might have even been enough to get the woman shot and killed, had he not been so pre-occupied at the moment.

Through tears, she glimpsed an older woman at the end of the first row of seats near the stage. She cried as hard as Lydia, holding tightly clenched hands to her pursed lips. It appeared that the old lady was praying. Lydia hoped that she was and that it was for her.

Then the guard squeezed her arm tighter yet, yanking her off balance toward the tiny space. It would've been no more frightening than if poisonous snakes had spilled from it. The guard shoved her in. She banged her head and her ankles, having to fold her body into a tight ball to fit, but she had to comply or suffer even more painful knocks and dings. The man obviously didn't care how much pain he caused, as long as he complied with Azziz's orders.

About to close the door, he hesitated and made his first real eye contact. His expression was smug. Although the man did not comprehend English, it was obvious he believed that she deserved this. To be born a woman in some Arab speaking countries must be a condemnation from birth, to live a lifetime being treated as property. He said something in his native language. Lydia didn't understand but had passed caring what the brute had to say. For the first time in her life, she thought how pleasurable it'd be to kill another human being.

As the door swung shut with a decisive wham, she caught a whiff of rancid breath, the final insult as light turned to absolute dark in an instant. Her knees were forced up and pressed against her breasts. Perspiration now tracked down her temples and forehead. Droplets formed and dripped from the tip of her nose. Her toes curled up against the opposite wall, and the low ceiling forced her head into a deep slump. The door and its opposing wall missed her shoulders by a fraction of an inch on either side. She worked her hands into position to hold away the walls, to keep them from closing in. Lydia would've sworn that her tiny prison had begun to shrink even more.

A crushing sensation consumed her.

Air felt as though it were being sucked out of the space. Breathing became difficult.

She didn't know if the phobia worked on her or if this cubicle was virtually airtight. It didn't matter. Either way, she couldn't breathe – certain she was about to suffocate, and then be crushed.

"Imagery, imagery, imagery," she stuttered. *Come on Lydia, put your head in another time and place far away from here. See the beauty, find the desirable... know only the wonderful.*

She fought to imagine beautiful and soothing places and scenarios. Invasive thoughts raced randomly, none comforting. The worst was a clear image of Benjamin lying wounded, maybe critically so. It forced a whimper from deep in her throat. Then a sudden image of that last phone conversation with her husband Bruce making snide remarks about her claustrophobia replaced that murmur, born of concern for Benjamin, with an angry growl. Finally, the God-awful bad luck of encountering ruthless terrorists overlaid even that image.

She mumbled, "Why did I come on this damn cruise anyway? Why?" She bounced her forehead off her knees.

Then it occurred to her – the marriage. Testing the bounds of a phobia had only been a side issue. It was supposed to have been time away from Bruce to think, free of his incessant badgering with that poor sense of humor – distraction-free time to assess the direction that the rest of her life should take, and whether Bruce should even be in that picture.

Was the marriage worth saving? That issue had been forced from her thoughts when she ran head-on into a brutal adventure she didn't ask for. The problem, her marriage, had not gone away, just temporarily set aside in favor of things more life-threatening. *Do I want to stay married to Bruce Hansard?* She had already determined before the decision-making process had been interrupted that there'd be no more sidestepping, just make a judgment call and then live with it. As unreasonable as it seemed, two potentially life-altering issues had been thrust upon her in the dark confines of a small equipment locker aboard a cruise ship, somewhere in the Gulf of Mexico. Choices had to be made, and quickly.

An unlikely calm settled over her. Her mind shifted into an analytical frame. *Visions of beaches or tropical paradises be damned, I have a problem to sort out, and I find myself with the time to give it all my attention without interruption.* She stared down into the darkness between her knees. Her breathing returned to normal, and the first thing she visualized was not Bruce or her marriage, but Benjamin. "Oh, Benny," she muttered, discovering a longing to be at his side – but not only because of his injuries, although she indeed worried and wondered just how serious those injuries were. *What a wonderful man he is… willing to give it all to ease another human's suffering. If Bruce even had a miniscule amount of what Benny has, he wouldn't treat me that way.*

That thought, those words, resonated as she carefully considered the depth of their meaning. *Could it be that Bruce only sees me as a comfort zone? If so, could that be his definition of love?* Suddenly, she realized she was outside herself and not scared at all. Just as quickly, she saw things clearly. She had no clue if she would survive this ordeal with the terrorists, but she now had more than just a hunch about her marriage; she had the answer.

CHAPTER 21

Sahid paced the captain's quarters, then slowed as he looked across the room through the window. In Arabic, he called, "Azziz, look!" Sahid hurried over for a closer examination of something through the rectangular Plexiglas portal of the captain's office. Bright sunlight drenched his face. The late afternoon sun had sunk to a severe angle and shone a harsh beam into the room.

Azziz pulled his calculating stare away from the uncooperative captain and strode over to join Sahid at the window. "Ah, good..." He nodded and softened as a deep sense of contentment came over him. The hard expression reserved for Mariostansi, the captain, relaxed. "Yes... very good."

"Good?"

Looking for only a second, Azziz made a move back toward Mariostansi. "You see, my brother, the Americans are taking our demands seriously. We now have visual proof." He hesitated long enough to glance once more through the window and swelled with pride at having drawn two small Coast Guard fast-response boats. They appeared to be holding a position several hundred yards out, bobbing in the Gulf swells. Then something else nabbed Azziz's attention far to the right. He stepped closer to the window and saw what appeared to be a Navy war ship clearing the horizon from the south. He straightened and took a deep breath of satisfaction. "Look, my brother, that is better still," he added, pointing to it.

"Does this not concern you?"

Azziz placed a calm hand on his friend's shoulder. "On the contrary, I am pleased. It would have been foolhardy not to expect naval boats to surround this vessel during negotiations. They will look for any opening to stall and gain leverage... possibly for a rescue attempt. You see, regardless of what the Americans say, their presence indicates that they take us seriously. That is a form of negotiation. I'd be concerned if they hadn't shown up."

Azziz's pleasant expression faded. He stepped back to once again give the Ocean Dancer's captain full attention and switched back to English. "Unlike our disrespectful host who seems unwilling to voice our demands to the Americans with the necessary urgency."

The captain slumped, hovering over an untouched and cooling cup of tea, appearing defeated. He lifted his head and looked to Azziz. In English with a thick Italian accent, he spoke.

"I have done all you asked. Have I not?" His tone was apologetic. "I have fulfilled my promise to the letter."

Azziz's eyebrows went up. "'To the letter'? You say that with a tone of pride in your voice. Surely you don't think that, in this case, doing what you have been told 'to the letter' is a good thing?"

"I asked the questions of the Americans you wanted, insisting they negotiate for the sake of passengers' lives. This is what I promised and what I have delivered. I don't understand your displeasure with what I have done on your behalf."

Azziz listened, lips pressing tighter. He took a sudden sharp draw of air, allowing his head to fall back. He looked momentarily to the ceiling and then back at the captain. "Yes, you have fulfilled the promise you made, 'to the letter', as you say. And my promise to you was that if you did as I requested, I would not kill you. Is this not also true?"

Hesitatingly the captain nodded, clearly uncertain where Azziz was going with the reasoning.

Drifting to the hot water urn under the window, he asked, "We are men of honor, are we not?"

Again the captain dipped his chin reluctantly.

Pulling the crisp white linen drape from beneath the urn, Azziz tossed it at the captain, "As honorable men, we keep our promises."

The captain held up the linen cloth, the unspoken question as to its purpose unmistakable.

"Oh yes, the cloth," Azziz said. "Keep it close, you'll need it."

"I don't understand," Mariostansi said.

"You will soon enough." Azziz rejoined Sahid at the window.

In Arabic, "I see no activity aboard the two small boats," Sahid said, "just men at the bow of both, watching this ship. They have binoculars and seem to be scanning the Ocean Dancer deck by deck."

"As we do them," Azziz said. "It will probably be all they do until they succumb to the mournful plea the captain's about to make. Then, my brother, the wheels of progress in meeting our demands should begin accelerating."

Keeping a watchful eye on the captain, Azziz walked around the desk behind him and addressed him in English. "Since we are men of honor, Captain Mariostansi, I am going to fulfill my promise to you as you have to me, 'to the letter'. I will not kill you. In fact, I'll not let you die, no matter how much you may want to."

The strange comment shocked the captain, and he quickly looked up at Azziz as his eyes grew wide. Then his breathing stalled and his face polarized.

Reaching quickly over the captain's shoulder, Azziz grabbed his hand, slamming his knuckles on the desk repeatedly until pain forced it open, palm down. "Sahid, remove his thumb."

"What! Why? No! Please! I beg of you," the captain wailed. He struggled against the iron grip on his wrist.

"I believe your next communication with the Americans will have the correct inflection for a fast response, and I will have preserved my vow not to kill you. I, too, am fulfilling my promise 'to the letter'."

"No!"

Azziz looked to Sahid.

Sahid had already begun drawing out the knife concealed under his tunic.

"If you please, my brother."

CHAPTER 22

Losing what could have been a rare opportunity with Nick took Trish's anxiety level to new heights. But this fretfulness had nothing to do with terrorist thugs controlling the ship, aside from the fact that it was they who were responsible for she and Nick ending up alone together. Under other conditions, almost anything imaginable besides the real reason, it should have been a good thing. This new angst created a contradictory reaction to desire; she released his hand so fast it might as well have been a burning ember. "Okay. I-I'll follow, you lead," she said. *What was I thinking? He's not interested in me – not with a wife and a teenager at home. He was just reacting to stress.*

As she stood rubbing sweaty palms on the sides of her shorts in the ship's conference room, she noticed that his stare at her lingered. It was soft, not like the conniving gleam of a player on the prowl. Then she remembered that as she had dressed this morning, thoughts of inspiring Nick's lust had inadvertently guided her clothing choice. She either took a page from her sister's playbook or was more like Sandy than she cared to admit. Even if she and her sister were alike, it was something she'd never mention aloud. The low-cut tank top and tight plaid shorts, apparel better suited to the gym, had been chosen specifically to draw his attention. But how he looked at her at this moment was not at all lustful. If he was not interested, his eyes lied. She didn't see Nick Brandon as someone who'd lie – and that included body language. She wanted to believe that what she saw on his face amounted to a thread of hope that she had a chance with this man.

He batted his eyelids as though regaining consciousness. "I suppose the first thing to do is get a peek up and down the corridor and see what's out there. Hopefully it's not swarthy men with machine guns over their shoulders." He backed away from her and turned toward the planning room door. He put an ear to it and listened.

As her eyes followed him, she saw that Nick had courage that he probably wasn't even aware of. She couldn't imagine what problems a wife would have with a man like Nick. She allowed her head to tilt; she fantasized various conjured heroic exploits as she watched him with his ear against that door. Of course, she was at his side in all scenarios.

Suddenly, it occurred to her that there were other things that needed her attention, things that could save her life, or end it. She had to set her mind to that and get it out of this sexual rut. Romantic thoughts could become a dangerous distraction, not the fanciful aside she was in the midst of – playing the smitten teen wondering if the boy liked her or not. It would have been so much easier if Benny and Lydia were still with them, or anyone else for that matter.

Apparently, Nick felt safe enough to continue on with his plan. He pushed the latch handle down and gently pulled. It squeaked. He stopped and glanced back, biting his lower lip. "I sure hope that's louder in here than it is out there," he whispered.

She ran to the wall separating the meeting room from potential dangers of the hallway and pressed her ear against it. "I don't hear anything."

"Whew. I think my heart skipped." He pulled on the door again, this time past the squeak to allow enough room to get a quick peek into the hallway. He slowly pushed his head around the door and looked, first one way, then the other. "I don't see anyone," he whispered, pulling his head all the way back inside. "Are you ready for this?"

Trish began nodding, slowly and then faster.

"Yeah, let's do it." She blew a careful breath through rounded lips and stepped in close behind him as he pulled the door full open. The hinges grated. His face contorted at the sound.

She noticed the look and blurted, "See something?"

"Shh." He waved her down. "All I see is a long corridor with doors on both sides similar to this one. It's unadorned, some things in shades of gray and white and others in bright red and stark blue – not exactly choices a decorator would make. I assume this deck, or this portion of this deck, was never intended for passengers' eyes."

"Any sign of people?"

He shook his head and took a single step across the threshold. "It appears deserted." He looked in the other direction.

Trish wanted to boldly step out behind him, but bravery was not tracking close enough behind desire. Waning courage chilled her. She hugged herself, rubbing her shoulders, and tried to take that first step but couldn't. From the time she was a small child, Trish had been fearful of the unknown, from walking into a darkened bedroom to simple separation from her parents for a few hours. She was cursed with an abnormally strong ability to visualize potential problems in gruesome detail. Sometimes, her imagination became so vivid that she'd vomit. She wondered if that might have been a contributing factor to agoraphobia.

Nick leaned back in. "Coming?"

The calm and encouraging sound of his voice caused the muscles in her legs to fire, but still her feet refused to move from that spot, as if her sandals had been nailed to the floor.

"You sure it's clear?"

"The only thing here is you, me, and our fears." Nick's nostrils flared as he smirked at her, extending a hand.

"Don't you be makin' fun of me."

"Sorry." He took her hand. "I'm scared, too. If you prefer, I'll go alone. Maybe you'd feel safer staying here."

Like a bolt, it hit her: Staying behind would be worse than anything she could imagine happening outside the room, as long as she could stay near Nick. "No way." She allowed him to guide her over the threshold into the unprotected hallway. "You'll not be leaving me behind alone and wondering where you are and what's happening. I want you in sight at all times. I don't need to add vomiting to my problems."

"Vomiting?"

"Never mind... let's go."

"Then let's get to the stairs behind that bulkhead I saw on the blueprint. It should be at the end of this hall." He began a stealthy glide down the corridor. Trish pranced along behind on the tips of her toes.

She suddenly remembered the man and his wife that were shot and killed in the auditorium. It came with a vivid flash image. And that had happened with infinitely less provocation than what they would be providing if caught loose outside the auditorium. She tried tossing the thought with a quick headshake. It was the last thing she wanted to be thinking about.

She focused on something much more pleasant: broad shoulders and the man they belonged to. She felt safe as long as he remained within arm's reach. Suddenly, conjured images of them in the throes of lovemaking transformed into a heart-pounding distraction. Still, it was preferable to visions of murder. Following close behind, her eyes traveled from his head down – thick brown hair that just touched the tops of his ears, normally parted on the left but at the moment hung mostly straight to just above his eyebrows, appearing to be about a week late for a haircut. The arms of his soiled golf shirt stretched tight over well-toned arms and a butt that did those khaki pants proud. He stood just over six feet, she guessed.

Suddenly, the fantasy was interrupted. She needed to pee.

"Nick!" she hissed.

He stopped and spun to face her, "What's the matter? See something?"

"I need to pee… and I need to right now. It's cooler out here than it was in that meeting room. That and too much coffee is working on me."

Nick deflated. Anxiety fizzled. "Pee?" A smile slowly came up stretching his mouth.

"We could be blown away by crazed gun-toting hooligans," she said with a sweeping gesture, "and you're grinning because I need to pee? Are you nuts?"

"Well… yeah, I guess I am. I know it's a normal bodily function but, somehow, in these circumstances it seems… odd and, frankly, sort of funny." His stare turned thoughtful. "Ya know, of all the dramatic adventure movies I've ever seen, I can't remember anyone ever needing a potty break as they ran for their lives. Even the toughest of the tough would eventually need to pee. Don't you think? I bet the directors of all those action movies just figured it was a waste of film to interrupt the action with, of all things, the hero needing to piss."

"Geez, Nick. You're turning into an idiot right before my eyes."

"I'm sorry." His smile never wavered. "Let's get through that bulkhead down there, into the stairwell, and see if we can find a cranny so you don't have to tinkle in the hallway; the only thing worse than being dead is being embarrassed and *then* dead."

"I can't believe you're enjoying this so much." She watched him again move swiftly down the hall. Her admiration suddenly lost a little gloss. *And so goes an infatuation.* She trotted to catch up.

Reaching the final door, he turned the locking mechanism and opened it. He ducked low and raised his feet high to step through to the other side. "Come on."

Trish followed him through and looked around the cramped space. The stairs were more of a steeply pitched ladder, angled upward. Next to them, an identical setup switched back then down. It was a simple chain, threaded through rings on evenly spaced pipe standards that served as a banister. The stairs between that chain and the wall would barely be wide enough to accommodate even Nick's trim girth.

Nick squeezed by her. Her breasts brushed his chest. As he moved laterally past her, she noticed the object of his sudden fascination, a hinged panel beneath the steep stairs.

"Let's check that out." Kneeling, he slid a latch, and the door swung outward easily. He peered in. The portal was only three and a half, maybe four feet tall.

"See anything?"

"Not sure. But there are lights, and it does look like it goes for some distance. Dedicated utility access, maybe? There are oodles and gobs of pipes, tubes, wires, and cables lining the walls on both sides, and plenty of room to stand and walk between them. It might be worth exploring."

Knees locked together, she couldn't stop the pee-pee dance. "I'll make a deal with you."

"What would that be?"

"You go ahead, and I'll close this cute little door behind you and pee." She raised an eyebrow and pointed a stern finger directly at his nose. "But you wait for me. Okay?"

"I can't believe you're thinking I wouldn't," he said duck-walking toward the low door and disappearing through the opening.

Closing the door behind him, Trish unbuttoned her shorts and slid them and her panties down. She squatted near the still-open bulkhead. Relief was near overwhelming. She sighed then shuddered. Suddenly, she heard a noise – voices. "Oh, shit," she muttered, forcing the last drops. She jumped up, struggling clumsily with the button on her shorts. Since the bulkhead opened outward, she had no choice but leave it open or be discovered.

Voices grew louder. She stood in a puddle of piss but gave that no thought, hesitating for only a second, thinking she might try to close the bulkhead anyway. She stepped to the side of the door and slowly craned her neck around to see the source. The low conversation was now very close. They spoke in whispers, still too far away to determine what was said or even the language. It was two men dressed all in black and armed, checking doors as they moved closer. She withdrew her hand slowly, opting instead to leave it as it was.

On her toes she moved swiftly to the hinged panel, sliding the latch on it, opening it and dropping down to crawl through.

Again she heard talk.

They were now within mere feet of the bulkhead.

She scurried on through the access door and closed it behind her. Nick stood about twenty feet farther in. "Nick," she said as loud as she dared, racing toward him.

"What is it?"

"Two men are almost to the bulkhead outside."

"Jesus!" He snapped glances side to side, forward and backward. "We have no choice but to go wherever this leads."

As they began to jog through the maze of conduits, pipes and such, a thought drilled Trish. "Oh crap!" she said, coming to a sudden stop.

Nick stopped so abruptly he slid a few more inches. "What's the matter?"

Whining, "The bulkhead door is open and there's a puddle of pee just inside. I marked a trail for them like… like some damn dog would. Could I have made it any more obvious?"

"No time to worry. Keep moving."

Before they'd run another ten feet, the unmistakable yet muffled pop-pop of a pistol stopped them in their tracks again, followed by barely audible screeches and wails from somewhere above them.

Nick jerked his wristwatch up. "Aw, hell!" he hissed, "Another hour has passed."

Trish's face distorted. She muttered, "Oh no… Benny and Lydia."

CHAPTER 23

The black behind Lydia Hansard's eyelids soothed her – safer than the true darkness of the cubicle. Unable to move beyond a partial twist or shoulder shrug in the cramped locker next to the stage, she held the walls away, still fearing they'd move in and crush her if she let go. But, for the moment, she remained calm. Control continued, tenuous but manageable for now. She tightrope-walked a thread, a delicate psychological balance easily tipped.

Her muscles ached in the cramped confines, the air stale. She perspired heavily. Her clothing was already saturated, but she was alive, and so was Benjamin. A small blessing, but at this point, every one counted.

She waited; for what, she couldn't say. Rivulets of sweat tickled as they tracked her face, neck, arms, and legs – everyplace except the deep scratch where Azziz's ring raked across her cheek when he backhanded her. There, it burned. The odor of diluting makeup and perfume had become mixed with a less pleasant smell in the cramped space that she could do nothing about.

Claustrophobia had begun losing its bite. As strange as it seemed, a terrorist on a cruise ship in the Gulf of Mexico had unintentionally thrust sudden clarity upon her that, as a by-product, lessened the strangling sensation of that other prison she'd been confined in – her own skin.

The problem may have begun as a child by an abusive stepfather, but it had been perpetuated and exasperated by another kind of abuse that developed with glacial slowness over many years – so much so that it came on unnoticed, until now.

After that troubled childhood, her husband, Bruce, had become the new focus and eventually the source of her phobia. Every cruel joke and demeaning remark pushed her farther down. The marriage itself had turned claustrophobic – a perpetual darkened closet she hadn't even recognized for what it had actually become. She hadn't recognized the walls of it as it shrank, because it was loosely masked by a velvet cover called love. Eventually, the union was no less confining than this tiny pitch-black storage cubicle. Even as she sat in darkness, her life had become easy to see for what it had become.

She now realized the walls of the closet, though close and uncomfortable, would not crush her. Her hands slid from them, and she draped them loosely over the peaks of her knees. Minutes ticked by as she tapped a rhythm on her legs with the tips of her fingers.

Without warning, the closet door jerked open. A whoosh of cooler, fresher air raised goose bumps on her arms. Light flooded in and blinded her. She shielded her eyes to better see what was coming.

As her eyes adjusted, she saw the barrel of a machine gun inches from her nose.

He barked something in Arabic.

She shook her head, not understanding.

He shouted it again.

She assumed he wanted her out. Unable to move quickly following her cramped confinement, she had to use her hands to push her stiffened legs outward and put a foot on the carpet. It was a mere step down, but muscles needed coaxing and a moment to relax the tension in them.

The man she now recognized as the assigned guard of the auditorium allowed no such indulgence. He reached and filled his hand with sodden and matted blonde hair, yanking her.

She tumbled out, squealing.

Grabbing for his hand, she attempted to lessen the strain on her scalp as she dropped to the carpeted floor, slamming down hard on the right side of her tailbone. Tears mingled with stinging sweat in her eyes as she grimaced, baring her teeth to the ceiling.

He brought the muzzle of the automatic weapon up, using it like a pointer, meaning for her to stand. She had no intention of disobeying and rolled onto hands and knees to begin getting to her feet, but it was a command that her body was slow to heed.

Before she had a chance to move from that position, he kicked her in the ribs.

She saw a bright flash and then almost blacked out as wind left her body in a violent rush.

Collapsing onto her side, Lydia curled, covering her midsection with both arms. If she could've drawn a breath, she would've wailed.

After a second or so, her vision marginally cleared, but the pain in her stomach remained sharp. Had something ruptured? Every move was like a dagger shoved in her gut.

Through swimming eyes, she glimpsed the faces of people sitting on the front row and saw that hers weren't the only tears flowing. Streaming eyes filled every seat. But she heard no open sobs – men, women, children, old and young. It didn't matter. They all cried.

She noticed the old lady in the first row that had encouraged her to be strong biting her lower lip, holding fast to both armrests. That's when it occurred to Lydia what was about to happen. She was next to be shot.

Pressing a hand into her ribs to lessen the agony, she used the other to push off the floor and struggled to sit up. The pain in her side remained intense. As a result, her face remained screwed down tight. With a grunt, she finally came upright.

Although he wouldn't understand, she chose to talk anyway, figuring it was the last chance to speak her mind. "I suppose this is where I should be begging for my life. But mercy from the likes of you wouldn't be the honorable thing to seek." She fought for a couple of good breaths. "Sympathy from you would be like selling my soul and siding with Satan!" Then she looked away and mumbled, "You son of a syphilitic whore."

He grinned – unflinching, showing deeply water-stained and yellowed teeth. He stood, straddling her as a disrespectful show of dominance. She looked up at his crotch. *How easy it'd be to smash those balls.* The image of pain on his face, the tears in his eyes, a criminal pig trying to catch an agony-filled breath, like a bully getting his due, made for a satisfying image worth dwelling on.

It suddenly seemed like a plan. Kick him and kick him hard; better yet, drive a fist into his testicles. That would be much more precise and make him double in pain; if even only for a fraction of a second. Could she control that machine gun long enough for someone to come to her aid? Would others react and jump in to help? She was weak. Advantage would be fleeting. In order for her plan to work, he must be swarmed before he sprayed machine gun fire into the crowd. She couldn't prepare anyone for what was about to happen without alerting her executioner, too. Did it matter? Her jaw tightened. She balled her hand into a tight fist away from his view. Her commitment to act hardened. She had to think of saving her own life first and just pray that others were reading her eyes and her mind and could see into her heart's intention.

Now was her chance, as he looked away and up the stairs toward where Benjamin lay.

She pulled her fist back for a haymaker swing to the groin, but the guard took two quick steps back – just beyond arm's reach – and stopped, all the while looking up the stairs between the rows of theatre seats. Her plan had abruptly soured.

For some inexplicable reason, he hesitated to kill her.

Lydia looked up the stairs to the intersecting walkway halfway to the main entrance to see that Benjamin had crawled out far enough to watch, while holding his good arm outstretched. He said something. But she only saw his lips move. She tried but couldn't hear the sound of his weakened voice.

The guard took another step away from her in Benjamin's direction. He grinned then pointed the gun at the old guy, while looking down at her. The unspoken question was clear. She wanted to be brave, to defy this man's cruelty, but she couldn't stop herself. Her face distorted and tears exploded from her eyes like shrapnel. "You animal! You want me to beg for my life by offering up the life of someone I love in trade? Is that it? Is that what you're implying?"

Ignoring her pain, she rose to her feet.

He didn't try to stop her.

She stumbled sideways then stepped in close to her would-be assassin. "I see clearly there is no reason to remain quiet or respectful. Your cause may be justified; I don't know. I don't even know what the hell your cause is and, quite frankly, don't care! You're no better than a predatory beast with a bloodlust that kills for sport." She spit in his face.

With menacing slowness, he wiped saliva from his jaw and stepped farther away. On that, his game had just ended.

She saw it in his eyes. All sarcasm left them, and they narrowed into resolve. He was about to follow through on the vow to take one life every hour.

Emboldened by Lydia's courage in the face of death, a young man in the front row wearing cowboy boots, tight Wrangler blue jeans with a wide belt, and big shiny buckle, came to his feet slowly. He stepped with a fast but stealthy glide toward the terrorist from behind, just as the thug raised the machine gun to end her life.

She noticed the young man's big square hands were scarred and gnarled. He'd obviously seen tough times, likely on the backs of bulls and in barroom brawls.

The young man reached to snatch the machine gun.

But the adversary must have seen Lydia's eyes follow the man and realized in time that someone was coming up behind him. His grasp on the weapon was secure.

They struggled.

The terrorist yanked his sidearm from the holster on his waist while still clutching the automatic weapon in his other hand.

Lydia grabbed for his wrist, but in a single motion he slammed her face with the side of the pistol and sent her whirling to the floor. Before the cowboy could stop it, the pistol was in his face and two quick shots fired – point blank.

The cowboy's body went rag limp and collapsed to the floor in a heap, dead instantly.

Lydia fell on top of the young man.

Shrieks and moans went up from the crowd.

She lifted his head. The back of his skull was gone, but his heart still pumped blood onto the carpeted floor. She didn't care about that. Blood streamed from between her fingers. He saved her life and deserved at least this moment.

"You sweet fool," she muttered and pulled his head to her chest.

His beating heart went still.

A rumble of agitated moans and squeals went on for several seconds across the expansive auditorium, but eventually faded.

She sobbed and looked up at the shooter.

"You filthy animal!" she wailed, as she continued hugging the body of the young cowboy. Blood mixed with sweat saturated her blouse.

In one swift motion, the terrorist yanked her off the corpse and tossed her aside. He fished in the cowboy's pockets and found identification. He then grabbed Lydia by the hair and dragged her across the floor.

She cried and screamed in pain. Even as he dragged her away, she saw Benjamin up the stairs. Pain stained his face, too. But this time, it was for her.

The guard threw her back in the closet, smashing her knee in the process, and slammed the door. She groaned.

Sounds of an agonized crowd died away.

She felt the ooze of sweat, now amended with the metallic smell of blood. The cut on the side of her face stung from the salty trickle. For the first time in her life, Lydia felt comforted by stale, cramped darkness.

CHAPTER 24

Nick sprinted down the utility access corridor, urging Trish, who ran just ahead of him, to move faster. A hand in the middle of her back was all that was necessary to get that message across. The cadence of her clicking sandal heels indicated that she was complying as best she could. Her footwear was never intended for a race.

In the background, the sound of heavy steel hinges on the bulkhead door now far behind them squawked. Sound traveled easily through this uninsulated, all-metal enclosure – a straight shot back to its origin. "Don't slow down, Trish." He had to find a place to hide. Otherwise, there would be no way to keep their presence a secret.

Running down the dimly lit passageway lined with pipes, tubes, conduits and wires, Nick heard a noise, growing louder, from the direction in which they ran. It was a deep, throaty hum – a large electric motor, maybe.

The footfalls of their escape had to be traveling just as easily back to that bulkhead door as the sound of it opening came to him. With its glossy gray metal walls and floor, the entire length of the corridor was an echo chamber. They might as well be tossing out bread crumbs and beating a drum to mark the way.

Besides being warm and humid, the air was stale in this un-air-conditioned space with not-so-inviting combinations of smells, the most pronounced of which was dank and mold mixed with that of fresh paint.

Nick's courage began faltering as gory possibilities snapped like a camera shutter in his head. Ratcheting desperation took his breath. Physical exertion played only a minor role. With his mind in overdrive, a course of action wasn't coming to him – every possibility incomplete.

The end of the corridor came abruptly.

"What do we do?" Trish's voice squeaked into a higher range.

"Don't panic," he said, as his darting eyes tried to detect useable crannies and make quick judgments on places that might conceal two adults.

She began to whine.

He put a hand over her mouth, offering a quick smile. He spoke as gently as possible. "We'll be okay if we keep our wits."

That was a line tossed out to him by a sergeant as they ran into the Iraqi desert after their tank had been disabled by a rocket-propelled-grenade. The fire that erupted inside the tank caused him to write off his life as lost. It was that sergeant who kept his head, exited the top hatch, and pulled him out, too. He was disoriented from the initial blast and, as they ran through the desert, Nick figured they'd die. That's when the sergeant saw his panic, stopped, grabbed him by the shoulders, grinned and said, "We'll be okay if we keep our wits." He remembered the calming effect those simple, blurted words had on him.

He then noticed that the source of the hum that he'd heard was indeed a large electric motor attached to a pump of some kind.

"What's that?" she asked.

"An inline pump; it's either pushing sewage out or pulling water in. Don't know which. But it's forcing liquid somewhere for some reason." It occurred to him that there was space behind it. The unit set to the side in a nook off the corridor with, maybe, enough room for the two of them to crouch behind it. "Come on."

He grabbed Trish's arm and yanked. After only a step, he put his hand on her back and pushed, urging her to move faster into position behind the big motor. He then shoved her down, forcing her to squat. He took the lead position most accessible to the straightaway around the corner to his left, preparing to be in position for any opportunity that should arise. He dropped onto his haunches.

Waiting tensed the muscles of his neck. His stomach roiled.

Contingencies marched through his head categorically, but it didn't take long. There were few – in fact, only one: He had to be the aggressor. Just hiding and waiting was even odds on a sure death for them both. The element of surprise was the only thing he had going for him, and he wasn't terribly sure about that. Either he got the jump on them and they might survive, or he didn't and they surely died. Even the upside was grim.

Trish sat with eyes forced shut, as if to pretend all this wasn't happening, wasn't real. She rocked back and forth while sitting on her heels, tightly clenched fists held to her breasts. He knew exactly what she was thinking: that when she opened her eyes, all this would be gone and she'd be in her bed at home, awakening from an awful nightmare.

It was also something Alli, his daughter, did often when she was younger, wishing away something undesirable. The youngster frequently had that look after her mother died. He vividly remembered the heartbreak of watching an impressionable child wanting to wake from a bad dream that wasn't a dream at all. He never counseled or criticized. He, too, had done it, unable to believe that Julia, the love of his life, was indeed gone and never coming home again.

Trish's hand found its way into his, eyes still closed. She sought comfort, but as he looked at his new friend, it was he who felt comforted. The feel-good moment was short-lived, though, as he realized how close he was to losing her, too.

An image of his second wife Evie popped into his head – one-dimensional, with no feeling attached. This close to death, his lack of emotion surprised him.

The sight of sudden movement shattered mental meandering. He looked for its source, finally noticing a bulging shadow that hadn't been there seconds ago. Or had it? It appeared between where they hid and the light bulb just out of sight that he remembered hung down the way, encased in a shatterproof globe.

Where he hunkered down, off to the side of the access way, his view was limited. All he clearly saw was the wall opposite where they crouched. His eyes remained fixed on the shadow. He studied every nuance of it. Was it a human form? Had it really just appeared? Or had it been there all along? He couldn't be sure and dared not look away. Even the tiniest movement could give him an advantage, if noticed in time.

His grip tightened on Trish's hand, but he didn't look to see if her eyes were still closed. He hoped they were. He didn't want her flinching or making sudden noises.

His knees ached from squatting and wanting to bring this episode to a conclusion.

The shadow moved.

Nick's heart stuttered.

His face became blood engorged as the shadow grew larger, although he still heard nothing.

If he'd ever have an advantage, this was it. He couldn't take the chance that the owner of that shadow would react quicker than he could. He had to make his move while surprise was on his side.

He eased his hand from Trish's grasp and rose fluidly.

Then his knee joint popped.

The shadow reacted.

Desperation replaced apprehension. He lunged and reached laterally around the corner for where the man should be standing.

He miscalculated and swiped at the air in front of a gun-toting figure in black.

He lost balance and fell forward onto his chest, knocking the breath from him.

He saw a boot next to his face, and then the point of a knee in his back.

Someone grabbed his hair and pulled his head off the floor.

Nick felt the sting of sharp cool steel at his throat.

Trish screamed, "Nick!"

CHAPTER 25

"Let me see if I have this right…" the tinny voice of the FBI negotiator said, and then paused.

Azziz kept his back to the speakerphone in Mariostansi's quarters, watching the American Naval warship sitting idle with Coastguard boats alongside it through the window with casual interest. The vessels bobbed and rolled in swells about three hundred yards out. Hands to his back, he patted the palm of one with the other.

"Please!" Captain Mariostansi wailed. "Do as they say!" The captain held his swaddled and thumbless hand close to his body, the makeshift bandage from a linen table cloth saturated in blood.

Keeping his eyes on the destroyer, Azziz regarded the captain's tone and demeanor, nodding. *So, dear Captain, you finally understand.* After another few seconds, he turned away from the window and offered the captain an affirmative nod on his way back to the speakerphone. He addressed the communication device.

"Go on, Mr.… I'm sorry, what did you say your name was?"

"Hargitay… Inspector Cliff Hargitay," came the reply from the speakerphone.

"Oh yes, Mr. Hargitay, my apologies. Please continue."

"You and your people have quite a laundry list of demands: all political prisoners held on suspicion of Al Qaeda ties released, pressure Israel to relinquish control of all occupied territories, recognition of Hamas, Hezbollah, Al Qaeda, and the Taliban as legitimate political parties, and on top of all that, a quarter-billion dollars wire-transferred into an account at the Bank of Dubai. Does that about cover it?"

Crisply, "Yes. That's all."

A knock at the door alerted Sahid. He opened it and took a card from the man. He handed it to Azziz.

Azziz swept his thumb over the photo of a handsome young man with angular features and wavy black hair sporting a Superman curl spilling down onto his forehead. He nodded approval to his man at the door, then to Sahid.

The courier withdrew from the room, never turning his back to Azziz or Sahid, and pulled the door shut behind him.

The speaker from the satellite phone crackled. "You realize that even if the United States wanted to negotiate in good faith, your demands are impossible to meet before you take the lives of more passengers, don't you?"

Still calm, Azziz replied, "I am aware of that, yes. As a matter of fact, as we speak and you stall, one more has gone to be with God. The time you take will be measured in human lives. It's not my place to offer advice on how you handle your business, but it might be advisable not to dawdle."

He waited for a response from the negotiator, but he heard only the hum of an open phone line.

"Are you saying that the all-powerful United States of America cannot accomplish this simple list of things in a timely manner?"

He moved to a small shelf of books and tipped one out to check the picture on its dust jacket. "The way I see it, all that must be done is to make a few phone calls, produce a single document with a government declaration, and then wire a bit of money… a pittance, by American standards. Surely, you don't find it impossible?"

"Time-consuming. Not impossible," Hargitay said, breaking a lengthy silence.

Azziz whirled around. "Then I will be the bigger man and show good faith first. I'll not take any more lives until seven o'clock this evening. And if fifty million dollars has been wire transferred into that bank account in Dubai on or before the deadline, you will have purchased time to meet the remainder of my demands. The length of time you will have bought is until seven o'clock tomorrow morning – an additional twelve hours with no lives taken." Azziz returned to the bookshelf, tilting out books one at a time, checking the selection. "That should give you plenty of time to meet the remainder of my demands."

"Mr. Baruk," Hargitay said, "I think we can work with that. Will you give me an hour before I call back to confirm the money transfer?"

"You have most of an hour anyway," Azziz said, walking back to the phone. He punched the button to end the conversation.

He turned and sauntered toward the window. As he walked by the captain, he peripherally noticed the pain showing in the man's rubicund-faced grimace. "You did well, Captain. I believe your performance was good enough to save your other thumb." He kept walking.

Sahid, standing near the captain, moved to Azziz's side. In Arabic, he said, "It seems, my brother, there may be cause to believe our conditions will be met."

"It was never my intention to have all the demands met – just the money." He glanced back through the window. The sun had sunk to a position that now cast a beam straight across the captain's quarters, striking the opposite wall, level with the window. Azziz shielded his eyes from the glare and again took note of nearby American forces.

"But Azziz, what about the prisoners, the political parties, and the Israeli pullout?"

"All in good time," he said, now facing his accomplice. "You see, Sahid, the Americans would never negotiate on those things. But if I hurl artillery shells at them, so to speak, and it's only a grain of sand that actually stings them, then that tiny bit of pain seems like nothing at all."

He draped his hands over Sahid's shoulders. "The fifty million dollars was all I sought from the beginning. Once the money is in our control, and while they discuss how best to put us off a while longer, we will summon our waiting helicopter and be gone. That deserted beach on Padre Island will make the perfect place to change our appearances and bury clothes and weapons. Then we'll fly to the mainland to be transported back to Houston, where we'll blend in for two weeks before we individually make our way home. We'll be in a bogus plumbing company truck en route to Houston before they even react to what we're doing. If they find the helicopter… so be it. It will have served its purpose. So, you see, the remainder of those demands have great value. We will have bought escape time. When they finally notice and scramble jets or get helicopters airborne, our own helicopter will be setting us down at our destination."

"With the Coast Guard and the Navy warship sitting idle out there, won't they see us leave?"

"Yes. We'll have a backup plan that requires a few hostages. If we need them, we have them; if we don't, we'll simply dispose of them somewhere on the way to Houston. With a little extra time and a few hostages, we'll be fine."

"Allah will bless your genius," Sahid said.

"Leveling a mountain begins with a single shovelful of dirt, my friend… or, in this case, fifty-million dollars."

CHAPTER 26

Nick had hit the floor of the utility access corridor hard, landing across a half-inch conduit strapped to the floor, the jab of it excruciating. But that discomfort, compounded by a knee between his shoulder blades, couldn't compare to the terror exploding in his brain of what was about to happen. The knife blade across his throat needed only to slide to sever his jugular vein.

He heard Trish scream, but it seemed distant. His hands drew down to hard fists. He scrunched up his face, closed his eyes and clenched his teeth, preparing for the inevitable end to his life. *I did the best I could.*

"Stop! Please don't kill him!" Trish shouted.

The man holding the knife spoke: "You're American?"

"Yes!" Trish said, her voice thready. She sprang up, but it was a clumsy ascent; she stumbled laterally from behind the humming motor large enough to conceal her. She awkwardly moved out from behind the electric powered unit, dancing her hands over the friction-heated housing of it. "Don't hurt him, please!"

The pressure of the blade against his throat lessened. He took advantage of his Adam's apple now being free to once again travel, and swallowed. The knee came away from his back. Only then did he again notice the bruising discomfort of the aluminum tube on the floor he fell across. He pushed up off the floor and massaged his chest, and then looked up and saw a sweet sight: a well-heeled U. S. serviceman. He rolled onto his back. The man stood straddling him, still prepared to overpower him if necessary. The guy clearly wasn't quite ready to believe the situation had been secured.

Nick, dizzy from relief, offered up a lazy smile. "I don't think I've had the pleasure. My name is Nick Brandon... from Houston. And you?"

The man caught the humor in the overly formal manner. He finally relaxed the all-business expression and smiled. "Petty Officer Ansel McAvoy of the Naval Special Warfare Command... at your service." As he sheathed the knife, he threw a thumb over his shoulder to another man in black commando garb standing farther down the narrow utility access aisle. "We're part of a Navy SEAL rescue unit."

Nick rolled to hands and knees, about to rise to his feet. "How'd you guys get on board undetected?"

"Not your concern, sir."

"Sorry."

"Not a problem, sir. We just need to stay focused on what needs to be done."

"Anything we can do to help?" Nick asked.

Trish came to his side and pulled him into a buddy hug. She pressed her head onto his shoulder and mumbled, "I thought you were a dead man."

His breathing had not leveled out yet. "You're not the only one."

"There is a way you might help us," McAvoy said. "Tell us all you can about the situation. We're aware the passengers and crew are held in the auditorium one deck up. But we don't know how many terrorists we're dealing with. Do you?"

"I've only seen six, maybe seven. I don't know how many are up there that I didn't see."

"I understand, sir; any more passengers or crew roaming around like you two?"

"Can't say, but I can sure identify the leader of that ruthless bunch." He waved an emphatic finger. "That son-of-a-bitch put a bullet through the brain of one of the Ocean Dancer's crew just to make a point."

"That could be useful, sir. We believe by his negotiating style that he arrogantly thinks he'll escape this ship alive. We'll only be giving him one chance for that. Either way, he'll not be allowed to leave a free man. For now, follow me, and let's find a safer place for you and your lady friend to stay while we take care of business."

"You got it." Nick grabbed Trish's hand and became almost giddy. "Whew. That was close. Thanks for hollerin' when you did."

A catty smile came up on her face. "What makes you think I did it for you? I would've been next, you know." She fell into step beside him as they followed McAvoy. "And, what did he mean by 'lady friend'? That has the ring of a kept woman or… or a pet, for Christ's sake, like I should be on a leash wearing a rhinestone collar."

Her concern was not as great as the words indicated – just nervous chatter. Her relief was obvious. She clutched his wrist and squeezed hard enough that he winced. "Sorry. Just wanted to make certain you knew that your 'lady friend' is in full compliance with the order." She saluted him and dropped her head onto his shoulder for a second.

"Yep. If you hadn't screamed when you did, I'd –"

"Shut up," she blurted, slapping her hands over her ears, "I don't want to hear it. It'll be hard enough to forget without you drawing a picture for me."

"Sorry, I didn't –"

"I know, I know; just drop it. I've grown accustomed to having you around. I – uh don't care to visualize this situation any other way at the moment."

He glimpsed her satisfied expression and turned full-on to face her. "Good to know."

McAvoy stopped and looked back. "Ma'am? Sir? We have to hurry. Time wasted is advantage lost."

They followed the petty officer and the other SEAL back to the bulkhead door and stepped around the puddle of pee in front of it, then over the high threshold into the roomier main hallway that split the deck they were on. Nick made an exaggerated point of looking back and down at the urine pool.

She poked him on the shoulder with an insistently stabbing index finger. "Not a word. Not one damn word, buddy."

McAvoy, spoke over his shoulder as he kept walking at a fast clip. "And you say you don't know if any other passengers escaped confinement from the auditorium?"

"I haven't seen anyone. But we've spent most of our time trying not to be seen. My opportunities to see anyone or anything have been extremely limited."

"For now, I'll assume you two were lucky." He stopped at an unadorned door, slightly wider than most, with a high threshold that opened out, instead of in as all the others did. A blue plaque on in it read: PERSONNEL ONLY. "These are crew quarters. Stay here and stay quiet. We'll be back to get you once the situation is contained and the danger neutralized." He ushered them in and closed the door behind them.

As Nick examined the space, he said, "Wow. I feel like a balloon losing air. If I continue to deflate, I'll collapse from exhaustion." He looked at Trish. "Honestly, I'm so tired I can barely stand."

"Do you think they can do it?"

"Do what?"

Take them out?"

His eyes drifted to the ceiling. "Well, if they fail, I see two other ways it might go. Number one, the terrorists get what they want and let us live... or number two, the U. S. military blows this ship and the terrorists out of the water – us along with it."

"I see what you mean."

"Don't worry. I think the SEAL team will have things under control in no time." He snapped his fingers as positive punctuation and then turned away, mumbling, "Humph, I wonder if blowing up the ship might actually be considered?"

"What?"

"Nothing. Get some rest; I'm going to."

The narrow room was long, and the bunk arrangement offered only the suggestion of privacy for each crewmember. Narrow steel partitions no wider than the bunks protruded from the wall at the ends of all the beds. At the foot of each mattress was a built-in metal combination dresser/chest of about two square feet, with three drawers. Every space was identical except for personal items.

Trish walked the line of bunks, examining each, then finally stopped and studied one in particular. Pictures had been taped to the wall beside the bunk, family photos perhaps. The people in them appeared Polynesian or Filipino. They seemed content and happy.

"I like this one," she said. "I'm getting a homey vibe from it."

"Whatever helps you sleep." He dropped onto the bunk opposite the one she chose and immediately fell over onto his side, facing her across the aisle. He stretched to his full length, moaned, and then offered her a quiet smile before closing his eyes and working his head into the pillow. "I actually think I might be able to relax now."

Although it was a simple statement of fact, he expected a response, but didn't get one. He popped open an eye to see that Trish had lain on the bunk opposite his. She was staring at him.

"What?"

"I was just thinking how close you came to... you know... dying, and how calm you seem right now. If that'd been me, I'd still be a trembling lump of gelatin, bawling my eyes out. Have you always been that way?"

"I thought we weren't going to talk about that."

"I can't help it. I have the disease of curiosity."

"Not something so easily forgotten, is it?"

"No, now answer the question: Have you always been like that? From my point of view, I'm looking at a man with genuine nerves of steel."

Nick realized she was right. He'd put it behind him in short order. He remembered that sergeant, his mentor, as they ran from knoll, to hill, to gully in the Iraqi desert under fire over a decade ago. As he ran, he saw a comrade take a bullet through his helmet, dead before he hit the ground. It shocked him to a standstill; he was unable to force his feet to run on. The sergeant grabbed his collar.

"Run, Goddamn it!" Then, what the sergeant said next deeply seared into his memory, as fresh today as then: "In this race, there is no rearview mirror! Don't stop for any reason!"

Bullets whizzed and ricocheted. Machine-gun fire rattled in stuttering pops, peppering the ground at his feet. The sergeant dragged him along and literally threw him into a shallow depression in the sand. Nick remembered babbling an apology, but the sergeant cut him off. "Look, when you're in a race for your life, looking back'll get ya killed, man! Remember Lot's wife in the story of Sodom and Gomorrah?"

"Of course."

"Keep your eyes forward at all times," the sergeant had said. "If you insist on watching the world at your rear, you'll miss the turn every time."

Nick's eyes came down to again meet Trish's. "No, I haven't always been that way. But a man I respected a lot, once upon a time, told me that worrying about the past in these situations is no way to survive long enough to experience the future."

She fluffed the pillow at her bent elbow and nestled her head into it. "You know, I think there might be a message in that wisdom for me." She closed her eyes. "I probably won't sleep, but it doesn't matter; this hard bunk feels like I'm lying on a cloud." As she moved her head around, searching for that sweet spot of comfort, she put her hands together and poked them between her drawn up knees.

Nick slowly opened one eye to make sure she wasn't still watching him. Her eyes were closed. If she was scared, he couldn't see it. In fact, she looked pleased. Satisfied, even. The rose in her cheeks from the tense moments had not entirely gone away, but the color only added to her beauty.

His opportunities to admire her had been limited and he didn't waste this one. It was so much more than ogling physical attributes, although that vision was certainly worth the sigh he just expelled. He wanted to think about the strong, intelligent woman that she was. As his eyes drifted up the length of her body, his gaze lingered on her face. He may have turned into that trembling lump of gelatin she spoke of if she hadn't been with him. A thought smoldered: Should anything happen to her, he'd stop caring for his own survival. His feelings for her had progressed from acquaintance, to patient, to friend, to something now that he hadn't the courage to put a label on. He just knew it was on the other side of a line he shouldn't be crossing but was willing to step right over if a comfortable occasion arose to do so. To make matters worse, the line kept moving, putting him on the wrong side occasionally without him having to do a thing.

He became drowsy. *That's a weakness I certainly need to keep to myself.*

Heavy eyelids took him down.

CHAPTER 27

Lying on her side, knees drawn up and awake but with eyes closed, Trish listened to Nick's deep, even breathing. She parted an eyelid, wanting the simple pleasure of peeking at the guy and, maybe, watching him sleep for a while. *Why are all the good ones taken?* And asleep he was – soundly snoozing. It had only been a minute or two since they decided to rest and, already, he was out.

She sat upright and crossed the ankles of her dangling legs over the side of the bunk. She watched him nap. Fantasies blossomed as she swung her legs in a girlish way. She crossed her arms, tilted her head, and dreamed of possibilities. The long dark bang fell into her eye when she did. From the corner of her mouth, she blew at it. With the precision of an electronic scanner, her eyes traveled from his head to his toes, then back again.

Her breathing quickened. *God help me, I can't stop fantasizing.*

She pictured them together as a couple, and that imagining came with sensations she refused to fight. Suppressed feelings began bubbling to the surface. She tingled. The setting was near perfect: They were alone, the stress of the situation had eased, and there were beds – lots and lots of beds.

She'd stopped dating because it became too much work. She tired of putting herself in situations where she had to explain her agoraphobia before a date even got underway. It would have been impossible to keep secret, so why risk becoming attached only to have it fall apart later? Crowded restaurants, concerts, theatres and nightclubs – all common to first and second dates – were relationship-killers for her. Meaningful rapport never had a chance – until now.

The rhythm of her swinging feet and an overactive imagination aroused her. As she drank in Nick, her eyes stopped below his belt buckle. *It's been so long.* She was on the verge of losing control. Breathing heavily, she clamped her jaws in a half-hearted attempt not to allow her lust to reel out of control.

She slid on her butt until her back came in contact with the cool metal of the wall behind her and drew her knees up. Her shoulder brushed a photograph taped to the wall. It was that Polynesian-looking man with his arm around a rotund woman of equally exotic appearance.

"If you've been on this ship for any length of time, I bet it's been a while for you, too," she whispered to the man in the picture.

Examining the photograph for a moment, a twinge of jealousy tightened her lip on one side. She wanted what she believed they had – a life. She draped her arms over the peaks created by her raised knees and closed her eyes. She tried to put her head in a different place. She might as well be trying to stop a runaway train, but try she must.

She heard a rustling and opened one eye.

Nick rolled onto his back but remained asleep.

The miniscule progress she'd achieved in putting romantic thoughts out of her head came to an abrupt end when she noticed that he must be having a really nice dream – because it showed. Conscious of it or not, Nick was aroused. "Oh... no."

After two false starts, she scooted off the edge of her bunk, stepped across the aisle, and sat next to him. She leaned over, until her nose came to within mere inches of his, and felt his breath. For a moment, luxuriating in that simple sensation, she turned her face to catch warm puffs on each of her eyes, her nose, and then her mouth. She gently pressed her lips to his.

His eyes popped open. Clearly startled, he recoiled, pressing the back of his head deep into the pillow. "What the hell...?"

Trish didn't move.

"I know this is inappropriate on many levels, given your situation and the problems we're dealing with, but damn it, Nick..." she said in a breathy huff. "If I'm overstepping some moral boundary then stop me now, because my body's in overdrive, and my good sense is someplace far, far away."

The shock on his face vanished. He reached with one hand and cupped the back of her neck. He pulled her face into his. Her tongue snaked between his lips as quickly as they met. She probed deep as she lay down beside him and then fluidly slid over on top of him. She hesitated briefly, looking down into eyes that were tracing the contours of her face and thought, *Heaven just might be reachable from here.*

***

At a loss for how much time had passed, Trish woke abruptly but couldn't say why. She remained motionless, lying spooned to Nick, her bare buttocks exposed from beneath the bed sheet to the walkway behind her. She lifted her head and looked over her shoulder down the narrow aisle between the bunks back to the door through which they had entered these crew quarters. She listened for several seconds and, hearing nothing, yawned and let her head wilt back onto the pillow she shared with Nick. As soon as her head touched down, she heard a muffled voice. It came from somewhere down the hall outside. "Nick," she said in a hoarse whisper. "Wake up."

He moaned and licked dry lips.

She placed a hand lightly over his mouth. "Shh."

The urgency finally made it through to him. He opened his eyes, lifted his upper torso, and twisted around to look at her. "What?"

"Someone's out there," she said. "I don't think the voices I heard were in English." She reached for her bra and panties.

"Did it sound close?"

She hurriedly dressed. "It sounds like someone is systematically checking doors. I bet those thugs are doing a sweep to find more crew or passengers… like us," she said.

"How could they have gotten by the SEALs?"

"I don't know. But you'd better get your pants on." She buttoned her shorts then snatched up the tank top and slipped it over her head.

Again, a clanking thud came from down the hall – each new sound methodically closer. It became clear that a room check was exactly what they were doing, and English was not the language spoken. Sitting on the edge of the bunk, Nick pulled his pants on, both legs at the same time, and rolled out of the bunk. As he pulled the shirt over his head, he examined their confines.

"If you're looking for a place to hide, I don't think you'll find one. We're exposed to anyone coming in… period," she said. "We're either in a bunk or in the aisle between them. It's just a long hallway. Christ, Nick, what're we going to do?"

"I don't think hiding under the covers will help."

"Damn it, Nick, this is no time for jokes!"

"It wasn't a joke. I was simply making the point that hiding is not an option," he said, while still looking up and down then back and forth. "We have to create an advantage."

"How? As soon as the door flies open, we'll be in plain sight and unarmed. The door doesn't even open inward." Her voice slipped into a whine. "Even hiding behind it to surprise them is out."

"Look," Nick said, "What's the first thing anyone does when they step into an unfamiliar room?"

"I suppose they look around. In this case, pointing a machine gun everywhere their eyes land."

"Exactly; movement will draw fire immediately. Here's my thought for a plan that may have a remote chance of working: I want you to sit on that chest of drawers with that bunk partition behind you. It's not very wide, but neither are you. And it's thick steel…" He stepped across the aisle and tapped the steel plate with his fingertips, "…substantially thick steel. Your job will be to have a pillow in your hand, and the instant you hear that door open, don't hesitate – toss it high and away. Remember, the key is to toss it high and to the opposite wall. Make his eyes follow it up and over. Got it?"

"O-Okay… I guess. Once I have gunfire spraying in my direction, then what?"

"Don't forget that you'll be protected by that steel plate at your back – that is, if you don't get curious and poke your head around to see what's going on. Keep extremities tucked in tight behind it. I'll be in more danger of ricochets than you will be from direct fire. The shooter's eyes will be fixed on the flying pillow. But that only buys me less than a second to act before he sees me. I'll be lying on my back with my head centered beneath the threshold that he'll have to step over to enter. I pray he advances as he fires. Body mechanics will make him stoop as he comes in and lower the machine gun to within reach. Then I can make a grab for the gun or his arms." He clenched his jaws and canted his head. "Can you keep your cool? Because it's gonna be dicey."

"I guess so."

"This is no time to fudge the truth. If I fail, we're both dead."

Her wide-eyed frenzy eased. "In that case, why worry? There's no choice."

Nick took two quick steps away, briskly massaging the back of his neck, and whirled around. "I don't know of a safer way, and I've got no more time to think about it. I'm sorry."

She forced a tiny smile. "All I needed was a glimmer of hope. Thanks for providing it."

"Okay then, get behind that partition."

Trish was already moving into position as he spoke. She heard the unmistakable sound of the door across the hall squeaking open, then rustling footsteps, rapid chatter, and the clank of the door closing. Their door was next. Nick put his finger to his lips. "Shh."

Her movement slowed and became fluid as she stepped up on the bunk and then sat on the chest that was not quite waist-high. She scooted back against the steel plate between her and the door, pulling a pillow to her breasts and hugging it like a teddy bear while squeezing her eyes shut, preparing for the inevitable.

Hearing nothing new, she peeked around the partition behind her toward the door and saw Nick lying on his back parallel to the wall and door, his head centered under the threshold looking up. He was exposed and unarmed. She figured there could be no way for him to be more vulnerable. It seemed unlikely this feeble plan would work.

She looked to the ceiling. *Dear God, this is an awful plan. Can you lend a hand? Amen.*

The latch on the door clanked as it was levered down.

She drew a breath and held it.

CHAPTER 28

Lying flat on his back, Nick placed sweaty palms against the floor to quell jittery fingers. He had one chance to get this right. When he made the grab for a weapon that might be firing and vibrating violently, it had to work the first time; there'd be no second. It had to be quick and solid, or he and Trish would be dead just seconds after a failure.

Maintaining calm was paramount. Still, his heart pounded in his ears, and the question of failure hovered and circled his courage like a vulture waiting at the fringes. Fight-or-flight instinct began kicking in; his desire to jump and run was strong.

A glance to the end of this cramped sleeping quarter, fifteen feet away, was all he needed to see to realize the idiocy of such an impulse; he could run to the end wall and be shot there, or burst out the door like Butch Cassidy and the Sundance Kid and be killed in a blaze of misplaced glory in the hallway.

Bare hands against automatic weapons, as implausible as it seemed, was the plan. The only weapon he had was the element of surprise, and even that was assumed. The last time he tried using surprise, he almost got his throat slit – and may have, if Trish hadn't screamed.

He lay on his back parallel to the wall, his upper torso positioned squarely in front of the door's threshold. When he extended his arms straight up, they were dead center in the doorway. Hopefully, the intruder would be leading the way with his firearm when he entered. He was betting his life on seeing the barrel of a machine gun or pistol first.

The envisioned scenario ignited a memory: He was eight years old, playing hide-and-seek with other kids in his neighborhood near his childhood home in Katy, Texas. He enjoyed being sought because scaring a scream out of the hunter was more fun than not being found. But that was then, and this wasn't hide-and-seek. *Focus, Nick, focus.*

He looked to his feet and wondered if the first glance by someone coming through the door might be to the right as that person stepped over the foot-high threshold. If so, those size tens suddenly seemed more like conspicuous umbrella stands attached to the ends of his legs. Someone with even adequate peripheral vision might notice his toes pointing straight up. He splayed them as wide as tendons and bones allowed, forcing his toes close to the floor. He needed a full second unseen; two would be better. But two full seconds would require a slow-witted gunman. He couldn't afford that assumption.

Sweat beaded on his forehead.

Noises in the hallway just on the other side of the wall became louder.

Rolling his head away from the door, he looked to the narrow steel partition separating the bunks that Trish hunkered behind atop that small chest. It stood out from the wall a mere eighteen inches, maybe. He saw no part of her body exposed, but then her head suddenly popped around it. She looked at him.

He waved her back behind the safety of the steel plate just as Arabic gibberish was exchanged beyond the door.

He removed his hands from the floor and rubbed them vigorously a last time along the sides of his khaki pants, working the knuckles of all ten fingers. He held his open hands palms-up toward the center of the door.

His mouth and throat went suddenly dry as he began to tense, pulling his body into a tight reflexive spring.

Realizing his own fear, he could only imagine how scared Trish must be. Unsettling thoughts of her gone from his life were incomprehensible. He had only known her a few weeks, but the length of time didn't matter. She was now part of his life, and he didn't want that to change. His focus shifted from self-preservation to Trish's safety. A flash image of their romantic encounter galvanized his courage. He didn't want to think that that moment would be the last.

His hands, ready to make the grab, were near eye level. He looked at them, front then back. Both had stopped shaking and had become rock solid. He physically felt fear leave him.

He had to rid his mind of extraneous thoughts, including Trish. *Just two scared people hookin' up. Just sex; that's all it was.*

A metal-on-metal clank next to and above his head startled him.

His eyes flicked away from his hands and up to the bottom of the door just above his head. He watched the door handle with unblinking intensity.

With a squeak, the handle began to turn down.

His focus went laser sharp and unflinching.

The door flung open abruptly, outward into the hall. Before he saw its owner, the barrel of a machine gun came into view above the high threshold over his head.

Now, Trish! Now!

Eyes fixed on the gun barrel, he saw it jerk higher.

She did it! She tossed it!

In a vibrating arc, bullets sprayed near-simultaneously in a fast left-to-right, then back again. The noise deafened him. His ears rang.

The barrel dipped down as the shooter leaned over to enter the room through the bulkhead-type door.

Summoning all speed, Nick grabbed the barrel with both hands. It was blistering hot, but he paid no mind. The acrid smell of gunpowder filled his nose.

The shooter reacted, jerking the weapon up and away.

Nick used that momentum as leverage to quickly leap to his feet.

They faced one another, weapon between them, four hands upon it. Nick held the barrel at an angle away from his body.

The shooter tried twisting the firearm around for a shot into Nick's gut.

Uh-uh. You're not getting that shot, you sonofabitch.

Nick broke eye contact with the gun and glimpsed his would-be killer. He was just a boy – no more than sixteen, seventeen at the outside. *God almighty! He's no older than Alli.*

The shock created dangerous hesitation.

The terrified boy tried wresting the gun from Nick's grasp, but the youngster didn't have the strength to get it done.

Nick noticed a man behind the kid and saw that that one was not scared at all – older and hardened. That man's upper lip rose in snarling determination, but he couldn't react. The kid blocked a clear shot.

It occurred to him that these people were so heartless that the other gunman in the hall behind the kid might shoot right through the youngster.

But he didn't. Why not?

Nick used his size and strength to his advantage and spun the boy and the machine gun around to face the other intruder. Still holding the barrel with one hand, he reached around the kid and yanked back on the wrist of the boy's trigger hand, sweeping the barrel upward as he did.

The gun rattled a response and drilled the older one from crotch to chest with four or five quick shots.

The terrorist slammed back against the wall across the hall. His hateful look vanished as if a curtain had dropped over his face. He lost control of his body. The pull on the trigger of his automatic weapon was reflex, not intent, as it peppered the ceiling.

Ducking low, Nick slammed the boy with a shoulder in the chest then violently slung the kid into the wall inside their quarters beside the door.

Air left the youngster's lungs in a rush.

Nick yanked the weapon from his grasp and slammed the butt of it into the side of the kid's head.

The boy's eyes rolled to white, and he collapsed to the floor. Blood streamed from the gash on his temple. He didn't move.

Nick flattened against the wall and held the machine gun close to his body, across his chest. Glancing repeatedly, alternating between the open door and the boy on the floor, he came to realize that the kid would be no threat for a while.

Breathing shallow and fast, he fluttered eyelids to clear sweat from his lashes.

The dying older man's hand still seized on the trigger. Bullets ricocheted and sang throughout the long, narrow crew quarters. Some hit the wall at the far end. Some bounced off the metal outside the sleeping quarters. The barrage of wild machine gun fire continued pounding the metal walls for a full second, maybe longer. Then it stopped.

Cautiously, Nick looked, then moved left along the inside wall. Not taking any chances, every step small and measured, he slid toward the door next to where he stood. He then craned his neck and looked around its edge. He saw a blood smear on the opposite wall, his eyes following it down. The man had fallen against it and slid into a sitting position, legs splayed wide, the machine gun lying on the floor between them with his finger still on the trigger. His stare was lifeless; he was dead.

Nick stepped away from the wall and stood motionless for a moment before spinning and facing the open doorway. He stepped quickly over the threshold into the hall – captured machine gun held ready to fire. He tightened his grip, preparing for the next intruder. He snapped glances one way, then the other. As tense seconds passed, he began to relax, coming to believe that the threat had been neutralized, at least for the moment.

Adrenaline drained away too fast. He began crashing, growing lightheaded. Stumbling backward, his heels kicked the threshold, forcing him to catch himself with a free hand before facing the open doorway. He then stepped back into the crew quarters and listed sideways as he clumsily headed for the nearest bunk, quickening his pace to make it before he fell from the sudden dizziness, convinced his butt would soon be introduced to the floor if he didn't. He collapsed onto a bed, mouth open.

There seemed to be too little oxygen. He gasped, placed the gun on the bed next to him, and fell forward, catching himself with hands on knees.

Trish stirred.

He noticed movement and glanced to the bunk opposite and one down from his. Her head appeared around the partition. She made no sound, but her face was distorted.

"It's over," he said, assuming that look on her face was an unasked question. But he saw her expression was pain, not fear. "What's wrong?"

She rolled around and fell onto the bunk on her back, squirming and arching high off the mattress. She was probing her stomach with both hands.

"What is it? What are you looking for?"

"Oh god, Nick! I – I've been shot in the back!" She whimpered. "I can't look. Did the bullets go all the way through me?" She searched her belly with fast hands for exit wounds. "It hurts so bad. Can you see blood?"

He rushed to her side and sat on the bunk next to her. "I don't see anything." He rolled her onto her belly. She yielded fitfully.

He eased her tank top up. There, across her lower back, was a straight row of four blood-engorged bruises, evenly spaced – but none of the wounds had penetrated. He looked to the metal partition she had been leaning against. He saw four matching protrusions where bullets had puckered the metal but had not penetrated. "Trish, I know you're hurting, but trust me, you're one lucky lady."

She looked up at him as if that were the stupidest comment she'd ever heard. The long, sweeping bang of dark hair hung squarely between her eyes. "How can you say that?"

She blew the hair away out of her vision with a disgusted puff and again writhed on the bunk. She reached around, groping for wounds on her back. "Excuse me for not feeling too damn lucky at the moment." Her face contorted. "Crap, that hurts!"

"I'm just saying, if that metal partition had been a sixteenth of an inch thinner, you wouldn't be in pain right now; you'd most likely be dead."

"But I've been shot. I feel it."

"Not quite; more like... hammered. Those wounds are blunt-force trauma from where bullets struck the partition and transferred that energy into your back with the force of a ball-peen hammer hitting you four times." He gently massaged the wounds. "Give it a minute. You'll feel better. I promise." He probed her back around each wound. "No broken bones that I can tell. But you'll have nasty bruises for a couple of weeks." He walked fingertips around one of the bruises.

"Ouch!" she hissed through clenched teeth. "*If* I survive a couple of weeks you mean."

"Don't talk like that."

Nick heard a noise.

The boy had begun regaining consciousness and was moving around on the floor.

"I need rope… or cord, maybe. Something to tie that kid up with."

"Rip a sheet into strips," Trish said, still more interested in her pain than his needs.

He pulled a sheet from one of the bunks and used his teeth to get it started, tearing it into a four-inch-wide strip.

The boy was coming around but clearly groggy, muttering something in Arabic, as if he spoke to someone. He wallowed and tried to roll onto his side.

Nick trotted to him and dropped to his knees. He flipped the boy over onto his belly and bound his hands and feet with the single strip. He pulled his extremities in close and finished with three square knots. The kid looked like a tied calf in a rodeo roping event, only reversed.

Nick sat back on his heels, resting his hands on his thighs, and wondered aloud, "Now, what the heck do I do with you?"

He pushed the boy back onto his side and studied the youngster. He was a good-looking kid, his smooth face glowing with youthfulness. Black hair, full on top, had been neatly trimmed in the recent past.

"What is it that makes you people so violent? If it's religion, how could anyone follow a god that'd allow it, much less advocate it?" He asked the questions of the boy but figured them rhetorical.

Suddenly, the boy's eyes opened, and that fresh innocent look went hard.

"I could ask all those same questions of you… American pig." He spat on the floor next to his head in Nick's direction. His eyes again dulled with pain.

"You speak English?"

"A great man insisted I learn it." He began struggling against his bonds but stopped abruptly, moaning from an obvious pounding headache. "It was my father. From a young age, he taught me that, in order to defeat an enemy, I must know him well – and that included language."

"I have to know why you think I'm your enemy before I'll even consider the possibility that you are mine. Why do you call me enemy?"

"When Azziz spoke, I listened. He said that what we do is the same thing as your patriots did in their war for independence over two hundred years ago."

"I don't see the connection."

"When American patriots were confronted with British forces – better armed, better trained and larger in number – the patriots changed the battlefield. They fought a war the British did not understand. It flew in the face of accepted standards of warfare of that day. The patriots no longer lined up against superior forces. They used guerilla tactics and hid behind trees and rocks. They inflicted damage swiftly, then blended with the background to fight again another day. We, too, fight for independence in the same way. We fight to be free of American control."

"Okay, you're overlooking many points in your obviously well-ingrained indoctrination of hate. But let's focus on just one, since you brought it up: The British forces and the patriots were military men. How many military people have you encountered on this ship? Frankly, son, there are precious few legitimate reasons for you and your people's presence here. But since you're a captive audience, I'll tell you what some of those reasons could be. Okie dokie? You hate western civilization and want to snuff out the culture. Or maybe, it's just that you hate Christians, and this is your way of pressing the Islamic extremist point of view. Convert or die, using God as an all-encompassing reason to slaughter people of differing ideologies. What kind of demented logic is that? Then, there's always a favorite reason, that really doesn't have religious, racial or ideological boundaries: Greed. Yep, good ol' money-grubbin' greed."

The boy's eyes fluttered on the word 'money'. "You know nothing of the purity of our cause! You –"

"That's it, isn't it? All of this is just a selfish grab for money. This is just a kidnapping on a grand scale." Nick sat back on his heels. "Well, I'll be damned."

"God will strike you down for your –"

"Shut up, boy! You don't have a clue what you're talking about. God created us and God has the right to strike us down, but if you'll notice, it's you and your people upstairs that are doing all the striking… not God. God strikes down people who needlessly destroy his creation. Crap, kid! An atheist could tell you that. How stupid can you be?"

Thrashing about, pulling against his bonds, the boy lashed out the only way he could. "Another will be executed soon – a woman that is frightened of that closet she was closed in." He sneered. "That should quiet your heresy."

On that comment, Trish stopped squirming on the bunk.

"He's talkin' about Lydia! They're going to kill her."

The boy grunted and strained, trying to break the improvised rope that bound him in an inverted circle on the floor, veins bulging on his neck. "This is why Azziz insisted I learn English, so that I'd know–"

"Azziz? He's the one that taught you to speak English? You mean the heartless bastard that took a pistol and casually blew a crewman's brains out? That's your father?"

The boy ceased to struggle. It was clearly something he should not have said. Belligerence vanished.

The sudden change in demeanor was not lost to Nick. He considered it. *Why would it be such a problem that we know Azziz is his father? Could it be that if Azziz knew his son had gotten himself into just such a situation, he might endanger them both? Interesting.*

"Well, since you're such an expert on our language, let me lay a little profane slang on you: You… fucked… up. You're in a world of shit. And, your so-called father, whom I'm sure is a wonderful parental figure," Nick rolled his eyes, "is going to pistol whip you to within an inch of your pathetic young life." Nick noticed the boy's breath wavered when he said "pistol whip".

He peered into the boy's eyes and added, in a calculating way, "That is, if he doesn't shoot you first."

Nick let that statement hang, noticing that that didn't seem to affect the boy as much as the thought of a beating frightened him.

Trish moaned. Discomfort from her injuries persisted.

Nick rose and walked to her, glancing back at the boy. *He sure seems to be afraid of an old-fashioned whipping. There's a story there. I wonder…?*

"I'm so sorry for being such a girl."

He sat beside her and offered a sympathetic look, realizing her pain and how courageous she'd been. "We all have different pain thresholds. It's nothing to be ashamed of."

She rolled onto her stomach. He lifted her shirt and danced his fingers over the edges of the four blood-blistered bruises across her lower back.

"Tell me when the pressure becomes too painful. I'm going to massage around those bruises and try to alleviate some of that throb." He began pressing with fingertips and then flattened his palms on her back and rubbed easy circles, careful to avoid points of impact.

Suddenly she shrank from his touch, sucking air between her teeth.

"Sorry." For several minutes he continued rubbing.

"You were right; that does feel better," she said, turning to look up into his face. "What about Lydia? What should we do?"

Nick raked his teeth over his lower lip as he continued gently massaging her. He kept glancing back, pondering the kid's fear of punishment. After a time, he leaned low and whispered into Trish's ear, "I've spent my career desensitizing people with phobias, but I think I may try to feed one and see what happens."

"Huh?"

"I think that kid is suffering from one. I don't know how severe it is, but judging by flash reactions to certain comments, it may be substantial."

She twisted her head around and looked up at him again. "You can do that?"

"Don't know, never tried, but it might be to our advantage if I can." He rubbed her back a few more seconds. "I'm going to stand and walk over to him. When I do, I want you to say in a loud voice that your injuries feel like your father just whipped you like he did when you were a child."

Questions lingered on her face.

"Just do it. Okay? If I'm right, you'll see soon enough why I'm asking you to say it."

"You're the doctor."

Nick leaned in very close to her ear. "I'm thinking the boy is afraid of punishment. He doesn't seem all that concerned about dying – just punishment. It's called rhabdophobia. Let's feed it and see if we can turn a baby phobia into a useable monster. Do what I ask… then watch."

She nodded.

Nick rose and began a planned walk back to where the boy lay. Trish rolled to her side, groaned and then spoke up. "Damn, Nick. My back feels like it did when my father whipped me with a willow stick when I was a kid." She pointed with her chin to the boy on the floor. "Is that what you're going to do to him?"

The boy's reaction was immediate. He fought to free himself, looking every direction he could, slinging slobber from parted lips. He whimpered. His eyes grew large. Sweat glistened on his face.

Although in pain, Trish was visibly amazed at how the simple comment scared hell out of the boy. But the surprise on her face settled fast. Given her own condition, she couldn't have been too surprised by his reaction.

Nick squatted beside the kid. "You know, son, the way you messed up this simple operation and," he nodded toward the closed door, "got your ruthless buddy out there killed, I'm really scared for you." Nick acted the part of a concerned friend, using every nuance of body language and facial expression to impart fear while setting himself up as the boy's protector and friend. "I'm so afraid your father will be angry, maybe mad enough to strip you naked in front of that crowd in the auditorium and whip you right there."

Nick rapidly rubbed his chin with a palm and worked at the appearance of contemplating ways to prevent unavoidable punishment. "There's got to be something I can do." He lightly pounded his thigh with a soft fist and looked away. *I should get an Oscar for this.*

The boy fought back tears, but finally broke and bawled. Veins stood proud on his temples as the strain of inconsolable fear caused his face to go bright crimson.

"If only I could prevent it," Nick said wringing his hands. "But what can I do? I'm just a man. You and your father want to kill me."

"Please! Let me go. I'll shoot myself so the blood will not be on your hands." The boy sobbed. He beat the side of his head on the steel floor.

"You don't understand. I work hard at not killing anyone, even in the direst of circumstances, unless my own life or that of someone close is threatened. That's your way, not mine. I prevent the taking of human life if I can. My conscience will not allow me to let you kill yourself." He rose and pulled off his belt. "But, I'm not above corporeal punishment. A kid your age shouldn't be trying to hurt people like you do. You should be taught a lesson."

The boy wailed. "No! Please! Not you, too!"

"What's the matter, son, wouldn't you rather preserve your life and get a little spanking instead?"

"Kill me! I beg you! Kill me!"

Nick dropped to his knees and grabbed the boy's face with both hands. "Look at me." He waited for a moment.

The boy's eyes remained shut.

And then slowly and forcefully, "I said, open your eyes and look at me."

The boy's eyelids relaxed and parted.

"I think I know how I can help. But you have to let me. Will you?"

Still crying, the boy did not immediately respond, but after a moment he nodded once.

"I'll make you a hero. I'll let you force me back into that auditorium at the point of an empty machine gun. I'll have you tied at the waist, the other end tied to my waist. If you try to run, I'll be the first to know. And so help me, if you try it, or yell out, I'll turn around and bitch slap you until the last breath leaves my body. Got it?"

The boy pulled his head down and closed his eyes. The thought of it happening in front of his superiors and all those people terrified him.

"I want you to walk me right up onto that stage where that guy is pacing with a machine gun, to within arms' reach."

The boy nodded.

"If you do it right, your father will have no cause to whip you, only praise you. Do you understand?"

He nodded again.

"What good can we do, walking back into a hornet's nest?" Trish asked.

Nick looked back at her. "There is no *we* in this plan – just me and the kid."

"Oh no, you're not leaving me here to wonder if you're dead or alive. I'm going–"

"No, you're not! If you're here, I'll know you're safe."

"What good is safe and alive if you're dead?" she shouted.

It was an angle Nick had not thought of. She'd fallen for him. He was stunned and forced to give Trish his full attention. His mouth tried to form a response, but no words seemed to fit. Finally, "Okay." He paused to carefully measure his next response. "You win. But if shooting starts, you do a belly-flop between rows of seats… right into someone's lap if you have to. Just put something between you and the end of that machine gun. Got it?"

A softened look graced her face. "Aye aye, Captain." She gave him a two-fingered salute.

Nick's seriousness did not waver. "Not good enough. You have to promise." He took a decisive step toward her.

"Okay, I promise. I don't think walking into a packed auditorium will be conducive to staying on my feet very long anyway. My knees will be pretty darned weak the second we step into that crowd." She pushed off the bunk and stood. "Now, back to my original question: How is it going to help Lydia if we march back into the middle of all that?"

Nick stared at her for a time then looked over his shoulder down at the boy, nibbling on the inside of his cheek. He scanned the whimpering kid's trussed body. Keeping his eye on the boy, he shrugged.

"I'm not sure. But another hour has almost passed." After a moment of quiet contemplation looking down at the kid, he continued. "Now that we know Lydia might be next, we again find ourselves short on options, especially safe ones."

"That statement doesn't exactly instill a tremendous amount of confidence in a girl. Can't you come up with a better idea than 'I'm not sure' and 'short on options'? You have a knack for scaring the hell out of me. You know that?"

"Sorry. I think out loud too much." He stepped away and then spun back. "How about pandemonium? Does that sound like an option?"

"Pandemonium?" She was plainly confused, but then the light went on. She arched her eyebrows, and the worry wrinkle on her forehead smoothed away. She finally understood the intent, although the infant that was to become a plan hadn't navigated all the way through the birthing canal yet.

CHAPTER 29

The plan was risky, maybe too much so. He had no way of knowing. All he was certain of was that something needed to be done – and it had to be soon, or they'd chance losing Lydia, and maybe Bennie, too. The comfort level he developed when the Navy SEALs showed up had vanished. He couldn't be sure that they saw the current predicament as desperately as he did. How could they possibly know? He assumed that the rescue unit was still assessing numbers before proceeding with an attempt. If so, Lydia would be dead by the time they were ready to move in.

Nick knelt beside the boy bound on the floor of the crew quarters. He trained his eyes on the captive while he considered what needed to be done. The longer he thought on the hastily arranged plan, the more it seemed like a death wish that'd accomplish little more than getting them all killed. Marching head-on toward a machine gun trained on him, held by a man more than willing to kill him, wasn't the sanest thing he'd ever considered. But the time had come for someone to step up and stop the madness. Aside from the SEAL team, wherever they were and whatever they were doing, he and Trish were the only ones available to take it on, and time was of the essence.

Sitting back on his heels, his stare at the boy transformed into an analytical examination. He was sympathetic to the kid's phobia; it was his nature and his livelihood. But compassion ran counter to what needed to be done. For Lydia's sake, concern for the kid must be shoved to near the bottom of his short priority list. The price of empathy might be costly. The boy had told him without prompt that she was marked for execution. And, since the kid knew of her claustrophobia, it was credible information.

What he concocted for the boy flew in the face of everything he'd worked hard to accomplish since that day in Bayside Mall ten years ago. Now, he considered risking a boy's mental health to save another.

As Nick considered consequences, frightening scenarios filled his head, all teetering to the bloody side. Somehow, he had to figure out a way for favor to tilt in his direction.

It was time to feed the phobia, take it to the limit, yet play a serious balancing game: keep the boy mentally ragged and edgy, but prevent him from going over the edge and losing control altogether. It was time to get it started. Nick drew a breath and huffed out the courage to get things underway.

"Son, I'm going to make you a hero in your father's eyes. Are you as devoted to this as I am?"

The boy whimpered. Though tense and red-faced, the youngster had lain quietly, looking up at Nick. The young man would rather die than take another beating from his father. There was great advantage in building on that, and as sad as that was, it was necessary.

Nick took it to the next stage, speaking calm, encouraging words, placing himself in the role of the boy's advocate and hoping for some level of trust. Each time he mentioned Azziz, beatings were referenced, to make the name and the act inseparable. Nick attempted to redirect the boy's hysteria toward his father.

The kid approached loss of reason even without fanning the fear. *Where is this kid's point of no return? I've got to be careful, very careful.* The youngster must fear his father most, but must also respect Nick enough to remain compliant to commands without question – such a precarious balance.

"Look kid, I have to have assurance that you'll let me help you. Otherwise, I'll have no choice but to walk away and leave you tied on the floor. I think you know what that means." Nick stood and dusted his hands. "You know what your father will do when he finds you like this, a hog-tied failure."

The boy fought against the sheet strips that bound him. Slobber forced from between tight lips strung in rivulets to the floor. Nick let him have the moment with no encouragement to calm down, hoping the young man would come to grips with the inevitable. After a time, the boy settled, still breathing hard. His head fell to the floor. "I'll do as you ask."

That's what I needed to hear. "Seriously, son, my only goal is to save our friend's life. I don't want to see anyone get hurt." Nick brought his inflection down to a soothing range, almost monotone. "I can't walk back into that auditorium and expect to be welcomed with a handshake and a hug. If what you and I do together prevents a needless death and stops you from being beaten by an angry father, then I'd call that success. Wouldn't you?"

He never took his eyes off the kid, searching for telling changes in behavior, no matter how slight. Then he saw it; a subtle deviation in the boy's eyes, contrary to belligerence or fear – something to be nurtured.

The boy then closed his eyes and went limp.

Nick read it as resignation.

The young man slowly began to nod. As he opened his eyes, they were already cast to the floor in shame. Within that humiliation, Nick noticed something else; a facial expression that seemed to go beyond acceptance. It might have been resolve; but to what end?

It stretched Nick's faith, but it seemed a positive, though subtle, change had begun. Time had come for that leap of faith.

Trish waved for his attention and tickled the air with a finger, signaling him over.

He backed away from the boy, gauging every move, every look. He finally turned and walked to where Trish sat, on a bed near the end of the long, narrow room lined with double and triple-stacked bunks. "How's the back?" he asked.

"Not stinging anymore. But it feels like Rocky Balboa worked my kidney over." She forced a smile. "I'll be okay."

"It'll keep getting better. What's up?"

She leaned in and cupped her mouth to his ear. "I don't trust that punk."

"I don't either."

"Then why are we doing this?"

Nick sat beside her. "That question takes us back to available options: There aren't any. This is it. Unless, of course, we throw Lydia to the wolves, and I don't think either of us considers that an option."

She sighed and let her eyes fall. "You're right. I'm sorry for sounding so selfish."

"I'm convinced Lydia will be dead in a matter of minutes if we don't act. So, I have to add just enough fuel to that boy's phobia to keep him amenable, but not so much that his knees buckle beneath him. If he melts into a blubbering jellyfish in that auditorium, we're screwed." He looked at the kid through sympathetic eyes. "Funny thing is, I really do want to help him."

Trish touched him lightly on the forearm. "Courage tempered by compassion; you're one special human, Nick Brandon."

"I'm glad you think so, but truthfully, I'm just scared and confused, hoping I'm not deluding myself. Anyway, I'm putting all my money on a long-shot bet that that boy has been searching for an opportunity to break the parental-abuse cycle, and that I can persuade him to trust me… an American he doesn't know. I smashed his face with the butt of a machine gun and hogtied him on the floor… not exactly a winning introduction." He pushed out his lower lip and looked at the boy again, shaking his head. "This is the hardest thing I've ever attempted. But if I don't try, what then?" He made solid eye contact with Trish. "Can I do it?" He shrugged. "Don't know." He held his gaze on her long enough for the words to develop a depth of meaning. He then took a quick deep breath, slapped his knees and sprang up.

She grabbed his hand before he took a step.

He looked down at her fingers wrapped tightly around his.

"Nick, no matter what happens up there," she said, nodding toward the deck above them, "I want you to know, while I have the chance to say it, you've been amazing… you *are* amazing."

His cheeks flushed. "Well, I –"

"You don't need to say anything; in fact, I prefer you didn't." She rose. With a finger, she pushed his chin to present his cheek to her. She kissed it and then rubbed it in with her thumb. "Now, let's get busy. What do you need?"

"Uh…" He stared for a couple of uncomfortable seconds. Part of him thought it was time to say something witty, but when he pulled the lid on that cookie jar, it was empty. All he had was another "Uh."

Finally, pragmatism kicked in. "Well, let me think… we need to untie him and lash him around the waist with a length of that sheet. Then tie the other end around my waist, leaving only enough room between us for the machine gun – butt of the stock against him, barrel against me..."

He paused and thought again about that moment between them. "What did you mean when you said, 'While I have the chance to say it'? We'll make it through this. You do believe that, don't you?"

She smiled. "Like I said, you've been amazing." She kept smiling and ripped another length from the bed sheet. "This sure is white. I wish it weren't so noticeable."

"Let me see..." He looked around and began rummaging through all the small metal chests of drawers near each set of bunks. "Humph. What can we do about that?" he muttered. After searching through several drawers, he produced a can of brown shoe polish. "This should do the trick." He handed it to her. "Once the boy and I are tied together, smear this over the exposed areas of the sheet strip. Maybe that'll provide camouflage... less noticeable than stark white anyhow."

"Good idea," she said, though her voice lacked enthusiasm. "You think they heard all the shooting down here?"

"Bet on it." He fell to his knees beside the boy and began untying knots, then hesitated. "I'm afraid to think what's happening to Lydia should we hear shooting up there."

"I don't want to think about that. What about us? Do you think they'll come down to investigate why the boy and that dead guy haven't returned?"

"The kid and the guy out in the hallway were probably supposed to be back at a pre-designated time, meaning we need to hurry and get up there. Our plan will disintegrate in a heartbeat if men show up here." He removed the binding strip of cloth from the boy and helped him sit upright. He then looked directly into the boy's eyes but spoke to Trish. "It would do this kid no good should that happen. His failure would be instantly evident. God help this lad if his father should discover that."

The boy winced and turned his face away as if Nick had struck him.

"No son, it's not me you need to worry about. It's your father's anger you should be concerned with. I don't hurt people if I can avoid it. It's your father who relishes inflicting pain to press a point. We need to prove you're a hero. That's what I'm planning for you."

The boy whined beneath his breath. "Hurry. Please."

He stood and pulled the boy up with him. "Stand right here. Don't move." He walked to the bunk where the machine gun lay. He disengaged the clip and jacked the chambered bullet out, plinking across the floor. He tossed the clip onto the bunk. After a stutter-step, he stopped and looked back at it. He whirled around and snatched up the clip, shoving it into his pants and feeling the cold steel against his buttocks. "Standing with my hands in the air in an open auditorium with guns trained on me would be the wrong time to think that I needed that clip after all."

"Yep, you've sure been amazing."

"Would you stop saying that?"

"Stop being amazing."

"You're going to get me overconfident."

"Sorry."

"Ms. Campbell, would you honor me by tying me and the lad together?" He held out the machine gun for her.

She reached for it. "Such formality." She took the firearm as if it might bite her. "It'd be my pleasure," she said and dipped her chin courteously, eyes remaining locked on his, as that long sweeping bang of auburn hair slid from her forehead to cover one eye. "Doctor Nicholas Brandon, I am at your service."

In the weeks he'd known her, this was the first time he saw her smile like that, one meant for him and not for something he might have done or said. He suddenly felt lighter on his feet.

"How is it that we're so calm with life-threatening danger waiting for us up there? How stupid is that?" she asked.

"It's not as stupid as you think." He watched her step behind the boy. "If we had many possible solutions to choose from..." He laughed sardonically and then frowned. "Hell, if we even had *one* other possible solution, things would be different. This... this whole thing would unnerve us. We'd be second-guessing the decision to the point of dread. It's that old fork-in-the-road dilemma – uneasiness created by choices, intensifying exponentially with each additional possibility. We're at peace with it because it's the only plan available to us. Make sense?"

"As odd as it sounds, yes."

"Please, let's not waste any more time," the boy said.

That broke the spell. Nick's eyes fluttered, as did hers. "He's right. We need to kick this plan over into second gear." He tossed her the strip of cloth he removed from the boy.

She pitched it over her shoulder as she stood behind the young man. After a quick examination, she pulled his tunic off and lifted his loose-fitting linen shirt. "Damn, Nick."

"What is it?" He stepped behind the boy to join her and saw what so disgusted her. Scars crossed at multiple angles, ridging across his back. Some had not healed and appeared only days old. The raised imperfections indicated that the original wounds had been deep, splitting skin to a bloody depth. "Your old man is cruel. That bastard doesn't deserve the title of *father*."

"Just hurry," the boy replied in thready voice.

"Right." Nick twirled a finger, gesturing for Trish to continue what she'd begun.

She wrapped the strip of cloth around the boy's waist twice, lightly crossing it over still-raw wounds from a recent lashing. She made sure not to tie it up too tight and then strung the long end through the trigger guard and several times around its barrel. "Step back closer," she instructed Nick. She pinched a pucker in the back of his shirt and began a tear in it with her teeth. She shoved the cloth through the small hole. "Hold your shirt tail up." She then wrapped it around Nick's waist. Her fingers seemed to linger on the bared flesh at his midsection. Then she pulled the gun snug into his back.

"Ouch!" He arched forward.

She kept working. "Hush." She continued wrapping it around him until only enough remained to tie off. She then smoothed his shirt down. Once complete, she backed away and examined the muzzle of the gun and the cloth where it disappeared through the torn hole in his shirt. "That's not bad at all; looks natural, if I do say so myself."

Nick looked over his shoulder. "Good work, but what about his hands? He might decide at a very inopportune time to break his promise."

"Hmm." She pulled the other strip from her shoulder. "Put your hand around the stock with your finger on the trigger." The boy complied. "Now, place your other hand on top of the barrel." He did as she said. She tied both his hands securely to the gun and then turned to Nick. "Anything else?"

Nick looked back again. "Just smear shoe polish on the sheet to break up that glossy white, and that should do it… I hope."

She popped the top off the flat, round shoe-polish tin, scooping it out and rubbing the cloth strips with it until the can was empty. "I think we're good to go."

Nick glimpsed her right palm and then paused for a closer examination. "Remember, we're going into that auditorium with our hands up. Do you really want your right hand looking as though you've been fishing around in a dirty toilet?"

"That's disgusting!" She looked at her hand. "But probably true." She dumped a pillow from its case and used the covering to wipe the hand. "What do you think the SEAL guys are doing right now?"

"Taking their time; searching the ship, deck by deck, and closing in on the auditorium. They won't show themselves until they know with reasonable certainty how many of those thugs there are and where they're situated. In other words, until they know that the advantage is theirs. I have a feeling that the two who escorted us here probably saw the kid and that other guy but chose to stay out of sight until they were more confident of what they would be dealing with when the time comes to act. I'm thinking they don't want an all-out gun battle erupting in a crowded auditorium. The mandate, I'm sure, is to preserve as much life as possible. Our challenge has been thrust upon us as a result of that approach. If they don't make a move until they hear shots fired inside the auditorium, that'll be too late for Lydia."

Trish drew a breath. "Time?"

"It's time." He looked back at the sad face of the boy. The youngster's head hung loosely from his shoulders. "Son, somewhere between here and there you'd better change that expression and man-up. That sad look is a sure giveaway that you screwed up. You have to shove me down that center aisle of the theatre like a conquering king. I'd be surprised if someone didn't reach from a seat on the aisle and slap you silly looking like you do right now."

The boy's head shied to the side and back. A stifled whimper died in his throat.

"Buck up kid. This is the only way to save yourself."

The young man pushed a shoulder up and wiped away a dangling tear from his tilted jaw. He straightened his posture and poked Nick in the back with the empty machine gun, shoving him forward.

"That's it, kid." He began walking, but after only a couple of steps realized how the bonds fixing him to the boy stifled flexibility. Should quick action be called for, he'd be severely hampered. He glanced at the open drawer from where the shoe polish came and saw a medium-sized, folded pocket knife, the largest blade probably three inches. "Trish, grab that knife. This excellent knot job of yours may need to be undone quickly."

Trish snatched it up, shoved it under the waistband of her tight plaid shorts, and followed them out the door. Once in the hallway, she quickened her step to walk beside Nick, examining the abnormal gait of both men. "That doesn't look natural. It looks like you two are dancing and both trying to lead."

"We're too jerky." He glanced back at the boy then looked forward as they continued to move toward the elevator down the hall. He looked around, searching for an idea in the air. "Kid, you've got to make this happen. I can't be dragging you along. You have to match my step and speed. If there should be any stumbling going on, it should be me, not you."

The boy ground his teeth. Frustration spilled out. "Haven't you shamed me enough?"

Trish threw an open palm into the air as if she were about to strike him. "Shut up!" The kid ducked away. She held the hand threateningly high. His gait immediately smoothed. "That's better."

Nick looked down the hall as they moved forward. "What's your name, son?"

"Shandahar... Shandahar Baruk."

"Baruk I'd guessed. I want you to remember one thing, Shandahar; we're not your enemy... never were, never will be. We wish you and your people no harm... never did, never will." He glanced back. "I hope someday you come to understand how precious life is. Man has no right to do anything but honor God's miracle." Nick suddenly stopped walking and looked back at the boy. "If you and I survive this, I hope we can become friends. I want to help you."

Shandahar remained quiet.

Even in the boy's silence, Nick saw that glint again, telling a story counter to his abused upbringing. Inside that kid lay an untapped reservoir of compassion.

A short time later, they stood at the elevator. Nick held his finger to the button. He looked at Trish. "Ready?"

She nodded briskly. "I guess I'd better be." She reached for the waistband of her shorts, securing the folded knife concealed there.

Nick pushed the elevator button. The up arrow on it lit, and an electric motor sounded off overhead. It began its journey down to their floor. He offered Trish a reassuring smile.

A ding sounded as the elevator compartment bottomed out. The doors parted. They stepped in. Nick and the boy turned so that he'd be facing outward when it opened. Every move they made seemed clumsy – every tiny misstep exaggerated. It'd likely worsen before it got better.

He glanced sideways at Trish. He was about to allow her to get into harm's way and suddenly felt stupid. He should have left her behind, regardless. He bit into his cheek until it stung. He whispered sideways, "Don't forget: Dive for the floor if shooting erupts. Don't get caught standing and gawking."

Without glancing over at him, she said, "Right." She then began to draw in a breath of courage, but cut it short when the elevator stopped.

Nick slipped his hand into hers. He looked straight ahead into the mirrored elevator door at them together, side by side.

Her nervous shifting eyes stopped on his reflection.

"If we keep our wits, we'll be okay. A person that I deeply respect once told me that I was amazing. It might help if you hung onto that belief." He flashed a silly, boyish grin.

The doors opened; his smile vanished. He whispered back to the boy, "Showtime and it's your show; push me into the hall."

"Trish, put your hands high in the air and remain in bodily contact with me, at my side at all times."

She nodded.

He raised his hands into the air as well, just as the boy shoved him with the machine gun into the hall.

A babble of Arabic came instantly from the closed double doors to the auditorium, still some distance away. The boy responded in their language.

Nick flushed as his heart stuttered. He hadn't considered that he didn't understand their language. The boy could say anything and he wouldn't comprehend it. "What did you tell him?" he whispered from the corner of his mouth.

"To open the doors and lead the way into the theatre. Otherwise, he'd be too close to us and surely see the bindings."

A renewed flicker of trust radiated through Nick. He watched the other well-heeled accomplice open one side of the double doors and walk into the auditorium ahead of them. As they came close, Nick dropped a hand and pushed the other door open.

He heard the rustle of many people turning to see who was coming to join them. Even as large as the space was, the air had grown stale with the odor of terrified bodies lingering. Once they were fully through the door, he heard Trish's breath grow rapid and shallow. His mind raced. *How can I feed one phobia and allay the fear of another at the same time?*

He glanced around the crowded room. It was the first time he'd been able to scope the entire room at once. It was huge and crammed full of people, standing, sitting, and lying in every available space. *For God's sake, how can so few of these goons successfully hold so many hostages? This is ridiculous!*

He stole a glance at Trish, wanting to reassure her, but chose not to chance it.

As they moved down the steps, Benjamin came into view, lying off to the side in the cross-aisle. As they passed, he rolled onto his hip for a better look. He held a grossly swollen arm close to his body. He was on the carpet in the area separating theatre seats below from reserve tables above. He lay below and in front of the table where they'd been sitting. Nick noticed that the tablecloth had slots ripped at its ends and that the table corners were shoved through haphazardly fashioned holes. It clearly had been done to preserve the secrecy of the removed air-conditioning register vent through which he and Trish had made their escape. *Lydia,* he thought.

"Benny!" Trish hissed. She took a sideways step as if she were going to drop to his side.

Benjamin gave her a warning wave away with his functioning arm.

"No, Trish," Nick whispered.

The gunman leading them, walking some distance ahead, made it to the stage and took the three steps up on to it, joining the lone pacing guard. Nick kept an eye on them both, seeking signs of suspicion. He saw no indication. They appeared pleased.

The one that had been clearing a trail through the crowd stepped beside the other gunman. Both of the terrorists now faced them. Shandahar continued to push him down the stairs toward the stage.

The boy said something to them.

They grinned.

It was clearly the arrogant smile of having foiled a plot. The men stood abreast. Each held a machine gun, muzzle up, close to their chests in an at-ease posture. The lone guard that had been pacing the stage wore a holstered automatic handgun in addition to a machine gun.

Nick's eyes moved from one terrified face to the next across a sea of them in the audience. He lingered on each as long as he dared, looking into as many eyes as the speed of their approach allowed. All his years of training were coming down to a single moment. He needed to see a particular set of eyes – an expression unlike the others. Hardly anyone turned to look at him. Fear of complicity had frozen their necks facing forward, and eyes downturned.

Then, as he walked by the second row up from the stage, he saw what he'd been searching for. In the third seat to his right, a young man – a senior in high school, or perhaps a college freshman – sat wearing a Chicago Bulls tank top and knee-length workout shorts. It wasn't simply the obvious strength displayed in the boy's bulging muscles. It was a calculating look – a gaze that locked onto Nick's. There was no fear in the boy's face. He was a jock. And Nick knew any star athlete worth his salt thought in terms of winning or losing – never playing to a draw.

There's the look – the need to win. Nick held a gaze on the boy, who was the right age to believe that death only happened to other people. He still lived in the age of immortality – a disease of deception unique to the teenage mind. Nick winked at him. The boy dipped his chin, affirming the signal.

Trish had not noticed.

The men onstage talked to one another, then spoke to Shandahar. The inflection indicated a question. Shandahar answered in three quick bursts of speech. One of the men laughed.

Nick's stomach was on the verge of cramping with fear – fear of not knowing what was said, and of how important it might be that he knows.

His hands still held high, he saw that Trish seemed to be walking strangely, knees knocking and occasionally clenching, as if needing to pee. *Aw, Jeez, Trish. Not again.* He inadvertently let his eyes drift upward and roll.

They stepped up the three steps onto the stage, and Trish dropped one arm and grabbed her crotch. The guards looked at one another. One of them spoke. The other laughed.

Shandahar whispered, "They think she desires them."

Nick cut a glance at her. He frowned. This time it didn't matter if they saw him or not. The message had to be immediately clear to her. *This is no time to be improvising. Stick with the plan.*

Suddenly, he heard a clunk and looked down to see that the pocket knife had slipped from the waistband of her shorts and worked its way down her leg, hitting the stage floor.

The two men did not know what to think about it – at first. Then the one that guarded the stage grew angry. He stepped brusquely up to her and slapped the side of her face with the flat of the gunstock.

She twirled away, stumbled and fell.

The crowd gasped.

She attempted to lift herself off the floor but fell back, lying limp.

The time to wonder what was next had passed.

Adrenaline flooded Nick's body.

He took a quick step, almost yanking Shandahar off his feet, and grabbed the barrels of both machine guns. Whatever advantage he may have had was as slim as his strength against two grown men, holding each with only one hand. He turned to where he knew the young boy sat. "Quick! Get up here! I can't hold them."

The boy in the Chicago Bulls shirt leapt up and sprang over the top of the seat ahead of him. The older woman beside him, likely his mother, screamed, "No, Bobby! No!" She reached for him but only grabbed air. He was already bounding up onto the stage.

Nick held the gun barrels with all his might, but one of the men made headway, coming around to point the muzzle at him. He grunted when his wrist twisted to a painful degree. The other man was not trying as hard. He went for the pistol at his side.

Bobby, the young man from the audience, grabbed the barrel of the machine gun that was now almost turned on Nick, and together, they shoved it aside. As the boy pushed the barrel away, Nick released his hold on it. With a quick, choppy punch, he hit the man squarely in the nose. The man's head snapped back, and Nick drove that same fist into his now fully exposed Adam's apple. He gagged and fell backwards, releasing his grip on the machine gun to hold his neck.

Bobby suddenly realized he clutched an automatic weapon. He had sole control of it and clearly didn't know what to do with it. He tossed it aside. It landed with a clank, sliding across the hardwood surface of the stage with a grating noise. The young man rubbed his palms on his tank top like the gun was diseased.

All this time, Nick still clutched the barrel of the other man's machine gun with one hand. Now he gave it full attention, trying to wrest the automatic weapon from the man's grasp. He looked down in time to see that Trish had managed to retrieve and open the pocket knife. She plunged it into the back of the man's hand when he went for the pistol holstered on his hip.

The guy let out a pain-filled roar.

This gave Nick a second to look back at the audience and saw hundreds of people watching as though it were a horror movie. They just sat, slack-jawed. "Get off your dead asses and get down here!" he yelled.

With a knife sticking in the back of his hand and dangling, the thug swung it roundhouse and hit Trish in the face, again sending her reeling backwards. She hit the floor with a splat of flesh against it. This time there was no movement; she was indeed unconscious.

The man had two choices: Release the machine gun into Nick's control, pull the knife from his hand and try again for his pistol, or continue the stalemate of holding onto the weapon. He chose to release the automatic firearm into Nick's control, contemptuously thinking he could get his pistol ready to fire before Nick turned the machine gun on him.

He slung the knife from the back of his hand and then went for the pistol.

But Nick didn't even try to turn the weapon and fire it. He jammed the butt of the machine gun into the man's forehead as soon as he had control of it.

It hadn't been the move the man expected. The stunned look blended smoothly with surprise. He staggered backward and fell on his butt.

Nick saw the knife on the floor. "Get the knife!" he shouted to Bobby.

People in the audience had begun to gather courage and were approaching the stage, but no one seemed interested in joining the fray.

The two terrorists were again getting their wits about them. The boy ran the few feet and snatched up the knife.

"Hurry!" Nick yelled. "Cut me loose from this kid."

The man Nick had smashed in the throat was the first to come around and was on all fours gagging, holding his throat and gasping.

The boy frantically sawed the sheet strip nearest Nick's back. Nick turned again to the audience. "What the hell are y'all waiting for?"

His attention was then drawn to the pistol on the floor, and before he was cut free, dragged Shandahar and the young jock along to get to where it lay.

After a couple of steps Nick lurched, stumbling forward as the sheet strip was cut through. He fell near the gun and snatched it up.

The man holding his throat still gasped for air but saw Nick going for the pistol and crawled to the machine gun a few feet away.

Nick rolled to his side and held the pistol out with both hands. He fired two quick shots. The man collapsed to the floor on his side. He was hit but had control of the machine gun and loosely pointed it at the teenager, who now advanced on him with the knife held high. The automatic weapon rattled a response.

The young man went down.

His mother yelled, "Bobby!"

The knife flew from his hand when he hit the floor. It slid toward Shandahar, who had been struggling to tear away the strips that bound him to the empty machine gun.

The terrorist was severely wounded and in pain but still had strength enough to swing the gun toward Nick. Nick sat up, took extra time to aim, and fired again. It was a well-placed shot to the head. He turned the pistol toward the other one, still writhing on the floor, partially conscious.

From behind came a whack across the side of Nick's head, driving him to the floor. A sharp pain bolted from his head down his spine. His hand sprang open and he dropped the pistol. Lights flashed. He lost focus. And for a second, he felt nothing at all. He couldn't move. Then both hands went directly to a searing pain behind his right ear.

He looked up, but his vision had blurred. As it cleared, he saw Azziz Baruk standing over him with Sahid Arrani at his side. They seemed calm, almost amused.

"So," Azziz said, "You are the hero of this gathering. There is one in every crowd." He looked to Sahid. "Is that not so, my brother?"

Sahid nodded.

Azziz then looked to the young man wearing the Bulls jersey lying nearby, still alive but nearing death. "Well, maybe two heroes in this particular crowd; it is a large group after all." Azziz walked to the surviving guard and pulled him to his feet. Blood streaked that one's face. He stumbled sideways but kept his feet as Azziz yanked him back straight.

Then Azziz turned to Nick. "Do you know how I handle heroes?"

Nick pushed up to a sitting position, still holding his head. He didn't care what the bastard had to say; it was a game Baruk played that'd end in his death, regardless what his response might be.

"I find it helpful to kill their friends, their loved ones, and their family... anyone close to them. It is a highly useful technique. It allows time for the hero to wallow in their mistake. Then... I kill them, too. There is no greater deterrent to others who might try the same thing."

He offered a hand to help Nick to his feet. Nick refused it.

"Please, allow me to honor your courage against overwhelming odds by accepting a helping hand up."

Nick ignored the comment and rose unsteadily under his own power. He rubbed the back of his head and stretched his stiffened neck, batting his eyes, still trying to regain a measure of lucidity. He needed his wits about him, should there appear one last opportunity.

Azziz looked to Trish, still motionless, sprawled on the hardwood floor of the stage.

"I think I shall begin with her." He smiled. "An obvious choice, don't you think?"

Azziz shifted attention to his son. His eyes narrowed. His speech went from calm to angry.

"Shandahar, come to my side," he ordered.

The boy hesitated.

"Do it now!"

Shandahar unwound the remaining strip from his wrists and dropped it to the floor. "Please, Father –"

"Not now. Your discipline will come later. I do not know what happened, but your bindings tell a tale of truth. You failed your assignment. That's all I must know for now."

Shandahar's face squeezed into a childlike contortion, but he shed no tears. His knees wobbled.

Nick saw and knew the immeasurable battle going on within the kid. He'd be beaten later. Nick was certain that one of those beatings would eventually kill the boy. But he didn't have time to wonder further about it.

Azziz dropped the machine gun, allowing it to hang loosely at his side by its strap around his neck. He unholstered his pistol as he stepped in front of Shandahar. "Now, my son, I am forced to continue your education and show you how to correct your error."

Nick's eyes swept the anguished faces of the audience and made their way back to Sahid, over to Azziz and finally to Shandahar. He had to do something, but what? Sahid's machine gun was trained on him. He would not be able to manage a single step before being mowed down in a hail of bullets.

Trish groaned. She rolled to the flat of her back and opened her eyes to see Azziz's pistol pointed at her head.

Nick saw no fear in her eyes – none at all.

Her head lolled to the side toward Nick.

Tears spilled from Nick's unblinking eyes as he looked down at her. Acid rose in his throat. He swallowed and muttered, "I'm sorry, Trish."

"I still think you're amazing." Her speech was slow and slurred. She smiled and closed her eyes. Her lips tightened to a straight white line as she waited for the inevitable.

Nick couldn't watch. He closed his eyes, too, squeezing tears out as he did. He no longer had control and didn't care about anything, except Trish. For her sake, he shouted to her executioner, "You heathen son-of-a-bitch!"

The gun discharged.

Nick flinched but didn't open his eyes to see the gruesome aftermath. He turned away to open them on Azziz, who was holding the gun high, pointed at the ceiling, eyes wide and fixed, as though surprised. His head tilted back at a severe angle and seemed locked in that position. The pistol slipped from Azziz's lazy grip, hitting the floor with a clank. He sank to his knees and fell over onto his face.

That's when Nick saw it: the pocket knife buried in the back of Azziz's neck. Shandahar, his own son, had severed his father's brain stem.

Sahid whirled away from Nick to face the boy, but he hesitated, disbelieving that Shandahar could've killed his own father.

That was the extra second Nick needed.

Nick reached around Sahid and grabbed the machine gun, with one hand on each side of Sahid's body.

Sahid clutched the trigger, and the deafening rattle reverberated through the large auditorium.

Nick fought to keep the muzzle at a safe angle away from people, but he was losing strength fast. He'd been through too much and simply did not have enough left in him to fight.

Sahid wrested the gun away and spun to face Nick. The firearm had no sooner been shouldered then a blast and spray of blood came at Nick. Sahid fell away, revealing Shandahar holding a pistol aimed to where Sahid's head had been.

Automatic-weapon fire suddenly erupted outside the auditorium, but only lasted a few seconds. Three short volleys until it stopped, and in came a welcome sight. Two Navy SEALs entered the auditorium, and Nick heard the sweetest words ever. One of the servicemen keyed a walkie-talkie and said, "The area has been secured."

Nick's knees buckled. No longer adrenaline-charged, he collapsed onto the stage floor, his nose only inches from Trish's. His body stretched out one way, hers the other. He looked at the knot on her head and the bruise on her jaw. He pushed hair away from her eyes.

She had no more strength than he did. "I hurt all over," she said. She didn't attempt to raise her head off the floor.

Although loose-lipped and eyes drooping, his obligation to show that his humor remained intact oozed out. "Now, what was that about me being amazing?"

"Odd time for a punch line…"

"I know. Is it working?"

"Amazingly, it is."

CHAPTER 30

The cheers and applause for the arrival of the Navy SEALs turned deafening in the auditorium as they marched en masse down the center aisle toward the stage, like conquering heroes. People crowded in, wanting to touch them as they passed, or shake their hands, or kiss them – whatever it took to make a personal connection with perceived saviors.

If Nick had had any energy left, he would have been pissed and chastising the audience loudly for overlooking what Trish, Shandahar, that poor student lying bleeding, and he had just accomplished. Although a welcome sight, the SEAL team only mopped up the excess outside the auditorium. Too weak to care that much, he still was annoyed at receiving nary a thank you for how close to death the four of them came. The naval rescue unit strutted like the sheriff showing up for the body count after the shootout in a B-movie western. They had made little difference in his survival or anyone else's.

The jubilant crowd continued popping up from seats and applauding, as if the curtain had just gone down on a show. He couldn't ignore one obvious difference: the pungent odor of residual fear from two-thousand-plus sweaty bodies.

Still stretched out next to Trish, Nick raised his upper torso and rested on an elbow. He attempted to look up the center steps beyond the approaching servicemen. Too many people choked the aisle to get an unobstructed view. He couldn't see Benjamin and wondered where Lydia might be.

His roving eyes stopped at the young man who had risked it all to save him and now needed immediate medical attention. He lay in a pool of blood and showed no sign of life. Nick struggled against personal discomfort, rolling over to hands and knees to crawl to the boy.

His mother, blinded by premature grief, ran tripping and stumbling, shoving her way through the throng and up onto the stage and collapsing to her knees at the boy's side. Nick wanted to let her have this moment, but with that amount of blood loss, the young man's survival depended on quick action. The kid had saved his life and may yet pay the ultimate price for doing so. The woman glanced at the boy's face and burst into a mournful wail, pulling him to her chest.

"Please, ma'am," Nick said gently. He pushed her off the boy. "I need to check his vitals and apply pressure to those wounds. The blood loss has to be stopped."

She wormed away from his touch and yelled into his face. "It's your fault! You hear me? Your fault! You've killed my Bobby!"

Nick put an ear to the boy's chest, then pressed the carotid with two fingers for a couple of seconds. "He's not dead. But you have to let me help him. There's no time to waste."

Still sobbing, she reluctantly yielded her place over her son. She sat off to the side on her heels and buried her face in her bloodied hands. Nick hesitated when he saw how distraught she'd become. It appeared she might not stop sobbing long enough to breathe.

The boy's worsening condition trumped her sadness. He placed an ear to the kid's chest and heard the faint beat of a strong, young heart. But it sounded distant and slow. Still down on all fours, Nick faced the crowd, intending to shout across the noisy assemblage for a doctor. He cupped his mouth and was about to do just that when a man in a white military-like uniform appeared from within the crowd and hurried up onto the stage. The uniform identified him as ship's personnel. In English but with a heavy accent, Spanish maybe, he said, "I am the doctor." He fell to his knees and began to examine the boy.

Nick withdrew in deference to the man's medical expertise. His own discomforts returned. With effort, he rose to his feet, listing sideways, equilibrium skewed. Without the adrenaline assist, his pains had become sharply defined – everything from a headache to throbbing feet. He wanted to sit and indulge his injuries, but once he saw Trish attempting to stand too, he hurried over to lend a hand.

"Take it easy," he said. "You took a couple of hard blows to the head." He pulled her up. "Frankly, I'm surprised you're even conscious. I'm sure you have a concussion."

"You don't need to tell me. My head is throbbing. I need an aspirin... maybe a handful." She held her head and swayed. A pained grimace spread across her face. "Crap!" Her knees wobbled and began to buckle. "...Head... spinning..."

Nick grabbed an arm as her knees gave way. He righted her and then pushed his face close to hers, examining her. "You and I need to be in sickbay, too, but not yet." He guided her to the edge of the stage. "Sit here. I have to find Lydia. Not seeing her around anywhere is scarin' the hell out of me."

He jumped off the two-foot high stage and threaded his way up the steps through the milling crowd, toward Benjamin. When the intersecting walkway came into view, he saw two passengers lift the old guy onto a makeshift stretcher fashioned from the same tablecloth that so capably preserved the secrecy of their escape route through the air-conditioning duct behind it. One of the SEALs was supervising the medical evacuation. "Benny?" His voice rose above the general din of a relieved crowd.

Benjamin drifted in and out of consciousness, lids heavy and eyes swimming in watery pools. Nick noticed the instant the older man caught sight of him, as the two burly male passengers moved him over onto the cloth, presumably preparing to take him to sickbay.

Benjamin forced a smile, extending his good arm to Nick. "Doctor Brandon. Thank God," he said laboring for breath, "it's you. I was frightened that you and Miss Campbell might have been killed. I couldn't see the stage. I didn't know."

"By His grace, we're fine." He looked Benjamin over head to toe. "In fact, I think we're in much better shape than you, my friend." He tried to smile. "Are you in pain?"

"No, as long as I don't move around I'm okay. It's just that I won't be doing jumping jacks for a while. That's all."

"Did you ever?"

Benjamin closed his eyes; his expression softened. "Eh, not so much." Suddenly, his face lost pleasantness. His eyes popped wide. "Lydia! You must go get her."

"Where, Benny? Where is she?"

"That tiny utility closet left of the stage, near the exit sign."

The men holding the makeshift stretcher carried Benjamin away, leaving Nick standing. As they moved, his hand slipped from the old man's grasp.

"Rest easy, Benny. I'll come find you later." He looked to one of the men holding an end of the sheet that Benjamin nestled in and then to the other one. "Take care of him; he's a damn good man."

"Don't ya worry, podna," the larger of the two men said, clearly and proudly a Texan. "Y'all just go on and take care of business. We've got your friend covered."

"Don't worry about me," Benjamin said. "Get Lydia. She's a peach, Nick... a real peach."

Nick watched for only a second as they carried Benjamin away, then turned and sprinted back down the steps toward the stage. He didn't get far before hitting a nearly impenetrable wall of people. After saying "Excuse me" a dozen times or more, he abandoned every pretense of manners and began shoving people aside. No one seemed to mind.

People celebrated – hugging, crying and releasing a variety of pent-up emotions. One elderly lady snared his arm and yanked him around. She locked his arms to his sides in a tight hug. She laid the side of her face on his chest and said, "God bless you, Mister."

He smiled. *Whaddaya know? Someone does appreciate what we did.*

"You're welcome," he said, peeling her arms off him to continue on. He pushed and shoved his way to the end of the seat rows in front of the stage and stepped between the first row and the platform. It was noisy.

Trish yelled, "Nick, what is it?"

He shouted "Lydia!" He stabbed the air with a finger toward the exit and the narrow door next to it, as he continued weaving through the crowd.

Trish rose from where she sat on the edge of the stage and joined him. They hurried over to the innocuous door a few feet from the left edge of the stage. Nick fumbled with the recessed circular latch and turned it counter-clockwise. The bolt receded from its hold. He yanked it open.

There Lydia sat, appearing much like an upright fetus in a womb, complete with a head-to-toe coating of amniotic fluid. She'd been stuffed into a space never intended to hold a human body, even one as slender and pliable as hers. Her back had been forced against one side, knees against her chest, and toes curled against the opposite wall. Her head rested loosely atop her knees. She did not respond when the door opened. With the support of it taken away, she wilted sideways into his arms.

"Lydia?" He gently lifted her out and laid her on the floor, kneeling at her side. "Lydia, can you hear me?" Cradling her head, he pulled an eyelid up, and the pupil reacted to the light. She was conscious, but those empty eyes indicated that clarity did not back the stare. Her skin was clammy and cool, her clothes saturated and clinging. He glanced up at Trish. "She's in shock."

As he and Trish tended to her, ship's personnel wheeled in cart after cart of bottled drinks. "Stay with her, Trish. I'll get water."

Nick stepped to the nearest exit next to the stage, where a young man in uniform pulled in a heavily laden hand-truck loaded with drinks, a case of water on top. He reached for it, then hesitated. He looked to the boy bringing it in. "You mind?"

"Take what you want, sir. All food and drinks are courtesy of the ship." The boy looked at Trish and Lydia a few feet away. "All medical attention will be provided free of charge as well." He flicked his chin in the direction of the women. "I suggest you and your friends over there take advantage of that and get to sickbay. It looks like all three of you can use the attention."

"You're right about that. The lady on the floor needs intravenous electrolytes, but I've got to try and get water in her now. She's seriously dehydrated."

The young man looked to where Trish hunkered over Lydia. "Yes sir, I understand. I'll take these drinks to a central location, then get you some help."

"Thanks pal," he said over his shoulder, already rushing back to Lydia's side. Nick fell to his knees beside her. "Move, Trish. Let's see if she'll take some water."

He twisted the cap off a bottle and drizzled water onto her closed mouth. She didn't respond, and that tiny bit of moisture spilled from the cleft between her sealed and dry lips. It trickled uselessly down her cheek. He tried again. This time, he smeared water over her lips and pushed a wet finger into her mouth, coating her teeth with it. She automatically licked her lips. He watched her tongue work inside her mouth. He pulled her lower lip out and poured the equivalent of a half-teaspoon on her gums. After a second, the Adam's apple traveled up, then down. She'd swallowed.

From the stage a few feet away, he heard a voice that he believed to be addressing him. He looked up and saw Shandahar sitting like a rag doll, upright, feet spread wide and both hands resting, palms up, on the stage. He slumped forward. That's when Nick noticed blood streaming from both wrists.

"American," Shandahar repeated, voice slurring. His lips were blue against the ghostly ashen pallor of his face, as life's blood drained from his body. There was not enough strength left in his facial muscles for expressiveness. His lower lip hung loose. "Thank you. Thank you for giving me courage to change who I am." His voice trailed. "I can die... in peace." He slipped from consciousness and fell over onto his shoulder, head banging the floor of the stage.

Nick saw the two SEALs blatantly ignore Shandahar. They checked the bodies of Azziz, Sahid, and the guard.

"Hey," he shouted, "Take care of the boy! Those guys are dead. He's not!"

He stuck the water bottle in Trish's hand. "Keep trying to get some fluid in her." He leaped to his feet and swooned. Fatigue tugged at him. But things remained to be done. He shook it off and jumped up onto the stage.

"We have things under control up here," one of the SEALs told him.

"Like hell you have!"

"Sir, please back away and get off the stage."

"What the hell is wrong with y'all? Don't you two realize if it weren't for that boy I'd be dead right now?" He then pointed at Trish. "That woman right there is alive too, because of him!" He threw his arms into the air. "God only knows who else may have died if that boy hadn't helped us intervene when we did."

Nick disregarded their order for him to leave the stage and rushed to Shandahar, shoving one of the SEALs aside as he did. He pulled his own tattered shirt off and ripped strips from it. He squeezed the deep lacerations together and tied them with cloth strips.

Pissed at the SEALs' lack of concern, he looked up and over his bare shoulder as he worked and continued scolding.

"This boy was as much a victim in all this as me or anyone else in this Goddamn auditorium! He wasn't evil." He flicked his chin toward Azziz. "That son-of-a-bitch lying dead over there was the evil one. This boy, Shandahar, neutralized his own father for you. He did your dirty work. He killed his father to protect me, for Christ's sake! I'll not sit idly and watch you let him bleed to death!" He finished drawing up cloth tourniquets tight above the wounds on both arms and sat back on his haunches. "Damn it, guys! Show some respect."

"Sorry, sir," one said. "We weren't aware of the role he played. We'll get him medical attention right away."

"Nick," Trish shouted. "I can't get Lydia to drink." The noise in the auditorium had not subsided.

As Nick stepped off the stage, he looked back at the SEALs. "Please guys, get the boy to sickbay. His is a life worth saving. Please believe that."

As he rushed back to Lydia, a number of men in white ship's uniforms burst through the double doors at the top of the stairs and at the exit near Lydia and Trish. All carried stretchers. "Good," he said. "Transport has arrived."

Two young men carrying one of the litters peeled off from the rest and walked in their direction. Nick was already slipping his hands beneath Lydia's shoulders, lifting her up, when the boys placed the stretcher on the floor beside her. "Let me do that for you, sir," one of them said, replacing his hands with younger, stronger ones.

Nick stood, backed away, and let the two young men take over. His muscles neared failure and were twitching. He barely had enough strength to control his body. He backed to the wall next to the small utility closet that'd held Lydia prisoner and leaned against it. He saw Shandahar loaded onto a stretcher. He whispered aloud toward the unconscious boy, "Thank you." And then his knees began giving way. He slid down the wall to land hard on his butt.

"Nick, are you okay?" Trish asked.

He saw and heard her plainly, but her voice seemed to echo in reverberation. His body was shutting down. Fatigue finally won out.

***

Nick woke on his back. When his eyes opened, he saw a single, circular fluorescent light overhead. At first panicked, not knowing where he was, he lay motionless. He tensed instinctively while attempting to determine time, place, and situation.

He was on a soft surface. That's all he could be certain of. He moved his eyes and then his head, slowly, trying to determine where he might be. He noticed he was not the only one in the room. There were others – all lying on the flat of their backs, like him.

With lightning speed, everything came back to him. He let his head fall to the left and saw that he was on a gurney. Lydia lay next to him with an IV needle in her arm, attached to a bag on a stand over her. Benjamin lay one over from her. He assumed Lydia was unconscious from loss of fluid, but he thought Benjamin might have been sedated.

He turned his head the other way, toward the front of the room. Lying some distance away was Bobby, the young boy that had leapt up onto the stage to join the fight. The doctor and two women in uniform were working on him. All three wore rubber gloves and surgical masks. The doctor's hands were blood-streaked. Nick watched him for a moment. The gloved hand, holding a pair of forceps, disappeared into a cavity in the boy's abdomen and back out. The forceps went back in and came up empty again. The doctor was likely attempting to remove a bullet and get bleeding under control.

On a large, stainless-steel table near the back of the room were sheet-wrapped bodies. He counted fourteen – terrorists and those hostages unlucky enough to be chosen for execution. He noticed the cowboy boots of one protruding from beneath a sheet. He then saw a pudgy arm covered in curly red hair and freckles that had slipped from under another sheet. Everyone else was totally concealed within white, starched cocoons, some with large bloodstains.

He lifted his upper body and leaned back onto his elbows. He then heard a moan and looked back at Benjamin, but it had not come from the old man. Shandahar was on the gurney next to Benny and apparently had regained partial consciousness. The boy's head fell rhythmically side to side.

Nick saw that the room was roughly the same size as the planning room in which he and Trish had holed up for a time. He looked beyond his toes and saw a few chairs scattered against the wall. Trish was sprawled in one of them, dozing. Her legs were straight out in front and crossed at the ankles, arms folded over her breasts, chin slumped onto her chest. She looked peaceful, breathing deep and even. Behind him was a long counter with cabinets above it, the countertop lined with medical supplies – bandages, disposable hypodermic needles, various salves, ointments, and bottled medicines. At the end of this arrangement was a series of four long but narrow doors, possibly pantry-like supply closets.

Suddenly, the monotonous beep of a heart monitor went constant. "No, damn it! No!" the doctor said in that Spanish accent. Even though a mask covered his mouth and nose, it was clear that the words came from between clenched teeth.

"Paddles," he ordered.

A cart with a defibrillator on it was hurriedly shoved to within arms' reach of the doctor. One of the women held two paddles out to him. He grabbed them. She squirted gel onto one. He smeared them together.

"Power up."

The machine beeped an alarm.

"Clear!"

He placed the paddles strategically and pressed the button. The boy's body arched then fell back. No one moved.

Nick saw no blips on the trailing screen of the heart monitor. It did not waver, tone constant.

"Again!" the doctor said.

Paddles in place, he punched the button. The boy's body convulsed a second time and then collapsed. Nothing changed. The boy was dead.

A lump swelled to the size of a golf ball in Nick's throat. Only exhaustion prevented a free flow of tears. The mother's words suddenly rang true. *It is my fault, just like she said.* He offered the doctor an unseen nod of admiration. Sickbay was not equipped to handle such intricate surgery. He felt drained all over again and fell back.

Trish came up on his blind side and slipped her hand into his.

"I know what you're thinking. I heard what the boy's mother told you. Forget that. It's not your fault."

Nick nodded but couldn't get a word out, choking when he tried. Technically it was not his fault, but emotionally, he'd have to live with the fact that it was his order that drew the boy into the conflict.

Trish placed her palms on both sides of his face and pulled it around to meet hers. "Don't do this, Nick. Don't let it eat you up."

He was in no mood to be counseled. He yanked his face from her grasp. He sat up and turned away from the boy and those gathered around the body. Trish was right. Guilt consumed him. He couldn't seem to get his mind elevated to a different plane. He attempted diverting his attention elsewhere.

"How's your head?" he asked.

"The doctor gave me a shot of some kind. I'm feeling no pain – just a little loopy, that's all." She pounded a fist into her open palm. "How can so few thugs cause so much damage and hold so many hostages?"

"That's the nature of fear," he said, staring at his dangling feet off the side of the gurney. "Those men knew that and fed on it. It drew the life force from everyone held captive in that auditorium. If it had only been one man, it would've still worked, for a time. Fear has saved many over the course of human history, but it has claimed countless lives, too."

He finally looked sideways at her sitting beside him on the gurney. "How did you manage to keep from collapsing from exhaustion?"

"Have you forgotten that I'm agoraphobic, Doctor Brandon? In that auditorium, I was wound tighter than a dollar pocket watch. I couldn't faint if I wanted to. I was thankful when you did, though."

"What do you mean by that?"

"Oh, nothing bad... really; I just meant that when you fainted it took my mind off my own problems."

"You must be a master at hiding it," he said. "I don't remember noticing that the crowd bothered you."

"It did."

"You waited until we were all in sickbay to crash?"

"That's pretty much it."

Romantic feelings began to simmer. He looked away and tried to ignore them, realizing they'd soon have to rejoin the real world – he with his marital problem in limbo, and Trish desperately needing a job without being dogged by agoraphobia. He still wanted to know her better, but doing so now without falling in love would be unlikely. To keep a cool yet respectful distance was the only solution. He had to return to a patient/doctor relationship, but he wondered if that would be possible now. Referring her to another therapist would be the responsible thing to do. He'd been handed the key to paradise and was now forbidden to use it. Even friendship with this magnificent creature had been rendered unworkable – and would never have been enough, anyhow.

As he thought on the dilemma, he stole glances, absorbing her appearance: dark auburn hair spiked on top, accentuating that bang sweeping across her left eye. She looked so young. Her long neck ended at lean yet muscular shoulders. His view of her was close – too close. The scent of her skin found his nose and, as if pulled into a riptide, he was drawn uncontrollably.

She turned to meet his advance, willing and ready.

He kissed her. Then, just as abruptly, jerked away.

"What the hell am I doing?" he blurted.

"You're doing what I hoped you'd do." She stroked his thigh.

"Trish, I can't." He lifted her hand away from his leg. "This isn't right. I have a wife and a daughter to consider." As he said it, his daughter's hateful opinion of her stepmother echoed. It seemed to offer a tailor-made excuse to allow guilt-free exoneration. Alli would like Trish. It was far too easy to see his daughter and Trish becoming fast friends. But that notion could not be allowed to take root. He had to deal with Evie before any decision like that could be made, and it was not for Trish's ears – and certainly was not Alli's decision to make.

A bland expression, accompanied by sad eyes, descended over Trish's face.

"I understand." She straightened and scooted a few inches away.

"I'm sorry, Trish. You're wonderful beyond words, but I made a wedding vow that needs to be heeded. I don't know if my marriage is salvageable, but I have to try."

"You're not a quitter," she said. She dropped her eyes to the floor as she wiggled her toes in her sandals. "I've seen that part of you; it's one reason you're so appealing. It was stupid of me to think–"

"Trish, if I thought –"

She put her hand over his mouth. "You don't need to explain. We are who we are…" She slid off the gurney, "…and that's the hell of it. But I refuse to regret the time we had."

He smiled. "No regrets?"

"Not one."

"Me neither," he said.

She walked back to her chair and sat.

Nick fell back on the gurney. It didn't take much to exhaust him all over again. He didn't want to move. He didn't even want to think, but that was an idle wish; his mind was in overdrive, and he couldn't stop all the swirling, interconnected thoughts flying around in his head.

He looked over at Lydia. She seemed peaceful, as if taking a nap. Her face was knotted and bruised, just as his and Trish's were. All four bore the marks of battle, and they'd survived. A rush of thankfulness for that blessing warmed him.

He then wondered what Lydia had to endure while he and Trish were off on an adventure. Then it occurred to him that she had faced her ultimate enemy, claustrophobia – squeezed into that tiny space and left alone? He wondered if therapy would have to begin anew.

He shifted attention to Benjamin. *And you; what happened to you? How'd you get that broken arm?*

He heard whispers and the rustle of a sheet behind him. The young female medical assistants and the doctor swaddled the dead boy to join those that had not survived. The lad was just another body to be thrown upon a pile.

The boy's name was Bobby. That's all he knew. He didn't even know his last name. The sight of that courageous young man sprawled and bleeding on stage was burned into his memory, and that's where it would stay for the rest of his life. He was sure of that.

He continued to lie on his side, curled, knees drawn up, hoping the debilitating thoughts that sucked his energy would go away and leave him be. He was tired of fighting terrorists and guilt.

The doctor's English seemed to worsen as he tired. He told his assistants, "Watch these people and page me if anything changes. I'm going to the Captain's quarters and treat his hand." He then mumbled something in Spanish as he stepped toward the door. The tone rang of sorrow – or regret, maybe.

Before the doctor left, an armed Navy SEAL came through the door of sickbay.

"How are things in here, Doctor?"

Nick raised his head when he heard movement on crisp sheets and noticed Shandahar regaining consciousness.

The doctor told the American service man, "We lost the boy, but everyone else is stable."

"They can rest easy," the young man in uniform told him. He nodded toward Shandahar. "Including this young one, we've accounted for all eight of the terrorists."

Shandahar became agitated at the pronouncement. Nick noticed a change in the boy's moan, but neither the SEAL nor the doctor seemed to care; they continued conversing right over the top of Shandahar's gurney. Nick sat up and slid off the edge of his rolling bed. He moved past Lydia's head then Benjamin's to stand at Shandahar's head.

The doctor and the SEAL stopped talking.

"What is it?" the doctor asked. "What are you looking at?"

Nick stroked Shandahar's cheek. "He's trying to tell us something."

Within a series of moans, the boy managed the word, "One".

"What do you think he's trying to say?" the SEAL asked.

Nick shrugged. "I don't know." He turned his attention back to the boy. "Shandahar, can you hear me?" He waited for a response but couldn't be sure if the boy understood. "What did you mean by 'one'? One what?"

Shandahar's eyes opened, but it was obvious he couldn't focus. From behind his head, Nick leaned over, held the boy's face upright, and looked down at him. The young man's eyes floated, unfocused and lazy, almost independent of one another. Though weakened by blood loss, the boy apparently retained enough presence of mind to comprehend what was said. His eyes finally stabilized on Nick. After swallowing, he spoke.

"There were nine, not eight."

CHAPTER 31

The young Navy SEAL stood stiff and tall in a black knit cap and vest over a black t-shirt and pants. Muscles stretched the tight-T and flexed in bulging lumps each time he moved. Had new perils been less of an issue, Nick could have been jealous of such strength and youthfulness. He was tired and wrung out, and he ached all over.

It wasn't necessary to tell the young professional anything. The message was clear. Once Shandahar's warning was out about a ninth man unaccounted for, the military man went into action. He grasped the semi-automatic rifle dangling from a strap around his neck and tossed it over his shoulder. A tiny microphone, at the end of a thin coaxial rod that had been pushed up and away from his face, he now pulled down close to his mouth. He pressed against the ear-bud and spoke into the mike.

"Team Leader, this is Devlin." He waited for a reply that didn't come. "Team Leader, this is Devlin in sickbay." He paused briefly again and then, "Urgent message, please respond." The young man's face constricted with growing concern.

Surely, Team Leader hadn't disabled his communication device this soon. Or did he? Nick's nervousness kicked up a notch, but it was just that fight-or-flight response that had become so well honed in the past few hours. He relaxed. This time, it wasn't his concern – a mop-up job for the SEALs. He and his injured companions were now safe.

"Team Leader, a threat exists. I repeat: A threat exists. Do you copy?"

"I must get to the Captain's quarters immediately," the doctor told Nick. "Blood loss from his severed thumb could become critical if left unattended much longer. Attempting to save that boy delayed me too long already."

"My name is Doctor Nick Brandon. I'm a clinical psychologist and not well-qualified, but if you take one of the medical assistants and leave one with me, the two of us can watch over the patients here."

The Navy SEAL began to move, then stopped mid-step. His tight face eased. He nodded in a show of support for Nick's quick offer to assist and then again pressed the ear bud. An easy smile stretched his lips, and he wiggled a thumb up, indicating that he finally had received a response coming through his ear-piece.

"That's right," the service man said into the tiny microphone at the corner of his mouth, "there is a continued threat, Team Leader. I have just been informed that our count was incorrect. There were a total of nine intruders, not eight. I repeat: Nine... not eight. One wolf is on the prowl. Do you copy?"

He stood silent for a moment as information fed into his ear. "Roger that, Team Leader." He pushed the microphone up and out of the way then turned his attention back to the doctor and Nick. "I've been ordered to rejoin the team to formulate a search."

"I must get to the Captain's quarters," the doctor told him.

"I'll escort you on the way to join my unit."

The serviceman turned and hurried to the door. The doctor followed closely, but hesitated at the threshold. He snatched up a short, steel pin dangling at the end of a small chain affixed to the wall beside the door, and pointed it at Nick. "Doctor Brandon, once we are out, shut the metal clasp on the door and drop this into its receiver. It'll be locked from the inside and keep you safe. It was intended for quarantine situations; I think this circumstance qualifies."

Nick flicked the 'okay' sign just as the two went on through and closed the door behind them.

Suddenly, it was quiet. "Well," Trish said, "here we go again."

He sauntered over and dropped the locking pin into the hole on the door's latch designed to take it.

"Yeah," he said looking around, hands resting on his hips. "I wonder if we need to find something to use as a weapon." Although the thought was out there, he didn't seriously expect to look for one.

Trish moved to the foot of Lydia's gurney and gently stroked her new friend's bare feet, which protruded from beneath a light blanket.

"I can't see a reason we'd need to." She looked at Nick with some alarm. "Do you?"

"This is a big ship; why would he single out sickbay as a destination? He should head for a place with more than one way in and one way out." He began walking down the row of four gurneys. "All we have here are three unconscious people, a number of dead ones, and, of course, you and me. We're no threat to anyone... except... maybe ourselves."

After a quick scan of the room, his eyes stopped at the air conditioning register that could not have been more than six by twelve inches near the floor. "Not even Harry Houdini could come in through that." He looked around again. "I bet if it weren't for that A/C duct, this room would be airtight. Even if the guy, for whatever reason, wanted in here, he couldn't make it happen. Oh, yeah, we're safe in here for sure." As he stepped to the head of Shandahar's gurney, he froze as a possibility struck him.

Trish looked at his shocked expression and then to the unconscious boy.

"Since that's the son of the leader and the only other survivor, do you think this boy is reason enough for him to want in here?"

"I just had that very same thought."

"Well, what do you think?"

"Well, maybe we'd better be prepared just in case. Inaction would be the ol' head-in-the-sand approach." He opened one of the cabinets above the counter. "Besides, we've made it this far by assuming the worst and preparing. 'If it ain't broke, don't fix it', I always say. So far, fear and planning has served us well. Besides, I'd just feel better with something sharp in my hands."

Until now, he'd paid little attention to the young medical assistant left to help him with the patients. He glimpsed the alarm on her face as she stood in the far corner of the room near the door, wringing her hands.

He closed the cabinet door and approached her. "I've never been known for great manners. I just now realized I haven't introduced myself."

"My name is Bonnie Sondervik. Do you think we – we're in danger?" she asked in an accent that Nick could not quite place. She was young, with no outstanding features. Her hair was washed-out blonde, fine-textured, and cut in a short, wedge style. A smattering of light-colored freckles covered her entire face. She was pasty pale, and although short and chunky, she had a cute, youth-inspired freshness about her. She stopped mauling her hands, but they trembled.

Nick reached for them, clasping them together between his.

"Danger? Nah. Not if we stay calm and stay together, hon; I think the danger will remain somewhere out there." He flicked his chin toward the door. "Trish and I were simply discussing a worst-case scenario. The actual chance of it happening has to be infinitesimal." He patted her hand. "Where're you from?"

She relaxed. "I'm from a small farming community about thirty-five kilometers south of Pretoria, South Africa…"

"Ah, an Afrikaner."

"Her head bobbled shyly. "Yeah… Afrikaner. Employment on the Ocean Dancer is my first time away from home. I'll turn nineteen in a couple of months and plan on going home and enrolling at the university next semester. I thought a six-month employment commitment would make a nice adventure before I have to get back to the books. But I never expected anything quite this dramatic."

"I said the same thing not long ago." His lip curled in a half-grin. "It has been some adventure; hasn't it? Try not to worry; okay?"

He winked at her and patted her hand between his. Still clutching it, he looked around and noticed Lydia's intravenous drip running low. Bonnie needed to be kept busy to keep her imagination under control.

"Why don't you give her another bag of electrolytes? She's trying to move. If we keep her hydrated, she may regain consciousness soon." He began to walk away then glanced back. "You *can* do that, can't you?"

"I'm not certified, but terrorists weren't supposed to be on this ship either." For the first time, she smiled, but it was weak and clearly anxiety-filled. "I've watched the doctor do it many times; I'm sure I can."

Nick returned her smile. "I'm sure you can, too." He developed an instant affection for the girl.

She had a mission and moved accordingly. "I'll get on it right now." The girl reached overhead into a cabinet, but then paused and looked back over her shoulder at him. "Thank you Doctor Brandon."

His smile broadened as he nodded. "When all this is over, would you share a carafe of coffee with me? I'd love to know more about life in South Africa, and what your hopes and plans are."

"And I'd love to tell you all about it."

He shook a finger at her. "Don't forget: You promised." His pleasant expression purposely lingered as he walked away.

Trish followed him and whispered in his ear, "Do you really believe what you told her... I mean about the danger staying somewhere out there?"

Nick presented her a bland face and answered with a quick shoulder shrug. He looked to the girl to make sure she hadn't seen his guarded lack of confidence. She still faced the cabinets, removing the packaging from an IV bag. Their luck had not been stellar, although complaining would be moot, since they were still alive. But there were situations, had they tipped ever so slightly another way, which could have become deadly. "Come on, Trish. Help me look for sharp things, just to have them within reach."

Nick walked directly to the blood-covered instruments used in that ineffective attempt to save a bullet-riddled teenager. All were strewn about in a tray next to the gurney that served as a makeshift operating table. He noisily shoved things around in the shallow, stainless-steel pan and snatched up a blood-streaked scalpel.

Trish rummaged through drawers and the cabinets above them behind the people on the gurneys. "Aha," she said.

"What'd you find?"

She held up a long, slender pair of scissors. "Not perfect, but I think I'd feel safer with this in my hand than that tiny little thing you're holding." She raised an eyebrow, nodding to the scalpel he held.

"Are you saying size matters?"

"Well... yeah," she said, as if it were the dumbest question she'd ever heard.

The young medical assistant blushed. "I hope you two are still talking about sharp objects."

Trish grinned and replied, "It's fine if you wish to believe that, dear."

The girl snickered and turned to finish her assigned task of replacing Lydia's IV. "It would appear South African girls and American girls have quite a lot in common," she mumbled with intent to be heard, giggling.

"Okay, okay, enough chatter," Nick said. "Let's get our chore done before we party." He opened one of the overhead cabinets and began shoving boxes around and taking mental inventory while looking for other potential weapons.

"American?" Shandahar asked.

Nick turned to the boy. "Call me Nick, son. You can drop the generic label."

"It is possible the other survivor feels honor-bound to rescue me."

"You really think he'd try?"

"I think so, yes."

"If he did get you out of this room, where would he take you? There's nowhere to go."

"You are looking at it like an American; I'm sure he believes he has reached a point of no return and has no plans to survive. This could be his last chance at martyrdom."

"That doesn't do a damn thing to keep me calm," Trish said.

"I'm sorry," Shandahar said, "but I feel his goal is to have me at his side and kill as many Americans as possible before we are killed ourselves." He gagged on his own saliva and coughed. "You are in grave danger just by being this close to me."

"If that's true," Nick said, "the SEALs won't even consider this as a destination for the guy. Like Shandahar said, they're thinking like Americans and probably believe he's looking for an escape route, which wouldn't be down here in the bowels of the ship. Right now they're probably searching all routes leading topside."

The young medical assistant said nothing, but Nick glanced to see that her hands were again shaking.

"How does that change our plan?" Trish asked.

"I think my scalpel and your scissors leave us woefully under-protected."

"You're right about that." She opened the first of the three long, narrow doors beyond the end of the counter and cabinets, looking for more substantial weapons.

Nick stepped in behind her. "What's in there?"

"Towels and sheets."

Suddenly, a thump came from behind the next door.

Nick grabbed Trish's shoulder and pulled her around to face him. He put his finger to his lips then pointed to the next closed door and spoke of unrelated things in casual tones. "Yeah, no shortage of linens and towels here." As he spoke, he pointed to a blood-soaked mop, standing in the corner of the room near the stainless steel table holding the pile of corpses. "If we have to be confined, it's best to have plenty of clean sheets."

Trish tiptoed over and retrieved the mop, then hurried back. Nick took it from her and slipped the scalpel into his hip pocket. He reconsidered; against his rear-end might not be the best place for a seriously sharp instrument, should an altercation break out. He pulled it from his pocket and stepped between Shandahar's and Benjamin's gurneys. He slipped the razor-sharp instrument beneath the sheet that covered Benjamin.

"Without a good supply of clean sheets, we're no better than animals," he said, continuing trite rambling as he pointed to the recessed circular door latch, gesturing for Trish to open it.

He saw that Shandahar had struggled up onto his elbow and was watching them.

It may have been thickening tension that caused Benjamin to stir. He moaned.

The young South African girl receded to the far corner of the room near the door, the only exit.

Trish held a firm grip on the scissors.

"Yes sir, I remember running out of clean sheets at home once." He gave Trish the go-ahead sign with rapid finger flicks toward the latch.

Hand shaking, she stuck her index finger in the recess and lifted out the spring-loaded half-ring, preparing to turn it to release the bolt and open the door.

Nick took a deep breath, adding as calmly as possible, "And, believe you me, when you run out of clean sheets…" She yanked the door open, and a machine-gun-wielding pair of hands fell out at the ready. "...you're screwed!"

The gun swung to the voice.

Nick came down as hard as he could with the handle of the mop against the man's knuckles. The gun fell to the floor.

Again, Nick came down with the mop, but he was a millisecond too slow.

The lone terrorist grabbed the mop as he exited the narrow closet and clumsily danced Nick back across the room, slamming him into the wall. The guy jammed the wooden handle across Nick's throat and pressed.

Weakened from exhaustion, Nick didn't have enough strength to stave off the attack. His fight now had been reduced to regaining the ability to breathe. He gasped and gurgled as the mop handle pressed ever tighter into his neck.

Holding the scissors high with both hands, Trish lunged and stabbed the point into the man's shoulder with her full weight behind it. It was the shoulder holding the most leverage on the mop handle against Nick's throat.

The man shrieked and whirled around, dropping the mop as he did. He shoved Trish, and she stumbled into the opposite wall and banged her head.

Before Nick could react, the man scooped up the automatic weapon and spun back to face him, scissors dangling from the back of his right shoulder like a stuck bull in a Mexican bullfight. But that didn't slow him down.

Nick had no choice but to submit. He raised his hands high over his head and backed away. The terrorist, unshaven with dark circles under his eyes, appeared as though everything he did was perfunctory, expressionless. The man was tired and near his physical limit, too. He secured the butt of the gun into the crook of his arm and pointed it at Nick. It didn't take an analytical genius to see that an execution was on his mind.

Shandahar babbled something in Arabic in three short bursts. The tone carried the cadence of an order.

The light of comprehension suddenly clicked in the man's eyes, as if what Shandahar said made perfect sense. He lowered the gun and backed far enough away so that he could see everyone in the room with a simple eye-sweep.

Still down on the floor, Trish was nearest him. She pulled herself up onto one of the chairs. He spoke harshly to her, waving the muzzle of the gun back and forth in front of her face.

She shied her head to the side, away from the business end of the firearm, and then shrugged. She didn't understand what he wanted of her.

"He wants you to move farther away so he can watch everyone at the same time," Shandahar told her.

As she moved away, the man released the foot brake on Shandahar's gurney, then pulled the boy to the opposite end of the room to be near him.

With a quick and, obviously, thoughtless yank, he reached over his shoulder and pulled the scissors from his upper back. He grimaced then growled, sucking in a great volume of air, clamping his teeth together until the pain subsided. Blood soaked a widening area on the back of his clothing. He had crazy eyes and held the bloodied scissors in a position to stab, eyes fixed on Trish. He stalked her.

Nick, still holding his hands over his head, asked, "What did you tell him, Shandahar?"

"I told him that if he fired that gun, he'd have an American force down here quickly, and we weren't ready. Martyrdom wouldn't be ours by killing a couple of American Navy men and a few ill-equipped passengers."

"Quick thinking."

"Don't thank me. He could still kill your lady-friend with those scissors. See how he looks at her? He's angry. He is disgraced by allowing a woman to have such an advantage over him as she did."

Nick became impressed by the boy's role-playing. Shandahar maintained an angry face. He spoke English in short, choppy phrases when speaking to Nick, clearly hoping his compatriot would believe that he chastised, ordered, or in some other way spoke down to the American. "I don't know if there's anything I could tell him... to stop him, if he wants to do that. Your lives are worthless to him. He doesn't care how he kills you, as long as he does it in a glorious way before going to be with God."

On that admonition, Trish shuddered. She sank down onto a chair as the man came to hover over her. She held her arms close together and poked her hands between her thighs crossing her legs. She cast her eyes to the floor, displaying subservient fear in response to the man's intimidating stance. She employed everything that crossed her mind to become small and insignificant.

The man pressed his lips tight, stabbed the air a couple of times with the scissors then bellowed, "Ahh!" He threw the scissors on the floor and kicked them away behind him. Maybe it was the pain in his shoulder or a glimmer of humanity that flickered, but he gave up on the idea and backed away, teetering slightly, to the stainless steel table where corpses were stacked like firewood. Loss of blood may have begun taking a toll. The red patch on his back now covered the entire right side of his upper body. He sat on the corner of the steel table, holding the machine gun ready to fire, but seemed to be taking a moment to clear his head.

"American…" Shandahar said, "I mean… Nick, if I survive long enough to be put in prison, do you think it would be close to you?"

Nick lowered his arms. "Taking into account all you've done, I might have some pull because of your condition. It is my specialty, after all."

"What condition do you speak of?"

"Shandahar, you've had a phobia beaten into you… literally."

"I don't understand."

"Has it never occurred to you why your mood, your attitude, your demeanor… everything that makes you who you are, changes dramatically when someone threatens to strike you?"

"I just thought I felt guilty for disrespectful thoughts about my father."

Nick smiled. "No, son, you have a medically verifiable condition called rhabdophobia – a rather severe case of it. My hope is that it's mostly tied to your father. If so, his absence may be more of a blessing than you can imagine at the moment. He was the source of your fear; you confronted it head-on and disposed of it… in the most literal way imaginable. That might mean a faster-than-normal cure. But I mean that in a clinical sense; it'll still take time to work through it. It'd be my profound pleasure to serve as your personal therapist.

When the time comes, I'll speak to the prosecutor and the presiding judge on your behalf."

The man no longer sat quietly. He stood and stepped forward. He said something Nick couldn't understand. As he moved, he listed sideways. He batted his eyelids and stretched his facial muscles. He was becoming lightheaded and rested his shoulder against the wall for a moment.

"He wants us to stop speaking," Shandahar said. "I'm letting my guard down and speaking in tones he does not trust."

Nick looked back at the guy, held up his arms in the I-surrender-pose, and nodded. He then backed into the opposite wall and leaned against it, crossing his arms over his chest. He prepared to wait it out and see what came next.

The intercom near the door broke squelch, and a tinny voice said, "Sickbay?" It was quiet for a few seconds.

"What do you think Shandahar? Do I answer it?"

The boy said something to the man, who was becoming increasingly irritable.

"I told him we must allow you to answer or raise suspicion. Be warned that although he doesn't speak English, he'll know you're conveying a message of another sort if you say more than a few words."

Again squelch broke on the intercom as Nick cautiously approached the speaker recessed into the wall near the door, all the while glancing to the armed man behind him. "Doctor Brandon, this is Petty Officer Devlin. Our search is continuing with no luck. I thought I'd check to make sure things are okay down there."

Nick held his finger to the talk button for a moment, trying to put together the right words. He finally nodded as if everything were fine and pressed the button, saying only, "The wolf is with us. Door locked from the inside." He continued nodding all the time he spoke, then released the button.

It was quiet for a moment, then a static-laced click was followed by, "Roger that."

Nick turned to the gun-toting man and employed body language designed to seek acceptance with a humble chin dip. He returned to his position, leaning against the wall a few feet from the head of Benjamin's gurney, the last in a row of them.

He finally looked away from his captor to Trish. He saw questions in her eyes. She wanted to know what was on his mind. He had no way to convey that he had no plan, other than to wait.

As he thought on the wisdom of doing nothing more than waiting, it occurred to him that with the door locked it'd take vital seconds for a SEAL team to get in. Trapped inside with this lunatic could be a lifetime in the most literal use of the word. Possessing no concern whatsoever for the value of human life, he'd kill everyone before the SEAL team could breach the lock. If that should be his only shot at martyrdom, he'd take it.

Nick finally understood that unspoken question in Trish's eyes. The agitation in her changing facial expressions spoke a universal language that unnerved him even more.

She had not noticed that the man guarding them paid her particular attention.

Holding a warning stare on her, Nick finally went so far as to frown and offer a faint headshake. But the quizzical look it drew from her shifted the man's attention to him.

The young medical assistant, standing quietly in the far corner of the room near the door, seemed to understand that Nick wanted Trish to relax and quit looking suspicious. She had a good view of them both and their captor. Hand down to her side, she lifted only her fingertips and waved from the wrist at Trish. But, it caught their captor's eye first.

It happened just as he had reached the end of his patience with the unspoken conversation among the three hostages. He sprang to his feet and moved on Bonnie.

Shandahar said something to the man but was waved off as he made an abrupt and sharp response in Arabic. He teetered sideways before righting his stance and continuing on to Bonnie's corner.

"He knows something is not right. I'm afraid he's going to make an example to prevent any plotting. I can't stop him."

"Hey you!" Nick yelled.

As the man unsheathed a long slender knife with a curved blade, he glanced at Nick.

The girl stepped back against the wall and literally tried to walk up it backward. She began to cry.

"No, please!" Tears exploded from her eyes. She wailed. The closer he came, the louder she cried.

Nick suddenly saw a mind's-eye snapshot of that young athlete leaping up onto the stage to help, and where that had gotten him. He glanced at the body of the lad wrapped in a blood-streaked sheet – dead. "Oh, hell no!" he shouted and began to sprint.

Trish took out after the man, too. "Stop, you sonofabitch!"

The man responded to Trish's voice and whirled about, but he saw Nick first and fired a quick volley of four or five shots. One caught Nick in the side, and one high on his arm. He spun away.

Trish lunged for the gun.

Not fast enough.

The guy swung it into her ribs, lifting her off the floor. She stumbled backward and collapsed, moaning and trying to breathe, mouth agape. She cried without tears or sound, from intense pain.

Still holding the knife in one hand, the man released his hold on the machine gun with the other, allowing it to dangle from the strap around his neck.

Bonnie screamed.

With no show of emotion, he reached for the cowering girl's blonde hair and yanked her chin away from her chest. He slid the blade across her throat. Her scream didn't stop, but transformed from a shrill cry into a gurgling bloody gush of air from the severed trachea. Blood pumped in spurts. As her eyes rolled back, she slid down the wall.

"You ignorant savage!" Trish yelled in spasmodic fits through pain. She tried crawling to Bonnie.

The girl's legs and hands twitched as she slumped to the side.

The man casually walked past Trish, wiping blood from the blade on his pants, then pointed it at her threateningly while speaking to Shandahar. She saw there was nothing she could do for the girl and changed directions, dragging herself across the floor to Nick.

The murderer rattled something in Arabic to Shandahar.

The boy came up to rest on his elbow. "He wants me to tell you that the only escape you can expect is by the same route she took." He fell from his elbow and collapsed back on the gurney. "I'm sorry."

Not worried in the slightest what the assailant thought, Trish pulled herself to her feet at the counter and grabbed two fists full of gauze pads. She dropped down beside Nick, lifted his ripped shirt and pressed a wad of them against the side wound.

"I don't think my wounds are dangerous, just painful," Nick said, forcing the words.

"Maybe not now, but if we don't get the bleeding stopped they might get that way."

"Yeah… I guess so," he said taking more of the pads from her and shoving them under the top of his shirt to the wound high on his left shoulder.

The man forcefully waved a finger at Trish and pointed to the chair where she had been sitting.

It was obvious he weakened further; he sat on the floor next to Shandahar's gurney, clutching the machine gun with what appeared to be a grip of desperation.

Reluctantly, Trish pulled Nick's other hand down to hold the gauze against his side.

"Hold them tight." She looked at the gunman. "If he's as close to losing consciousness as he appears, he might shoot us simply because we're too close together… or to make sure we're dead before he goes out. I'd better get back to my chair."

She rolled over onto hands and knees. Her ribs had been brutally battered twice today, first across the back and now on one side. Pain was evident in every move she made. She struggled to simply stand.

As Nick pulled himself back toward the wall with one hand and fought to sit up, he wondered if that last blow had broken her ribs. That kick she took was hard; surely, one or two had to be cracked, at least.

Blood saturated the gauze pads he held over his wounds. During a few seconds that the pain was bearable, he looked to the girl. Blood ran from the fatal slit pooling beneath her head; her stare, wide and fixed, still bore a look of terror – fear she no longer felt. Her only crime was waving at Trish. Then his gaze went to the row of gurneys that held Lydia, Benjamin, and Shandahar. Finally, his eyes settled on Trish.

It might have been pain, exhaustion, mourning for Bonnie or a combination of them all; whatever it was had put tears in Trish's eyes.

He thumped his head against the wall behind him and squeezed his eyes shut. *Dear God, what next?*

CHAPTER 32

The intercom in sickbay clicked. A hollow hum and electronic crackling from the small speaker bolted to the wall sounded an open line, but a full second passed before a human voice came on and said, "N... 2... O."

Nick heard it plainly, then waited for clarification. It didn't come. After a second of static filled silence it clicked off. Nick didn't understand and glanced to Shandahar in time to see the boy respond to his compatriot, rolling his head to the side, looking down at him and shrugging his shoulders. He didn't understand either.

The expression of the injured man on the floor seemed to indicate he believed it to be a cryptic message. He blinked clarity back into his eyes and straightened his posture, despite weakness from blood loss from the stab wound in the shoulder.

Trish didn't look up. Her curiosity had already ended in one death – a good-intentioned South African girl, Bonnie Sondervik.

The man continued losing blood but could still scatter gunfire if he had to. He said something in a quick burst of Arabic. Shandahar translated it.

"He believes it's a coded message and thinks our time to act is running out."

Nick didn't offer body language that might indicate acknowledgement. He went about checking his wounds, both located on the right side, one bullet hole just above his love handle and another through the trapezium muscle, just missing the clavicle. Both holes were clean. The bleeding had almost stopped. This luck, like all the rest today, came in a backhanded way. It seemed he and his friends paid hefty prices to earn the good fortune of survival. It sure as hell didn't come served up on a silver tray. They had worked at it, and hard.

The man said something else to Shandahar. The boy looked down at him and nodded lazily. "He thinks that a plan needs to be made while his strength holds," he told Nick in terse fashion, disguising its true meaning. To add to the charade, he spat on the floor in Nick's direction.

Nick continued looking dejected, as if criticized. Although the hostage-taker didn't understand the message from the intercom, it was enough to prompt him into conversation with the Baruk boy. As they spoke, Nick thought on the symbols. *N2O... Where have I seen that before?* He suddenly remembered his last trip to the dentist's office, recalling the label on the tank near his chair. He'd been bored, sitting with gauze pads bulging one cheek, reading every chart, diploma, and label within limited view from his semi-reclined position. It occurred to him that that label was N2O-O2. The symbol spoken over the intercom was just the first part of that. *I'll be damned. They're going to flood this room with pure nitrous oxide.*

Sickbay's air conditioning register vent was located near the floor. It could have been the reason the rescuers decided to try it, hoping that he'd realize what was about to occur and take precautionary measures to move away from it. The duct happened to be nearer the gunman than Trish and only about three inches off the floor. Pure nitrous oxide could be lethal in large doses. Heavier than air, it tended to pool at the lowest point in an enclosed space, as sickbay was. Preparation had to take that into account. He had to assume the rescuers only guessed at how much to pipe through the system.

Although farther away, he, too, was on the floor like his captor. He had to get his head as far from the floor as possible. Trish already stood, but hunkered over, holding her injured ribs and leaning against the wall.

"Shandahar?"

The boy interrupted his conversation with the man. "What?"

"Ask him if it'd be okay to have Trish help me up on to that empty gurney."

Shandahar relayed the message. The man looked first at Nick then to Trish. It was plain he didn't see it as a threat, given Nick's injuries. He nodded then tossed a finger from Trish to Nick, giving his okay.

"Tell him thank you, Shandahar." He began maneuvering into position to get on his feet with as little pain as possible. He waved Trish over. "Give me a hand, would ya?"

The man resumed talking to Shandahar but watched Trish, his disdain for her clear in those squinty eyes. He would not be forgetting that it was she who had buried a pair of scissors in his back. If the thug lashed out in a lethal way, it'd surely be directed at her first.

As soon as she laid hands on him she said, "I'm not going to be much help. I think I have a couple of broken ribs. I can barely lift my arms, much less a grown man."

"Doesn't matter; hush and listen. They're going to flood this room with nitrous oxide."

"Nitrous oxide?"

"Laughing gas. But it could be dangerous. When you walk away, go back toward the young girl and pretend to pray over her."

Trish looked to the body of Bonnie Sondervik. "I won't be pretending."

Nick offered a respectful nod on that comment. He, too, missed the girl, a person he hadn't even gotten the chance to know. "When you get there, stay put. Don't come back in this direction." He struggled up onto the gurney and lay down, hoping it'd be high enough that he'd still be conscious after the gunman succumbed to the gas.

Trish shuffled toward the lifeless body.

The man berated her in his language.

"Shandahar, tell him she's just going to pray for the girl's soul. Surely, he can understand that."

After the boy had told him, the gunman settled and let the automatic weapon fall back into his lap.

Nick continued looking around, wondering if there were other ways to improve their chances. In these circumstances, this was as good as it could be. Then he caught a whiff of a sweet smell in the air. He lay flat on his back and purposely began breathing shallow.

A minute, maybe two, passed. Nick heard a commotion. The gunman had begun reacting to the gas. The guy rolled his head around, looking at things only he could see. He spoke in casual tones, as if describing something, most likely hallucinating. Blood loss sped up and intensified the effects of the gas on him.

Trish seemed normal, still facing away, standing over the body. Then he noticed that she slowly pulled the tail of her knit tank top up to cover her mouth and nose. Nick felt a sudden euphoric rush, and the pain of his wounds vanished. He raised his injured shoulder and stretched sideways. He felt only a minor twinge from two bullet holes, no real discomfort at all. *Man, that gas is some good shit.* He became giddy at his Tommy-Chong-style humor.

"Whass happenin' ta me?" Shandahar asked. "I...I'm floating."

"Don't worry, son," Nick said, "I promise everything will be okay... hunky dory... peachy keen." He snickered.

Everything will be okay... okay... okay. Nick's mind wandered. *Everything will be okie dokie. There's no place like home. I want to go home, Toto. It's time to click my heels together.* He snickered again.

The gunman wilted over onto his side, mostly out.

Nick saw the man wallow in a semiconscious state. He found it amusing and grinned. "See what happens when you're a bad boy and behave like the crap-for-brains you are?" He chuckled.

"I feel strange," Shandahar said. "Am I dying?"

"No," Nick said. "You're just flying high on some good gas. So am I." Then it occurred to him they needed to let the rescuers know to stop it or risk killing them all. "The door, Trish. Unlock the door." *The door... da door... door me no more.* The word became hilarious. He couldn't prevent ridiculous thoughts. He held the bullet wound on his side and laughed.

Trish pulled the pin and yanked the handle. Even before she could retract her hand, it flung open, and two of the SEAL team rescuers wearing gas masks rushed in, taking sentinel positions on each side of the door. Two more masked team members rushed in between them, heading straight for the terrorist on his side. They disarmed him and cuffed his wrists.

Nick let his head fall back onto the flat pillow on the gurney. "I've had a helluva day, boys. Even my nap was interrupted." He stifled a snicker, blowing slobber from between clenched lips.

Trish frowned and then clucked her tongue, slowly shaking her head. "You're a rambling mess, Nick Brandon." She looked thoughtfully at him for a moment lying on the gurney. "Are you going to remember what you're saying? I bet not."

"If it's not one thing it's another," he said, flailing his arms. He laughed as they escorted Trish out the door and followed her closely with a train of gurneys into the hall.

Trish slowed her pace and allowed Nick's gurney to catch up. She patted his shoulder. "Even gassed, I can't believe everything is so funny to you. How can you be happy?"

"Happy? Who? Where?" He rolled his head back and forth, searching. "Bring 'em over here and I'll slap the smile right off their face. Can't they see we're in some really deep caca?" He paused and frowned. "Wait a minute. The deep doo-doo is being wheeled out ahead of me with a stab wound in his back." He snorted, stifling a laugh. "Nothing left here but the stink." He fanned his nose. "Whew." He blew spit from between pursed lips, only pretending to stifle a laugh. Then he abruptly dropped the happy look. He grabbed her wrist and took on a sudden seriousness. "It is over, isn't it?"

Trish plainly thought about that and it relaxed her. "Yeah… this time I think it really is."

Nick lifted his head high enough to see one of the SEALs push a gurney with the last terrorist on it, the final threat. As he watched, he said, "I've had all the rest and relaxation I can stand. Let's go home."

CHAPTER 33

Standing on the steps at the main entrance of Galveston's John Sealey Hospital, Nick basked in the comforting warmth of this late spring day with his daughter Alli. No more frigid air conditioning ducts or fear-induced chills. Semi-tropical humidity filtered the sun's rays; still, cotton-ball clouds pushed racing shadows over the ground. He turned a three-sixty while drawing a breath of the muggy air; the joy of simply being alive and capable of enjoying such pleasures filled him. Freedom to live as he saw fit put a delicious smell in the heavy Galveston air. He smiled, aware of how lucky he was and hoping he never lost that gratitude. There's no greater reason to refocus one's life than almost losing it.

"What the heck are you doin'?" Alli asked.

"Just takin' time to smell the roses, kiddo."

"What roses?" Her eyebrows went up over a mock look of ignorance.

"You know what I mean." With a sweeping arm gesture, he added, "Magnificent day, isn't it?"

"Careful," she said. "You don't want to make those wounds start bleeding again." Her face went bland. She shuddered then squeezed her eyes shut.

"What?"

"I just had a flash image of something I never want to imagine again. Dad, I almost lost you, too. I'm not emotionally equipped to be without Mom *and* you. I'm far too young to be thrown into this world alone."

Nick wrapped her up into an embrace. "You're a lot stronger than you think you are. I've seen many teenagers with psychological hang-ups, some severe. Believe me, you're nowhere near any of them. Your constitution is strong. You, kid, are disgustingly normal – a run-of-the-mill teenager to the bone."

She slapped him on the back. "Oh hush."

"Give yourself some credit. Seriously, you could handle a whole lot more than you think."

With arms still wrapped around him, she gathered two fists full of shirt at his back, refusing to let him out of the embrace.

"I'm having trouble believing that. Forgive me for being cynical." She pulled her face away from his chest and looked up at him. "Cynical? Is that the right word?"

He peeled her arms off and stepped back, but did not release her hands.

"Yeah, but it's misplaced, because I know normal, and you're it. Trust me." He kissed her on the forehead. "Come on," he said turning and pulling her along, "Let's get up to Benny's room. They'll be discharging him soon. I want to be there to fulfill my promise to drive him home."

"Benny, huh? Sounds chummy."

"Not just him... all three of them; it's amazing how close we've become. Lydia and Trish have earned my respect and lifetime friendship, too. Those three are the most courageous people I've ever met, and in more ways than you can imagine. Each one of them went toe-to-toe with their worst fears on that cruise. Then, when the chips were down, each of them was willing to give their life for the other. That's a bond you don't often see, especially among people who were only acquaintances until then."

A devious smile came upon Alli's face. "So... you like all three equally, huh?" She lifted an eyebrow. "I saw the fireworks in that tiny little space between your face and that Trish chick when y'all parted at the docks last week. I thought I'd have to call in the Jaws of Life to pry you two apart." With an easy laugh and bouncing eyebrows, she continued, "Evie noticed, too. I had the pleasure of watching the witch's reaction."

"Hey, don't call your stepmother a witch." He paused. "Seriously, was I that obvious?"

"Duh."

"It's a complicated issue... Trish and me, but it's not something I'll be sharing with you anytime soon."

"Ooh, that sounds wonderfully scandalous."

"Maybe someday I'll tell you about it, but not today. I have loads of work to do repairing a faltering marriage – that is, as soon as I figure out what caused the stumble in the first place. I owe it to Evie to try. Love brought us together in the beginning; maybe it can bring us back together now."

"Gross. You should just dump her."

Nick raised a disciplinary finger but had no chance to speak. Alli threw both hands into the air, quickly adding, "But whatever...I won't say any more."

She whirled around and pranced playfully toward the hospital's automatic sliding doors, then mumbled in a voice to be heard, "But that Trish is pretty hot." She blew a breathy whistle.

You got that right, kid. Nick cast a crooked grin as he followed her through the doors and said no more. It was time to just let that subject go dormant, before Alli began making sense.

Trish happened to be only one reason, but a huge one, that he had so much trouble keeping his mind on his job once he returned to work. Many times a day he lost concentration, becoming entranced by compelling thoughts of her that just would not go away. His mind's eye was 20/20. And now, as he walked through the hospital reception area, there she stood in his imagination once again, offering up a distracting, romantic, rosy blur, like a black hole for every other thought.

He held the elevator for an elderly woman with a walker. Alli followed the old woman in. Nick fell in behind. He punched the number requested by the older woman and then the number of the floor where he knew Benjamin's room to be located.

All the while, clear thoughts of Trish randomly flashed. He couldn't prevent what had to have been a goofy smile.

As the elevator traveled up, Alli glanced to him, did a double-take, and stared. "You're thinking about her, aren't you?"

"None of your business." He kept right on smiling.

"Right," she said, drawing out the word. "What room is your friend in?"

He rolled his eyes and dropped an arm over her shoulder.

She nuzzled her cheek into his arm.

The smile for Trish metamorphosed into a frown; it disturbed him that he couldn't seem to force his thoughts over onto Evie. It actually took conjured images of Alli's mother Julia, Alli herself, or even problems with patients to pull his head away from the well-traveled rut in his brain that Trish had carved.

It had become impossible to continue on as Trish Campbell's therapist, but he struggled with following through and making that happen. He couldn't take the initiative and arrange another therapist to take over, all the while knowing it would be the proper and professional thing to do. A selfish streak burned through him. He procrastinated, wanting to reserve it for a time that he could tell her in person, just to be near her one last time. But was he emotionally equipped to resist her if he went to see her? Ethical questions were too easily brushed aside. No better example of "Damned if you do and damned if you don't" had ever existed for Nick.

He walked down the long hospital corridor with Alli at his side, past the nurses' station, until Benjamin's room appeared on the right. The door was open. Nick knocked, but only in passing, as he walked on in. "Hello?"

"Doctor Brandon," came the cheerful voice of Benjamin as he and Alli rounded the blind corner created by the bathroom. The old guy sat on the edge of the bed, buttoning his shirt with one hand.

Lydia sprang up and approached Nick from the only chair in a corner across the room. Without hesitation, she threw her arms around him and hugged him, then kissed him on the cheek. "It's so good to see you again. You're our anchor, ya know that? How're the bullet wounds?"

"Almost healed; they were clean. How about you?"

"Just mild heatstroke, no long-term damage; once I rehydrated and the mineral loss had been replaced, I was good as gold and sassy as ever." She massaged her ribs. "But I'm still sore where that guy kicked me."

"You know, Nick, you didn't have to go through all this trouble just to get me home," Benjamin said. "Lydia and I had already talked about hiring a shuttle."

"What trouble? Y'all are my friends. This is a treat, not trouble."

An awkward silence followed. Alli elbowed him in the ribs.

"Oh, I'm sorry, I haven't introduced my daughter. This is Alexandra. She goes by Alli."

Lydia didn't hesitate to hug her either. "You guys are like family. It's good to meet you, hon."

"You, too, Lydia. Wow, I suppose there's no better way to bond with people than to almost die with them."

Walking stiff and slow, his arm in a sling, Benjamin placed a finger on the side of his nose and said, "Somehow, Miss Brandon, I have a strong feeling our friendship would have grown strong even without such a fateful encounter." He winked. "Just not quite as fast."

Lydia moved to Benjamin's side. "Friendship is a good word, but Benny and I have much more than that." She rubbed circles on his back as she held a long gaze into his eyes. "Our future is together."

"Yes, quite true," Benjamin said. "I already had a good friend in Carol Rourke, and a wonderful irreplaceable friend she is, too, but…" He kissed her lightly on the lips. "…Lydia is my love."

"I suppose we'd better get your things down to the car," Nick said, becoming uneasy with the starry-eyed romance in Lydia's eyes. He figured if they waited any longer, he might witness a moment that'd certainly be none of his business.

As Nick drove over the bay bridge, he heard Benjamin's breathing quicken. He glanced in the rearview mirror. "Are you okay Benny?"

Benjamin kept his eyes closed. "Let me answer by saying that I'd better not quit therapy anytime soon."

"You have a standing weekly appointment," Nick said, then smiled at his friend in the mirror. "And there'll never be another bill… not from me. You deserve at least that much." He paused. "And that goes for you, too, Lydia. There'll never be another fee for your therapy, either."

"I don't think I need it anymore."

"Seriously?"

"I think not. Something snapped inside me when I was locked up… but in a good way, a very good way. I had plenty of time to contemplate the reasons for my fear under the worst circumstances imaginable – the abusive stepfather and a suffocating marriage. The former began the problem forty years ago, and the latter perpetuated then built upon that claustrophobia. It became clear, sitting in the dark, sweltering confines of that storage locker, that I had to break with my past." She reached across the seat and patted Benjamin's leg. "That meant creating a new future. Doctor, I believe I can say, with ample confidence I might add, that I'm cured."

CHAPTER 34

Nick stood at the front door of his home, committed to reconciling with Evie, but questioned whether it was what he truly wanted. Alli's concern rang in his ears. *"Are you sure Evie is what you want, what you need?"* A simple question that carried more weight than Alli would ever know.

He arranged this day so there'd be no distractions and no excuses. Evie had argued against the discussion, but he'd insisted, and she finally acquiesced. This conversation was needed and carefully orchestrated to happen within the next few minutes; the future of their marriage depended on the truth coming out. But, now that the appointed time had arrived, thoughts began a not-so-merry dance in his head, calling into question the wisdom of leaving no out to postpone. His willpower to follow through wavered.

He had no clues as to how they'd conquer this marital problem, and he was rapidly becoming apprehensive to even try. This suddenly seemed about as hopeless as stopping a psychotic, arrogant, and narcissistic Lebanese thug from blowing a man's brains out in front of an audience in a packed cruise ship auditorium. *What am I afraid of – that the marriage will be saved, or that it will end?*

Alli had fought him on it.

"Let it die," she had said. "It wasn't much of a marriage anyway. Walk away and don't look back."

But, even as he had scolded her for saying it, she was more convincing than he would ever admit. He had been left wondering if the advice of a sixteen-year-old might be profound logic, or just sounded appealing for selfish reasons.

Still standing at his front door with his hand on the knob, he couldn't shake doubt. As pro-and-con thoughts layered, his will to fight for the marriage weakened further. *Maybe this marriage needs to be euthanized. Alli might be right.*

He sighed and stared a moment longer at the brass knocker on the front door to his home. His gaze shifted down to the key in his other hand. Inserting that key and turning it might well be equivalent to opening Pandora's Box.

If he hadn't bribed Alli with a substantial amount of shopping money to stay away from the house for the afternoon, she'd have certainly attempted sabotaging his efforts with Evie. She loved him so much she actually hesitated, but only for a second, before prancing off with a fistful of cash and a twinkle in her eye to go the mall with friends.

Finally, he slowly inserted the key, turning it and the knob at the same time. He then gently pushed the door open, not wanting to be heard until the last vestige of hesitation left him. Having made a career of treating phobia sufferers, here he stood, afraid of confronting a five-foot-three-inch, hundred-and-five-pound woman. It occurred to him he was on the verge of a panic attack. He had to remind himself of advice he'd given to others countless times: Fear doesn't come from the event, but the anticipation of it.

He stepped over the threshold, literally and symbolically. Standing in the foyer, he noticed how sterile and empty his home seemed, and despite warm late spring temperatures, it also felt chilled. He, again, struggled against hesitation.

Do what ya gotta do, man. Get on with it!

He began walking down the hall. As he did, the desire to get it over with strengthened fast. He picked up the pace.

As fresh determination swarmed him, he announced in a bold voice, "Evie, I'm home. It's time for that talk."

***

Sandy Campbell came into the room from the kitchen, holding a glass of wine with a limp wrist suspended from well-manicured fingertips. She watched Trish's back for a moment and then sat on the sofa, pulling one leg beneath her. The gaze at her sister took on more the air of a diagnostic examination. She sipped and smacked her lips before setting the glass on an end table.

"Hey sis, you've been staring out that window for almost an hour. Should I be worried? You've been acting strange since I picked you up at the docks in Galveston. Havin' bad flashbacks... nightmares... or something like that?"

Trish sighed. "Something like that." After a moment she faced Sandy. "I'm fine, really." Her eyes danced evasively in their sockets. She tossed her head around with a nervous smile and again turned her back to look out the window. "At least, I will be. I just need time to get past... well, time to sort through some issues."

"The least you could do is shower and change clothes. Jesus-H, girl, you've been wearing those sweat bottoms since yesterday, maybe longer. Since I'm your sister, I can say this: There's a little green, odorous cloud following you," she said, as if narrating an episode of Twilight Zone. " You're raunchy, girl. Get a grip, then get a shower." She dipped her head humbly. "Of course, I tell you this with love."

"I know," she replied blandly.

"Trish, you're starting to scare me. Any other time, you would've attacked me over a comment like that. What's wrong? Did those terrorists do more than you're telling? Are you traumatized? Did something happen that's so horrific you won't talk about it?"

"Yes, yes, and yes," she said looking across wooded Memorial Park from her sister's second floor apartment.

Sandy sprang off the sofa to her feet. "Crap! Were you raped?"

"No, nothing like that; just beaten, kicked, and mauled; I suppose that could be considered typical terrorist treatment. Damn if I know. The things that ruthless bunch did I can get past. I can deal with that stuff."

Sandy sat back down, retrieving her wine glass. "Then what is it?"

Trish said nothing.

"Come on. I'm your sister... family, from the same flesh and blood. If you can't talk to me, then who can you talk to? Doctor Brandon? Should I call him to discuss some other form of therapy for you?"

Trish whirled around. "You're not going to talk to Nick about anything, got it?"

"Nick? Not Doctor Brandon anymore?" She set her wine glass on the low table in front of her. Her jaw went slack, and her lips parted. "That's it. Isn't it? There's something between you and that doctor."

Trish stepped quickly to the sofa and sat on the opposite end from Sandy, staring.

"Spill it, Trish. I want to know everything."

Sandy saw the questions in Trish's unblinking expression. As her only sibling, she knew that Trish wondered how much to share. Everything? Nothing? It was clear she didn't know which way to go.

Sandy broke the silence. "I thought Doctor Brandon was married."

Trish's eyes finally fell away. "He is. I don't think you need to be terribly intuitive to figure out the rest of my problem from there."

"Well... maybe I can help you sort through it. What happened on that ship? I take it there was more than just being held captive, seeing people murdered, and the occasional spurt of bravado?"

Trish held a guarded pose, but eventually relaxed with a quick exhale. "Look, we were scared and alone together for a time. We were exhausted and not at all certain we'd survive. We... Nick and I... had a moment."

Sandy snapped stiff and straight. "Oh my God, you had sex with a married man?"

Trish sprang to her feet and hugged herself, offering tightly closed body language. "I knew it was a mistake talking to you about this!"

"No, no," Sandy said, reaching for Trish's elbow. She held on, then gently pulled her back down. "It just shocked me, that's all. It's not what I expected to hear. I thought you may have just been infatuated with him for his courage, his looks, and whatever else goes into the package that makes up Doctor Nicholas Brandon."

"Your tone made it sound like... like it was something tawdry. It wasn't that at all." Trish reluctantly returned to the sofa and sat. "Like I said, it was just a moment between us. The problem is, I can't let that moment go. I can't get past it. How often does a girl find a guy like that? One with a big caring heart, brave and intelligent, and... oh God...to look like he does, too... That man is the *total* total package."

"Then go after him."

Trish shook her head. "Humph! You're my sister, all right… never met a man she wouldn't stalk."

Sandy seductively tossed her shimmering blonde hair and licked her lips with a grin. She playfully slapped the air between them.

"Go on. You're such a flatterer." After a moment, she let the smile fade. "I'm serious. If he means that much to you, for Christ's sake, go after him."

"It's complicated. I can't."

"Hell, Trish, you've lived your whole life complicating things. It's time to simplify."

"You're going to make me explain every detail of this, aren't you?"

"Yep."

"Okay, here's the deal. Nick is married for sure, but the marriage is shaky. It was troubled before I entered the picture. It was my lust that caused the encounter on the ship. And, it was likely his tenuous marriage that caused him to give in… or it could have been that he didn't think he'd come off that ship alive, or it might have been exhaustion that prevented him from pushing me away. I don't know why it happened, but it did. And I'm glad it did!"

Sandy patted her knee. "Settle down, Trish, but keep talking." She scooted closer, retrieving her wine glass on the way, and postured as though listening to a deeply romantic audio book.

Trish looked to Sandy's wine. "I need one of those if I'm going to get through this."

"Be my guest," Sandy said gesturing toward the kitchen. "But don't stop the story. You've got me hooked. I'm into this."

Trish rose and began walking away but continued, "That's what made me think that this whole thing may be too complicated to pursue, because I instigated it, and the circumstances were extraordinary…" She glanced back. "…Yet I can't shake the notion that a relationship is possible, no matter how remote the chances."

She walked into the kitchen, poured a glass of red wine to the brim, and then returned to stand at the opposite end of the sofa from where Sandy sat.

"Okay, you think you have no chance of getting the guy, but that doesn't explain why you're giving up." She took a sip and struck a pose of smugness, poking her nose in the air. "Therefore, my opinion stands." Her smile wilted as she weighed her next words carefully. "Seriously, if you think there's a glimmer of hope –and by your admission, you do – go after him. Someday you'll hate yourself if you don't try."

"When I said 'no matter how remote the chances', I didn't mean I thought I couldn't have him if I wanted him. I'm almost certain I could."

Sandy frowned. "Could you be any more confusing?"

"Look, you need to understand. That means hearing the whole story. I'm not going to club the guy and drag him off to my cave." She sat. "Try to see this from my perspective, not yours."

That elicited another sarcastic grin from Sandy. "I suppose you might have a perspective worth listening to."

"Shut up and listen. If I get within ten feet of that man, it'd be like a giant electro-magnet. Our bodies would slam together in an embrace, and I'm sure I wouldn't have to say much at all to make him mine. But I know he wants to work on his marriage. Do I really want him under those circumstances? It would just be romantic heat, a flash in time… like on the ship. In the end, he'd resent me for not respecting his wishes. He'd always have questions that he may have let the better relationship go over a moment of head-spinning passion. If I have him, I want all of him… mind, body, and spirit, forever." She sighed. "Unfortunately, I can't convince myself that I should be so noble."

"You poor idealistic fool; without risk, there is no life at all. Do you really want to live the rest of yours like a freakin' amoeba? If you deny yourself this, you might as well. Every decision you make has consequences. I know that, and you know that. If you never take chances, then getting nothing and having nothing is exactly what you deserve."

"Now *you're* scaring *me*. That made too much sense."

"Oh, for Christ's sake, Trish, for once in your life take a chance. Sure it's a leap of faith. So what? That so-called complication you spoke of doesn't mean diddly. Go after him! How many times must I say it?" She noticed Trish coming around to her way of thinking. "I'm tellin' ya, sis, it's the prudent thing to do."

Trish gnawed on a cuticle. "I could at least talk to him, I suppose. But I really should do it before therapy day after tomorrow."

CHAPTER 35

Nick and the young court-appointed attorney stepped into the heavily fortified meeting room. It was the Special Housing Unit of the Federal Detention Center near downtown Houston. A guard stood in the corner, hands clasped together to his front.

Shandahar, the teenage son of Azziz Baruk, dressed in an orange jumpsuit, sat with hands cuffed atop a long, narrow steel table, waiting. Everything was painted in shades of gray. The boy stared at the tabletop as his head slumped, eyes dull as the walls.

His father, Azziz, finally had achieved what he wanted – worldwide notoriety. But he'd never know it or enjoy its attention. Nick didn't know much about the Islamic faith but had heard martyrdom included the reward of seventy-two virgins. If Azziz did get seventy-two virgins, Nick wondered, *virgin what?* Surely, even Allah would not see Azziz Baruk as a soul worthy of reward. There are places in all faiths reserved for people who leave this earth with hearts as black as his.

Nick set aside his low opinion of Shandahar's father. The boy was his personal savior and deserved his full attention as such. He smiled at the boy.

"You look much better than you did in sickbay on the Ocean Dancer."

The boy raised his head only high enough to glance up.

"The color in your face is good." He examined the bandages where the self-inflicted wrist wounds were. "Are they healing?"

This time Shandahar offered the courtesy of eye contact.

"Yes. Thank you." He remained expressionless. "You're looking well, too."

"I have potentially good news for you, Mr. Baruk," the young attorney blurted, topping Shandahar's words. With a slap of leather against the metal tabletop, he dropped a briefcase on it near Shandahar and removed a stack of papers, splaying them in a wide arc. He talked as he searched through them. "Doctor Brandon here put together a convincing argument that your condition played a major role in your participation in the attack on the Ocean Dancer. Rhabdiphobia, I believe he called it." He finally yanked a particular sheet of paper that had been ripped from a legal pad out of the pile with scribbling at odd angles all over its face. "Ah! Here it is. It's the fear of being bitten." He glanced at Nick for confirmation.

"Beaten, not bitten."

"Oh... can't read my own writing."

Nick settled back, planning on allowing the young attorney to have his moment.

"Nevertheless, the layers of scars on your back are evidence of forced complicity. Any judge should take that into account. Mr. Baruk, that's strong support of our argument in your favor. Your father may as well have signed a confession absolving you of guilt. The scars on your body are as good, maybe better, than his signature, and will stand as solid defense testimony even in a case as serious as this one. Once I explain the conditions of your participation, your chances for a lesser sentence should improve dramatically."

Nick thought Shandahar would be happier with the news. As the attorney spoke, he watched them alternately. The fresh-faced attorney was the one who was pleased. He saw none of that in Shandahar. It could have been the young lawyer's inexperience and youthful appearance, but Nick became concerned that inability to sway even his own client might not bode well in front of a judge. A federal panel in a terrorism case will be harder to convince than any other jury. He vowed at that instant not to stray too far from the case and to stay in contact with this young attorney, Daniel Ellingham. Shandahar's future might come crashing down as a result of an inexperienced decision made in haste. Ellingham's over-exuberance could lead to a conclusion opposite their intention.

Now that he had been granted expert witness status for the defense and attending mental health professional, Nick was confident that he'd be allowed greater access to Shandahar. He and

Trish Campbell, for sure, and possibly Lydia Hansard and Benjamin Robenstein, too, might not be alive and walking around today if it had not been for the heroic actions of this young man. Ellingham would be foolish not to count on the testimony of his travel companions.

The attorney sported a recent haircut, a new three-piece suit, freshly shined shoes, and manicure. This boy was right out of the box and untested. Nick didn't need to be told. He saw it. The attorney rattled on and on, lacing the barrage of information with enough legal jargon to confuse even him, while never adequately explaining anything.

"Look, Shandahar," Nick finally interrupted, "What Daniel is trying to say is that even though jail time cannot be avoided, maybe lengthy confinement can." Nick looked to Ellingham. "Sound about right?"

"Yes sir, exactly. This is certainly no slam-dunk case for the prosecution." The young attorney leaned across the table in Shandahar's direction. "As I understand it, besides Doctor Brandon, you have over a thousand eyewitnesses that saw you personally put an end to the brutal murders."

Still, Shandahar said nothing. Instead, he picked at a thumbnail with his index finger while absently stroking the sutures on his wrist from the suicide attempt. Without looking up at either of them, he finally spoke.

"I have no country, no home, no family... no friends. I am alone." He looked up at Nick. "If I walked out of this building today, where would I go?" His head drooped again. "Forgive me for my lack of gratitude. I know you are working on my behalf, and I should be grateful."

Up until now, it had been difficult to look at Shandahar and see anything but a fully mature man. At this moment, his youth and immaturity glared; just a lad in need of a family, a father – a real father. The only thing that kept the boy from crying had to be lifelong indoctrination demanding stoicism.

Nick glanced to Ellingham, whose slackened jaw was all he needed to see to know that the young man was taken aback by Shandahar's lack of verve and didn't know how to respond. He'd expected a different response and didn't get it. Nick saw the attorney's reaction as inflexibility, a danger of inexperience. As legal counsel, the young man should've rolled with it and turned it into an advantage.

Nick took the lead and revived the conversation.

"Shandahar, that day on the stage in the auditorium, the raw courage you summoned was magnificent. The judges, the media, the general population… everyone needs to know what I already do. Federal court can be your forum and the right time to let the world know about it, and I want to help you have that opportunity. I have friends who'll gladly testify, and I bet hundreds who were there will step forward, too. You were an unwilling participant and, when the chips were down, did the right thing. You'll have the opportunity to show that you despise terrorism and the unwarranted taking of human life and were willing to offer the ultimate sacrifice to stop it." He glanced to the young attorney. "Give Daniel a chance. He's working on your behalf. And, don't forget, you placed your life on the line for me. I'll be here for you, no matter what."

After a long pause, Shandahar nodded.

"And about that perception that you're all alone," Nick said, "I'd be proud to call you my friend after all this is over. And, as your friend, I'll do whatever I can to ensure that the balance of your life is more satisfying and happier than it has been up until now. Deal?"

Shandahar looked up. Finally, there were tears.

"Thank you."

His hands began to shake.

Nick rose and walked around to Shandahar's side, put an arm over his shoulder and hugged him. He whispered to the boy, "I promise this with all my heart… friend."

Shandahar shuddered and wept openly.

A guard peered through the reinforced window of the meeting room door. He knocked on the glass, beckoning Nick over with a twirling finger. The electronically controlled lock on the door buzzed, echoing in the featureless room. The guard flung it open and poked his head in. "Doctor Brandon, your cell phone rang three different times. I shouldn't have, but I answered it. I hope you don't mind."

"Not at all."

"I apologize. It was a reflex, and since I'd already done it, I told her I'd see if you could answer."

"No problem." Nick pushed away from the table. "Remember Shandahar, life can only get better. Depend on it, and depend on me. I'll see you soon and often."

Nick followed the guard out the door and down the hall to the check-in desk, where his personal belongings had been left in a numbered tray, including the cell phone. He snatched it up. "Hello?"

There was a long pause. "Nick?"

"Trish?"

"Yeah. Can we get together? I need to talk to you."

He hesitated. *No* was the answer screaming in his head, but he heard himself say, "Where?"

"How about my sister's apartment; do you still have the address?"

"I've got it."

"I hope you don't mind driving over here."

"Not at all." He pinched the bridge of his nose and screwed up his face, realizing even as it came out of his mouth that he shouldn't be doing it. His heart guided his response. "When?"

"Now'd be great… but if you can't make it… I'll understand."

"I'll see you in about forty-five minutes."

CHAPTER 36

Nick wrung his hands over the top the steering wheel repeatedly, finally stopping, but held it with a white-knuckled grip as he sped toward Trish's sister's apartment just off the downtown side of Houston's Memorial Park. The trip around the loop seemed long – too long. He pushed his car to legal limits, eager to see her again. Succumbing to a wanton, sexually charged desire threatened. Although aware, he couldn't bring himself to care about that. A web of connected but contradictory thoughts diluted purity of motive, making his foot heavier yet on the accelerator. A rush goaded by the need to act while courage held.

Taking the Memorial Park exit, he hurried across the wooded area, seldom using the brake and squealing tires at every curve and turn. If a cop had been nearby, he would have earned a citation, but he didn't care; he just ached, believing this to be his last shot at determining from which direction romantic winds blew. He had to know. And it had to be now.

He'd never used the word *love* around Trish. How could he? The romance of that relationship could be counted in minutes. Yet, her image attached to everything he saw, felt, did, touched, or thought. Only a fool would think themselves in love after a few minutes of unbridled lust.

Fool? Really?

The depth of his feelings was real; he was sure of it. He rolled a hand into a fist and hit the steering wheel. Desire to tell her that he loved her was pure – no caveats. But could he do it? Should he do it? *Maybe I am a fool.*

The winding street, through tall pines, forced him to slow the car. Strong sunlight winked at him as he drove by the trees. The flora seemed out of place in the heart of such a crowded and busy city.

The ambience was peaceful. It took the edge off the frenetic pace as he approached the apartment complex where Sandy Campbell rented an apartment and, more importantly, where Trish lived. His palms perspired. One at a time, he rubbed them on his pant legs. Expectations had begun to pressurize. He feared it, yet wanted it. It was intoxicating.

He wheeled into a parking space directly in front of her apartment. Throwing the gear selector into park, Nick began to leap out, but then froze with the door still closed, hand on the handle.

He looked up to that second-floor window. Should he even be here? It wasn't appropriate. *Come on, Nick, do the right thing and drive away... just leave.*

He couldn't do it. Right or wrong, here he sat. Whether by lust, love, or a combination of both, losing control began to seem like it wasn't such a bad thing.

Twice he attempted to get out of the car, and twice he failed, trying to map out in his head what needed to be said and how to say it, or whether anything needed to be said at all. The right and wrong of it kept getting in the way.

The critical crossroad he dreaded had finally presented itself – one way, Evie: predictable, the scenery familiar and comfortable but not necessarily desirable; the other, Trish: totally uncharted but extremely alluring. The acid of indecision was burning a hole in him.

A face appeared in that second-floor window. It was Trish. She'd spotted him and waved for him to come up. Hesitating was no longer an option. He tossed up an obligatory smile and wave, then made all the moves to exit the car. She turned away from the window, and he again fell back against the seat. He needed just a few more seconds to assemble courage.

Like an Olympic ski jumper, he began rocking back and forth, until the perfect motion had been achieved. He threw open the door and was on his feet beside the car before better sense kicked in. Having made the first move, the walk to the exterior flight of stairs became easier.

Halfway up, he glanced at the window with the curtains pulled back, which lent a reasonable view of the interior of the apartment. He noticed Trish's shadow as she walked across the room. Suddenly his legs went leaden.

He kept moving, arriving at the door to her apartment. As he held a fist to the door, ready to knock, he paused and thought: *Never have I had so much trouble with such a simple task in my life.* He knocked twice – the raps light, with no conviction.

His fist barely cleared the door from the second knock. She opened it so fast, suction from the sweeping door moved hair that had fallen over his forehead. What he beheld definitely tipped the scale of choices away from the course of his life up to this point.

Trish wore black pants, snug at the waist and opening to billowy legs, topped by a loose-fitting white silk blouse with long sleeves that ballooned near the wrist, to complement an elegant yet casual look. Gold hoop rings dangled from her ears that matched a cluster of thin, tinkling bracelets on her left wrist. Her short, dark hair was as free as ever, just like her – short and spiked on top but had that long, sweeping bang partially covering her right eye. Sweet perfume wafted out to greet him, evidence that she'd carefully prepared for this moment. Nick's heart took a fast slide to his stomach.

"Hi Nick." She stepped aside. "Come in."

"I-uh… I'm sorry I took so long to get here." His gut tightened at such a lame statement.

"You said forty-five minutes. You made it in thirty-three."

To know the time so precisely, she had to have been watching the clock.

"Thirty-three, huh? You're sure it wasn't thirty-four?" He began to relax.

"Oh hush." Her cheeks flushed at having her eagerness discovered. Her eyes fell, and she turned away. "Would you like something to drink?"

He wondered briefly about the wisdom of adding alcohol to an already undermined will to keep a respectful distance. But it was born of guilt. Like all decisions since she called, this one, too, was not made from an analytical review of the facts. "What's the choice?"

"I'm going to have a glass of Cabernet, but if you'd like me to mix up something, I have gin, tequila, and rum."

"Do you have some tonic water and lime?"

"Sure do. Sandy keeps the liquor and mixes well stocked. How about gin and tonic with a squeeze of lime?"

"Perfect."

Trish moved into the tiny kitchen and talked across the counter. He remained in the living room. "Have you had nightmare problems since the cruise?" she asked.

"No. Have you?"

"Not of the sleeping variety. But I do get nauseating images of peoples' faces that that lunatic shot and, of course, of that poor girl in sickbay getting her throat cut." She shuddered. "The name Bonnie Sondervik and that sweet face of hers will follow me for the rest of my life, I'm afraid."

"Yeah... I know what you mean. Me, too."

He turned away, hoping she read the body language. Her chosen topic was not what he wanted to hear.

She came around the counter separating kitchen from living room and handed him the drink. He sipped it.

"Mmm, good; you certainly know your way around a gin bottle."

Her eyes steadied on him. She cooed, "Among other things."

He was in the process of taking another sip and had to force it down to keep from choking. He cleared his throat and quickly recuperated. He met her gaze, but then immediately looked away. To look directly into those eyes would be like staring into the face of Medusa.

He saw a wall clock in the kitchen over her shoulder and chose to concentrate on that for no other reason than to have something to focus on besides those gorgeous brown eyes.

He took a step back.

"So, you're having a bit of trouble with gory images?" It wasn't what he cared to talk about, but it was the first thing that came to mind, so he blurted it. He turned and walked to the window overlooking the wooded area beyond the parking lot. His eyes followed a blue jay as it glided from one tall pine tree to another. "You seem to be keeping it in the correct perspective."

She took a large drink from the wine glass in her hand.

"As far as blood and gore goes, I guess I am. But there's so much more that I can't get a handle on. No matter where I am or what I'm doing, I see Nick Brandon. I – I'm helpless against it. I can't control it and it's driving me crazy." She took a deep breath. "Now, it's out there. I've said it."

Nick abandoned his view of the park through her apartment window and took the plunge. He faced her without regard for consequences. He set his glass on a lamp table and walked toward her until their auras mixed. "You, too? I've had a helluva time trying to get you out of my head." He placed his hands on her upper arms and rubbed them slightly, wanting to pull her in to a full embrace, wanting to kiss her, wanting to get lost in her and never be found. "But I have to admit that I haven't tried very hard. You're just too alluring, too pleasant to think about; I'm compelled, and, like you, I can't control it."

Trish stepped in closer. Her eyes studied every square centimeter of his lips as she moved in for the kiss.

He didn't know from where it came, but an inkling of willpower showed up just in time. He stepped back and turned his head to the side and down. "I'm sorry... so very, very sorry... but I can't do this."

She nodded and let her eyes fall to the floor between them. "I know. I just had to hear you say it aloud and to my face before I could let you go. I'm sorry I put you through it. Sandy talked me into being selfish about it. I hope you don't think badly of me for trying."

"Oh, Trish, no... a thousand times no; my feelings run just as deep, I swear. It's just that... well, it's complicated."

"'Complicated'. That's a mighty big word standing between us. But, I knew it before you said it." She walked back to the kitchen and set her wine glass on the bar. "Is there any hope for us... out in that murky future, I mean?"

"At this moment..." He couldn't finish the statement, and just slowly shook his head as it wilted forward.

Trish offered a slight affirmative nod. "Don't say any more. I understand."

"Evie and I had that talk. She had a brief fling with her best friend's husband and was guilt-ridden over it. That's what made her act so strange before the cruise. Once it was out in the open, I couldn't very well keep you a secret."

Trish looked up, shocked. "You told her about us?"

"Don't worry. The frankness of our conversation was more therapeutic and calming than anything else." He paused. "We're giving the marriage another chance."

Trish's eyes floated in watery pools, otherwise expressionless. "Then I should beg your forgiveness because I..." She drew a deep breath. "I've fallen in love with you."

Nick couldn't say anything or risk giving away a truth he now felt he should keep to himself. So, he simply tapped his heart with a finger, kissed it and pointed it at her.

She offered a knowing smile and wiped away an escaping tear. "I realize that continuing on as my therapist is out, but if you ever decide to take your star patients on another cruise, can I go, too?"

"I have a feeling it'd be boring without you." He smiled and turned toward the door.

"Don't forget me, Nick."

Standing in the open door with his hand on the knob, he looked back.

"How could I? You're not the only one that fell in love on that cruise."

He closed the door behind him.

THE END

MORE GREAT READS FROM BOOKTROPE

Don Juan in Hankey, PA **by Gale Martin** (Contemporary Comic Fantasy) A fabulous mix of seduction, ghosts, humor, music and madness, as a rust-belt opera company stages Mozart's masterpiece. You needn't be an opera lover to enjoy this insightful and hilarious book.

Sweet Song **by Terry Persun** (Historical Fiction) This tale of a mixed-race man passing as white in post-Civil-War America speaks from the heart about where we've come from and who we are.

Memoirs Aren't Fairytales **by Marni Mann** (Contemporary Fiction) A young woman's heartbreaking descent into drug addiction.

Skull Dance **by Gerd Balke and Michael Larocca** (Thriller) An atmospheric tale of international nuclear espionage, intrigue and heroism, twisted politics, terrorism, and romance.

Deception Creek **by Terry Persun** (Coming-of-age novel) Secrets from the past overtake a man who never knew his father. Will old wrongs destroy him, or will he rebuild his life?

Paging Dr. Leff: Pride, Patriotism, and Protest **by Gabriel Constans** (Biography) A biography of Dr. Arnie Leff, Vietnam veteran and activist, who has fought for community health and a workable drug policy.

… and many more!

Sample our books at:
www.booktrope.com

Learn more about our new approach to publishing at:
www.booktropepublishing.com

CPSIA information can be obtained
at www.ICGtesting.com
Printed in the USA
FFOW03n1948250314
4436FF